THE BATTLE WAS ON!

Darcey wrestled for control of the door latch, as determined to exit as Kane was to keep her there. When she pulled, he pushed. When she struck out with a doubled fist, he ducked. When she tried to kick him in the shins, he leaped sideways and then slammed her back into the closed door.

Darcey gasped as Kane crushed his muscular contours against her wriggling body to hold her in place. When his eyes took on the sheen of polished silver and he stared at her mouth as if it was the first one he had ever seen, Darcey panicked. "Don't you dare try to kiss me, damn you," she said. "I'll scream these walls down around us!"

"When?" His raven head inched deliberately toward hers. "Before, during, or after I kiss you?"

Darcey managed to say her piece, but she forgot to scream while she had the chance. And when his sensual lips rolled over hers with a gentleness she hadn't anticipated, it was impossible to scream at all. . . .

FEEL THE FIRE IN CAROL FINCH'S ROMANCES!

BELOVED BETRAYAL (2346, $3.95)

Sabrina Spencer donned a gray wig and veiled hat before blackmailing rugged Ridge Tanner into guiding her to Fort Canby. But the costume soon became her prison — the beauty had fallen head over heels in love!

LOVE'S HIDDEN TREASURE (2980, $4.50)

Shandra d'Evereux felt her heart throb beneath the stolen map she'd hidden in her bodice when Nolan Elliot swept her out onto the veranda. It was hard to concentrate on her mission with that wily rogue around!

MONTANA MOONFIRE (3263, $4.95)

Just as debutante Victoria Flemming-Cassidy was about to marry an oh-so-suitable mate, the towering preacher, Dru Sullivan flung her over his shoulder and headed West! Suddenly, Tori realized she had been given the best present for a bride: a night of passion with a real man!

THUNDER'S TENDER TOUCH (2809, $4.50)

Refined Piper Malone needed bounty-hunter, Vince Logan to recover her swindled inheritance. She thought she could coolly dismiss him after he did the job, but she never counted on the hot flood of desire she felt whenever he was near!

CAROL FINCH

MOONLIGHT ENCHANTRESS

ZEBRA BOOKS
KENSINGTON PUBLISHING CORP.

This book is dedicated
to my husband Ed
and our children
Christie, Jill, and Kurt . . .
with much love.
And to Tim Novosad.
Reach to where the eagles fly!

ZEBRA BOOKS

are published by

Kensington Publishing Corp.
475 Park Avenue South
New York, NY 10016

First printing: May, 1992

Printed in the United States of America

Chapter 1

Independence, Missouri
1866

Like a restless cougar, Kane Callahan wore a path across the plush carpet of his walnut-paneled study. Most people meditated in a seated position, with their eyes closed, but Kane always found that stamping around with his hands clasped behind his back stimulated his powers of thought.

Powers of stewing, Kane qualified with a disgusted snort. Curse that Melanie Brooks! He had been called away on official business and wham, Melanie up and married some strutting dandy from St. Louis. Not a note of explanation, not a word, not a warning, nothing! After their year-long engagement—an arrangement that made no demands on Kane—Melanie had grown tired of waiting for him to return from one of his many assignments that took him from one side of

5

the country to the other.

"Women," Kane muttered acrimoniously. There wasn't one among them who was dependable and trustworthy. History had repeated itself in the Callahan family. Kane's mother had abandoned his father when Kane was the vulnerable age of thirteen. And even more unforgivable was the fact that his mother had left Kane's three-year-old brother behind as well. Kane and Noah had been forced to cope with the emotional blow and they had been dragged up and down the Missouri River while their father built his riverboat empire and brooded over his wife's betrayal.

And now Melanie Brooks had destroyed what little faith Kane had in women to begin with. His male pride had been severely dented, and frustration was eating him alive. He wasn't sure he had ever loved Melanie, but she had proved to be enjoyable company, as far as women went. And Kane had intended to relinquish his Gypsy lifestyle and sit back to enjoy the fortune that had been left to the Callahan brothers. But then Melanie had found herself another man—one Jonathan Beezely. True, she had fussed and whined because Kane's secretive ventures called him away unexpectedly. But damn it, there had been a war going on. The problem was that Melanie, social-minded butterfly that she was, hadn't noticed the war or allowed it to interfere with the posh parties she attended, with or without her betrothed . . .

Kane jerked up his raven head as Giddeon Fox extended a silver tray that held a snifter of brandy and a crystal goblet.

"I thought you might be needing this just about now, sir," Giddeon speculated.

Hollow laughter rumbled in Kane's massive chest as he closed the distance between them to pour himself a drink. "I'm all for drowning my troubles," he agreed as the flask clanked against the goblet. "But I'd prefer to drown Melanie Brooks."

"I'm sorry I was unable to stuff her in your bottle," Giddeon apologized with faint sarcasm.

A hint of a smile bordered the servant's lips as he watched Kane gulp down his drink in one swallow. "Would you care for another, sir?"

Kane expelled a harsh breath and focused glittering silver-blue eyes on the man who had been in the service of the Callahan family for nigh on fifteen years. "Must you always be so formal and proper, Giddeon?" Kane inhaled another drink and poured the third.

A smile tugged at the corner of Giddeon's mouth, but he stifled it immediately. Ordinarily, Kane Callahan was the epitome of self-control and never stooped to petty complaints. Unfortunately, Melanie's abrupt marriage to another man had caught her former fiancé off balance. Kane was not his old self and grumpiness didn't become him.

"I will try to be more informal, if you wish, sir . . . Kane."

Kane heaved an audible sigh and glanced apologetically at the mild-mannered servant. "And I will try not to be so peevish."

As Giddeon patiently waited for Kane to polish off

his third brandy and return the goblet to the tray, he glanced toward the foyer. "There is a gentleman here to see you who says he is a former client of yours. He has come all the way from St. Louis to speak with you."

"I'm not sure I want to see anyone from St. Louis, former acquaintance or not," Kane growled. "I suddenly find I bear a grudge against that city."

"I hardly think all of St. Louis should be held accountable for your woes," Giddeon replied blandly. "It seems to me that your frequent absences did more to dissolve the relationship between you and your fiancée than your competition in St. Louis. And it is not as if your clandestine missions are necessary for your support. You and Noah could live out your lives on the dividends of your investments without indulging in one day of labor."

Kane frowned at his servant's plainspoken remarks. He knew Giddeon had never approved of the lengthy and oftentimes perilous journeys that took Kane away from Independence. But the servant was not in the habit of rebuking him, either. What had gotten into Giddeon?

"Is this going to turn into a long-winded lecture or shall we call in my guest?" Kane mocked dryly.

Unabashed, Giddeon allowed a grin to surface on his lips. "You are the one who asked for informality, Kane," he reminded the younger man.

Kane shrugged his frustrations aside and chuckled at the lanky man who stood as tall and straight as a flagpole, with silver tray in hand. "I did at that,

8

didn't I, Giddeon?"

"Yes you did, si—Kane," Giddeon confirmed with a stoical nod. "And while I'm at it, may I suggest that you decline whatever proposition your would-be client requests of you. Stay home for a change and find yourself a woman to court instead of concerning yourself with everyone else's problems."

Having said his piece, Giddeon pivoted on his heel to summon Kane's guest.

Stay home? Kane sniffed distastefully at the thought. The unexplainable restlessness within him refused to be appeased. As many places as Kane had been the past decade, he still hadn't found that part of himself that seemed to be missing. Even as lovely, vivacious, and seductive as Melanie Brooks was, she hadn't been able to fulfill this restless need within him. Honest to God, there were times when Kane swore he was just like his mother. He, too, just couldn't seem to remain rooted to one particular spot.

To satisfy his need to roam, Kane accepted assignments from here to yonder. He had infiltrated the Southern lines during the war to gain valuable information for the Union troops. He had even discovered a traitor in Philadelphia who had devised a most cunning scheme to elicit information from the wives and daughters of military and government personnel and sold it to the desperate Southern troops. When the war ended, Kane had been called upon countless times to travel from one locale to another to solve problems for the government and individuals in private enterprises. Although he was always anxious to

9

return home to see Giddeon and Noah, he just couldn't seem to stay in one place for very long . . .

A curious frown furrowed Kane's brow when he recognized the stout, red-haired man who buzzed into the office like a bumblebee. Patrick O'Roarke cast him a brief nod of greeting and plunked into the tufted chair across from Kane's marble-topped desk. Kane's keen gaze swept over Patrick's expensive garments and then settled on the diamond stickpin that peeked from his black silk vest. Patrick reeked of wealth. He was a shrewd, aggressive man who had built his own empire in the stage and freighting business. O'Roarke Express offices were scattered from Missouri to California and all areas in between. Kane had dealt with Patrick before the war when he was handling investigative assignments for private citizens rather than the federal government.

"I want to hire you to solve some of my biggest headaches," Patrick announced without preamble. His assessing gaze flooded over the swarthy, six-foot-three-inch, two-hundred-fifteen-pound package of brawn and steel-honed muscle who had eased a hip on the edge of the desk. "I'm prepared to pay you a fee of five thousand dollars and a two-thousand-dollar bonus when the assignment is completed."

An astounded whistle drifted across the room, causing Kane and Patrick to swivel their heads toward the open doorway. There, propped leisurely against the wall, stood Noah Callahan, who was obviously bedazzled by the staggering offer his older brother was about to consider.

10

"Don't let the door hit you on your way out, Noah," Kane insisted, flinging his brother a stern glance.

"If he won't take the case, Mr. O'Roarke, I will," Noah said before easing the door shut behind him.

"Your younger brother has gone into the investigation business, too?" Patrick queried as he resettled his gaze on Kane.

"Noah has aspired to follow in my footsteps," Kane grumbled in explanation. "I've discouraged him, but he is persistent. Noah seems to think what experience and action I allowed him to see in the war has earned him his stripes. I'm still dragging my feet where he is concerned."

Patrick surveyed his host with quiet admiration. He knew perfectly well that Noah idolized his older brother, and with excellent reason. Kane Callahan, alias Jack McCord and Peter Flannigan—and who knew how many other names he had employed the past decade to ensure secrecy—was the stuff legends were made of.

Kane was an inventive spymaster, a federal as well as private detective. He was the kind of man who made up his rules as he went along, and he was dynamic and powerful enough to enforce them. His deadly calm in critical situations, his shrewd perceptiveness, and breathtaking boldness were absolutely phenomenal. With his cold daring and incredible powers of observation he could solve the most difficult cases with remarkable ease.

So impressive were his abilities that he had been hand-picked to serve as a secret agent on President

11

Lincoln's staff. This much-sought-after detective had also served Wells Fargo, Adams and Company Express, Rhodes and Lusk's Express, to name only a few on his impressive list of credentials. All his clients praised his keen, unerring instinct and unshakable control in the face of adversity. For the past year Kane had worked for the Department of the Treasury, solving cases that less competent investigators had been unable to crack. When shipments of gold were stolen en route to federal mints, Callahan was called in to track down the money and the fugitives who had confiscated it.

Kane displayed the most remarkable technique of blending into his surroundings like a chameleon. He seemed to be at ease in any disguise. At thirty-two, Kane had experience galore and a unique ability to portray endless roles as if he had been born to them.

And cunning! Patrick sighed in silent admiration. He felt better already, even before he unfolded his troubles and dumped them in Kane's lap. This highly praised master of many faces would solve Patrick's problems somehow or another. Kane was legendary in his skills and abilities. He had the reputation of pursuing his assignments until he met with success.

"Just what is the problem, Patrick?" Kane prompted when his client continued to peer up at him without elaborating.

As if all the tension were spilling out of him, Patrick slumped in his chair and expelled an enormous sigh. "The problem is Denver," Patrick declared irritably.

A deep skirl of laughter rumbled in Kane's chest. "If you've come here to request that I blow the town off the map, I doubt the government will approve. They bought out the private mint owned by Clark and Gruber in '63. The private mint had even sent to Philadelphia to purchase coining equipment. The company had coined almost six hundred thousand dollars in ten-dollar mint drops, which were stamped 'Pike's Peak Gold,' before they sold out. The Treasury Department even confided that the private firm's mintage was worth more than the government's because it was so pure."

"I'm well aware of all that," Patrick muttered. "I've been transporting gold dust and coins to the mint before and after it sold to the government."

"Then you are also aware that blowing Denver to smithereens and destroying the mint are assignments I cannot take," Kane teased the brooding entrepreneur.

Although Kane had mastered the ability of setting his own personal frustrations aside when discussing business, Patrick had not. He was clearly troubled, and his tone of voice and facial expressions testified to his deep concerns.

"The city stays," Patrick grunted, refusing to be amused. "But the highwaymen who have been preying on my stage and freight lines have to go. They are giving my company fits. For almost six months, the gold I transport to the Denver office to be weighed and delivered to the mint for coinage has been held up by these pesky thieves. One of them, a man who calls

13

himself the Courtly Highwayman has single-handedly robbed my stages and leaves infuriating thank-you notes. But he finds himself in competition with a more ruthless gang of outlaws who terrorize stage passengers and injure my guards. The problem is that law enforcement is still unorganized and understaffed. I contacted the Rocky Mountain Detective Agency, but they have so many cases already and not enough manpower to be three places at once. Desperadoes are running rampant in that frontier territory. And I'm sorry to say that the rougher elements of Denver protect their own. It is the honest citizens of Denver who are being victimized by ruffians. The entire town needs to be swept clean of riffraff."

Patrick paused to inhale a deep breath and plunged on. "I need someone who can infiltrate Denver without being looked upon with suspicion. Because you have refused to allow the press to photograph you or disclose your true identity, you have always been able to go where other detectives cannot. I don't need an investigator; I need a master detective like you!" he added emphatically.

Kane shrugged off the accolades. "How much have these desperadoes cost your company?" he asked curiously.

"Four thousand in less than six months, not to mention the cash that seems to disappear from the office itself!" Patrick muttered resentfully. "But that is only half my problem."

A frown plowed Kane's dark brow. In his various dealings with Patrick, he'd never seen this sturdy

14

Irishman in such a stew. "What's really bothering you, Patrick?" he questioned point-blank.

The simple inquisition seemed to set Patrick off again. He shot out of his chair and thrashed around the room like a wounded rhinoceros. "My daughter is my foremost concern," he blurted out as he raked his blunt fingers through the mop of bushy carrot-colored hair. "I made the mistake of permitting Darcey to talk me into letting her involve herself in my business affairs after my wife died. I suppose it was my way of coping with my loss and helping Darcey cope with hers. I'll admit I have pampered and spoiled Darcey to the extreme because she's all I have. I sent her to the finest schools in Philadelphia and catered to her when she requested a position in our firm that is usually given to a man. But since her return from the East almost two years ago she's become a whirlwind of activity. My God, the girl works harder than I do!"

After erupting in a burst of frustrated temper, Patrick plopped back into his chair and scowled. "My express office in Denver has shown far less profit than any other agency. Darcey, in some need to prove herself as competent as any man, deputized herself to put the Denver agency in proper working order.

"Although I refused to give her my permission, she packed up and rumbled off to Denver to show me and the rest of the world that she can overcome any obstacle in her path. Not only has she undertaken the task itself, but she has put herself in an area that is teeming with thieves and thugs and only God knows what all. I want her home where she belongs!" His

15

voice approached an exasperated roar.

Now Kane understood why Giddeon Fox had difficulty stifling a grin when the master of the house muttered, stewed, and stamped about. Another man's woes never seemed quite as serious as one's own. Patrick, a highly successful man who had proved himself capable of handling almost any situation, had been frustrated by . . . What else? A woman. They, after all, were the root of all evil. And if not actually the root, Kane bitterly stipulated, then females were the twigs on the tree of trouble.

"So . . . you are offering me seven thousand dollars to locate your thieves and persuade your daughter to come home," Kane summed up.

"Persuade?" Patrick erupted in an explosive snort. "Darcey is unpersuadable . . . Is that a word?" he added, then, with a dismissive flick of his wrist, he flung his own question aside and forged ahead. "My daughter is very determined and as deeply rooted as a Colorado pine, I'm sorry to say. It will take more than logical coaxing to get her back where she belongs."

It wasn't difficult to ascertain where the young chit had inherited her character traits. Kane could look at the father and visualize the daughter. A repulsive shiver skittered down Kane's spine when the vision rose up before him. It wasn't a pretty sight! Not by any stretch of the imagination could Patrick O'Roarke be labeled handsome. His features were too bold and meaty and his thick body reminded Kane of an oversized barrel. But Patrick O'Roarke was a most impressive man who would move heaven and earth to see his ideas through in all his business endeavors.

Patrick had plunged into debt to buy out several small stagelines. He refurbished coaches and added well-stocked relay stations to channel mail, gold shipments, and passengers to their destinations. He had purchased trail-hardened horses from the Army to pull the coaches over rough terrain. When the Army sold surplus stock that cost fifty dollars a head, he shrewdly bought them for fifteen dollars each and obtained one-hundred-thirty-dollar freight wagons for twenty dollars apiece.

The relentless Irishmen had expanded to operate more than thirty-five hundred miles of stagecoaches and freight wagons in Kansas, Missouri, Nebraska, Colorado, Arizona, and California. Patrick was making money hand over fist.

When United States mail contracts had been up for grabs, Patrick had elbowed his way past his competition to receive a staggering subsidy of four hundred thousand dollars. If Patrick promised delivery of goods or mail by a certain date, his vows were kept. And from the sound of things, Darcey O'Roarke was a chip off this determined, persistent block.

Kane tossed his musings aside and focused his steel-blue eyes on the Irishman. "Are you suggesting that I employ *force* to return your daughter to you?" Kane questioned.

"Not by force, either," Patrick muttered sourly. "If she is uprooted and carted back to St. Louis against her will, it would only make her more determined to trot

17

back to Denver to complete this mission she has undertaken."

"Then what *are* you suggesting?" Kane demanded to know.

Patrick threw up his hands in resignation. "How do I know how to handle my firebrand of a daughter? If I had handled her correctly she wouldn't be in Denver in the first place! *I'm* not the ace detective who is renowned for getting things done when nobody else can. I'm no good at that sort of thing. Heavens! I even wrote and *begged* her to come home before she gets herself into trouble. It didn't help one whit."

His wide green eyes drilled into Kane. "I don't care what kind of scheme you have to devise to send her running back to me. If it means kidnapping her yourself and scaring the living daylights out of her, then do it."

"Kidnap her?" Kane croaked in amazement. "That's a mite drastic, don't you think?"

"You don't know my daughter," Patrick declared. "She is out to prove to me, to the world, and to herself that she can tackle and conquer any task. She demands to be accepted on her own terms and she has made the faltering Denver express office her crusade."

Kane was well aware that Patrick was far more concerned about his daughter's welfare than about the pesky criminals who were cutting into his profits. His staggeringly generous offer of seven thousand dollars testified as much.

"Retrieving runaway daughters is hardly my line of business," Kane reminded Patrick. "I usually deal with

18

hardened criminals and secret activities concerning conspiracies against the government and its Treasury department."

"Eight thousand dollars." Patrick upped the offer. "She's my daughter, for chrissake! She's my only heir. Do you think I have built my company only to give it away when I have no more need of it?"

Suddenly, he slumped in his chair and sighed heavily. "I suppose a man just has to have a daughter of his own to understand what I'm undergoing. I'm worried sick about Darcey. Capable, headstrong, and resourceful though she has proved herself to be, she is tripping on the borderline of disaster in Denver. In fact, I'd bet she has considered hunting down those bandits herself. I honestly don't know what that girl thinks she needs to prove to me or to herself. She has become obsessed with making money since her return from Philadelphia. But I can't love her more than I already do, so there has to be more to this than wanting my affection and acceptance. She's had those things every day of her life!"

Kane wavered in indecision. He really had no need to accept this case. There were several competent detectives in Denver who could handle Patrick's problems. And, having thoroughly soured on women after Melanie's betrayal, Kane wasn't thrilled about dealing with the female version of Patrick O'Roarke. Besides, kidnapping wasn't his style, even if every female on the planet deserved to be abducted and shoved off the edge of the earth for putting men through hell before Judgment Day. As far as Kane was concerned, women served only one purpose—to satisfy a man's physical needs—and he wasn't going to let himself forget that anytime soon. Melanie Brooks had certainly done her part in reaffirming his cynicism about the fairer sex.

"I think you should look elsewhere for assistance," Kane advised after giving the matter a moment's more consideration. "I can give you the names of several reputable investigators who—"

The door banged against the wall and Noah Callahan burst inside. He drew himself up proudly in front of Patrick. *"I* will take your case," he volunteered with more enthusiasm than common sense.

Kane glared daggers at his younger brother's inflated chest. "Eavesdropping doesn't become you," he scolded.

"Perhaps not," Noah concurred with an unrepentant glance at Kane. "But the tactic serves its purpose in investigation, does it not?"

"Out!" Kane's muscled arm shot toward the door. "it seems I have overlooked teaching you your manners. Giddeon is right. I need to stay home and tend my own household."

Embarrassed and deflated, Noah slinked out of the room.

A trace of a smile finally surfaced on Patrick's full lips. "How old is Noah?" he wanted to know.

"Twenty-two," Kane grumbled in reply. "He thinks he has the world by the tail. I'm afraid he isn't mature enough to realize how little he *does* know about life and its pitfalls."

"And would you send him out alone to track down vicious criminals? Did you feel no concern whatsoever when Noah joined the Northern troops?" Patrick questioned wryly.

Kane leaned close to relay the confidential remark. "I worried myself sick about him, if you must know." He wasn't about to be overheard by the ears that were undoubtedly plastered to the hand-carved oak door. "The truth is I pulled every string available to ensure that Noah engaged in very little fighting. He was delegated to destroy railroad lines, cut telegraph wires, and demolish bridges with a guerilla band. I'm afraid I haven't been around enough the past few years to train him properly and then war broke out and—"

"Then perhaps you do understand my worries about Darcey in an untamed territory so far away from home," Patrick cut in. "She is twenty-one years old and has decided to grab the world by the horns."

Patrick O'Roarke was a shrewd man. He'd spotted Kane's vulnerable spot in one minute flat and scored a direct hit. Noah was all the family Kane had. He had been his brother's keeper through those trying years when neither of them understood why their mother had deserted them and their father was obsessed with building his company to compensate for his crumbled personal life. Kane and Noah had followed their father up and down the Missouri while he developed a network of steamboats. It had not been an easy life and Kane had come away with volumes of experience, some good, some not. There had been times when he had been called upon to soothe Noah's fears and

21

comfort him while he cried for his mother. And all the while Kane himself had been crying on the inside but was forced to behave like a man and not let his sorrow show.

"It's worse for me, you know," Patrick continued, milking Kane's sympathy for all it was worth. *Anything* to get this master detective to consent to the offer! "A young woman alone in a faraway city is easy prey for unscrupulous men, especially in those mining communities in the Rockies where there aren't enough females to go around. She could be set upon by lechers who hunger to appease their animal lusts, but she is too naive and sheltered to be able to realize the truth until it's too late."

Quite honestly, Kane didn't think Patrick had all that much to stew about. If Darcey had inherited her father's puffy features and a thatch of red hair that was reminiscent of a bristly brush, her homely looks would be her chaperone.

"Ten thousand dollars and all expenses paid," Patrick bartered. "And take Noah and Giddeon with you. Maybe the three of you can find a way to corral those bandits and get my daughter to come home."

"No, Patrick," Kane said firmly. "This case isn't for me. I'm considering giving up my profession. As Giddeon has pointed out, I couldn't even spend all my inheritance if I lived to the ripe old age of eighty. Money is hardly a factor."

Patrick cursed under his breath. If he thought he could have accomplished the feat of slamming Kane to the carpet and pinning him down until he screamed his

22

consent, Patrick would have done so. But the mere size and stature of this midnight-haired man was intimidating. Kane Callahan was not only incredibly skilled with a various assortment of weapons, but he was also adept with his fists, or so the rumors went.

Patrick had only seen Kane in action once, but he had made quite an impression. Kane was always the predator, never the prey. In the face of battle he exploded with lightning-quick reflexes, amazing agility, and unequaled strength. And he had the uncanny ability of vaporizing into shadows in the batting of an eyelash. Some of his daring feats had been hailed as phenomenal, under his many aliases, in various newspapers, where his praises were sung. Kane was remarkably effective in his profession. His fugitives never saw him coming and wouldn't have known who he was even if they had. He just materialized from nowhere to apprehend the wiliest of thieves or to destroy conspiracies against the struggling government after its war-torn years.

Patrick unfolded himself slowly from his chair. He was determined to utilize another tactic. He wasn't about to give up on Kane Callahan. "Very well then, you leave me no choice but to hire Noah. He has made it clear that he will take this case, despite his lack of experience. If he should perish in the line of duty then . . ." He let the remark dangle in the air, leaving Kane to visualize his own frustrating conclusions.

That did it! Kane wasn't about to send his kid brother on this mission, not without proper guidance and training. Hanging out one's shingle did not a

23

detective make! A man had to learn to think like his quarry, to understand what made men tick. He had to plot and plan and consider every minute detail of the chase and capture. Noah was young and inexperienced. He would go off half-cocked, relying on his enthusiasm rather than good sense. Kane had learned the hard way in the beginning, that enthusiasm wasn't always enough and he'd never forgotten those lessons. He had a knife wound in his ribs and a bullet hole in his shoulder as proof that he had twice taken a desperate fugitive for granted. Since then, Kane had never considered a man unarmed or subdued until he was standing in shackles, stark-bone naked. And even then, a violent, half-crazed criminal would attempt to bite off an ear or finger just for spite.

"I'll take the case for half the amount," Noah announced as he zoomed into the room.

"No you won't," Kane boomed, bringing his brother to a dead stop. His glittering silver-blue eyes bore into Patrick. *"I'm* taking this case."

"I rather thought you would," Patrick replied with a sly grin.

"For ten thousand plus expenses and not a penny less," Kane growled, infuriated that Patrick had backed him into a corner. Very few men had been able to do that, and Kane was most uncomfortable with the position; it went against the grain.

"I thought money wasn't an issue," Patrick taunted as he swaggered toward the door.

"When you maneuver me into doing something I don't want to do, it will cost you," Kane shot back.

Patrick paused at the door to glance over his shoulder. "Now that I've been assured my daughter will be in competent hands and the bandits will soon be behind bars I can rest a lot easier." His smug smile vanished. "I know you aren't in the habit of taking desperadoes for granted. But don't take Darcey for granted, either. You may find that rounding up the highwaymen is mere child's play compared to uprooting my daughter when she has dug herself in."

"No woman can be that difficult to handle," Kane snorted, still out of sorts after Patrick had gotten the best of him.

One bushy red brow elevated to a challenging angle. "Not difficult?" He chuckled heartily. "Wait until you've met my daughter, my friend. You may be forced to eat your words."

Witch O'Roarke probably had a hooked nose and bushy red hair that flared over her flat bosom, Kane mused spitefully. Who in the hell would tamper with a harridan like that? Kane shuddered at the hideous vision that leaped to mind. She probably had a face that only her father could love and a body that a man wouldn't want to touch for fear of being cursed for life!

"Keep me abreast of any developments. I'll also expect a full report on Darcey's activities." An audible sigh gushed from Patrick's lips as he turned squarely to face Kane. "What a relief it is just knowing you'll be there to ensure that my daughter comes to no harm until she is safely back in my arms."

A muted growl erupted from Kane's chest. He had been cleverly manipulated by a shrewd businessman who had spent years perfecting the technique of getting exactly what he wanted. Patrick O'Roarke always knew which strings to pull in his dealings. That intuitive gift had gained him a fortune. He seemed capable of handling everyone except his own daughter. Kane supposed he did hold an advantage over Patrick in that respect, for Kane wouldn't allow his heart to rule his logic in the case of Darcey—the witch—O'Roarke. Kane would make sure that firebrand returned to St. Louis. Patrick could depened on it.

Kane frowned as a fleeting thought dashed through his head. "By the way, Patrick, have you ever heard of a man by the name of Jonathan Beezely?"

Patrick rubbed his chin in thought and then grumbled under his breath when the name struck a chord of recognition. "Indeed I have. He is one of the founding investors in Edward Talbot's new railroad company. Confound railroads anyway." He scowled. "Darcey keeps telling me I should invest in the wave of the future, but I'm sticking to the stage business. I'd rather not associate with those cocky upstarts like Talbot and Beezely . . ." His voice trailed off and he glanced bemusedly at Kane. "Why are you asking about Beezely? Is he under investigation?"

Kane's shoulder lifted in an enigmatic shrug. "I just wondered if you had ever heard the name. He married a friend of mine," he answered, striving for the most indifferent tone he could muster.

When Patrick ambled out the door, Noah wheeled around. "When are we leaving for Denver?" he wanted to know.

26

Kane surveyed the young, energetic boy . . . *Man* he reluctantly corrected himself. Noah was busting at the seams with eagerness to follow in his older brother's footsteps. Perhaps it *was* time and this *was* the assignment to permit Noah to tag along. Kane could teach Noah the basics during their trip to Colorado and drill him on the finer points of investigation.

"Sir . . . Kane," Giddeon piped up. "I don't think it wise to include Noah. He needs someone to look after him while you're attending to—"

"Have you ever been to Denver, Giddeon?" Kane broke in.

"No, I haven't, nor am I inclined to muck about the raucous town Mr. O'Roarke described," Giddeon replied with a distasteful sniff.

A smile spread across Kane's lips as he folded himself into his chair. "Pack your bags, Giddeon. You and Noah are coming with me."

"But, sir, I . . ." Giddeon tried to protest, but it did him no good whatsoever.

Kane flung up a hand to forestall the blustering servant. "We'll be Denver-bound by the end of the week. See that you're ready."

While Noah jumped for joy at the prospect of learning the business which had brought his older brother such fame, Giddeon grumbled in complaint. After Noah whizzed off to gather his belongings, Giddeon lurched around to confront Kane.

"I cannot for the life of me imagine myself clomping around the gold fields, assisting you in any manner," Giddeon muttered.

Kane grinned at his disgruntled servant and long-time friend. "You will provide the elegance and dignity that the rough young territory seems to be lacking."

"And you are merely utilizing this case to distract yourself from your unfortunate romance with Melanie," Giddeon predicted. "I'm beginning to realize that you simply cannot stay put, even if your feet are nailed to the floor. I swear you were born under a wandering star!" Having delivered his parting shot, Giddeon drew himself up in a manner that would have done the Army proud and marched out.

Kane's thick black brows furrowed ponderously. Maybe he was using this case as a distraction to forget the feelings of hurt and betrayal, but Kane had always felt the need to roam. His wealth had never appeased him. Being engaged to Melanie hadn't really satisfied him, either. Nothing had, except the challenges of the hunt, the desire to rid the world of men who defied laws. It was, after all, a noble cause, Kane reassured himself. He had found his niche in life and he couldn't argue with the success he'd had. Settling down to a wife and family might have suited some men's nature, but not his. He was damned good at what he did, even if dragging home belligerent imps to their concerned fathers wasn't quite his specialty.

Another picture of Witch O'Roarke formed in Kane's mind and he cringed. He wasn't the least bit anxious to make that termagant's acquaintance. Sharing Darcey O'Roarke's company on the return journey would probably sour him against all women forevermore.

And maybe that's just what I need so I don't forget how much trouble women are, Kane decided. After tolerating Patrick's pugnacious daughter, Kane would be ready to swear off women for the rest of his life. And maybe Giddeon wouldn't be harping at Kane to settle down after he'd gotten his fill of Darcey O'Roarke. There was that definite possibility!

Chapter 2

Denver, Colorado Territory
1866

The tinkling of the bell that hung above the express-office door prompted Darcey O'Roarke to glance up from the neat stack of credit vouchers she was alphabetizing. Vivid green eyes lifted over the top of the wire-rimmed spectacles that were perched on the bridge of her upturned nose. Although Darcey only needed her glasses for reading and working with numbers, she wore them constantly. They gave her a studious, businesslike appearance that helped her project the image she desired. In her opinion they detracted from her God-given looks, as did the prudish, high-buttoned gown she wore. Above all else, she was a businesswoman, and she never wanted her male clients to forget that.

Darcey assessed the neatly dressed gentleman who

ambled in off the street and then she inwardly groaned. When Peter Alridge showed up, business always screeched to a halt.

"Good morning, Miss O'Roarke," Peter greeted, tipping his derby politely.

Darcey studied Peter's tall, thin frame and the expensive but ill-fitting clothes that hung on his emaciated torso. "May I help you?"

She knew she couldn't. Peter only came to visit his brother, who worked as an accountant in the express agency. Darcey resented his periodic interruptions, for they invariably put Lester Alridge and everybody else behind schedule.

"I just came by to speak with Lester for a moment," Peter replied.

If only it was for a *moment*, thought Darcey. They would be lucky if Peter sauntered off in less than a half hour.

"Is your law practice progressing slowly today?" she questioned as she double-checked the vouchers.

"Yes, I'm sad to report," Peter confessed with a deflated sigh. "One would think in a town such as this that there would be more cases to be tried in the People's Court. But with law enforcement being what it is, there are far more unsolved crimes than trials."

Peter certainly had gotten that right. The robberies that plagued the express stages were frustrating Darcey beyond words.

"I'm sure you are distressed over the fact that Sheriff Whitcomb was wounded during his pursuit of the outlaw gang that robbed the O'Roarke stage last week," Peter commented as he propped himself against the counter.

Darcey nodded affirmatively and reversed the order of the vouchers she had stacked incorrectly. "I went by to check on him twice and to thank him for his efforts in our behalf."

"With Whitcomb out of commission and Deputy Metcalf in command of the field, the town is falling into even worse ruin than it already is in," Peter went on to say.

Before Peter talked her leg off for lack of nothing else to do, Darcey gestured her auburn head toward the hall. "Lester is in the accounting office trying to learn my new system of bookkeeping. I would appreciate it if you wouldn't detain him too long. We have a great deal of work to do."

When Peter moseyed on his way Darcey rolled her eyes heavenward. She would have preferred that Peter not kill time at the agency. After all, Peter and Lester shared a cottage on the west side of town. It wasn't as if they had no opportunity to see each other.

"I see that no-account lawyer has arrived," Owen Graves observed with a ridiculing smirk.

Darcey pivoted to see Owen sprawled negligently in his chair, doing what he did best—very little—while he made eyes at her.

"Mr. Graves, I am trying to run an efficient business here," she reminded him curtly. "Just because Peter comes in on occasion to bother his brother is not your cue to take another break from your duties to stare at me as if you were the rat and I was the cheese."

The appreciative leer that had settled on Owen's face became an instant glare. "When *I* managed this office, we did our tasks without working our fingers to the bone. I, unlike you, am not married to my job." A goading smile quirked his lips as he looked Darcey up and down, wishing he could find something about her dazzling good looks and curvaceous figure to criticize. There was nothing. "But then, I suppose you feel compelled to keep my nose to the grindstone so I won't notice you're an attractive woman. I do believe you resent being a woman more than you resent my attention."

Darcey compressed her lips to prevent lashing out at the demoted manager, who thrived on irritating her. He was getting very good at it, Darcey was sorry to say. The first week after she'd arrived, Owen tried to flirt with her. When she rejected his advances, he began patronizing her in an effort to return to her good graces. The third week, he had resorted to antagonizing her. In return, Darcey had heaped mounds of work on him to assure him that she was the one in control of the floundering office and that she was immune to his shallow charm. Their already deteriorating relationship had gone even further downhill.

"For your information, Mr. Graves," Darcey replied with a condescending frown, "I feel compelled to keep you busy because you are being paid a full day's wage. In return, I expect a full day's work." She scrutinized him and his tailor-made garments from over the rim of her spectacles. "I am awaiting the day when the fruit of your labor matches the meat of your salary. At the moment, you seem to be as much a distraction as Peter Alridge and I'm not even paying *him* for what *he* doesn't do around here. And if this office's budget and margin of profit weren't so far out of balance I wouldn't have to be here at all. The fault falls directly in your lap." Darcey directed his attention to the bills of exchange that set before him. "Now get back to work."

Having been properly put in his place, Owen glared at the paper in front of him. "Foul-tempered little shrew," he muttered, half under his breath.

"I heard that," Darcey hissed, flinging him a mutinous glare.

Clamping a firm grip on her temper, Darcey wheeled back to total the figures on her vouchers. One of these days, she was going to fire that self-acclaimed Casanova and save the company part of the profit it had been losing. Owen Graves, in her estimation, was excess baggage. He had no self-discipline to speak of, he took it as a personal insult when a woman refused his amorous attentions, and he couldn't balance an account to save his soul. Why her father had hired that arrogant blond windbag was beyond her.

Darcey made a mental note to discuss Owen's lack of industriousness and incompetency when Patrick came to check on her next month. She was certain the office would be a far far better place without Owen in it. And he could take Peter Alridge with him when he went, Darcey spitefully tacked on. Neither of them seemed to be able to get the hang of working a full day. Lester was having enough difficulty learning Darcey's book-keeping system without his brother dropping in to distract him . . .

"Why don't we call a truce? We could get better acquainted over lunch," Owen suggested, switching tactics again.

Darcey assumed that Owen spoke in his most provocative voice. Either that or he'd suddenly developed the purr of a tomcat.

"I'm sure you will like me better once you get to know me." Owen assured her huskily. "I can be very interesting company . . ."

Darcey seriously doubted it. Owen was trying to woo her into easing up on him. He didn't treat her as if she were his employer. It would be a cold day in hell before that Don Juan sweet-talked her into letting him shirk his responsibilities in the office or charmed her out of her stockings!

"We are not taking time for lunch today," Darcey declared in a no-nonsense tone. "Your two-hour lunch break yesterday put us an hour behind."

"You are only jealous because I was detained by a very agreeable young lady who happens to appreciate me for what I am," Owen taunted her.

Darcey pirouetted around to prop her elbows back against the counter. "Do tell me the woman's name," she requested in a tone that dripped syrup. "I'll be sure to look her up. Since I haven't been able to figure out what you are besides a waste of time, maybe she can point out what saving graces you might have."

The barb struck Owen's cocky hide like a porcupine quill. With a muffled curse and a poisonous glare, he abandoned his attempt to melt the frost that encased this ice maiden's heart. Darcey refused to be charmed or even goaded into behaving the way normal women should behave around men. It really got Owen's goat to be demoted and then spurned by the very female who had replaced him! But if Darcey intended to make his life hell, he intended to reciprocate in like manner.

The day was only half over, Owen thought spitefully. By the end of it, he intended to salvage his bruised pride and ridicule that termagant into quitting her job and running back home to her father, where she should have stayed in the first place!

After Darcey had insulted Owen sufficiently into working, she strode over to fetch the scales to weigh the gold dust. Her flickering green eyes strayed to Owen's back, mentally visualizing where to stab this pest of a man.

Damn men everywhere! Darcey silently fumed. She was tired of being treated as if she were an empty-headed twit who couldn't see through men's infuriating ploys. Men balked at the thought of women being intellectually equal to them. And Owen, like so many of his gender, refused to accept Darcey in any other capacity except "woman." Owen tried to toy with her as if she were placed on this earth to serve no purpose other than cater to men.

Well, Darcey had been trifled with once and it was never going to happen again. She was immune to rakes like Owen Graves. He could accept her for what she was—his new employer—or he could find himself another job. Darcey would give him one more month to adjust. And if he couldn't, she would file a report to her father, requesting that Owen be replaced. It would serve that rascal right. Curse him! He was spoiling their business relationship because he couldn't cope with working for and with a woman!

Kane Callahan sank down in his chair in the saloon and found himself sticking to the furniture. So much whiskey had been slopped around the tavern that customers couldn't sit down without becoming physically attached to their chairs. Sighing in disgust at the unsanitary conditions, Kane scooted sideways in search of one clean spot. There wasn't one to be found.

After riding the stage west two weeks earlier, Kane, Noah, and Giddeon had purchased horses at a small ranch that also served as a relay station east of Denver. The threesome had taken a few days to familiarize themselves with the area. Kane had found the nearby mining communities very much as Patrick had described them—rough and rowdy and waiting for dignified elements of society to catch up with them. Begrudgingly, Kane had admitted that this was no place for a city-bred woman without a man's protection. And rough as this place still was in its seventh year of existence, it had definite possibilities if law and order could get a foothold.

Kane had set up headquarters in a three-room cabin in a mountain valley northwest of Denver. The cabin perched above the well-traveled road which O'Roarke Express employed to transport supplies, mail, gold dust, and passengers from one locale to the other. With field glasses in hand, Kane had scouted the area, speculating on probable sites for holdups. Then he had ridden into Denver to establish himself as a gambler while Noah and Giddeon remained at the cabin, keeping an ever-watchful eye on robbery suspects.

Kane believed that a detective could wheedle the most information by infiltrating a community and becoming one of the masses. He fully intended to lay as low as possible during his assignment. People always became leery when directly questioned by investigators and law officials. It was as if they believed themselves to be suspect simply because they were interrogated for information.

Following that theory, Kane had dressed the part of a gambler and frequented saloons and gaming tables night and day. The valuable information he had gleaned from unsuspecting customers at the taverns had led him to believe one of the local thugs was responsible for part of the robberies that plagued the express company.

A man who went by the name of Grizzly Vanhook appeared to be the most likely suspect. According to the general consensus, Griz was the kind of man who would be involved in criminal activities. But no one had substantial proof, and "Griz" always had more alibis than a tiger had stripes. From what Kane had ascertained thus far, Griz and his two cohorts had no visible means of support but they were never without a pouch of gold nuggets to pay for their drinks. The oversize galoot intimidated everyone with whom he came in contact. Griz Vanhook was a rudely obnoxious bully when he was sober and even worse when he was drunk, which he was more often than not . . .

Speak of the devil, Kane mused as Griz and his two foul-smelling henchman lumbered into the saloon. The Criterion Saloon was one of Griz's favorite 'watering holes'. The two-story frame structure on Larimer Street boasted the town's most elegant dining hall and a hotel that could house as many as one hundred boarders. It also provided dancing and gambling for those who wished to partake in those activities. The windows were etched with floral designs and the wine cellar was always stocked to capacity.

Griz frequented the saloons one and all. He divided his time between the Elephant Corral and the Louisiana Saloon, both on Blake Street, and the Cibola Hall and the Criterion. No one who knew Griz liked him. He was just one of those individuals who could swagger into a room and offend everyone in it in five minutes flat.

In the four days Kane had been in town, Griz had arrived upon the scene, either coming or going from one tavern to the next, making a nuisance of himself. It was becoming increasingly difficult for Kane to stand aside and watch this scoundrel daunt and threaten everyone in his path. But in Kane's attempt to blend into the rougher element of society without inviting suspicion, he was forced to hold his temper and keep his seat. It wasn't easy. Natural instinct warred inside him while he watched Griz shove bodies out of his way to reach the bar.

And sure enough, Griz hadn't been in the saloon a full minute before he started causing trouble.

Griz clomped over and half sprawled on the bar. With a snort and a growl he slammed down a pouch of gold dust and demanded a drink. When the bartender turned to fetch the bottle from which all the other customers were pouring drinks, Griz drew his pistol. The barkeeper nearly leaped out of his clothes when he pivoted to see the barrel of a pearl-handled Colt staring him directly between the eyes.

"Don't give me that rotgut you serve yer regular customers," Griz snarled drunkenly. "I want the good stuff."

Kane felt his hand reflexively inch under the table toward the pistol that hung on his hip. Tensely, he waited to determine if Griz was going to be pacified when the quaking barkeeper retrieved an uncorked bottle from the shelf behind him. Kane had already decided he would defend Griz's victim, even if he did blow his cover and that burly brute bade his natural instinct to react. Kane could not imagine why the citizens of Denver had allowed this scraggly ruffian to live so long. He was a full-fledged menace. Unfortunately, most everyone in Denver was terrified of him and feared brutal retaliation for speaking out against him.

Griz finally holstered his pistol and cast the barkeeper the evil eye. "And don't try to serve me that rubbish again, neither," he scowled in warning. "Or I'll see to it that ye're the deadest man who ever lived in Denver."

41

Keeping an ever-watchful eye on the surly hooligan, Kane plucked up the deck of cards in front of him and absently shuffled them. His years of riding up- and downriver on his father's steamboats had gained him hours of experience in every card game known to man. In his youth, Kane had been taught to deal and play with the best gamblers in the business. He knew all the tricks of the trade and he had learned how to read and mark decks so he could deal a winning hand.

While Griz and his cohorts were guzzling whiskey faster than a distillery could brew it, the deputy sheriff ambled inside and parked himself at Kane's table. Leisurely, Kane dealt the deputy a handful of aces and watched the younger man gape in disbelief.

"How'd you do that?" Pup Metcalf queried incredulously.

With a noncommittal shrug, Kane retrieved the cards, shuffled with experienced ease, and dealt again. Pup, who fit his nickname and was the image of a gangly canine with ears that jutted out from the sides of his head, marveled at Kane's skills.

Kane silently appraised the man who hadn't shown himself to be much of a law official. The boyish expression on Pup's stubbled face was more of a joke than a threat to the rough elements of Denver society. As far as Kane could tell, the only duty Pup performed with any respectability was checking stores and saloons after hours. He was the symbol of lax order and an unstable justice system and nobody paid him much attention except Kane, and he had his own secretive reasons for doing so.

Pup glanced briefly at the bar where Griz and his henchmen were propped, slopping another round of whiskey into their glasses. It was obvious that Pup preferred not to tangle with the burly baboons who made nuisances of themselves wherever they went. In fact, Pup usually tried to steer clear of Griz. When trouble erupted, Pup usually vanished, to appear again only after things simmered down.

"All seems to be well around here," Pup declared before tugging the watch from his vest pocket. "I guess I'll go make my rounds in the streets."

One of the local patrons, who was sitting behind Pup, burst into a horselaugh when he overheard the deputy's comment. "You don't fool us none, Pup. You've got your eye on Miss O'Roarke. Just about the time she closes the express office and heads back to her hotel, you make your rounds."

"A citified lady like Miss O'Roarke needs protection," Pup said defensively. "Somebody has to keep an eye on her."

Kane couldn't imagine why. He had visualized Witch O'Roarke more than two weeks earlier and he couldn't fathom why anybody would cross paths with that homely imp unless absolutely necessary. He had intended to deal with her after he investigated the most likely robbery suspects. And the prime candidate was at the bar, drinking himself blind.

"Aw, come on and admit it, Pup," the saloon patron teased unmercifully. "You're sweet on the lady. We all know it."

"I gotta go," Pup mumbled as he surged out of his

43

chair and propelled himself toward the door. "I've got more responsibilities than I know what to do with now that Sheriff Whitcomb is laid up."

And Kane was reasonably certain who was responsible for bushwhacking the sheriff. His steely gaze swung back to the bar. The ambush was Griz's doing. Kane was prepared to stake his reputation on that. After so many years of experience, he could almost recognize trouble at first sight. And Griz Vanhook had trouble written all over him.

When Griz swung around and muttered something about finding a woman to ease his needs, Kane tensed. It would probably be Witch O'Roarke's misfortune to be strolling down the street at the same time the drunken Griz went wenching. He knew Griz wasn't very particular when it came to women, and if the scoundrel tried to molest her, the incompetent Pup would feel obligated to come to her defense.

Grumbling over the fact that he felt responsible for a woman he had yet to meet and a young deputy who lacked the necessary skills of a lawman, Kane gathered his feet beneath him and stood up. With any luck at all, Griz wouldn't make a scene and Witch O'Roarke could ride her broom all the way to the hotel without mishap.

No such luck . . .

Darcey scurried down the street toward the hotel after putting in a twelve-hour day at the express office. Since her arrival in Denver she had thrown herself into the task of ensuring that the office ran like a well-oiled clock. Unfortunately, the agency was in such a state of disorganization that it was losing as much money as it made. Even though the company charged five cents for delivery each way and five cents for insurance coming and going, money was being lost in the shuffle. To compound the problem of poor office management and a baffling bookeeping system, robberies were cutting huge gashes in profits.

Lester Alridge, the company accountant, had the most peculiar technique of recording transactions Darcey had ever seen. There always seemed to be a financial breakdown between Owen's lackadaisical manner of filing and registering the day's activities in the ledgers. After six weeks of scouring the books and ledgers, Darcey still hadn't figured out exactly where the problem lay, but there definitely was one!

Not only did the company show a loss, but it was difficult for her to tell which customers had been extended credit. O'Roarke Express not only provided services to pick up and deliver freight, supplies, mail, and gold, but it also acted as a bank for its regular clients. Darcey had no qualms about extending credit, but she was annoyed with Owen's lack of attention to recording loans. That in addition to her refusal to be wooed by his scant charm had instigated the problems between them.

Their working relationship was as fragile as eggshells. The argument they'd had late in the day had been fueled by the one they had before noon!

Darcey heaved a tired sigh. Absently she adjusted the plumed hat that set atop the bun on her head and then scanned the mile-high city. Denver, which had once been two independent settlements—Auraria and Denver City—was located beside Cherry Creek, where it flowed into the South Platte River at the foothills of the Rockies. Pike's Peak loomed like the gateway to heaven in the distance, surrounded by the craggy ridges that were bathed in deep-purple shadows.

Although this seemed an unlikely location for a city, it boasted more than five thousand residents and had become the trading center for surrounding mining areas. The natural vegetation consisted of scraggly cottonwoods and the chokecherry scrubs whose bitter fruit had given the creek its name. Neither Cherry Creek nor the river contained enough water to bear boats of significant size, except when devastating floodwaters gushed down from the looming mountains. Two years earlier the city had very nearly been washed away by torrential waters that uprooted buildings and turned the streets into swamps. But despite the community's drawbacks, gold had been discovered and the town flourished.

Supplies were freighted in from the east and the area had become a bustle of activity. Stamp mills had been established to pulverize ore so gold could be extracted by chemical treatment. The city claimed twenty-nine wholesale and retail houses, fifteen hotels and boardinghouses, and twenty-three saloons. In addition, there were eleven restaurants, two schools, two theaters, and one newspaper. There were also doctors, lawyers, tailors, barbers, and shoemakers. Everybody seemed to be making money except O'Roarke

Express office . . .

"Good evening, Miss O'Roarke," Pup murmured, jostling Darcey from her reverie.

Darcey recognized Pup Metcalf's slow, monotone drawl the instant he started speaking. As usual, she nodded a greeting which did nothing to invite further conversation. But Pup didn't take the hint.

"I thought I'd walk you back to the hotel to make sure you got home safely," Pup said as he hastened his clumsy step to keep up with Darcey.

In all his days, he had never met a woman who set such a fast pace. Darcey didn't saunter or mosey anywhere, and she never broke stride from the instant she breezed out of the express office until she veered into the hotel lobby. Pup marveled at this bewitching lady's high level of energy. She always seemed determined of purpose and nothing slowed her down.

"Nice evening, isn't it?" Pup commented for lack of much else to say.

According to Pup Metcalf, every evening was a nice evening. Every conversation began in the same repetitive manner. Since Darcey had no intention of encouraging the incompetent young deputy she merely nodded without smiling.

Bolstering his nerve while keeping the fast pace Darcey set, Pup blurted out his invitation. "I thought maybe some night . . . when you had the time . . . we might take supper together."

Pup was rather shy and awkward around the female of the species, but he had developed a serious infatuation for this particular female. Darcey was very standoffish and remote. Her cool detachment did not invite the attention of men, even though most men were anxious to give it. And if Pup was lucky, he would be the recipient of only a civil smile, and not one which could be considered friendly or receptive. But he kept trying and hoping she would notice him.

Darcey very nearly missed a step when Pup asked her to dine with him. Her dark lashes fluttered up as she glanced at the unfashionably dressed deputy. "I'm very busy, Pup," she replied, offering no encouragement whatsoever. "In fact, I—"

Her breath came out in a groan when she rounded the corner and plowed into Griz Vanhook's bulky body. Repulsion shot down Darcey's spine the instant she came within sniffing distance of him. Griz smelled like a brewery. And what was even worse was that Darcey was certain the repugnant beast had never engaged in bathing of his own free will. It was poignantly obvious that personal hygiene was not one of Griz's foremost concerns. Merely touching his filthy clothes caused Darcey to cringe.

Although Darcey had every intention of removing herself from Griz's close proximity, he snaked out an arm to yank her back to him. His bearded face puckered in a lusty leer, displaying two rows of decaying teeth which boasted noticeable gaps between the ones he had.

An indignant squawk erupted from Darcey's lips as she launched herself away from the repugnant brute. But Griz had the strength of two men and he lunged forward to jerk Darcey full-length against him. His

48

head descended toward hers to steal a kiss. His mouth was like a frog's—lipless and wet—and the smell of perspiration and liquor caused her to gag on her breath.

Never had she been more infuriated and disgusted! She had been approached by a score of men since her arrival in Denver, but no one had dared to treat her so abominably. She had long ago learned to deliver glares that could freeze a man into a block of ice and discourage him from forcing his presence on her. But nothing worked with Griz Vanhook. He was a menace to society and a threat to all womankind. He took what he wanted because he was big enough and mean enough to get away with it, especially with his oversize henchman to back him up. Most folks tried to ignore Griz's existence, but Darcey couldn't, not when he was all over her.

Chapter 3

"Let me go!" Darcey shrieked indignantly.

"You heard the lady!" Pup barked as he stalked forward to protect Darcey from harm.

Before Pup could pry Griz loose, the two henchman grabbed him and restrained him. But Darcey wasn't waiting for assistance. She had always made it a point to handle her own affairs, and she bit a chunk out of Griz's stubby hand in an effort to free herself from his bone-crushing grasp.

With a drunken roar, Griz backhanded Darcey across the cheek. Her senses reeled from the teeth-rattling blow and she stumbled backward, tripping over the hem of her skirt. Although she flapped her arms like a windmill to regain her balance, the heel of her shoe dropped off the edge of the boardwalk. Darcey landed with a thud and a whoosh of breath. The expensive bonnet that perched upon the knot of auburn hair went skidding in the dirt.

51

"I'll teach you to tangle with me, tigress," Griz snarled as he staggered forward to clutch the bodice of Darcey's mint-green gown. "You've been prancin' 'round town like a queen holdin' court far too long. I ought to take you where you lay and teach you yer place."

"Try it, Griz, and you'll answer to me . . ."

Kane Callahan's rumbling voice only hinted at the raw fury that pulsated inside him. He had been stunned to the bone the moment he spied the five-foot-three-inch bundle of beauty and vivacious spirit who had dared to resist Griz's advances. So startled was he, in fact, that it had taken him several seconds to react to imminent danger. The woman Kane had erroneously envisioned as a hook-nosed, scraggly-haired witch was anything but!

Although Darcey was wearing wire-rimmed spectacles that had been completely bent out of shape by Griz's blow and a prim gown that shouted all sorts of things about her aloof personality, she was gorgeous by anyone's standards. It looked to Kane as if this she-cat dressed in an effort *not* to draw attention to all her comely assets. But nothing could downplay her natural beauty. Kane honestly wondered who she thought she was fooling. Any man with eyes in his head would notice her in one second flat. Kane was no exception.

Darcey O'Roarke had a curvaceous figure that would have stopped a gold rush. To add to her lure, she possessed the face of an angel and the greenest eyes ever. Kane was vividly aware of why Pup Metcalf was drooling over Darcey and why Griz had been overcome by animal lust. This female drew men like magnets, whether she wanted their attention or not.

Griz's murderous growl jolted Kane from his meandering thoughts. When Griz's bloodshot eyes swung to the man who had dared to cross him, Kane focused absolute attention on the wooly menace whose fist was knotted in the fabric of Darcey's gown.

"Back off, stranger, if you value yer life," Griz ordered in a whiplash voice. His beady eyes bore into the intruder like a worm into an apple. "In case you ain't heard yet, I'm the toughest man in town."

"That was before I got here," Kane amended with deadly menace.

The remark produced the effect Kane hoped it would. Darcey was momentarily forgotten when Griz's reputation was challenged. The burly gorilla lurched around to glower directly at his foe.

"You want to back up them words, son of a bitch?" Griz sneered.

Darcey, who was already so furious she couldn't see straight, bolted to her feet and thrust herself between the two men whose hands were hovering over their holstered pistols in fatal threat. Although she had never seen the raven-haired giant who loomed over Griz, she recognized his type at a single glance.

Undeniably handsome and incredibly masculine though her would-be rescuer was, he was decked out in the typical fashion of a gambler who preyed on hard-working miners. And yet, though she was most reluctant to give it, his sheer physical presence demanded her attention and admiration.

53

The challenging remark he'd made to Griz indicated he was quick on the draw. He intended to bolster his reputation by sending Griz on a one-way trip to hell with a well-aimed bullet through the heart. Not that Darcey didn't relish the idea of launching Griz into the eternal inferno, mind you, but no one was going to stage a showdown over her!

"I refuse to be a party to this gunfight!" Darcey spumed.

"Darcey, get out of the way!" Pup warned as he strained against the chaining arms that held him.

Kane didn't spare the outraged female even one glance. His glittering silver-blue eyes were fixed on the bearded scalawag who was attempting to stare him down. And even without looking, Kane could feel the crowd that was gathering on the street, waiting with bated breath.

"Pick up the lady's bonnet and apologize," Kane demanded in a tone that rustled with ominous threat.

"Fetch it yerself, stranger," Griz jeered in defiance.

Impasse. Neither man intended to budge an inch.

"I said . . . pick it up . . ." Kane repeated. His voice was as cold and foreboding as a tombstone.

"Not on yer life, you meddlin' bastard," Griz growled poisonously.

Darcey muttered several unladylike curses under her breath and then stamped toward the object in question. Furiously, she stomped on the expensive bonnet and then wheeled toward the two huge men who stood toe-to-toe and eye-to-eye. "I hate that hat," she screeched at them. "I wouldn't wear it again, even if either of you handed it to me. If you want to kill each other, then find

54

another excuse . . ."

Griz found one all right. He reached for his pistol with a vicious snarl, but to his stunned amazement, Kane had drawn his Colt with lightning-quick speed and was pointing it at Griz's heaving chest in the time it took to blink. Griz's pistol hadn't even slid out of its holster!

"Pup, why don't you escort these men to jail to sleep off their bout with the whiskey," Kane suggested, sending the two henchmen a warning glance. He had nothing to worry about on that count. The two men who had captured Pup were gaping at Kane in fascinated disbelief after he'd outdrawn Griz, who had proclaimed himself to be the fastest gun this side of the Continental Divide.

Pup wormed himself free, drew his pistol, and nudged the two hooligans toward the sheriff's office. Two of the more courageous miners in the crowd stepped forward to lend assistance, but they were reluctant to approach the seething Griz Vanhook. His murderous gaze drilled into the man who had dared to confront and best him in front of the crowd of spectators.

"You'll live to regret this, stranger," Griz vowed malevolently.

"*You* won't if you continue to harass decent women in the streets," Kane countered with a glare hot enough to melt rock.

Griz's mutinous gaze shifted to Darcey. "You ain't seen the last of me neither, woman," he vowed spitefully.

When the two miners hesitantly grabbed Griz's arms

55

to herd him to jail, Griz shook himself loose. "Keep yer hands off me," he muttered as he staggered off, but not without flinging Kane and Darcey one last I'll-get-even-with-you glower.

Kane had dealt with enough desperadoes in his time to know better than to holster his weapon until long after the confrontation ended. Only when Griz disappeared into the sheriff's office and the crowd converged around it did Kane shove the Colt into its normal resting place.

With careless ease, Kane sauntered over to pluck up Darcey's squished bonnet. He dusted it off and reshaped it as best he could. But when he extended the hat to her, Darcey promptly dropped it as if it were a live coal and again trounced upon it with a vengeance.

Kane glanced sharply at her and frowned. All he had tried to do was salvage her bonnet, but the feisty minx glared at him as if he'd committed some unforgivable sin.

"A simple thank you would have sufficed," Kane snorted as he watched the defiant hellion attempt to stare *him* down.

"I did not invite you to come to my rescue," she snapped in cold disapproval. "And don't ever try to use *me* to further your reputation as a gunslinger. I was managing quite well by myself until you showed up to make things worse than they already were."

A burst of incredulous laughter exploded from Kane's lips. "Managing by yourself?" he parroted sarcastically. "Is that what you call being backhanded and very nearly raped?"

Darcey put out her chin in a militant fashion. "If you expect me to heap praise on you for your daring, you are wasting your time. Men like you and Griz Vanhook have given Denver a bad name. I prefer never to see him *or* you again."

Kane couldn't help but admire Darcey, even if she was annoying the hell out of him. Honest to God, she had more vitality and spunk than could be contained within the expected limitations of womanhood. This green-eyed, auburn-haired firebrand was everything Patrick said she was, and more. With her bewitchingly elegant features, alluring figure, and undaunted courage, she was every man's dream ... *Except mine,* Kane quickly amended. After his dealings with Melanie Brooks Beezely he had decided to swear off women for the next century.

When Darcey proudly drew herself up, dusted herself off, and pelted down the boardwalk, Kane automatically fell into step behind her. He told himself it was only an instinctive reaction, that she needed his protection, whether she wanted it or not. But Kane refused to admit he was drawn by the gorgeous minx. She was part of his assignment—nothing more, nothing less.

"What do you think you're doing?" Darcey demanded when she shot a glance over her shoulder to see the muscular giant following like her shadow.

What he was doing was becoming hypnotized by the graceful sway of feminine hips and incredibly fluid lines of her whole body. In fact, he was, at that very moment, visualizing how this shapely goddess would

57

look in the altogether while he was doing things that would have earned him several slaps on the face.

Instead of admitting the truth, he responded, "I'm seeing to it that you get home safely."

Darcey spun around to assess the handsome wastrel whom she had decided to dislike on sight. He was a man, after all, and a gambler and gunslinger to boot! He was one of those good-for-nothing tumbleweeds who blew into saloons to drink Taos lightning, gamble away fortunes, beat up other patrons, and even occasionally try to kill them.

"You are seeing that I get home safely?" she fluted flippantly. "Isn't that rather like sending the lion to guard the lamb?"

A wry smile quirked Kane's lips. He gave this sassy imp the once-over twice, impressed by all he saw and anxious to see more. Kane decided she was more woman than the average man could handle, but from all indication she was a repressed maiden who would avoid men at all possible costs. In fact, she seemed to make a conscious effort to offend a man and send him on his way. He would need the tough hide of an elephant to protect himself from her needling jibes.

"No," Kane drawled in belated contradiction. "From what I've learned about you thus far, I'd say it's like sending the lion to guard the *lioness.*"

If Kane expected Darcey to be insulted by the comment, he was disappointed. She accepted the remark as a compliment. After all, it was her goal in life to prove herself as competent as any man.

A smile grazed Darcey's heart-shaped lips, making

her bright-green eyes sparkle like polished emeralds. Kane strangled on his breath. This imp had the most devastating grin he'd ever seen. It was as if the sun itself had been confined to the space she occupied. Lord, all this time Kane had visualized Darcey as a wild witch. What a mistake that had been!

"I would much prefer to be considered a lioness than a lamb, Mister . . ." She paused, waiting for him to fill in the blank, which he did in a low, seductive voice that could melt a woman's heart if she wasn't guarding it closely. But Darcey was guarding her heart, and she always would. She had been burned once and she had vowed to avoid all fires henceforth and ever after.

"Callahan, Kane Callahan," he supplied as he bent at the waist and dropped into a cordial bow.

Before coming to Denver, Kane had contemplated using an alias and then discarded the idea. He knew no one in the area and the war was over. He had never employed his given name on another assignment, but as far as he could tell, it made no difference what anyone called him during this particular mission. He wasn't planning on being here very long anyway. After targeting Griz Vanhook as his prime suspect, Kane intended to let Griz catch himself in his own trap. Then Kane would conveniently vanish, letting someone else take the credit for Griz's capture.

Darcey frowned. Where had she heard that name before? Probably on a wanted poster somewhere between here and Missouri, scoundrel that he un- undoubtedly was.

Shaking off her pensive thoughts, Darcey squared

her shoulders. "If you do consider me to be more capable than a timid lamb, Mister Callahan, then it hardly seems probable that I need your protection. Good evening, sir," she said before continuing on her way.

Despite the fact that Darcey was unappreciative of his attention and his intervention on her behalf, Kane swaggered up beside her. Before she breezed through the hotel lobby and clambered up the steps, Kane clasped her elbow. "Have you had supper yet?" he questioned out of the blue.

"No, but I—"

"Neither have I." Kane propelled her through the hall that led from the hotel lobby to the adjoining restaurant.

Darcey did not appreciate being touched by a man in any manner—impersonally or otherwise. "I prefer to dine alone." Darcey insisted as she wriggled her arm free from the lean brown fingers that had closed around her forearm.

"I prefer company myself," Kane informed her, grinning inwardly at her belligerent resistance.

Kane had never met such a difficult she-male. He was happy to say he had never lacked for feminine attention when he wanted it. Even Melanie Brooks had found him amusing company until she tired of waiting for him to come home and marry her. But the way this green-eyed elf was behaving, one would have thought he had contracted leprosy!

When Kane shepherded Darcey into the dining hall, she stubbornly set her feet and refused to budge from the spot. From his towering height, Kane grinned down at the rebellious minx. "You have nothing to fear from me. It is highly unlikely that I would attempt to take unfair advantage of you in a restaurant teeming with patrons. I'm only trying to be a gentleman, my dear," he informed her with a disarming smile.

"I'm sure that pretending to be a gentleman is difficult for you, considering your true nature," Darcey sniped. "And I am not *your dear.*"

"Would you like to be?" Kane couldn't help but tease her.

"Not hardly!" she spouted up at him, giving him her most frigid glower. To her dismay, she realized Kane was immune to frostbite. Nothing she said or did seemed to faze him.

Another ornery grin dangled on the corner of his sensuous lips as he reached out to tilt her chin down a notch. "Then am I to understand that you have no objection to my taking advantage of you as long as I don't refer to you as *my dear?*"

Green eyes spit fire and brimstone. "I object to you, period, end of sentence," Darcey assured him bluntly.

And what infuriated her to no end was the fact that she felt as if this ruggedly handsome wastrel was amusing himself at her expense. Darcey detested making a fool of herself. And what was infinitely worse was having someone else do it for her!

Bright ringing laughter bubbled in Kane's throat as he uprooted his stubborn companion and towed her toward an unoccupied table in the corner. "It seems to me that we could both do each other a great favor, Darcey—"

"Miss O'Roarke," she corrected with a glare.

"Darcey," he continued, flagrantly ignoring her attempt to remain formal. After all, he had spent years trying to break Giddeon of the annoying habit of calling him sir. "If I am seen associating with you, the townspeople will think I possess a smidgen of decency. And they might decide you aren't the ill-tempered harridan they thought you were."

The comment caught Darcey off guard. Too stunned to react, she permitted Kane to stuff her into a chair. As he folded his muscular frame into the seat across from her, Darcey peered inquisitively at him. "People think I'm a harridan because I have taken control of the express office in an effort to make it run smoothly and efficiently?" she questioned incredulously.

Kane was extremely adept at analyzing people and searching out their weaknesses in order to throw them off balance. In his profession it was a beneficial technique. Darcey O'Roarke was such a feisty, defensive sprite that a man had to startle her long enough to crack her protective shell. She was also as stubborn as the proverbial mule. And let's not forget that she was as independent as the American flag, Kane reminded himself with a grin. The only feasible way to disarm her was by proceeding in reverse. She could not be handled in all the customary ways a man would approach her, not with her remarkable bulwarks of defense.

"It appears to me that you have a low tolerance of those who don't think and behave exactly as you do," Kane predicted, forcing Darcey to pause a moment for self-inspection. "According to my theories, a shrewish woman's problems can be boiled down to two ailments—a sour stomach or a disappointing love life. Which is it in your case?"

Kane had gone way too far with his teasing remark. He could almost see that wall of reserve go up around her like an impenetrable shell. He had put Darcey back on her defense so quickly that it made his head spin. Sparks were flying from those enormous green eyes that were fringed with sooty black lashes and an agitated frown puckered her elegant features.

"My temperament and my love life are none of your business!" she hissed.

Kane cursed under his breath. He had just begun to make headway and then he had taunted her on a subject that had obviously hit a raw nerve. It left him to wonder why she was cynical toward men. But now, he decided, was not the time to pursue that line of questioning, even if his curiosity was killing him.

The waitress's arrival forced Darcey to clamp a stranglehold on her temper. The audacity of this rapscallion! He was one of the lowest forms of life on the planet. Kane was like a vulture waiting to feast on those who had found gold in the hills and came to town to celebrate. He was beneath contempt! She, on the other hand, performed a valuable service for the mining community.

"What would you like to eat, Darcey?" Kane questioned, jolting from her self-righteous deliberations.

"Your heart, boiled," she replied, acquainting him with her look of contempt.

63

The waitress burst into a snicker and Kane flashed the plump matron his most charming smile. "She's only kidding, of course."

"No, I don't think she is," the waitress contradicted. "Miss O'Roarke has proven herself to be intolerant of men, in case you haven't figured that out yet."

After ordering their meal, Kane eased back in his chair and flung Darcey a mocking grin. "There, you see. You do have a reputation of putting men off without good reason. I hardly think that could be good for business."

Darcey gnashed her teeth in frustration. This rake infuriated her beyond belief! "I am running an express service, *not* a bordello, Mister Callahan," she reminded him caustically.

"Lucky for you that you aren't," Kane smirked. "You would drive all your business away."

"I do not have to sit here and tolerate your insults," she spewed indignantly.

"Would you prefer to stand up then?" he teased unmercifully.

"What I would prefer is for you to disappear into a cloud of smoke and grant me a moment's peace!"

"And what I would prefer is for you to accept yourself for what you are instead of trying to hide behind those cock-eyed glasses and that outdated gown which is a hundred years too old for you," Kane dared to say. "But they don't detract from your beauty, you know. Not one whit. You happen to be a very lovely woman, despite your nasty temperament. Most women would kill for your dazzling looks and delectable figure."

"I am not *most women!*" Darcey spluttered in outrage.

"I can't argue with that," he chuckled.

Both Darcey and Kane fell back to regroup when the waitress set two plates in front of them. In fascinated disbelief, Kane watched Darcey rotate her plate so that the various foods sat like the numbers on the face of a clock. The venison was at twelve o'clock and the fluffy potatoes were situated at three. She plucked up the steaming biscuit and moved it to nine o'clock so that the slices of candied apples lay at half past the hour. And to Kane's further astonishment Darcey began eating in a clockwise manner—one food at a time.

Talk about organized and particular! Kane had never seen the like. He had the devilish urge to reach across the table and spin her plate so that the potatoes slammed into the candied apples, which wound up at high noon instead of half-past the venison. No doubt, this chit would refuse to eat again until all her foods— none of which were allowed to touch each other if she could help it—were in their proper places.

"That is the most ridiculous thing I've ever seen," Kane blurted without thinking.

Darcey glanced up, unaware of her unconscious method of organizing everything in her life, including her plate of food. "What is?"

Kane gestured his fork toward her platter. "That. What happens if the cook accidentally places your vegetables where your meat is supposed to be?"

"Then I simply move the . . ." Her voice trailed off and a becoming blush stained her peaches-and-cream complexion. Her embarrassment quickly transformed into irritation and she glared holes in his teasing grin. "Is there anything I do, Mister Callahan, that does not draw your criticism?"

When their eyes met for that one brief instant, something very peculiar happened. Even Kane's keen, analytical mind couldn't explain it. He felt as if he'd been hit by a lightning bolt. The jolt caused his brain to malfunction momentarily, and it took a second to recover from whatever had caused the phenomenal sensation to whiz up his spine to boggle his mind. It was a feeling of . . .

Kane shrugged off the strange thought that dangled helplessly in midair and focused on Darcey's enchanting face.

"It seems I *have* been unnecessarily critical," he said apologetically. "But if nothing else, I greatly admire your spirit."

The unexpected compliment put the faintest hint of a smile on her lips. "You do? Even after I tell you my spirit is as organized as my dinner plate?"

Kane hated to admit it, but he was utterly fascinated by this female. Darcey possessed several quirks of personality that stood out like leopard's spots. She was hot-tempered, defensive, independent, and organized to a fault, to name only a few. But she was still the most intriguing paradox of femininity he'd ever come across. For some reason, Kane felt ashamed of himself for harassing her unmercifully. He supposed it had become a habit with him because of his profession. He had ridiculed those fugitives who had settled into lives of crime like ducks in water. For too many years, he had sat in judgment. Now he was condemning this saucy sprite just because she had decided to carve her own niche in this man's world. He was being unfair to her. Darcey wasn't the kind of woman who flirted with men, only with disaster. There really wasn't anything wrong with that, Kane supposed. He had never wanted to be like everybody else, either, come to think of it.

Impulsively, Kane reached across the table to tip her bewitching face to his apologetic smile. "Forgive me, Darcey," he murmured softly. "It appears I need a great deal of practice in behaving like a gentleman. I was teasing you and I'm sorry if you got the impression that I disapproved. The truth is that I like your spunk. You are what more women should aspire to be."

The tenderness of his touch and the huskiness in his rich baritone voice knocked Darcey sideways. The man had a sensual appeal that oozed from his pores. He could crumble a woman's defenses with a bone-melting glance of those silver-blue eyes. And when he reached out to touch her it was like the whispering wind on her skin. Darcey involuntarily shivered in response to this enigmatic man who displayed a sensitivity and gentleness she hadn't expected from him.

Owen Graves had attempted to ply her with his meager charm the past several weeks, but he was nowhere near as effective as this midnight-haired rake. But the fact remained that Darcey was not in the habit of falling prey to a man's disarming smile or seductive touch, not since Michael . . .

The painful thought caused Darcey to flinch and

withdraw into her defensive shell. "Shall we finish our meal, Mister Callahan?" she chirped, distressed by the unexpected crackle in her voice.

They ate in silence. While the minutes ticked by, Darcey became increasingly annoyed with herself for sparing this rogue discreet glances at irregular intervals. The man disturbed her so much that she felt very unsure of herself for the first time in years.

Callahan . . . Darcey frowned meditatively. She was certain she had heard the name before. But where? She had no idea! Yet, what was infinitely more distressing than a name ringing a distant bell was the ever-growing fascination she felt for the gambling gunslinger. Since her humiliating experience with Michael Dupris, Darcey had avoided any type of romantic involvement with men. Even her father hadn't known of the heartache she'd suffered during her days at the elite finishing school in Philadelphia. She had buried the hurt deep in her heart and vowed never to allow a man close enough to make a fool of her again. She had been too naive and innocent to deal with the cunning, deceptive masculine mind. Now she knew how it felt to be used and betrayed and she'd never forgotten that painful experience.

And then along came a man who was far below her station in life—a wastrel, a rake, a pistolero, and only God knew what else! She didn't trust his intentions for a second, of course. And yet she felt physically attracted to him. He had hair as shiny and black as a raven's wing and long, thick lashes that any woman would envy. His eyes were the most incredible shade of silver-blue. She had seen them flash like ominous lightning bolts in the heat of battle. And in gentler moods they turned baby blue. Not only did Kane Callahan stand six feet three inches tall and tower over his foe like a formidable mountain, but he was also the most well-sculptured package of brawny muscle Darcey had ever encountered.

What a paradox the man was, Darcey decided. He seemed well educated and yet he moved in the circle of society which she detested and avoided like the plague. And why would a man such as this seek her out for companionship when she had made it clear she wanted nothing to do with him, that she had nothing to give?

"Is something troubling you, Darcey?" Kane questioned after watching the multitude of conflicting emotions chase each other across her lovely face.

Darcey shook herself back to reality. "You," she admitted honestly. "I'm having difficulty figuring you out."

With graceful ease, Kane rose to his feet and dropped several gold coins beside his plate. After flashing Darcey a charismatic smile, he assisted her from her chair. "There is nothing to figure out, my dear. I'm only concerned about your safety in this raucous town."

"Aren't you just." The defensive shield went up again and Darcey agilely removed herself from his light grasp on her arm—a careless caress which had the most peculiar effect on her pulse.

An audible sigh rolled from Kane's lips as he followed the standoffish she-male through the hall and up the flight of stairs to her room. "If I might offer a few words of advice . . ."

"You may not," she inserted without a backward glance.

His hand folded around her elbow to turn her on the landing above him. They stood eye to eye and Kane couldn't help but uplift his hand to trace the expressive mouth that he suddenly found himself wanting to kiss.

"A dignified lady like you doesn't belong in a town like this," he told her, squelching the insane urge to kiss her right there where she stood.

If he knew what was good for him, he would treat her like his kid sister, and look upon her the same way he did his younger brother. Lord! That was going to take concentrated effort on his part.

Darcey bristled defensively at his remark. "And just where is it you think I belong, Mister Callahan?" she demanded to know.

"Kane," he corrected for the umpteenth time.

Darcey ignored his request to use his given name. "I suppose you, like most men, think a woman's place is at home, waiting on her master hand and foot."

Another chuckle bubbled in his massive chest. Her belligerence was both aggravating and amusing. "I doubt you'd be content in any man's shadow, independent as you appear to be," he contended. "But Denver definitely doesn't suit you."

How dare this ne'er-do-well try to tell her how and where to live her life! "I'll thank you to mind your own business and let me handle mine."

When Darcey wormed loose of his grasp, hiked up

her skirts, and stormed off, Kane expelled an exasperated breath. Patrick O'Roarke was right. This girl was damned near impossible! But Kane was as determined to complete his assignment as Darcey was to make the express company prosper. And she was not having the last word, as she seemed eager to do, either!

Hell-bent on his purpose, Kane stalked up the steps in Darcey's wake. She wasn't going to spout at him and walk off! By damned, he wasn't going to let her get away with it. Darcey O'Roarke was the kind of a woman who would test a man just to see how far she *could* push him. Well, she was about to find out that she had pushed Kane Callahan as far as he intended to go!

Chapter 4

"Look, lady," Kane muttered as he stalked after the five-foot-three-inch terror in green satin. "If you can't defend yourself against men like Griz Vanhook, you'd better find someone who can, or you won't last long. You seem to have a self-destructive tendency that refuses to let you back down from anything, even when it would be a helluva lot wiser to do so."

Hurriedly, Darcey fished into her purse to retrieve her key and stabbed it at the lock. "Are you offering your services as a bodyguard?" she questioned in a distinctly unpleasant tone. "If you are, I'm not the least bit interested, Mr. Callahan."

"Kane," he corrected gruffly.

When he breathed his name down her neck, Darcey thrust her shoulder against the door in hopes of removing herself from his close proximity. Because of recent, unseasonable rains and the excessive moisture in the air, the door had swelled to such extent that force had to be applied to open it. With a determined thrust, Darcey plowed into her room and wheeled to slam the door before her unwelcome guest breezed in. Quick as she was, she was way too slow. Kane slid inside with snakelike agility.

Darcey stared at the looming giant who stood more than a foot taller than she did. The last thing she wanted was to be enclosed in her suite with a man. Especially this one! He had already proved himself capable of standing up against the toughest desperado in the territory. And Kane Callahan could obviously make mincemeat of her if that was his want. Curse it, why wouldn't he just go away and leave her alone?

"So that's it, isn't it?" she sniffed when the light of understanding suddenly dawned on her, or at least she thought it had.

"What's it?" Kane questioned, wondering how any man could carry on a normal conversation with a woman who jumped from one topic to another like a confounded grasshopper. He didn't have the slightest inkling what in the hell she was talking about!

Darcey glared accusingly at him. "I've heard about your kind in frontier towns where law and order has no foothold. You're one of those unscrupulous men who are handy with a gun and who offers to protect shopkeepers from rapscallions. First you assure me that I can't take care of myself and suggest I slink meekly out of town. And when I refuse, you offer me protection. When I reject the offer and your exorbitant fee, then I will be forced to live in fear of my life and the destruction of my place of business." She inhaled a

74

deep breath and surged on. "And unless I miss my guess, which I doubt I have, you are in cahoots with Griz Vanhook. Why, you probably staged that entire incident with that ruffian just to set me up!"

Kane stared goggle-eyed at her. It was glaringly apparent that this high-strung female had been harnessed to a runaway imagination that wouldn't quit. He had never met anyone who made such hasty leaps of certainty into the most damning of all possible conclusions. Always expect the worst; that was Darcey O'Roarke's motto.

"Are you this cynical and mistrusting every day of the week, or just on Wednesday?" Kane smirked flippantly.

"Just Wednesday," she smarted off. "On Thursday I'm as sarcastic as you are. Maybe worse," she added on second thought.

A muted growl erupted from Kane's throat as he reached over to slam the door shut. For a long moment he glared at this overly defensive chit who was everything her father said she was and more. "Look, honey, you . . ."

"Don't call me honey," she protested as she wrestled for control of the door latch. If he was staying, then by damned she was leaving. This room was nowhere near big enough for the both of them. She was *not* going to be closeted in this suite with this infuriating man and that was that!

The battle was on! Darcey was as determined to exit as Kane was to keep her there. When she pulled, he pushed. When she struck out with a doubled fist, he ducked. When she tried to kick him in the shins, he leaped sideways and then slammed her back into the closed door.

Darcey expelled a pained moan when her head collided with solid wood. A startled gasp erupted from her lips when Kane crushed his muscular contours against her wriggling body to hold her in place. It only took a moment for Darcey to realize how futile it was to resist this man. Kane was one hundred percent male, all muscle and formidable strength . . . And she was in serious trouble!

Kane hadn't meant to mold this spitfire's luscious curves against him, but she had forced him into it when she resisted him. And now that they stood full length of each other, feeling the accelerated beats of each other's hearts, his anger melted into a stark awareness of the desirable woman who was plastered against him.

His gaze dropped to the delicious curve of her pouting lips. She had the most beautifully sculpted mouth. At close range, the temptation of taking her lips under his and kissing her senseless had the most intriguing appeal.

When his eyes took on the sheen of polished silver and he stared at her mouth as if it was the first one he'd ever seen, Darcey panicked. "Don't you dare try to kiss me, damn you!" she hissed, struggling in vain for freedom. "I'll scream these walls down around us!"

"When?" His raven head inched deliberately toward hers, eclipsing the light and suffocating her with the alluring scent of his cologne. "Before, during, or after I kiss you . . . ?"

The warm, powerful threat of his masculine body pressing intimately against hers rattled her to the extreme. "All of the above," she fluted, her voice two octaves higher than normal.

Darcey, who always preferred to have the last word, managed to say her piece, but she forgot to scream while she had the chance. And when his sensual lips rolled over hers with a gentleness she hadn't anticipated, it was impossible to scream at all. She felt as if she had mortar in her lungs. She was being entrapped in the aura of rugged masculine appeal that encircled this seductive rogue.

Sensations she hadn't allowed herself to experience in her twenty-one years of existence bombarded her. His tongue traced her lips and then delved into the dewy recesses of her mouth to steal what little breath she had left. The firm grasp he held on her became a tender embrace. She felt like ice melting over a slow-burning fire. Darcey expected to experience the same revulsion that engulfed her when Griz Vanhook had assaulted her. Indeed, she would have preferred it. But that, unfortunately, wasn't the way it happened. Kane had become a gentle giant whose seductive methods of persuasion were far more devastating and impossible to resist than brute force. Darcey felt her defenses crumbling without understanding why. She wasn't even sure she liked this arrogant, domineering stranger, for crying out loud!

Kane, who was a master at anticipating and predicting the outcome of most encounters, was thrown off course by the startling direction his confrontation with this hellcat had taken. He had intended to look upon her as his kid sister. He had planned to convince her to pack up and leave town before she lost her life and her unblemished virtues. But when he kissed her she went to his head like potent wine, not to mention the devastating effect she had on the rest of his anatomy. Suddenly *he* was her greatest threat! *He,* the man who had been offered ten thousand dollars to protect her and send her back to her father— Kane's client!

Good God! Where had he gone wrong? And worse, why was he entertaining ideas of scooping this delicately formed sprite up in his arms and taking her to bed to appease the monstrous need that had sprung up out of nowhere to engulf him? Hell, hadn't he sworn off women indefinitely? And if he had, why was he harboring thoughts of being this bewitching maid's first experience with passion? Had he gone mad? Obviously! But damn it, everything he did to her seemed new and incredibly sensual to her. He could feel her traitorous body responding, trembling in awakened awareness. That aroused him more than he already was, if that were possible.

The conflicting thoughts that were buzzing through his head stung like a wasp. Cursing his lack of self-control, Kane hastily retreated. Darcey half collapsed against the door in an effort to maintain her balance after this skillful rogue had kissed her until her knees turned to rubber and her brain turned to mush.

Kane sucked in a ragged breath and pivoted before he embarrassed the both of them with the vivid evidence of his arousal. "Despite what you're probably thinking, being the skeptic you are, I had not intended to do that," he insisted in a voice that rustled with an unappeased desire he was having difficulty controlling, even when he made a conscious effort to do so.

Breasts heaving, Darcey braced herself against the door and gaped at the profile of this ruggedly handsome rake who had invaded her privacy, stormed her defenses, and left her sizzling with erotic sensations she didn't want to feel, in places she didn't even know she had! A muddled frown knitted her brows when she took time to consider what had happened and what *could* have happened. Kane could easily have taken complete advantage of her. With his strength, she couldn't have stopped him if he had decided he wanted more from her than a steamy kiss that caused her mind to malfunction.

"You didn't?" Darcey chirped like a sick cricket.

It had taken her so long to respond to his comment that Kane, a little shaken up himself by what had transpired, couldn't even remember what the hell he'd said!

"I didn't what?" he croaked. It infuriated him to note the hungry desire that pulsated through his entire body had also strangulated his vocal chords.

"You didn't mean to kiss me?" she prompted, her voice still on the unsteady side. "Why not? I thought that was what all men wanted from women—to steal a kiss, to take a tumble in bed . . . whatever they can get to prove their superiority over females."

As was his habit when he was frustrated, Kane fell

into his restless pacing routine with his hands clasped behind his back and his head downcast to monitor the rapid pelting of his feet. Darcey O'Roarke's dazzling appearance and vital personality had thrown him for a loop. Kane felt the need to walk off his tormenting craving for this minx until he had gotten himself in hand.

While Kane beat a path across the floor, Darcey watched in mounting amusement. She knew she had several failing graces, many of which Kane seemed to delight in bringing to her attention. But he was nowhere near perfect, either. Although she did her pondering while sitting down, drumming her fingers and staring off into space, he stalked from wall to wall. She was overly organized and ritual-prone, but Kane Callahan was methodic and analytic. She had noticed that during dinner, but he had put her on the defense immediately and she never had the chance to point his defects out to him. And if *she* was independent, *he* was domineering. He seemed the type who walked in and took over lock, stock, and barrel whether anyone invited his leadership and his opinions or not. Darcey was definitely one of those individuals who did *not!*

When Kane glanced up to see Darcey grinning in mocking amusement, he froze in midstep. Expelling an explosive breath, Kane raked his fingers through his wavy black hair and let his arm drop limply by his side.

"If you know what's good for you, you'll get the hell out of this town as fast as you can get out. Since you don't seem to know what's best, I'll tell you," Kane volunteered. Willfully, he ignored the curvaceous imp who had the knack of arousing him without even trying! Lord, he still couldn't breathe normally after they had shared that mind-boggling, body-throbbing kiss.

"You simply don't fit in here," he told her frankly. "Most decent women in town have husbands or fiancés to protect them from harm. Those with loose morals have cribs in the red-light district of town. But you don't fit into either category. What happened with Griz tonight will become a constant threat to you. The man seems the type to hold grudges and he is known for his violent temper. You could wind up dead . . . or worse . . . if you stay."

Darcey strained against the swollen door until it creaked open, and then gestured for Kane take himself off. "Thank you for your concern," she replied in a tone that was anything but appreciative. "Good night, Mr. Callahan."

"Kane, damn it!" he snapped in exasperated correction.

"Good night, Kane damn it," she obliged with a ridiculing smile.

Kane couldn't say exactly why he did what he did next. Like a striking snake, he reached out to jerk Darcey against him. His lips came down on hers in firm possession, determined to kiss her blind, to ease the intermingled frustration and desire that hounded him to death. He knew he wasn't accomplishing one solitary thing except making himself even more aware of the unwanted attraction that had sprung up between them. Darcey certainly didn't want to be kissed, or so she had said in the beginning. But her body was delivering subtle messages of its own and his body was responding with an urgency that nothing seemed to be able to control.

Before Kane knew it, he was savoring and devouring her honeyed lips. His questing hands were moving on their own accord, itching to delve beneath her prudish gown to explore her voluptuous curves and swells.

Darcey gasped at the feel of his caresses roaming over uncharted territory. Her heart pounded against her ribs. Sensation after traitorous sensation swamped and buffeted her, causing her to respond to his masterful kiss, leaving her aching for his skillful touch.

It was downright terrifying to realize what a potent spell this silver-blue-eyed wizard could weave around her in less time than it took him to mold her into his muscular contours. Her senses exploded with his musky fragrance. Her body tingled when it came into contact with the rock-hard wall of his chest and the lean columns of his thighs. A fog of unexpected pleasure swept over her and Darcey found herself kissing him back when that was the last thing she ever meant to do.

Her will had suddenly become his own and she could no more control the sensual blossom of desire that unfurled inside her than she could fly to the moon.

For several breathless moments Kane abandoned all hope of controlling himself. Suddenly he couldn't even remember the meaning of willpower. It was as if he'd never possessed any in all this thirty-two years. His body had rebelled against his brain and he was a captive of primal needs that demanded appeasement.

Finally, logic won the battle over lust and Kane pried himself loose from the world's greatest temptation—a green-eyed minx who could make a man forget his ultimate purpose for being in Denver in one second flat.

"I didn't mean to do that, either," Kane muttered, incensed with himself for losing control, the second time in less than ten minutes. "For the life of me I can't imagine why I did."

Darcey took offense to his remark. "I can't imagine why you did, either," she sputtered. "It wasn't as if I invited it!"

"But you didn't do much to fight it," Kane growled back at her.

Darcey reacted without thinking. Her palm connected with his tanned cheek, leaving fingerprints on his face. "Get out of here and don't ever come back!"

"I can't imagine why I would ever want to," Kane bit off as he stalked past her. "You are one impossible woman."

"And you are a most infuriating man," Darcey assured him before she slammed the door behind him with a decisive thud.

Breathing heavily, Kane spun around to glare at the door and the billy goat of a female behind it. Well, so much for logical persuasion, he thought. Patrick O'Roarke had proved himself right again. Darcey had more determined will and inner drive than any woman rightfully ought to have. Sure enough, that auburn-haired hellion was as firmly planted in Colorado soil as a pine tree. Her bark was impenetrable and her needles pricked like sharp spikes. But what was infinitely worse was that Kane couldn't reason with her because his lusty needs kept getting in his way. Like a blundering fool he had grabbed her to him and impulsively kissed her, not once but twice! Honest to God, he would never make headway if he kept getting sidetracked by that delicious body of hers and those petal-soft lips.

With tremendous effort, Kane turned himself around and inhaled a steadying breath. Damn it, he hadn't acquired his legendary reputation by folding his tent and skulking away at the first sign of difficulty. Somehow, he was going to find a way to convince Miss Stubborn-as-a-Mule O'Roarke to pack up and leave town. One way or another, he was going to deliver her to St. Louis where she belonged. And by the time Kane accomplished his mission, he had the inescapable feeling he was going to earn every penny Patrick planned to pay him. That was one bull-headed female . . . who possessed such irresistible lure that Kane found himself doing things that could get both of them in way over their heads.

Lord, he'd just made things worse. He hadn't wanted to be quite so aware of Darcey as a woman, but after this incident he was as aware of her hidden charms as one man could get! Well, he was just going to have to get a firm grip on himself and ensure that he never allowed his male needs to overrule his purpose ever again.

Chewing on that noble thought, Kane stamped off. He could use a drink . . . or three . . . to forget the taste of kisses that melted on his lips like thirst-quenching wine. After a few glasses of whiskey he wouldn't remember the feel of Darcey's curvaceous body imprinted on his, the way he had boldly caressed . . .

"Blast it, get hold of yourself," Kane growled as he stomped down the steps. He was in Denver on business and that was the beginning and end of it. He was *not* going to become emotionally involved with that gorgeous firebrand!

Even as the determined thought rattled through his brain, Kane had the unshakable feeling he had just heard the echo of famous last words.

Chapter 5

When Kane's footsteps faded into silence, Darcey slumped in relief. She would have died before she admitted it aloud, but her lips still tingled from that rapscallion's sensual kiss. He may have been a cardsharp and gunslinger but he definitely hadn't spent all his times shuffling cards and wielding a pistol! Sweet merciful heavens, when he kissed a woman she knew she had been thoroughly kissed. Why, the man had probably forgotten more about kissing a woman blind than Darcey would ever learn in her whole life.

Not that she wanted lessons in passion, mind you. Darcey had come to the conclusion that love was grossly overrated. Her bittersweet romance with Michael Dupris in Philadelphia had taught her that. She had innocently offered her heart to a rake who knew nothing of fidelity, who had used her because of the wealth she could offer him. When she caught Michael in a most compromising situation with his paramour—one Darcey never even knew he had—

she had held him and all men in contempt thereafter.

And then along came a charming wastrel who had awakened her slumbering passions. Darcey reprimanded herself severely for becoming aroused by Kane Callahan's steamy kisses and bold caresses. She should have felt nothing but repulsion, yet the taste of his kiss still lingered on her lips, even when she tried to wipe it away. The scent of his expensive cologne clung to her hair, her flesh. Every breath she inhaled was still thick with the scent of him! Curse it, it still felt as if his muscled body was imprinted on her skin.

Disgusted with the entire evening, Darcey struggled to open the swollen door and called to a passing maid to fill her tub. Within a quarter of an hour, Darcey plunked into her bath to rinse away the taste and smell of the man she had her heart set on hating for a dozen good reasons. If Kane Callahan dared to come near her again, she would crash through walls, if she must, to avoid him. She was *not* going to get involved with any man ever again! She had come to Denver for one purpose. She wanted to prove to her father and the world that she could manage the family business and repay the money she had lost in Philadephia because of Michael's shrewd manipulation. She was her own woman and she would never stand in the shadow of any man . . .

Her thoughts screeched to a halt when she realized how quickly Kane had analyzed her. The man possessed incredible insight. All the more reason to take a wide berth around him, Darcey advised herself. Good Lord, he seemed to know what she was thinking even while she was thinking it. It would never do for him to know what she was feeling! And what she felt was . . .

Darcey gulped hard and scrubbed away the lingering male scent that still clung to her flesh. What she felt, Lord forgive her, was an unwanted, illogical attraction to that suave giant with entrancing silver-blue eyes and engaging smile.

"You were every kind of fool once, Darcey O'Roarke," she chastised herself before dunking her head in the tub. "Don't ever be again. It should be glaringly apparent by now that you are a miserable judge of men. The less association you have with them, the better off you'll be!"

Resolved to that cynical philosophy, Darcey dried herself off and plopped into bed. Tomorrow she would dress and venture to the express office to attend her tasks. And she wasn't going to spare that annoying Kane Callahan a single thought. Theirs had been a brief, unpleasant acquaintance, and it was over as quickly as it had begun. She had seen the last of that midnight-haired gambler and he of her!

Since Giddeon Fox was unavailable to fetch Kane the drink he definitely needed, he bought himself an entire bottle of Denver's best whiskey and took it to his room above the Criterion Saloon. Even after swallowing several gulps of brandy, thoughts of Darcey O'Roarke still clouded Kane's mind. The liquor couldn't smother the taste of her kiss or numb the vital parts of his male anatomy to the tingling pleasures they had enjoyed. It shocked Kane to be so instantaneously attracted to a shrew like Darcey. She was, without a doubt, a man-hater. She possessed peculiar table habits—like eating in a clockwise manner and setting each piece of silverware just so beside her plate. And defiant! Not to forget incredibly independent and sassy, either, Kane added sourly. In time, all her quirks would drive the most stable man crazy.

Although it would have been to Kane's best interest to avoid all future contact with that sprite, she was the crux of his mission in Denver. Kane was prepared to bet his inheritance that Darcey was entirely innocent of men, too. That should have been incentive enough for him to keep his distance unless absolutely necessary. He had always purposely steered clear of virgins. And Darcey definitely lacked experience. It showed in her reluctant and yet tantalizing kiss. But ironically, that lack of experience left Kane wanting to teach her things about the magic between a man and a woman. Taming a firebrand like Darcey would test the most competent and patient man, that was for damned certain. Not that he even wanted to tame her, of course. This was all merely hypothetical speculation and a... waste of his time.

Kane let out a long sigh and swallowed another glass of brandy. Lord, he wished Giddeon and Noah were here to distract him. He didn't want to be alone with his thoughts when visions of Darcey O'Roarke kept dancing in his head.

Restlessly, Kane climbed to his feet and paced the small room located above the saloon. How in the hell was he going to convince that determined female to leave town before she was toted out in a pine box? She had challenged Griz Vanhook and the man wouldn't forget that. In fact, that burly brute would probably harass Darcey until he . . .

A wordless scowl passed Kane's lips. The thought of that feisty spitfire being assaulted by that heathen turned Kane's mood black as pitch. If only he had concrete evidence that Griz was behind the robberies that hounded O'Roarke Express, he could dispose of him. Griz definitely belonged behind bars, but he always had an alibi and witnesses to swear he had been nowhere near the scene of a crime.

Kane poured another drink and paced some more. What tactic could he utilize to rout Darcey before all hell broke loose? "Think, man," he scowled at himself. Force wouldn't work. Friendly persuasion had fallen flat on its face. As Patrick had warned him, Darcey's stubborn resistance increased in direct proportion to the obstacles she confronted.

A wry smile hovered on Kane's lips as a fleeting thought skittered through his mind. Perhaps he just wasn't using the right kind of persuasion. Maybe he could woo her into trusting him enough to accompany her out of town. Kane had never considered himself a lady-killer, but he had been confident enough of his abilities before Melanie bruised his male pride black and blue. If he courted Darcey until she began to like him . . .

No, that wouldn't work, Kane thought sensibly. If he did manage to make Darcey fall in love with him, then he would have to hurt her to make her go crying to her father in St. Louis. But what other practical option was available to him? None that he could think of, he was sorry to say.

"Curse your hide, Patrick," Kane muttered to the empty room. "You assigned me an impossible task!"

And then Kane recalled Patrick's smug grin as he'd swaggered out of the office that day almost three weeks earlier. Like a fool, Kane had declared that no woman could be difficult to handle after dealing with hardened criminals for a decade. And, with green eyes twinkling, the stout Irishman had said: "You haven't met my daughter . . ."

Now that Kane had met Darcey O'Roarke, he felt as if he had slammed into a brick wall.

"Women!" Kane grumbled acrimoniously. "If a man wants a woman to stay, she leaves in a cloud of dust. If he wants her to go, she won't budge from her spot. I swear, a mule is less contrary than the female of the species!"

On that frustrating thought, Kane downed another drink and paced back and forth across his room until he very nearly wore himself out. But even exhaustion didn't cure his dilemma with Darcey, not that he really expected it would!

"Miss O'Roarke, the gold sh-shipment just arrived," Lester Alridge informed his new boss. "S-since you are double-checking the accounts, I'll help Owen weigh the nuggets b-before delivery to the mint."

Darcey marked her place in the ledger with her index finger and glanced up at the accountant who had been an employee of the office since it opened four years earlier. Lester was a small, frail man of thirty or thereabouts—five years younger than his brother, Peter had informed her during one of their many conversations.

Although Lester slicked his straight brown hair back, several recalcitrant strands stuck out on the top of his head like the plumes on a turkey. The thick round glasses that were perched on his triangular-shaped nose made Lester appear bug-eyed. Lester's physical appearance definitely suited the role he had assumed in life. He didn't look as if he could handle anything more strenuous than sitting at a desk, counting money, and tallying accounts. He was meek, mild, self-conscious, and he stuttered nervously when he was forced to communicate with other humans. Lester functioned best, as far as Darcey could tell, when he was enclosed in his closet of an office, totaling columns of numbers.

Setting the ledger aside, Darcey rose from Lester's desk and gestured for him to assume the task of crediting and deducting funds from various accounts. *"I'll* weigh the gold," she insisted before breezing out the door.

Lester opened his thin lips to voice a comment, reconsidered, and then scrunched down into his chair. Darcey spared the accountant no more thought as she aimed herself toward the main counter of the clapboard office where the demoted manager was randomly dropping pouches of gold on either side of the scales.

"I figured you'd want to do this yourself," Owen grumbled sourly. "I'm sure our previous system doesn't suit your high standards."

Darcey glared poison arrows at Owen. He still

hadn't recovered from the fact that he had been demoted and rejected. The arrogant dolt still hadn't gotten it through that chunk of wood he called a brain that she was all business and no nonsense. And she'd had just about enough of his snide remarks.

Darcey picked up the sacks of gold dust and plunked them down in an orderly fashion—from small to large. "Do you value your job?" Darcey questioned point-blank.

Owen gnashed his teeth until he very nearly ground off the enamel. "I don't recall hearing any complaints about my ability to weigh gold until you showed up," he muttered in a resentful tone.

Clamping an iron grip on her temper, Darcey elbowed Owen out of the way to work the scales. After recording the weight, she spared her glaring associate a brief glance. "Complaints about the inefficiency in this office are the very reason I'm here, as if you don't know. We are in the business of providing a service to the community and making money while we're at it. Under your loose supervision, this office has been doing neither."

Owen glowered at Darcey's satin-clad back. As pretty as she was, she was a royal pain in the ass. "I suppose if I had thought to stuff a few snakes in the company strongboxes to discourage thieves from stealing gold shipments, as you did, I wouldn't have been demoted."

He wished he had thought of that ingenious idea instead of this female who possessed all the necessary character traits that would also qualify her as a prison warden. The technique had worked splendidly to quell trouble until word spread and the thieves began to prepare themselves to face serpents when they pried open the strongboxes. But the first few times the thieves reached inside and came up with a snake, the stage drivers and guards had been able to thwart the robberies.

In addition to that clever scheme, this highly organized and imaginative female had revamped every stage and freight wagon schedule to ensure that not one minute was wasted. The change in schedule also served to throw would-be thieves off track. Darcey closely supervised every facet of the stage lines. After visiting the stage stations, she had demanded fresh coats of paint on the buildings and that the most sanitary conditions possible be provided for travelers. She had insisted on first-class accommodations, meals, and equipment. Employees who didn't pull their weight were replaced. Some of the replacements, of course were women. Darcey had seen to that.

"Did you wish to voice another petty complaint?" Darcey prompted when Owen merely stood in her way, halting her efficient process of packaging the gold which was to be delivered to the federal mint.

"Do by all means get on with it," Owen cooed pretentiously. "I hate to stand in the way of such monumental progress."

"At least you recognize efficiency when you see it," Darcey parried with a mocking smile. "That is a start."

Owen's fingers hovered around her neck, but he managed to squelch the urge to strangle the sassy imp. She had the infuriating knack of flinging insults and she irritated Owen to the point that he couldn't think of a suitably nasty rejoinder, short of sputtering curses at her. And that would inevitably cost him his job.

When Owen stamped off to help the customer who had entered the office, Darcey grinned mischievously to herself. She delighted in antagonizing that cocky buffoon. Owen was a womanizer and she sorely resented his attitude. Some men openly invited ridicule. Owen Graves was one of the most deserving candidates she'd ever encountered. Kane Callahan was another.

While Darcey was meticulously plodding through her precision-honed system of converting and recording the gold, a messenger arrived from the telegraph office. The first note was from her father, a brief plea to return home because he missed her terribly. Darcey smiled affectionately at her father's message. Each week Patrick made contact, requesting her return, and she sent off her weekly reply. She had no intention of leaving Denver until she could account for the loss of profit in this floundering office and put the Denver agency back on its feet.

A spasm of unintelligible hisses spewed from Darcey's lips where her eyes blazed over the second telegram. The Courtly Highwayman who operated alone had struck again. This time he had halted the stage on a remote and tedious stretch of road in the mountains. He had hauled the company strongbox from the coach, hitched it to his mule, and made off with an undetermined amount of gold. As always, the lone bandit had refrained from stealing cash and jewelry from the stage passengers and had left his customary thank-you note to O'Roarke Express for supplying him with funds to keep him in the manner to which he had grown accustomed.

Darcey had taken giant strides in ridding the freight and stage lines of thieves, and still there were two thorns in her side. One thief treated passengers with respect and kindly thanked the guards and driver for delivering the loot to him. The other thorn was the ruthless gang of outlaws who left a trail of blood behind them, as well as frisked and sometimes wounded passengers who tried to defend themselves.

"More trouble?" Owen queried, casting Darcey a smug glance. "It seems that sometimes even highly efficient methods are no match for thievery."

Darcey eyed the assistant manager suspiciously. "And how do you know this telegram is a notice of a robbery?"

If she didn't know better, she'd swear Owen had offered information to the thieves. In fact, he could be the mastermind who was bleeding the agency dry. Owen was probably cutting himself in on the loot at the company's expense. No doubt he wanted Darcey to look bad so her father would drag her home and leave the office in Owen's incompetent hands.

Owen shrugged his shoulder before negligently bracing his elbows on the counter. "It cannot be a message stating the light and love of your life has abandoned you, since you loathe men and don't have even one beau to your credit," he replied with wicked delight. "So naturally news of robbery is the only thing that could possibly cause a woman in your managerial position such distress."

It was with considerable effort that Darcey refused

to snatch up a pouch of gold and hurl it at the haughty blond-haired baboon. But better yet, she would scour the ledgers for proof that Owen had been swindling money from the company and passing information to thieves. Perhaps she should switch the schedules again without informing Owen. If it threw the thieves off track for a couple of weeks, she could be reasonably certain Owen was participating in the holdups.

"You are correct," Darcey admitted, casting her musings aside. "There has been another robbery. You have allowed yourself to become complacent about such things, as if such occurrences should be expected and overlooked. I, however, take robbery as a personal insult. Perhaps if you would take your employment here more seriously instead of mucking about, wasting my time and yours, we could get along better and ensure that this company functions to its full capacity."

Owen stormed toward his cubicle of an office with such haste that his coattails flapped behind him. Darcey snickered to herself before sifting out the next pouch of gold dust. Now perhaps she could complete her chore without interruptions. Owen was more of a nuisance than a help. And if he was going to bombard her with hostility, then she would give as good as she got. But she was *not* buckling to his ridicule. She was made of sturdy stuff and she was determined to endure whatever pitfalls she encountered. After all, a woman's greatest penance in life was tolerating the presence of men like Owen Graves and Kane Callahan before she earned her wings and flew through the pearly gates.

*   *   *

Cautiously, Kane eased open the door of the pigsty Griz Vanhook called a room in the dilapidated boardinghouse. Before sneaking out, Kane made sure that no one saw him leaving. Griz and his henchmen were locked in jail after harassing Darcey and Kane had investigated the room. To his dismay, Griz had been clever enough to dispose of any evidence that might link him to the O'Roarke Express robberies. Kane hadn't counted on Griz being so cunning. The man's strongest point wasn't brains, but he was obviously a little smarter than he looked. The ruffian hadn't been careless enough to draw more suspicion by stashing stolen jewels, credit vouchers, and gold sacks stamped with the O'Roarke insignia. If Griz was the leader of the bandit gang, he had certainly covered his tracks well.

Although Kane felt the need to ride off to the cabin where he had stationed Noah and Giddeon, he wasn't ready to leave town just yet. He had thrust a pair of field glasses at Noah and sent the would-be detective to patrol the stage route and make note of any suspicious characters who lingered in the area. Even though it was time to make contact with Noah and Giddeon, Griz would be released from jail at nightfall and Kane anticipated more trouble.

Bearing that in mind, Kane checked his timepiece and ambled down Larimer Street, past the Criterion Saloon, which was teeming with patrons. He fully intended to escort Darcey from her office to her hotel, just in case Griz showed up to satisfy his vengeance. Of course, convincing Darcey to accompany him any- where would be no small feat. The past few days she had made a spectacular display of avoiding him. And considering her penchant for theatrics, Kane decided to invite her to the opera house to watch a performance by a traveling troupe that had arrived in town to entertain the citizens. Surely she wouldn't object to a harmless evening in his presence. At least he hoped she wouldn't, even if he'd have to do some fancy talking to convince her to accompany him to the theater.

Darcey had just finished sorting out the wooden crates of gold which would be hauled to the mint when Kane sauntered into the office at closing time to fling her a flirtatious smile which she purposely ignored. Since she was the only one left to tend the agency, she was forced to indulge Kane in conversation.

"May I be of assistance or did you just strut in off the street to make a pest of yourself?" she questioned, unwillingly admiring Kane's expensive black jacket, matching breeches, and gold silk vest which was probably bulging with his winnings at the gaming table.

Kane smothered a grin as he glanced around the immaculate office. The place shouted efficiency and organization. It had Darcey's stamp of order all over it. Customer ledgers and office supplies were placed in rows, all in alphabetical order, of course. Nothing was out of place. Even the scales had been wiped clean of gold dust and returned to their proper location between the other necessary equipment that began with the letters *R* and *T*.

Amused, Kane fixed his gaze on the prim and properly dressed young woman who wore another high-collared gown that screamed a few more things about her personality. Things like *Don't touch. I have no intention whatsoever of drawing the attention of men.* But Darcey O'Roarke, with her glorious mass of auburn hair, intelligent green eyes, and curvaceous figure couldn't disguise her many assets unless she stuffed herself in a gunny sack. But she seemed to consider her breathtaking beauty the curse of her life. Men naturally gravitated toward her and she resented it.

"I asked you a question, Mister Callahan," she prompted, shifting awkwardly beneath those probing silver-blue eyes that stared a little deeper than she would have preferred.

"In the first place," Kane began as he leisurely propped himself against the counter, "I did not strut in here. In the second place, I do not consider myself a pest."

"You, of course, are entitled to your opinion," she said flippantly.

Kane willfully overlooked the sassy remark and continued. "I came in to invite you to dinner and to the theater. But if you are too busy this evening alphabetizing your wardrobe, I will certainly understand." A devilish grin quirked his lips when Darcey flashed him a venomous glare. "I was hoping you could fit me, *K* for *Kane* in between *J* for *jewelry* and *L* for *lingerie.*"

"Your wit is only half of what it should be," Darcey countered, unable to bite back the makings of a smile.

For all his faults, this raven-haired rake was clever with words and always ready with a devastating grin that could tug on a woman's heartstrings. But Darcey had no intention of falling head over heels like a hopeless romantic ever again. She was immune to Kane Callahan.

"I'm relieved to see your lovely face doesn't crack when you break into a smile," Kane teased as he reached over to trace the velvet-soft curve of her lips.

Darcey winced and pulled away. Curse it, the slightest touch from him rattled her to the extreme. His caresses triggered the same sensations he had aroused on a night she preferred to forget. If he kept this up, Darcey would have to grow a shell to protect herself from his deadly charm.

"Just exactly what is it you want from me?" Darcey questioned. "You assured me the other night that I was not your conquest, that what happened between us simply happened. So what are you doing here when I insisted I did not want to see you again?"

Kane wasn't about to tell her he was concerned about her safety. She scoffed at what she thought was none of his business, even though he had been highly paid to make her personal welfare his foremost concern.

"Perhaps I simply long for the pleasure of your company," he murmured in a low, caressing tone.

"Pleasure?" Darcey stared dubiously at him. "It seems to me that you always find as much fault with me as I do with you. What, may I ask, is the pleasure in that?"

Was there no way around this quarrelsome female?

102

She even sought to induce an argument about their quibbling, for pity sake! Determinedly, Kane conjured up his most persuasive smile and presented it to Darcey. "Despite our diametrical differences, I find you an interesting companion. I just thought you might enjoy a little harmless conversation, a good meal, and an amusing play at the theater, that's all."

Darcey chewed on her bottom lip and contemplated his offer. She had worked herself into exhaustion since her arrival in Denver. Perhaps she did deserve a diversion. The theater would be a welcome distraction. For one night she would forget about the unbalanced books, the unsolved robberies, and her mounting problems with Owen Graves. Besides, she had spent the afternoon poring over the ledgers until she had worked up a ferocious headache. Enough was enough.

"Very well, I accept," she announced before she began her orderly ritual of closing the office. "Are you going to ridicule me again if I eat my evening meal in a clockwise fashion?" she wanted to know.

"Probably," Kane chuckled as he watched Darcey zoom around the agency, putting every last pen and paper in its place. "Are you planning to mock me for the unpardonable sin of being born a man?"

"You can depend on it." Despite her resolve to remain cool and detached in Kane's presence, Darcey felt another impish smile playing on her lips.

Laughter echoed around the office as Kane watched her radiant grin light up the shadowed room. "I feel better already, just knowing I was the reason you cracked a smile. I think this will prove to be a very interesting evening for both of us," he remarked as he ushered Darcey toward the door.

Interesting was not the appropriate description for the evening they were about to have. But Kane hadn't been blessed with the gift of foresight. If he had, he would never have opened the door to plunge into the surprise reception which awaited them.

Chapter 6

"Well, well, look who we have here, boys," Griz Vanhook snickered to his burly henchmen. "If it ain't my two favorite people in all the world."

Darcey knew perfectly well that she and Kane were anything but! Archenemies was nearer the mark. Griz had come to settle the score, with his brutish friends as his reinforcements.

Before Griz could latch hold of her, Kane thrust himself in front of Darcey like a shield. His steely gaze never wavered from Griz and his drunken cohorts for even a second. "Go back inside and lock the door, Darcey." His very tone brooked no disobedience, but it was wishful thinking on his part to assume Darcey would meekly comply to the command.

"This is my fight as well as yours," Darcey said courageously.

Kane gnashed his teeth and swore under his breath. He should have known this hellion would court catastrophe for the mere challenge of it. Kane was certain she had never backed down from anything in all her life. It just wasn't her nature to break and run. She would stay to the bitter end, even if it killed her . . . which it very well could.

Griz staggered forward. His dark eyes narrowed murderously on Kane. "I don't take kindly to bein' left to rot in that filthy calaboose. And you're the two who saw to it that me and my friends got stuffed in there."

Kane's gaze leaped to Griz's gun hand, which hovered over his holster like a honeybee over a flower, and then he glanced back to his nemesis's eyes. In his dealings with vicious desperadoes, Kane had noticed the eyes always signaled the split-second decision to draw. Griz, however, was drunk and that made his actions more difficult to predict. Kane had been in these tense situations before. He was an old hand at showdowns and gunfights and he had conditioned himself to react with instinct and intellect, not emotion. But this time he had Darcey's safety to consider. Now, not only did Kane have to be quick and competent enough to protect himself from these three pistoleros but he also had to be proficient enough to protect Darcey, all in the same moment.

While Kane stood there evaluating every choice, Darcey pushed past him to prevent another showdown. "We are not going to have a repetition of the revolting scene we had the other day . . ."

She had barely gotten out the last word when Griz lunged at her. Kane took advantage of Griz's preoccupation with Darcey. He came uncoiled like a human spring and made a spectacular leap at his foe. Griz found himself propelled backward by the exploding force of the man who had charged at him full steam ahead. A mutinous growl erupted from Griz's curled lips when he slammed into his pistol-packing friends, sending them all sprawling into the dirt in a tangled heap.

Kane had decided that thrusting himself into a knock-down-drag-out fight was a safer mode of battle than exchanging gunfire with Darcey underfoot. He might get the hell beat out of him and then shot later, but there was always the outside chance that Darcey would see the necessity of dashing down the street to summon the deputy who usually waited around the corner to escort her home.

A pained groan tumbled from Kane's lips when a doubled fist plowed into his jaw. Like a carpenter pounding nails, Kane threw repeated punches at the three faces that sneered at him. For several minutes the four men exchanged beefy fists. Kane, being out-numbered three to one, tasted more than his fair share of them.

When the barrel of a pistol flashed before his eyes, he knocked the weapon away, causing it to discharge. In the near distance Darcey let out a yelp. Reacting to Darcey's startled squawk was Kane's downfall. He swiveled his head around to ensure that the stray bullet hadn't struck her. Before he could ascertain whether she was still on her feet, another meaty fist caught him on the side of the head, rattling his teeth and his senses.

A gasp of dismay gushed from Darcey's lips when she scrambled back to her feet after deftly dodging the bullet. Although she had marveled at the explosive, volcanic force Kane possessed when he leaped on his foe like streak lightning, she winced in sympathy when he took a bone-jarring blow. Determined to lend assistance, Darcey circled the pile of men with a makeshift weapon in hand, hoping to club one burly brute or the other over the head. Kane had been doing a magnificent job of holding his own until he glanced around to check on her. Darcey cursed herself soundly for yelping in fear when the pistol exploded. Because of her, Kane was getting the tar beat out of him!

Growling like a panther, Darcey raised her club and hammered the closest head. Thank the Lord it wasn't Kane's! A dull groan tumbled from one of the henchmen's lips as he rolled in the dirt and lay there like a slug.

"Damn it, Darcey, go fetch the deputy!" Kane scowled as he cocked his arm to deliver a powerful blow to Griz's bearded jaw.

Darcey hesitated. She had been operating under the theory that Kane wouldn't get shot if she were there to oversee the battle. It was similar to the adage about a watched pot never boiling. But Kane's growled command contradicted that theory and left her wavering in indecision.

"*Now,* damn it!" Kane roared the instant before an unseen blow knocked the wind out of him.

Darcey dropped her club like a hot potato and shot down the street. The exploding pistol had already alerted Pup Metcalf, who whizzed around the corner to investigate. He and Darcey collided in midstep, sending Darcey skidding backward in the street.

Pup stared, horrified, at the young woman whose petticoats had flipped over her head, displaying an indecent amount of bare leg. When he reached down to hoist her back to her feet, Darcey practically dragged him after her in her haste to save Kane from certain disaster.

By the time they returned to the scene of battle, one of the henchmen had grabbed both of Kane's arms and Griz was kicking him to splinters. When Griz reached for his pistol to shoot his battered foe at close range, Darcey reacted more quickly than the rattled deputy. Pup was still fumbling for his pistol when Darcey jerked up his Colt and took quick aim. In her eagerness to save Kane's life she didn't take time to focus on her target. She missed Griz by a mile. The bullet sailed over his wooly head and ricocheted off the hitching post where the desperadoes had tethered their horses.

When the horses reared in fright, Griz glanced over his shoulder and made his hasty decision. A crowd had spilled out of doorways and surged down the street behind the deputy and Darcey. If Griz satisfied his need to blow this meddling bastard to kingdom come he would be charged with murder. There were too many witnesses on hand and he didn't have time to intimidate any of them into refusing to testify against him.

"Come on, Tom," Griz snapped at his cohort.

Leaving their unconscious companion to fend for himself, Griz and Tom dashed toward their horses. Gasping for breath, Kane floundered to retrieve his pistol. Although he considered himself an excellent marksman, he had difficulty focusing on the fleeing desperadoes. His left eye was swollen shut and the vision in his right eye was severely blurred. Despite the handicap, Kane took aim and fired. Even though he

109

hadn't been able to get a clear shot at Griz's departing back, Kane winged Tom Hatch. The outlaw toppled from his horse and screamed curses when Griz abandoned him in an effort to save his own worthless hide.

A wave of humanity swept down the street to take the two desperadoes into custody. But it was Darcey who dropped to her knees in front of Kane, peering at him with anxious concern.

"Are you all right?" *Stupid question,* Darcey scolded herself. One glance at Kane testified to the fact that he had seen better days. He had the makings of a magnificent black eye, two bloody lips, and he was clutching his ribs as if they were cracked in at least two places. There was also a noticeable goose egg that was in the process of hatching on the left side of his head.

"This is all your fault," Kane grumbled out the side of his mouth that hurt the least. God, he ached in places he didn't even remember he had. He had been involved in hand-to-hand combat in his time, but this was positively the worst! He usually tried to even the odds before plunging into a melee, but it had been impossible in this instance. "If you would have gone back inside like I told you to do in the first place—"

"You'd be dead," Darcey said with perfect assurance. "I suppose you think you could have taken all three buscaderos on at once and emerged the victor. Isn't it just like an arrogant man to think he can launch an attack on every gunslinger in the country and walk away unscathed. You aren't courageous, Kane Callahan. You are downright foolish!"

Kane sagged back to the ground and inhaled a

careful breath. His insides felt like mashed potatoes. "What I could use right now is a little sympathy instead of a lecture." He expelled a miserable groan. "Let's just forget whose fault it was, shall we?" he suggested.

"Well, it certainly wasn't mine," Darcey sniffed, unable as usual to prevent herself from having the last word.

Kane rolled his eyes and sighed audibly. With extreme effort, he dragged his noodly legs beneath him and staggered to his feet. To his surprise and relief, Darcey wrapped a supporting arm around him to steady him.

"We'll get you to a physician and patch you up. Then we'll put you to bed," Darcey insisted.

Pup Metcalf lumbered over to inspect Kane's multiple scrapes and bruises. "I'm afraid the local doctors aren't around to offer first aid. There was a mining accident at one of the stamp mills and the physicians aren't expected back until tomorrow."

"Then fetch me a carriage," Darcey ordered, taking control of the situation with her usual efficiency.

Like the obedient puppy he so strongly resembled in appearance, the deputy loped down the street to do Darcey's bidding. In less than two minutes Pup was back with a borrowed carriage and assisted Kane into the seat.

While Pup and the other members of the community gathered their prisoners and marched them to jail, Darcey aimed the buggy toward the closest physician's office to collect the necessary medical supplies, despite the doctor's absence.

When Darcey halted the carriage in front of her

hotel, Kane frowned. "Now what?" The world was spinning around him and he had the urge to lie down until he got his bearings. All Darcey's hasty starts and stops weren't doing him one whit of good.

In a single bound, Darcey was off the buggy, waiting to assist Kane to his feet. "You can convalesce in my room until you feel well enough to make your way home . . . wherever that is."

Kane gaped at her. "I don't think that's a good idea. You have your reputation to consider," he reminded her.

Darcey flung him a withering glance and latched on to his arm. "My reputation, being what it is, will probably do more to quell gossip than to incite it."

Kane managed a feeble chuckle as he eased onto the boardwalk. "Amen to that."

Darcey bristled at his teasing remark. Why it annoyed her, she couldn't say, but it did. "I'm not completely ignorant of men, you know," she felt compelled to say as she shepherded Kane into the lobby. "And I wasn't always as cynical, either. I even fancied myself in love once, and once was more than enough to cure me."

"So that's it," Kane said with an understanding nod.

"What's it?" Darcey quizzed as they trudged up the steps, side by side, arm over arm.

This close personal contact with Kane rattled her more than it should have. Curse it, she couldn't even keep up with the conversation when they were draped all over each other like Spanish moss.

"That's why you hold all men in contempt," he speculated. "The rest of us have to pay penance because

112

of the betrayal of one man."

A smile stretched across his swollen lips, causing him considerable discomfort. It suddenly hit him like a sledgehammer that he was guilty of the same offense. He had sworn off women because of Melanie Brooks. They were birds of a feather. The only difference was Kane was older and wiser and he hadn't carried his bitterness to the extreme. No doubt Darcey had been more vulnerable and at a very tender age when struck and wounded by Cupid's arrow. And ten to one, she was still carrying a torch for her lost love.

After blurting out her foolish remark about being in love, Darcey slammed her mouth shut like a drawer. Damn her runaway tongue. She had never discussed or even hinted at her heartbreaking relationship with Michael to anyone until now. And when Kane was feeling better he would probably harass her unmercifully about it.

Well, she would make no more references to her first and last bout with love. It was over and done and it was nobody's business but her own. Darcey had always felt awkward about sharing her innermost thoughts. Neither did she feel comfortable with these unwanted feelings of affection she harbored for this gambling gunslinger. *My God,* thought Darcey. *I was actually afraid for him when he nearly got himself shot and killed trying to defend me!* And if the truth be known, she had felt far more than compassion and sympathy.

Quickly, Darcey squelched her traitorous thoughts. She was only playing the good Samaritan. Kane had come to her defense and she was returning the favor by offering to nurse him back to health. It was as simple as that. At least Darcey hoped it was. *It was!* she convinced herself as she fumbled for the key. She was *not* going to get emotionally or romantically attached to a man she knew so little about. And *that,* she decided right there and then, was *that!*

A relieved sigh tumbled from Kane's lips as he eased his battered body onto Darcey's bed. He hurt to the ends of his hair after Griz and his cohorts had pounded him into putty. Lord, maybe Giddeon Fox was right, thought Kane. Maybe it was time he gave up his rough-and-tumble life and left the task of tracking and apprehending criminals to younger men. At thirty-two, Kane had been shot up, shot down, and knocked around a few times too many. Already, some parts of his body woke up slower than others. If he kept up this dangerous way of life that helped to cure his restlessness he wouldn't live to enjoy his father's inheritance. But taking the easy way out had never been Kane's style. He'd always loved a challenge and this time he'd paid for it but good!

"Ouch . . . damn it, that hurts!" Kane nearly came straight up out of bed and right through the ceiling when Darcey dribbled stinging antiseptic on his cut lips and scraped cheek.

"I'm sorry," she apologized as she set the antiseptic aside. "I'm not very good at this."

"Ain't it the truth," Kane grumbled in pain.

"Well, you don't have to be sarcastic," Darcey snapped defensively. "I was only trying to help!"

"That's the same thing Napoleon's advisers said at

Waterloo," Kane muttered grumpily. "And you know what good that did *him.*"

Darcey sank down beside her cranky patient. A wave of compassion flooded over her as she surveyed what had once been a ruggedly handsome face. To be perfectly frank, Kane looked like hammered hell.

"You certainly have your fair share of abrasions, contusions, cuts, and scrapes," she murmured sympathetically before she reached for the antiseptic once again.

"And leave it to you to list all my battle scars in alphabetical order," Kane muttered irritably. "I'd rather you kiss me where it hurts instead of burning the fire out of me with that damned antiseptic."

Even when Kane Callahan was cranky, cross, and injured, he still maintained his incorrigible wit, Darcey noted. Despite the situation, Darcey broke into an elfin smile. As gently as possible, she wiped away the trickle of blood that clung to his bottom lip. "You really are a daredevil," she admonished teasingly. "No doubt, my kisses would be worse than the antiseptic."

Long black lashes fluttered up to peer into the elegant face that hovered above his. As confident and efficient as this saucy nymph was, she seemed to be the only one on the planet who was oblivious to the devastating effect she had on men. As bad as Kane felt at the moment, he wouldn't have minded being the recipient of her kisses. In fact, it would probably cure what ailed him. This curvaceous sprite could make *any* man forget the pain that pulsated through him.

When Darcey loosened the buttons on Kane's shirt to inspect him for other wounds, he swore there wasn't

115

enough air in the room to fill a thimble, much less his lungs. He watched Darcey blush at the sight of his hair-matted chest. He saw her inquisitive gaze sweep down his belly to the band of his breeches in unguarded feminine appreciation. Suddenly, Kane felt another ache, one that had nothing to do with Griz Vanhook's beefy fists and kicking boots.

Darcey told herself that her eyes were only on a medical inspection to locate other abrasions that demanded attention. But the sight of Kane's utterly masculine chest, the washboarded muscles of his lean belly, and the crisp thatch of hair that trickled down to disappear into his breeches seemed to hold her gaze like a powerful magnet. A pale scar curved around his ribs and a small indentation caused by a bullet marred the whipcord muscles on his left shoulder. Other than that, Kane Callahan was pretty nearly perfect. His sensual appeal radiated from him like heat from the sun!

A warm sensation trickled down Darcey's spine as her fingertips splayed over the discoloration caused by a hard kick to the abdomen. When Kane groaned unexpectedly, Darcey's wide-eyed gaze bounced up to the pained expression that was stamped on his battered features.

"Did I hurt you again?" she questioned in concern.

Did she ever! Kane cursed his instantaneous and highly explosive reaction to her untutored touch. What was there about this sassy, overly particular, cynical female that caused him to respond so violently? True, Kane had decided to woo her into leaving town with him, even if he did have to dent her pride when he abandoned her. But if all he thought he was doing was devising a way to lure Darcey away from trouble, he was kidding himself. Honest to God, she had the most incredible knack of making him forget his purpose, one for which he was being exceptionally well paid!

"I want you to be on the first stage out of here," Kane demanded, removing her lingering hand before she burned him up with a fever she didn't know how to cure. "If Griz shows his face in town again, he'll come gunning for you. We'll go together . . . anywhere . . . so long as it's away from here."

Darcey's backbone stiffened like a ramrod. "I will not run from trouble and shirk my responsibility to the express company," she assured him in no uncertain terms.

"If you had any sense you would," Kane scowled.

"You can call me a fool if you like but—"

"Fool," Kane obliged with a ridiculing snort.

Darcey flung him a glare that would have frozen the tropical jungles of the Equator.

Kane expelled a long sigh and scolded himself for being so irritable. His emotions were at war with each other and that inner battle was spoiling his disposition. Darcey desperately needed to get out of town and out of this room. Her very presence was tormenting him and causing a conflict between his professional obligations and his personal desires. Not only was Darcey O'Roarke going to have to contend with Griz Vanhook, but she also might find herself fending off the very man who'd been sent to defend her!

Lord, so much for swearing off women, Kane thought deflatedly. This self-imposed celibacy was beginning to take its toll on him. Kane didn't want

117

medical treatment nearly as much as he wanted to lose himself in Darcey's honeyed kisses. He wanted to teach her things she didn't know about men.

"My, but you do turn into a sourpuss when somebody beats you to a pulp," Darcey pointed out. "I think the best thing to do is get you out of this gun belt so you can rest comfortably. And perhaps a half a bottle of whiskey will take the edge off your nerves."

An embarrassed gasp bubbled in her throat when her hand accidentally bumped against the private part of his anatomy in an effort to remove his double holsters.

Kane cursed fluently. Now there was no question whatsoever about the effect she was having on him. He'd have had to clutch a pillow in his lap to cover his obvious state of arousal. And he would be doubled over, screaming in pain in another minute if she didn't move away and allow him to draw in a breath that wasn't thick with the scent of her enticing perfume.

Darcey shrank away and her face flushed bloodred. As well educated as she was, her father had never sat her down to explain the facts of life. The first thought that occurred to Darcey was that a well-aimed blow to the groin had caused swelling, similar to the goose egg that bulged on the side of Kane's head.

"It seems you've been bruised in other places . . ."

Another hot blush spattered across her cheeks and heightened noticeably when Kane burst out laughing at her ignorant remark.

Talk about naive! Good Lord, she was far more innocent of men than she would have him believe. In fact, she didn't seem to know beans about the change a man's body underwent when aroused.

"If you aren't completely ignorant of men, then you're pretty damned close. This condition has nothing to do with fighting and everything to do with thinking what it would be like to have you in my bed," Kane blurted without thinking.

Darcey gasped in profuse mortification when the light of understanding dawned on her. It humiliated her beyond words to have Kane know how little she really did know about the male of the species.

Kane didn't think her bewitching face could turn a deeper shade of crimson than it already was. He thought wrong.

As if she were sitting on a bed of live coals, Darcey bolted to her feet and presented her back. "I'll go fetch the whiskey," she croaked. "I think we both could use a drink."

When Darcey buzzed out the door Kane groaned in dismay. He and his big mouth! Darcey had just begun to let her guard down with him and he'd botched up by mocking her innocence. The blow to the side of his head had obviously scrambled his brain and played havoc with some of his more noticeable bodily functions. And damned if Patrick hadn't proved himself correct again. Even after Kane had analyzed this she-male until it had given him a king-size headache, he still was at a loss as how to handle Darcey. Hell's bells, these days he couldn't even handle *himself!*

119

Chapter 7

Feeling as unstable as a two-legged chair, Darcey paused in the hall outside her room. Inhaling a steadying breath, she uncorked the whiskey bottle before crossing the border into dangerous territory. Although she had never partaken of anything stronger than dinner wine in all her twenty-one years, she decided there were times when whiskey was the answer. Staring at the amber liquid in her glass, she took a quick swallow. A sputtering wheeze passed her lips. She sucked air and turned blue. Lord, it felt as if liquid fire had seared down her throat to smolder in the pit of her stomach. But still her nerves were frazzled. She definitely needed another drink and she wasted no time in taking it.

With each new encounter, Darcey found herself more attracted to a man she knew better than to even like. Kane wasn't her type, that was for sure. And he also suffered the same annoying foibles that plagued the rest of his gender. He perceived Darcey as a woman only, not an associate, companion, or friend. And although Kane had once declared he had no intention of seducing her, he had been affected by her nearness. That had become embarrassingly obvious!

Darcey downed another gulp of whiskey and struggled to breathe.

She hadn't wanted to notice how masculine Kane Callahan was, how his muscles flexed and relaxed beneath her inquiring touch.

She gulped another jigger of whiskey with considerably more ease than the first three swallows.

And when her hand had brushed across Kane's lap . . .

She gulped another drink. She had to get a firm grip on herself, and quickly! From this moment forward she was going to consider Kane as just another member of the human race. Theirs would be a strictly platonic relationship and she would observe all the limitations she had established for herself when dealing with men. Kane was a shiftless gambler and a daredevil gunslinger and she was a wealthy heiress with a noble mission in life. They mixed as well as oil and water.

Resolved to that sensible philosophy, Darcey shouldered open the swollen door to her room. Despite her self-inspiring lecture, her gaze fell helplessly to the provocative expanse of Kane's chest the instant she walked in. The sight of him disturbed her and put her heart on a drumroll. She couldn't have looked away if her very life depended on it.

To make matters worse, the four drinks she'd guzzled had taken more than the frayed edge off her nerves. The whiskey had also numbed the workings of her brain.

"You have a very magnificent chest. I'm sure the rest of your body . . ." Darcey covered her mouth and blinked like a startled owl. Curse it, she hadn't meant to say any such thing! How did that betraying thought leak out?

The blundering comment wasn't helping Kane cope with his own wayward thoughts. From the moment he'd ventured too close to this temptress she had become an itch he couldn't quite reach to scratch, a mathematical equation he couldn't quite puzzle out. He'd been afraid their rocky relationship was going to build to this climactic point. He'd warned himself against such dangerous notions. But hell, when such a bewitching woman stared at a man in open fascination, what was he to do? Damned if Kane knew!

Darcey helped herself to another drink. Her fifth. But who was counting? Darcey certainly wasn't. She was desperately trying to ignore the thoughts that poured through her soggy mind.

"Gimme that bottle," Kane demanded impatiently. "I'm the one who got beaten black and blue."

Darcey jerked the bottle out of his reach to take another quick drink. "And I'm the one who had to *watch* you get beaten black and blue." Her voice suddenly sounded as if it had rusted and her nose was plagued by the most peculiar tingle. But better that she experience tingles there rather than in places she hadn't realized she'd had until Kane Callahan walked into her life to turn her wrong side out, she reckoned. And being inebriated had to be better than feeling the attraction to this midnight-haired rake with his entrancing silver-blue eyes!

Before Darcey could replenish her glass again, Kane propped himself up on an elbow to grasp the bottle. After consuming a generous portion of whiskey straight from the flask, he sank back and sighed heavily.

"After a few more drinks I'll go back to my own room. In the meantime, you start packing," he ordered gruffly. "We're leaving Denver."

"You may be, but I most certainly am not!" Darcey announced with her customary obstinacy. "That grizzly miscreant isn't going to frighten me away. And besides, you can't go anywhere. You're hurt, in case you've forgotten."

Kane grasped her arm and yanked her toward him. Unfortunately, Darcey tumbled off balance and wound up half beside and half atop him. Her hand was braced on his bare chest and her bent knee wedged intimately between his thighs.

Kane felt as if he'd been scorched with a hot branding iron. The tantalizing scent of her perfume clouded his senses to such a degree that Kane forgot what he'd intended to say before he dragged her toward him. All he could remember was the feel of her luscious body molded familiarly to his and how long he had been without a woman.

When their eyes locked, Darcey tried to draw a breath. It was a hopeless cause. She could no more breathe than she could untangle her gaze from his eyes. And when she finally did muster the willpower to tear her gaze away from the silver-blue pools that visually seduced and emotionally unnerved, her attention strayed to the sensual lips that were only a hairbreadth away from hers. For days she had avoided any close contact which might result in more kisses like the ones which had caused an explosion of her senses. But now, temptation was staring her directly in the face.

She had assured herself she never wanted to repeat those titillating embraces, but after the whiskey had dulled her mind, she began to wonder why she'd taken such great pains to avoid Kane. He stirred something within her that she thought Michael Dupris's betrayal had killed forevermore. This handsome gambler had set spark to her feminine yearnings. He had made her aware of, and vulnerable to, her own wanton desires.

Kane was thoroughly convinced that restraint, noble as it was for the soul, was hell on a man's body. He'd tried to maintain a respectable distance from Patrick O'Roarke's daughter, but he had depleted his last ounce of willpower. He needed to kiss Darcey's dewy-soft lips. It should have been his reward for restraining himself the last half-dozen times he'd wanted to take her in his arms and drown in her innocent kiss.

His lips rolled over hers, oblivious to the pain caused by the blows to his chin and jaw. Her kiss was the healing balm that soothed the soreness from his body and ignited the fires that simmered in his blood. A groan of unholy torment rattled in Kane's throat. He could feel her breasts boring into his chest, feel her hips moving in innocent response over his.

Kane had been without a woman for more weeks than he cared to count. He'd refused to buckle to his lusty needs for this green-eyed elf for what seemed forever. Now, he ached for her up to his eyebrows. He felt like a volcano that was about to erupt. Wanting Darcey had become his obsession. A flame of desire for her burned him inside and out. The attraction surpassed anything Kane had ever experienced. It made no sense whatsoever. And yet, the feel of her lips surrendering to his kiss felt incredibly right.

Darcey closed her eyes and mind to all except the wild, breathless sensations that throbbed through every fiber of her being. Her foggy senses took flight when Kane deepened the kiss. His hands tunneled beneath the hem of her gown to make stimulating contact with the sensitive flesh of her thigh. Flames flickered in the core of her being and burning desire melted what little resistance she had in her liquor-numbed mind.

With each bold caress, her defenses slipped another notch. When his index finger drifted over the fabric that covered the rose-tipped crests of her breasts, another coil of white-hot desire unfurled inside her. Sparks danced on her spine and her body burst into sweet flames. She gave herself up to the tantalizing sensations. Her traitorous body had taken complete command, making her a prisoner of her own awakened needs.

Despite the stabbing pain in his ribs, Kane twisted sideways to bring Darcey down beside him. He kissed her hungrily then, his questing hands refusing to be still for even a moment. He explored her feminine curves and his imagination ran wild. He could envision what she would look like lying naked in his arms. She would be absolute perfection, a dream come true.

Kane cherished every silky inch of flesh he exposed as he eased the sleeve of her gown down her arm. His gaze dropped to the creamy swells of her breasts that strained against the lacy chemise and another wild wave of desire buffeted him. His lips feathered over the dusky peaks he'd unveiled and a sigh of pure pleasure echoed in his throat. His hands moved restlessly, wanting more . . . and more. He tasted her, touched her, savored her with a growing urgency that was eating him alive.

He'd never felt so unsteady in all his life! He had no control whatsoever. It was as if his iron-clad will had never even existed!

As shadows of darkness drifted across the room, Kane knew he was battling a hopeless cause. He had visualized himself making sweet splendorous love to Darcey so many times the past week. Now she was in his arms and that delicious fantasy was only a whisper away from reality. Kane had drunk a little too much whiskey, too, and being with Darcey, touching her, caused his body to throb with longings so fierce and demanding that they banished all thought. Helplessly, Kane surrendered to the forbidden yearnings.

A tiny moan trickled from Darcey's lips when she felt Kane's greedy kisses burning a scalding path across the sensitive tips of her breasts. His slow, tantalizing exploration caused spine-tingling sensations to ribbon through her. Instead of pulling away from his caresses and kisses as she should have done, she arched toward him, reveling in the deliciously wicked pleasure that bubbled up inside her. Another gasp broke from her throat when his masterful hands glided over the ultrasensitive flesh of her thighs to arouse her beyond bearing.

Suddenly she was no more than a shell which housed the hot, pulsating needs that only this man could appease. Her betraying body welcomed his intimate exploration and shamelessly begged for more. Monstrous yearnings mushroomed inside her and she felt herself yielding to him. Over and over again he drew her to the edge of oblivion and then pulled her back to arouse her until she lay there, teetering on the brink of maddening urgency. Darcey swore she had died at least twice, and yet the torturous craving for more never subsided. Divine torment built like a brewing thunderstorm, prolonging, heightening, and intensifying the pleasure until her nerves and muscles screamed for release.

Even when Kane's muscular body glided over hers to take intimate possession, she didn't push him away. The sensual heat of his masculine body moving suggestively against hers was so devastating that she couldn't muster the will to resist for even a second. He had made her want him so desperately that even dying was no great sacrifice in exchange for the sublime rapture he offered.

When Kane braced his arms beside her, Darcey's lashes swept up to study the bruised and battered, but undeniably handsome, face that hovered above hers. Kane reminded her of a sleek, muscular panther. When he moved he never seemed to expend one unnecessary ounce of energy. Now, his glowing silver-blue eyes were upon her, watching her watch him, watching her eyes flicker with the same indescribable need that blazed through him.

"I tried," Kane rasped as he combed the tangled auburn tendrils away from her enchanting face and stared into her fathomless green eyes. "Know that, little nymph. I really did try not to want you the way I do now . . ."

His lithe body moved over hers, gently guiding her thighs apart with his knees, causing Darcey to tremble in breathless anticipation. "I can overcome anything else for you, but I can't overcome the fact that I am a man and you are a very desirable woman."

Kane had no experience with virgins, but he knew he had to restrain himself or he would frighten her into resisting him. If he didn't tenderly guide her over the hurdle of initiation, he would confirm her cynical opinion of men. What was meant to be a moment of unequaled splendor could become a painful nightmare for this innocent maiden.

Ever so slowly, Kane molded his muscular body to hers, granting her time to adjust to the feel of flesh absorbing flesh. Lord, it was all he could do to prevent himself from ravishing her. But he had vowed to be gentle and considerate, even if it killed him.

Darcey flinched when she felt the penetrating thrust of his powerful body invading hers. The haze of mindless pleasure shattered like glass when his masculine body blended with hers. Darcey's cry of anguish died on her lips when his mouth covered hers with tender expertise. He kissed away the initial pain he'd caused her and whispered promises of the rapture to come. And just as suddenly as the pain had invaded her

129

senses, it ebbed, replaced by a flickering, ever-growing sensation that blossomed like a fragile flower opening to warm sunshine.

Tenderly, he taught her innocent body to move at his command. He taught her the gentle cadence of feminine need communicating with masculine desire. Ever so gradually, Darcey found herself caught up in the sweet hypnotic rhythm, like a river gliding around each meandering bend until it cascaded over a sparkling waterfall to plunge into infinity.

With each driving thrust of his muscular body, Darcey could feel herself being absorbed until she was a living, breathing part of his phenomenal vitality. Powerful undercurrents of passion surged through her until she was swirling in a whirlpool of oblivion. Her arms fastened around his neck and she held on for dear life. She was like a drowning swimmer, uncaring if she was rescued. Sensation upon ineffable sensation engulfed her as she submerged in a sea of inimitable pleasure. Breathlessly, she clung to the one stable force in a careening universe of sensual darkness.

hen Kane felt Darcey surrender to the tidal wave ssion, he lost the last smidgen of control. Passion t forth like an erupting spring, dragging the last ce of strength from his body. Spasms of ecstasy meled him. The shudder that consumed him ked his very soul and shattered every thought. They ng together like two mariners on a storm-tossed sea, iting for the winds of passion to ebb.

After what seemed forever, Kane's foggy senses ared and he peered down at the flushed face and orious mane of auburn hair that fanned on the pillow. A mist of tears glistened in Darcey's enormous green eyes. Kane regretted those shimmering tears and the initial pain he'd caused this innocent elf. But he couldn't bring himself to regret the delicious splendor he had discovered in her silky arms. For one so innocent, Darcey seemed to know instinctively how to pleasure a man. Her responses were so natural, so uninhibited, so delightful.

But oh, there would be hell to pay for what he'd done. Kane was sure of it. Patrick would kill him if he knew Darcey's highly paid bodyguard had stolen his charge's virginity. And Darcey herself would probably consign him to hell when she regained control of her senses. Come dawn, she would be asking herself all sorts of questions. Guilt, confusion, and resentment would supply those answers. But Kane knew that passion such as this was the exception, not the rule.

As experienced as Melanie Brooks had been, she couldn't compare to this spirited, emerald-eyed sprite who had ardently responded to his lovemaking. Darcey O'Roarke was a dozen kinds of passion seeking release. She had returned his caresses and kisses with eagerness and lively imagination.

Darcey was vaguely aware of the smile that quirked Kane's lips, but her overindulgence with the whiskey and the heady intoxication of the lovemaking had taken its toll. She had been running on pure determination and raw nerves for almost two months. Exhaustion had finally caught up with her. Although she sought to keep her eyes open, darkness engulfed her. Suddenly she was drifting through the same erotic fantasy she had experienced in Kane's arms, allowing another sweet, hypnotic dream to take up where reality left off.

An amused smile pursed Kane's lips when Darcey sagged limply in his arms. Carefully, he eased down beside her to marvel at her enchanting profile in the moonlight. Kane reached out to trace his forefinger over the swanlike column of her neck and then glided his thumb over the rose-tipped buds of her breasts.

Perfection. Absolute perfection, Kane mused as his admiring gaze flooded over every satiny inch of her flesh. His eyes beheld what he had possessed, what no other man had discovered about this iron-clad violet. Beneath that stubborn, defensive shell lay a beautiful, responsive woman. Kane tried to conjure up even one woman who could match Darcey's limitless spirit and natural beauty. In comparison, even Melanie ran a distant second. Darcey was an odd but intriguing combination of imp and angel. And, no doubt about it, the incredibly passionate angel would retreat behind that impish shell when Darcey roused from sleep. She would regret this intimate tête-à-tête, sure as hell. Dedicated man-haters were just like that. Darcey would blame him in hopes of soothing her own guilt and embarrassment would hound her.

A weary sigh tumbled from Kane's lips as he eased his head onto his pillow. He draped his arm over Darcey's hip and cuddled ever closer. It seemed he had two choices. He could leave now and allow Darcey to cope with her tormented feelings all alone or he could weather the inevitable storm and force her to discuss what had happened.

The only problem was that Kane didn't have the

slightest idea what he was going to say to make things easier for her. But staying seemed the wiser choice. Besides, Kane wasn't sure he could have dragged himself out of bed, even if a fire had been lit under him. His battle with Griz Vanhook and his two henchmen had cost Kane considerable strength and a good deal of pain. What energy he had left had been expended in splendorously delightful but physically exhausting passion. And besides, cradling Darcey's voluptuous body in his arms during her gentler mood was a temptation too great to ignore.

This . . . ah . . . this was paradise, Kane mused with a contented sigh. Never before had he been so inclined to linger after the lovemaking was over. The nagging restlessness he usually experienced had evaporated in a cloud of hazy pleasure.

On that drowsy thought, Kane followed Darcey into sweet dreams. He had given so much of himself in the attempt to make certain she endured only minimal discomfort during her voyage into womanhood that he had nothing else left to give. All the tenderness he possessed, he had generously offered to her. And only sleep could replenish his strength.

Chapter 8

A shallow sigh tripped from Darcey's lips as she made her groggy ascent from sleep to wakefulness. A throbbing headache drummed at her temples and she feared she would need a crowbar to pry open her eyes to greet the morning sun. The slight movement beside her brought her awake faster than she intended. She could feel the warm, hair-roughened body beside hers and reality hit her like a pile of falling bricks.

With a mortified gasp, Darcey jerked up the sagging sheet and clutched it around her before bounding out of bed. In the process of covering herself, she had inadvertently bared the brawny giant who had been lounging beside her. Wide emerald eyes flooded over Kane's power-packed frame and her face flushed beet red. The previous night, bathed in moonlit shadows, their romantic interlude had seemed so pleasurable, so right. But in the blaring light of day, and without the numbing effect of whiskey to cloud her thinking, Darcey was horrified by what she had done. Curse it, she had allowed herself to become his casual conquest!

Another embarrassed groan burst from her throat when she spied the telltale stains on the sheet, the very same ones that had captured Kane's attention. When he glanced up to meet her embarrassed gaze, Darcey died a thousand times over. What he had taken from her had nothing to do with love, only with temporary physical possession. All he had wanted was a warm feminine body, not the emotions and personality attached to it. Why, to hear him talk, he didn't even like her all that much. He was constantly pointing out her quirks of character. But seducing a woman—any woman—was as natural to him as breathing.

Darcey felt incredibly awkward, self-conscious, and infuriated with herself and with this seductive rake who had made her want him so desperately. *Made* her, mind you. She would never have succumbed to the wanton desires of the flesh if Kane hadn't used his remarkable powers of masculine persuasion on her. Never!

Kane braced himself for the worst. He could tell by the cavalry of emotions that were galloping across her animated features that Darcey was on the verge of battle. It was just as he predicted. Guilt and humiliation were leading the attack and Darcey was having one helluva time coping with the intimacy that had transpired between them.

Hurriedly, Kane formulated his thoughts, praying the right words would leap to his tongue before Darcey split apart at the seams and there would be no reasoning with her.

"Don't spoil the magic we discovered in each other's arms," Kane murmured as he eased onto an elbow to

136

peer into her crimson face. Grimacing in pain, Kane swung his long legs over the edge of the bed and stood up. "What you and I shared—"

With a yelp, Darcey wheeled to face the wall, but the unnerving vision of Kane standing there, stark-bone naked, had supcrimposed itself on the wallpaper like a life-size portrait. "I don't wish to discuss what happened during my temporary lapse of sanity," she croaked, her voice nowhere near as steady as she'd hope. "I just want you to leave . . . *now!*"

A devilish grin dangled on the corner of his lip as he ambled toward the bundle of sheets from which only a tangle of curly auburn hair protruded. "I think we should discuss what happened . . . *now,*" he insisted.

"Will you kindly don your breeches," Darcey bleated, feeling his naked presence behind her, in front of her, beside her. *Everywhere,* curse it! "Perhaps you are accustomed to carrying on conversations in the buff, but I am not!"

"I understand how you feel," Kane whispered, feeling tremendously inadequate, but compelled by the need to try to say something appropriate.

Damn it, this wasn't any easier for him than it was for her. He wasn't sure how to broach the ultrasensitive topic, either, and he hated not being in control, despised feeling incapable of dealing with such a touchy situation. Touchy? Lord, it was all those intimate *touches* that had gotten them where they were now.

"No, you *don't* understand!" Darcey wailed in contradiction.

Agilely, she sidestepped to avoid close contact with

Kane. She was contemplating crashing through the wall to escape him and her own humiliation. "You couldn't possibly understand how I feel. You aren't a woman and this obviously wasn't the first time you—"

Darcey glanced over to see the wide expanse of his hair-matted chest, the long contours of his muscled thighs, and his bare hips. She lost her train of thought and her nerve. With a quick snap of her head that sent a cascade of auburn curls rippling around her, Darcey refocused on the wall.

Since Darcey was having such a difficult time, Kane came to her rescue to complete her dangling sentence. "The first time I've been with a woman? No, it isn't," he answered honestly. His hand glided over the thick strands of her tangled hair and he expelled a sigh. The pause was dead, showing no potential sign of life. "Considering all that's happened the past week, I think we should pack up and leave. And if—"

A war party of frustrated emotion attacked Darcey, anger was chief among them. "Leave with *you?*" She pivoted to glare into Kane's bruised features. Curse it, she was so furious that she was tempted to blacken his other eye! "Leave and do what? Travel from one mining camp to another while you swindle men out of the gold at the gaming tables? Are you suggesting I become your paramour until some other female happens along to cause a flareup of that incurable disease known as roving eye? No, thank you! I'd rather take a bullet in the chest first."

"And you probably will if you don't get the hell out of town," Kane snapped more harshly than he intended.

Honest to God, there was no way to carry on a civil conversation with this firebrand when she was in a snit. She never listened to reason even when she was being sensible. And she was so infuriatingly contrary that if he told her *not* to jump off the nearest cliff, she'd do it just to spite him.

"I fail to see how being shot down in cold blood could be any less painful than being seduced by a rakehell like you!" Darcey spouted. "You said yourself that you're accustomed to women's beds, that I was only a smile and a lusty moment of time you were killing while you recuperated."

"I said no such thing!" Kane blared at the impossible imp. "As always, your imagination has taken you on a wild-goose chase. If memory serves me, you were a willing participant in what happened. You wanted me every bit as much as I wanted you, and don't you dare deny it!"

Darcey would have admitted nothing of the kind, even if he held a gun to her head! In a fit of temper, she came uncoiled like a rattlesnake. Kane caught her doubled fist before it connected with his good eye—at least the better one, which was only partially swollen shut! When she shrieked in outrage and attempted to hurl herself away, Kane yanked her against him to glare into her puckered features.

"We are leaving town—you and me, the two of us together, and that is that," he growled into her defiant face. "In fact, considering what happened, I think we ought to get married while we're at it. It seems the logical thing to do."

"Married? Logical? My eye!"

Darcey feared she was becoming hysterical. She had never been hysterical. She had always coped with every situation without losing her composure. But she wasn't coping well at all now and damn it, she *was* hysterical.

"Oh, what sacrifices you men make to salvage the soiled reputation of deflowered virgins, especially the ones who are known to have money," she spumed. "You know my father owns the express company. And you, being the kind of scoundrel you are, would leap at the chance to wed wealth," she accused in an explosive tone. "Then you could stash me somewhere out of the way and wander all over creation, satisfying your need to whore and gamble and do whatever else you rapscallions do!"

Leave it to this spitfire to tangle logic in a Gordian knot, Kane thought irritably. Always the cynic, always infuriatingly suspicious and defensive—that was Darcey O'Roarke. Well, he ought to tell her who and what he really was. He couldn't help but wonder how she would react if she knew her father had paid him handsomely to cart her out of this potentially dangerous situation she found herself in. No doubt she would blast away at her own father for scheming to rout her from Denver.

Yet, angry as he was, Kane couldn't quite bring himself to blurt out the truth, even if it would have gotten him off the firing line. For some reason he felt the insane need for this feisty hellion to accept him for what he appeared to be, to accept the fact that they had shared something special, no matter who or what either of them were. Damn it, this hotheaded vixen had begun to make a difference to him. And honest to God, Kane

140

didn't even know why! Darcey made him so furious sometimes, he couldn't even think straight. But still he gravitated toward her like metal to a magnet and longed to recapture the sweet splendor he had discovered in her arms.

Kane had lingered too long in thought. That was a critical mistake, he soon found out. Darcey clutched at her sheet and raced across the suite to grab the lantern as her makeshift weapon.

"Get out of my room and out of my life!" she hissed as she heaved the projectile across the room.

With deft footwork, Kane dodged the oncoming missile and grabbed his breeches. He had barely stuffed one bruised leg into his trousers before Darcey snatched the pitcher off the commode and put it to flight. It barely missed his ruffled raven head and crashed into the wall, splattering on the floor in a million pieces.

"Will you calm down!" Kane snapped as he reached for his shirt and then leaped backward like a mountain goat to avoid the small table Darcey had hurled at him.

"I won't calm down until you get out of here," she spewed, green eyes blazing like a forest fire. "Marriage indeed! I'm swearing off men and whiskey for the rest of my natural life."

"My God, what else is there left?" Kane smirked and then skedaddled toward the door, scooping up his boots along the way. His attempt to soothe her raging temper with humor didn't work worth a damn. She refused to be amused. The flippant remark only left her incapable of coherent speech and she spouted several unintelligible curses at him.

In another burst of fury Darcey threw the empty vase she held in her hand. Porcelain flew in all directions at once. Kane made his exit, and not a moment too soon.

Employing the door as a shield, Kane poked his head back inside. He was reasonably certain Darcey had thrown everything at him that was possible to throw. And even then, she had hurled her makeshift weapons in alphabetical order—the lantern, the pitcher, the table, and the vase. To him, it would have made more sense to throw the vase and then heave the small table on which it sat. But then, he wasn't plagued with Darcey's organized mind. All that was left now was the wastebasket which couldn't inflict all that much pain on him, small as it was.

"When you come to your senses and realize what a fool you are making of yourself, we'll sit down and talk," Kane told her, stifling the amused smile he knew would set her off if it accidentally surfaced on his lips.

Except for the wastebasket, Darcey had depleted her stockpile of weapons, but she was nowhere near out of boiling fury. The nerve of this man! How dare he propose to her! He was no more anxious to have a wife than he was to have his neck fitted for a hangman's noose. And she wouldn't have married this silver-blue-eyed rapscallion if he was the last man in the universe! Kane cared nothing about her. She was only another conquest, one who could bring him a fortune to squander. Well, he'd never get his greedy hands on the O'Roarke fortune, not in a zillion years!

"There will be no talking because I'm never going to speak to you again . . . ever!" Darcey sputtered. To emphasize her declaration, she jerked up the waste-

142

basket and threw it at the dark head that protruded from the edge of the door. "Now get out and stay out!"

Kane slammed the door before the object smacked against his skull. It was glaringly apparent to Kane that Patrick O'Roarke had sent him on an impossible mission. There was no reasoning with this human wildcat. Kane hadn't been able to persuade, coax, plead, or seduce Darcey out of town. And now that he had fallen out of her good graces, she had declared him one of her archenemies. Guilt, suspicion, and humiliation hounded her every thought. Concerning the scoundrel she presumed Kane to be one of the lowest forms of life on earth.

Expelling a frustrated breath, Kane rammed his feet into his boots. Stiff and sore though he was after his battle with Griz, not to mention his skirmish with Darcey, he limped down the hall. Honest to God, nothing had gone according to plan this week, especially his dealings with that green-eyed horror. And why the devil had he proposed marriage to her anyway? Probably because it was the gentlemanly thing to do after he'd stolen her innocence. His generous offer had only incited Darcey's fury. Kane wasn't sure why she had reacted so violently to the proposal. A firm, unequivocal *no* certainly would have sufficed!

After veering into the dining hall, Kane ordered a hearty breakfast. While sipping his coffee he reviewed all his choices. The situation called for drastic measures. Kane had been reluctant to employ strong-arm tactics at the onset of this assignment, but he had exhausted every last tactic other than forced abduction. Maybe Patrick was right again. Perhaps scaring the living daylights out of that wildcat was the only conceivable way to send her running back to her father's open arms.

Kane's thoughts trailed off when Darcey, dressed in one of her high-collared gowns and matching pink silk hat, sailed into the dining hall to take her morning meal. Despite his frustration, Kane broke into an amused grin at Darcey's remarkable display of ignoring him. She refused to glance in his direction or acknowledge his presence in any manner whatsoever. In that stubborn, intractable mind of hers, he no longer existed and neither did their previous night together.

Well, by damned, he *did* exist and she would know to what extent before the week was out! Darcey despised him now but she would have more than enough reason to loathe him when he finished with her. He'd see to it that she begged Patrick to find a new position for her in the home office in St. Louis. Darcey O'Roarke may be a tough nut to crack, but Kane Callahan was an expert when it came to difficult cases. That wall of stubborn defiance was about to run headlong into an unstoppable force. Kane had every intention of moving that curvaceous mountain of contrary femininity, even if had to take her out of here one shovelful at a time! But, if it was the last thing he ever did he'd remove her from this mile-high city and track down the thieves who preyed on O'Roarke Express.

Calling upon her theatrical ability, Darcey pretended not to notice the sinewy giant who sat on the

144

opposite side of the dining hall. It had taken considerable effort to breeze into the restaurant as if nothing out of the ordinary had happened. Guilt hounded her every step of the way. Humiliation stung her pride like a hive of wasps. Not only had she shamed herself in Kane's arms but she had lowered herself into throwing a temper tantrum to evict him from her room.

Curse his handsome hide! He had probably decided to make her the target of his seductive attention since the moment he learned who she was. Oh, he was a sly one all right. Kane had led her to believe his intentions toward her were honorable, or at least as honorable as a shiftless wastrel's could be. He had come to her defense a time or two to try to convince her that he was sincere in his concern for her safety. And when she let her guard down he had taken full advantage. Why, he had even played upon her sympathy while he was recuperating from battle. Darcey couldn't bear the demoralizing realization that she had been conned by a master. No doubt Kane had expected her to wail and beg for a proposal of marriage to salvage her pride and reputation, then he would have wed her to get control of her fortune.

Darcey could see it all now, just as it had been with Michael Dupris. Getting his greedy hands on her money had been Michael's goal, too, adventurer that he was. He had courted a young, innocent heiress who was out from under her father's wing for the first time. Michael had wooed her and painted pictures of a bright, blissful future. And naive and trusting as Darcey had been at eighteen, she had believed him. But Michael and his paramour had set Darcey up for the kill. Luckily, Darcey had happened upon them and sprung the trap before it had closed around her foolish neck.

Now, three years later, she had found herself in a similar situation. Her encounter with Kane Callahan had only reinforced her belief that all men had ulterior motives where women were concerned. They took all they could get, damn them.

Well, Darcey *was* swearing off all men forevermore. She couldn't trust any of them except her father. And if she hadn't been so intent on proving her true worth to Patrick she would have packed up and hurried home. But she was not leaving Denver until she had made a success of this office and quelled the difficulties on the stage route.

Muttering, Darcey spun her plate so that each food was in its proper place—meat at the top, potatoes at the bottom and bread at . . .

Her dark lashes fluttered up to see Kane peering at her with a mischievous grin. Even at a distance he was ridiculing her. Damn him, he didn't know how little effort it would have taken to scoop up her plate and hurl it at him. He had rattled her in ways no other man had ever been able to do. Even Michael Dupris was no match for this cunning giant with his magnificent black eye—one she wished *she* had given him!

With a silent oath and a venomous glare, Darcey stabbed at her food, wishing Kane Callahan was lying on her plate. She would have delighted in cutting him into bite-size pieces and making a meal of him!

Men! They were such nuisances. And if her mortifying ordeal with Kane wasn't enough for one day, Darcey had yet to face Owen Graves's mocking scorn. Her headache would be in full bloom by nightfall; she'd bet her fortune on that.

With as much dignity as she could muster, Darcey gracefully rose from her chair and made her regal exit from the restaurant. If she never saw Kane Callahan again that would suit her just fine. He would be no more than an unpleasant page from her past. She would not dwell on their brief liaison; she would forget it completely.

Darcey decided defiantly she would never look back, never remember Kane Callahan. She would take all her pitfalls in stride and never spare What's-his-name another thought as long as she lived.

Chapter 9

For three days, Darcey threw herself into attempting to correct every problem at the express agency and dedicated every spare moment to forgetting Kane Callahan ever existed. It didn't help matters when Owen Graves taunted her every chance he got. Owen was sly with his insults. He had learned just how far to push Darcey before she completely lost her temper. Having flown into such an embarrassing tantrum once that week, Darcey guarded against any rash decisions or impulsive outbursts that might have more to do with her liaison with Kane than with Owen and the express company.

A half hour before noon a telegram arrived to report another robbery attempt which, thankfully, had met with failure. According to the report, a lone highwayman—and not the usual courtly one who left thankyou notes—had tried to escape with a large shipment of gold that was headed for the main office in Denver. But the guards had been able to fend off the attack and the shipment, though delayed, was due to arrive by evening.

Knowing she would be forced to work late, sorting credit vouchers, weighing gold dust, and counting cash, Darcey rushed through her tasks with as much efficiency as possible. Owen grumbled about having orders spouted at him, and performed his duties at his own accelerated rate of inefficiency.

Darcey had tried to train Owen to employ her organized system of filing but he refused to conform to it. And then there was the quiet, meek Lester Alridge who tried to please Darcey but who never quite caught on to her newly revised system of bookkeeping, either. But luckily, Lester's brother had kept his distance the past few days and the employees could work with minimal distractions.

By closing time Darcey was exhausted and she still faced several tedious hours of work. The stage shipment arrived a few minutes after the sun went down and Darcey's spirits sank with it. There was a mountain of work to be done and reports of a robbery to be filled out.

While Darcey labored over her duties, Lester lingered by the door after Owen had left for the night. "There is very little reason for me to go home. My bb-brother hasn't been around all day and I have ss-seen nothing of him. He must bb-be bb-busy with a client," Lester stuttered awkwardly. "I'll be happy to ss-stay and help you record the transactions."

There were times when it was quicker and easier for one to do things oneself. This was one of those times.

150

And besides, Darcey wanted to be alone with her thoughts. Customers had been hopping in and out of the office like jackrabbits all day and she'd had little time for introspection. She needed time alone far more than she needed Lester's assistance.

"Thank you, Lester. I appreciate the offer," she replied with a tired smile. "But you go on home. I can handle this."

"I cc-could list the vouchers and file the report in the ledgers while you weigh the gg-gold," Lester volunteered, his gaze failing to meet Darcey's. Self-consciously, he twirled his plug hat in his hand and stared at the toes of his shoes. "I don't mind the extra hours, really I dd-don't."

"Perhaps another time," Darcey murmured before turning toward the mound of pouches that lay on the counter. "I'll see to this matter myself."

Nodding mutely, Lester scurried out the door to take his evening meal.

Heaving a weary sigh, Darcey bolstered her energy and plunged into the task of weighing gold that would be processed at the mint. Only a single lantern burned atop the counter while she labored. The office was surrounded with shadowed silence, barring the occasional clink of the scales and the thud of gold-filled pouches.

An unidentified rattle from the back door of the office caught Darcey's attention. She stood perfectly still, barely breathing, as she pondered the reason for the unexpected noise. The faint creak of the door sent her pulse leaping. To her knowledge the express office

151

had never been robbed, but she wasn't optimistic enough to think it couldn't happen. And she was just pessimistic enough to expect a robbery to occur while she was alone in the office. That was simply the kind of luck she'd been having of late.

Bracing her courage, Darcey tiptoed across the main room toward the narrow hall that led to the accounting and storage rooms. A fleeting shadow caught her attention and she froze on the spot. Before she could inch back toward the counter, a bulky form leaped at her, knocking her to the floor. Darcey opened her mouth to emit a blood-curdling scream, but a gloved hand clamped over her lips, smothering her cry for assistance.

"If you move, lady, you're as good as dead," the hoarse voice snarled in threat.

All Darcey could see as she was yanked up by her hair was a masked face and a long canvas duster that concealed the body inside it. She didn't need to see the pistol that had been rammed between her ribs. She could feel it! Her alarmed gaze flickered over the flour sack that served as the bandit's mask. She couldn't prove positive identification, but she swore by the voice that rustled beneath the flour sack and the foul smell that emanated from the canvas duster that the intruder was Griz Vanhook. Just as Kane had predicted, he had come back to seek his vengeance on her.

"Fetch the gold," the thief ordered gruffly.

Darcey thought it over and decided her chances of surviving this holdup were slim. And since that was the case, she had nothing to lose. "Fetch it yourself," she flung in defiance.

With a muted growl the highwayman backhanded her, sending her stumbling against the counter for support. Before Darcey could orient herself and make a mad dash toward the door, the bandit launched himself at her. The pistol jabbed her in the throat and she gasped to inhale her last breath.

"Now do what I told you," the desperado sneered.

Begrudging every step she took, Darcey inched toward the pouches of gold that she had neatly stacked beside the scales.

"Hurry it up. I ain't got all night" came the impatient command.

Darcey was reasonably certain she had encountered at least one of the thieves who had been preying on the stage line. She suspected Griz Vanhook was involved in the holdups since he seemed to have no type of work to support his drinking habit. But neither she nor the deputy had been able to prove Griz and his cohorts were responsible for some of the robberies. Now that Griz was alone and his friends were locked behind bars, Darcey knew her suspicions were correct.

Lord, she'd give most anything if she could remove this menace from society, but Darcey had the inescapable feeling that if anybody was going anywhere it would be her. After all, Griz was the one holding the pistol. All she had was fierce determination and that wouldn't stand up all that well against a loaded six-shooter.

"I said hurry up," Griz snarled, giving her a painful nudge with the barrel of his Colt. "Put those pouches in—" His voice trailed off into a muffled oath when the creak of the front door caught his attention.

Lester Alridge was definitely having misgivings about reentering the office to help Darcey. Despite her insistence on handling the gold shipment herself, Lester had intended to help her. What he hadn't expected, after his hasty meal at a nearby restaurant, was walking into a robbery in progress! Courage wasn't one of his nobler traits, but Lester nevertheless fumbled for the snub-nosed pistol he kept tucked in his vest pocket in case of emergency. And this was definitely an emergency!

Darcey's frantic gaze bounced from the masked highwayman to the wide-eyed bookkeeper who had inadvertently stumbled into harm's way. She doubted Lester could shoot his way out of a gunny sack, much less gun down a ruthless bandit. Taking that into account, Darcey moved like streak lightning to take advantage of Griz's distraction. Employing the pouch of gold she had clutched in her hand, she whacked the bandit on the head, hoping to give Lester enough time to take aim and fire. The outlaw cursed fluently and swung the barrel of his Colt toward Darcey and then back to Lester.

The office was suddenly as silent as a graveyard. Lester stood pointing his pistol at the thief who was pointing a weapon back at him. Darcey held her breath and prayed. Oh, how she prayed! She would have lunged at the bandit to misdirect the shot but she was afraid she'd become the victim of Lester's bullet. She could be dead, no matter what she chose to do.

*　　　*　　　*

Kane expelled a wordless scowl when he rounded the corner of the bakery to see the lanternlight flickering in the express office. He had come prepared to stage a holdup of his own and forcefully rout that stubborn minx from Denver before she got herself killed. Kane was five minutes too late. A gunman loomed beside Darcey, bearing down on the frail man who hovered half in and half out of the office.

Like a cannonball, Kane shot into the street to position himself so he could blast away at the bandit. But before he could call anyone's attention to his presence, the thief cocked the trigger of his pistol and Lester fumbled to answer the oncoming bullet.

Reflexively, Kane snatched up his Colt to do what he doubted Lester could do on his own—hit his target. Kane gritted his teeth and waited. He knew there would be damned few allowances for mistakes in this crucial situation. He had only one chance to save Darcey's life and there were too many outside influences which could contribute to disaster.

Pistols barked simultaneously, making it impossible to determine how many shots had actually been fired. Fortunately, Kane's aim was as good as his eyesight. His bullet whizzed through the open door, missing Lester by a foot. After scoring a direct hit on the highwayman, Kane slipped away as quietly as a shadow.

The bandit buckled at the knees in disbelief and dropped like an anchor. Before he could satisfy his fury and dispose of the quaking little man who clung to the doorjamb for support, Darcey kicked the pistol away and instinctively ducked when it misfired.

When the bandit pitched forward on the floor, Darcey jerked the flour sack away to determine if her suspicions were correct. Sure enough, they were. Griz's wooly face was caked with flour and a dull gleam of vengeance glowed in his dark eyes. A blank stare curtained his face and he collapsed at Darcey's feet, never to rise again.

Even though her heart was pounding, Darcey wobbled over to retrieve the sack of gold she had hurled at Griz and replaced it on the counter where it belonged.

"I'll go fetch the deputy," Lester volunteered in a strangled voice.

Darcey nodded in compliance. She was shaking so badly from fright that she didn't trust herself to speak without croaking in the same manner Lester had.

While Lester scuttled down the street to summon Pup Metcalf, Darcey sucked in air in great gulps, hoping to gain control of her shattered composure. Odd, she had never been quite so frightened after Kane Callahan happened on to the scene of disaster. His confident presence had fortified her courage. The night she and Kane had confronted Griz and his cohorts outside the office she had been more determined to come to Kane's defense than to flee for her own safety. But now, without Kane's strength, Darcey felt like a quivering jellyfish!

Thank the Lord this most recent ordeal was over,

Darcey breathed raggedly. She needed a few minutes to recover . . .

A strangled gasp was ripped from her throat when a steely hand clamped around her. Curse it, there was more than one of them, Darcey realized bleakly. One of Griz's gang had been waiting by the back door and had sneaked in to take up where the leader of the brigands had left off.

The bandit, whose dark mask and wide-brimmed hat concealed every feature of his face, dragged her toward the counter to scoop up the pouches of gold. With swift efficiency, the highwayman tucked the sacks in the pockets of his long duster. Darcey would have bit at the hand that clamped around the lower portion of her face but the wily thief had the foresight to cram a wadded handkerchief in her mouth first. She couldn't sink her teeth into anything that would cause her captor pain. Even when she wormed and squirmed she had no effect on the diligent bandit. He held her clamped to him as if she were his second skin and went about his business of stealing every last credit voucher and sack of gold. And when she kicked him in the shin, the odious cur retaliated by kicking her back. And to infuriate her all the more, he jerked her spectacles off the bridge of her nose and squashed them into the floor.

Despite every attempt Darcey made to free herself, she was dragged to the back of the office and slammed roughly against the wall. The blow to her skull and spine invited an instant headache. In amazement she watched the bandit jerk another gag from his pocket and lash it over her mouth. Within a matter of a few seconds he had also fished into his pocket to retrieve a rope to bind her wrists and ankles.

A stab of horror penetrated Darcey's mind when the highwayman snatched up the tarp he had brought with him to wrap her up as if she were a mummy. The possibility of being abducted, molested, and murdered in some obscure region of the mountains had never occurred to her until this gloomy moment. Considering the terror she knew awaited her, Darcey would have begged for Kane Callahan to walk back into her life after he had disappeared from town two days earlier. She would have *begged* him, mind you!

Darcey was sure she was about to become the victim of a fatal assault perpetrated by an entire den of murderers and thieves. She would never see her father again. And he wouldn't know what had become of her. By the time Lester returned with the deputy she would have vanished into thin air.

A dull moan rumbled beneath Darcey's gag when she was lifted up and flung over the bandit's shoulder like a feed sack. In swift strides she was carried into the alley and draped over a horse, giving her a perspective of life that had been turned upside down in a matter of minutes. God help her, she was going to suffer all the torments of the damned and she would never awake from this horrifying nightmare!

After the highwayman mounted his own steed, he grabbed the reins to Griz's horse and led Darcey through the inky black shadows of the alley. As soon as the outlaw found open road, he kicked his horse into a gallop. Darcey was grateful she hadn't taken time for supper. Each time the pommel of the saddle and the jogging horse jammed into her abdomen she swore she'd lose every meal she'd ever eaten. Without one smidgen of concern for her comfort the bandit thundered over the rocky path toward the mountains that loomed to the west of Denver like grotesque shadows.

Sickening dread engulfed Darcey when she realized Kane Callahan's prediction had come true. He had warned her to leave town before she sacrificed her life for her noble crusade. Now the mission of putting the express office back on its feet seemed of no importance. Survival was her foremost concern.

Darcey groaned when the horse stumbled over the rocks. She got an unnerving bird's-eye view of the steep precipices that overlooked the narrow chasms in the mountains. All her tireless efforts to make her mark on society and prove herself as good as any man, including her father, had been in vain. She would die all alone in Colorado. Her limp body would be hurled over a jagged cliff and left to the wolves and vultures.

No doubt Kane Callahan would gloat over the fact that he'd told her so. But, being stubborn to the core, Darcey had refused to listen. Kane would love this, damn him. Of course, he really didn't care what happened to her. She had been nothing more than a prospective meal ticket to luxury. Sooner or later he would charm the petticoats off some other wealthy heiress and convince her that he was sincere about his marriage proposal. Darcey wondered how many times in the past that rapscallion had employed his tactic of deflowering innocent girls and then proposing marriage to them. Surely she wasn't the first. In fact, Kane might have been married a half dozen times already and might have squandered his unfortunate wives' money.

Darcey slumped defeatedly against the saddle and let her chin bang against the horse's ribs. Dull misery enshrouded her. This was the beginning of the end. Her future was bleak. Life as she knew it was over. *This,* she realized, was her one-way journey into the jaws of hell!

Pup Metcalf's boyish face displayed the full extent of his concern as he dashed down the street toward O'Roarke Express. He shuddered just thinking of the terrifying ordeal Darcey had endured.

When Lester Alridge finally caught up with him on the far side of town, Pup had beat a straight path to the office. Behind him, Lester wheezed to catch his breath.

The instant Pup stepped into the office, his worried gaze penetrated the shadows, searching for the bewitching auburn-haired woman who had become the object of his affection. Unable to locate Darcey, Pup strode over to survey the corpse that was sprawled on the planked floor.

An anxious crowd had formed a wave that surged down the darkened street.

"Who shot Griz Vanhook?" one of the bystanders questioned.

"I did," Lester announced, unaware that it had been

Kane's accurate aim that had felled the grizzly renegade.

A ripple of astonished murmurs swept through the crowd. Word of Griz's death flooded down the street. No tears were shed over the fact that the town's worst menace had been permanently felled. In fact, Lester—the most unlikely hero among them—was applauded for his bravery. Cheers echoed down the street, chanting Lester's name. He was lifted upon two sturdy shoulders and carried around like a conquering warrior returning from battle.

While the townsfolk celebrated the death of their number-one nuisance, Pup circumnavigated the office and back rooms searching for Darcey. He half expected to find her slouched in a dark corner, after having fainted from her near brush with disaster. But after a thorough search of the agency, Pup turned up nothing. Darcey had vanished from sight.

By the time Pup reentered the main room, Griz's body had been removed and the crowd had drifted down the street to the nearest saloon. The celebration had begun and the sound of a tinny piano and whining fiddles filled the crisp evening air. Toast after toast was being made to the man who had shot Griz Vanhook.

Befuddled by Darcey's disappearance, Pup scurried past the milling crowd and aimed himself toward the hotel. After knocking on Darcey's door twice and receiving no answer, Pup whizzed back downstairs to interrogate the clerk. He chastised himself for not thinking to quiz the hotel proprietor first before

161

wasting his time and energy running up and down the steps. His lack of experience as a deputy was showing and his concern for Darcey's safety was clouding his thinking.

To Pup's dismay, the proprietor reported that Darcey had not returned to her room; he knew that for certain since he hadn't left his desk. Pup dragged the hat from his head and raked his fingers through his crop of sandy-blond hair. Where in the hell could she be? Pup knew Darcey couldn't have run to Kane Callahan for comfort because Kane had stopped by two days earlier to announce his departure from Denver. According to Kane, he had decided to amble through the nearby mining camps in search of a few high-stakes poker games.

Pup had been surprised by Kane's announcement and also a mite relieved. As much as he liked the charismatic gambler, he sensed a growing attraction between Kane and Darcey. Pup hadn't gotten anywhere with that standoffish beauty and he didn't need the competition of Kane's dynamic presence.

Shrugging off his meandering thoughts, Pup scuttled through town. He hoped that by now Darcey would have ventured back to the office from wherever the devil she'd gone. But to Pup's mounting concern, the express agency was just as he'd left it—empty.

He ambled around the room aimlessly. His footsteps halted beside the scales which rested upon the counter beside the opened ledger into which Darcey had recorded her evening transactions. Drawing the lantern closer, Pup noted the entries Darcey had made.

Frowning puzzledly, Pup glanced from the bare counter to the empty box in which the pouches of gold should have been stacked for delivery to the mint.

A knot of apprehension twisted in the pit of his belly when he started adding two and two together. Knowing Darcey O'Roarke's penchant for organization and orderliness, Pup was certain she would have finished her task and put her equipment away before leaving the office. In the two months Darcey had been in Denver she had never once left the agency without replacing her books or returning the scales to their rightful place on the shelves.

Pup shot out the door like lightning and raced down the street to locate Lester. By the time Pup came upon the recently crowned king of Denver, Lester had been toasted to the hilt and was groggy with whiskey. Without preamble, Pup grabbed Lester by the lapels of his coat and jerked him out of his chair to fire several questions that Lester's dazed mind couldn't decipher.

"Hey, Pup!" someone hollered from behind him. "Take it easy on Lester. We just gave him the key to the city and named him Denver's hero."

Pup didn't care what Lester had been given. He needed answers!

Lester blinked like an awakened owl when he was uprooted from his chair and held upright by two clenched fists that crinkled his jacket. To combat the fear that had seized him when he'd confronted Griz, Lester had gulped glasses of whiskey like water. His thoughts were already in a tangle before Pup began bombarding him with questions.

When Pup received only a glassy-eyed stare for his efforts, he gave the frail bookkeeper a hard shake. "Answer me, damnit!" he demanded urgently. "Did you stash away the gold sacks that Darcey had been weighing before you left the office?"

Again Lester blinked and fumbled to digest the inquiry. "Gold? Oh, the gg-gold." Lester frowned, but his facial muscles were so numbed by liquor that the expression sagged on the left side of his face. "Well, no, I dd-didn't. Miss O'Roarke told me to gg-go fetch you."

"And what about after we arrived at the office?" Pup persisted. "Did you put the shipment of gold away before you trotted off to celebrate?"

Lester gave his disheveled head a negative shake. "I dd-didn't have a chance. I was picked up and carried away. I ss-supposed Darcey would have seen to the task. She is very efficient," he slurred out.

"She is also very *gone!*" Pup blurted in exasperation. "I can't find her anywhere and the gold pouches are missing."

His booming voice brought quick death to the conversation and bubbling laughter that had filled the saloon seconds before.

With a grim expression that matched his apprehension, Pup released Lester, who promptly plunked into his chair like a sack of flour. Pup wheeled around to make his bleak speculation to the saloon at large.

"Miss O'Roarke is nowhere to be found. I turned the town upside down looking for her." He paused when a ripple of whispers rushed through the stunned crowd. "Although Lester shot Griz, part of his gang must have been waiting in the alley. The shipment of gold and all the credit vouchers are gone. Miss O'Roarke has been kidnapped and the gold was stolen a second time!"

By the time Pup finished rattling off his speculations, his voice had risen to a frustrated roar. Sharing concern for Darcey's safety, bodies surged out of chairs and a stampede of humanity thundered down the street. After another thorough search of the area, several of the townspeople spotted the tracks in the alley. From what Pup deduced, two horses had stamped around in the dirt and two sets of tracks had left imprints in the alleyway—Griz's and an unidentified outlaw who had obviously accompanied Griz to town. Pup had the inescapable feeling that Darcey had been carried away, since no footprints matched the dainty size of her feet. She had either been knocked unconscious or . . . Pup gulped in anguish, fearing the worst.

"I need volunteers for a posse!" Pup shouted.

Within a few minutes several obliging men had returned with their mounts to lend assistance. Unfortunately, Pup didn't have the slightest inkling in which direction to ride. The tracks of the missing horses had veered into the street to mingle with other prints. Pup was so frustrated and worried about Darcey that he wanted to pull out his hair strand by strand.

Muttering a curse, he wheeled his steed around and galloped back to the saloon to rout Lester. "You hightail it over to the express office and send off an all-points bulletin," he demanded hurriedly. "And then put the agency back in order. I'm leaving you in charge of the office until O'Roarke is notified of his daughter's disappearance. I'm sure he'll be counting on you to assume command since you're the one who tried to prevent the burglary."

"Me?" Lester squeaked, goggle-eyed. "But what about Owen Graves? He was the manager bb-before . . ."

"You're the one who shot Griz Vanhook," Pup snapped. "You gained instant fame. Miss O'Roarke demoted Owen. I'm sure she would want you in charge after you came to her rescue. And you know how particular she was . . . is . . ." Pup cursed the dreary thought about Darcey and her future, or rather her lack of it. "Just run the office the way she always did!"

Nodding in compliance, Lester levered himself out of his chair and weaved through the saloon. Pausing at the door, he drew himself up to assume his new role as one of the pillars of the community. With head held high and a slight wobble in his strut, Lester propelled himself down the street. Now he was a man of distinction and he had a job to do for Darcey. She would have wanted him to carry on in her efficient, orderly manner. The only problem was . . .

Lester missed a step when a discouraging thought buzzed through his brain. Well, he would just have to deal with all the difficulties his new position entailed. The community was depending on him to continue providing the service of transporting freight, gold, and mail and making stage connections. Denver needed

166

him. Darcey was counting on him!

Resolved to live up to the expectations that had been heaped on him, Lester marched down the street. From this day forward he would rise to his full potential! He was famous, after all. He had displayed courage in the face of danger and he had shot Griz Vanhook! He was a hero, a legend in his own time!

Chapter 10

While Pup Metcalf was thundering off in the wrong direction, relying on his underdeveloped instincts as a law officer, Kane was staring out the holes of his mask to survey the mountains that loomed ahead of him. Silently, Kane weaved through the narrow passes he'd scouted in the two days since he'd left Denver. Although Kane had been leading his upended captive between the jagged precipices for three hours, he still hadn't communicated with Darcey. He dreaded informing her that he was the bandit who had abducted her from the express office. The fact was, Kane was still trying to collect his composure after the nerve-racking robbery of the express company.

Watching Darcey defy death at Griz Vanhook's hand had rattled Kane. He had only been allowed a split second to fire before the fumbling Lester Alridge made his courageous but disastrous attempt to save Darcey's life. Even now Kane could feel the wild desperation that had pulsated through him when he aimed around Lester's narrow shoulders to target the burly bandit. He'd held his breath for what seemed forever, hoping beyond hope that Lester wouldn't accidentally shoot Darcey by mistake.

Kane couldn't have cared less that Lester had erroneously credited himself for disposing of Griz. In fact, the less attention Kane drew to himself during an investigation, the better he liked it. As far as Denver was concerned, Kane Callahan was just a drifter, a gambler looking for a high-stakes poker game to support himself. Kane had endeared himself to the townspeople by standing up to Griz and the other unruly desperadoes, but now Lester was the talk of the town and Kane had been forgotten. That was good, since Kane didn't want anyone to suspect him of stepping in to abduct Darcey after he'd shot Griz. Darcey's disappearance would have to remain a mystery until Kane had located the elusive Courtly Highwayman who had been harassing O'Roarke Express.

As for the vicious gang of thieves who'd stolen gold and mail from the stage, the problem had just been resolved. While Kane had been scouting the mountains west of Denver, he had seen another bandit attempt to waylay the stage. Kane had recognized Griz Vanhook's horse on sight, as well as the battered canvas duster and the flour sack that concealed his wooly face. When Griz's first attempt to rob the stage was thwarted by the guards, Kane hadn't expected the scoundrel to circle back to town to recover the loot directly from the express office.

Some detective he'd turned out to be! He should

have predicted a man like Griz Vanhook would pull such a daring stunt. Considering Griz's personal vendetta and lust for Darcey, Kane should have second-guessed that pistolero.

Fortunately, Kane had returned to town in the nick of time to stop Griz. If he had delayed even a minute, Lester Alridge would have been dead and Darcey . . .

Kane swiveled his head around to stare at the wildcat who hung upside down on the saddle. Kane supposed he should feel sorry for her after all she'd been through this evening. But Kane couldn't muster much sympathy. That defiant sprite deserved the scare tactics he was using on her and he intended to frighten the living daylights out of her before he was through.

After the tantrum she'd thrown in her hotel room three days earlier she deserved to suffer such torment, thought Kane. Sometimes she made him so frustrated he considered strangling her. But Patrick O'Roarke hadn't offered to pay Kane ten thousand dollars to wring his daredevil daughter's neck, but rather to save her from disaster . . . which he just had!

Darcey had been saved from certain death, even if she wouldn't bother thanking him for it, but she still had a few lessons to learn before Kane sent her running back to her father's protective arms. As Patrick had said, only terrifying memories would prevent Little Miss Determination from hotfooting it back to Denver the first chance she got. Kane intended to solve every problem that would prompt Darcey to return to Colorado. If the company was running efficiently and the bandits had been captured she would have no reason to dawdle in Denver.

With Griz Vanhook dead and his cohorts locked in jail, Kane had only two problems left—Darcey, and the gentleman bandit. Of course, Darcey would wind up hating him more than she already did. Unfortunately, the tempestuous relationship between them was a hazard of Kane's crusade. Darcey would have all the more reason to rush back to St. Louis and her father . . .

Muffled squawks erupted from Darcey's gag, dragging Kane from his deliberations. Hell, he might as well get this over with. There was no sense prolonging the inevitable. He couldn't hobble that viperous tongue of hers forever. She was ready to blow off steam and he might as well let her spew.

Resigned to listening Darcey rant and rave, Kane pulled his steed to a halt and swung to the ground. In grim anticipation, he strode toward Griz's horse which carried the lovely but infuriating pain in the . . .

Another round of muffled hisses and curses resounded along the craggy peaks that glowed in the moonlight. Reluctantly, Kane yanked the gag from Darcey's mouth and braced himself for the barrage of outraged curses.

After Darcey called her captor every loathsome name in the book, she glared at the concealed face beneath the broad-brimmed hat and black mask. "Be warned, you despicable swine, my father owns O'Roarke Express! When he learns of my abduction, he will have every law official and master detective in the country on your trail! He'll hound your every step until he hunts you down like the despicable cur you are. Then he'll hang you from the tallest tree in Colorado and shoot you full of bullets. Even if you run to the ends of this earth he will track you. You will never enjoy a moment's peace. There will be nowhere you can hide to avoid my father's vengeance."

"Is that so, darlin'?" Kane replied in the slow, lazy Southern drawl he had utilized in espionage missions during the war to infiltrate enemy lines. Several times in the past he had been forced to perfect the accent that made him sound as if he were Southern born and bred. Now it helped him conceal his identity from this fuming wildcat.

"Yes, that's so," Darcey sassed her captor. "Hell will have nowhere near the fury of my father!"

During the last hour of her ride, Darcey had resolved to go out of this world in a blaze of glory rather than in sniveling tears. If she were going to meet her Creator, she preferred to go here and now, not ten miles later. She was a determined fighter and she didn't give a whit if she had to take on the devil himself. Anger and frustration had won out over fear and Darcey was good and mad.

When Kane grabbed her by the hair of her head and lifted her face up to meet his unrecognizable stare, Darcey grimaced in pain. But only for a second. She glowered at the disguised bandit, wishing she could claw the concealing mask to shreds, along with the face beneath it—whoever the devil it belonged to!

"And just what, darlin', do you think all these threats are gonna do you?" Kane drawled in mocking disdain. "You'll be dead long before I ever will be."

Darcey sputtered furiously and attempted to wriggle

loose, but the ropes held her fast. "I'll be waiting at the pearly gates to ensure you don't get in," she smarted. "Knowing you'll be frying over the hottest fire in Hades will make me eternally happy."

This was going to be even more difficult than Kane had imagined. This she-cat was supposed to be frightened within an inch of her life, but contrary as she was, she got mad when it would have made more sense to be scared.

"Well, it seems to me that yer *daddy* would pay handsomely to get you back—though why he'd want you has got me baffled," he added with a smirk. "Maybe I'll just send yer *daddy* a letter and see if ye're worth as much as you seem to think you are."

Darcey blinked and gaped at the masked desperado. She hadn't considered the possibility that he would steal all the gold in the office and also demand a ransom for her return. Not that she would be returned. She was absolutely certain she wouldn't be. If this miscreant rode with Griz Vanhook, he was just as ruthless as the ringleader. Damn, she should have listened to Kane. He warned her she'd wind up neck-deep in disaster one fine day. *This* was the one fine day!

"I'd say you ought to be worth about ten thousand dollars," Kane mused aloud. After all, that was the price Patrick had put on his daughter's auburn head.

"Ten thousand?" Darcey croaked. "That's outrageous."

A low rumble of laughter rippled beneath Kane's mask. "Ye're prob'ly right, darlin'. Sassy witches like you prob'ly ain't worth even a thousand dollars to anybody but their daddies. I'd give more for a well-

174

used whore myself."

If Darcey could have wrested her hand loose she would have slapped the insulting rascal silly! Since she couldn't, she had to settle for glaring flaming daggers at his concealed chest that was covered by a long canvas duster similar to the one Griz had worn. To Darcey's further frustration her captor released her head and reached up to whack her on the derriere.

"Of course, if I've a mind to, I could teach you how to satisfy a man. Maybe you'd be worth more if you used this shapely body of yers to pleasure men instead of antagonizin' them."

"I'd rather be dead!" Darcey spewed poisonously.

Kane cupped her chin, forcing her to arch backward to meet his goading chuckle. "That, darlin', can easily be arranged *after* I've taken what I want from you."

For the first time in a long while, Darcey allowed someone else to have the last word. Her imagination was running rampant. She kept visualizing the horrifying encounter this merciless renegade suggested. He wouldn't be as gentle and considerate of her as Kane had been when he introduced her to passion. She had scorned Kane and herself at the time, but she would have gladly run into Kane's arms if it would free her from this lusty devil's clutches.

Chuckling wickedly, Kane moseyed back to his horse and swung into the saddle. "When we get to my cabin, you can work yer wiles on me, darlin'. And if you try real hard to please me, I might even—"

"You may take what you want eventually," Darcey hissed spitefully. "But I guarantee, you'll have a fight on your hands!"

175

Kane snickered devilishly again. "There are ways to ensure a woman don't fight back," he told her bluntly. "I can take what I want from you and there won't be a damned thing you can do about it, believe you me." There. Let her chew on that frightening possibility awhile and see how sassy she was!

Darcey gulped over the lump of fear that clogged her throat. Again, she had allowed this bastard the last word because her tormented mind was too busy envisioning the most hideous tortures known to womankind. Would she be lashed to a bed and beaten to unconsciousness? Would she be subjected to the worst offenses imaginable at his cruel, disgusting hands?

A wave of nausea rose in her throat. For the first time in two months, Darcey wished she'd listened to her father when he pleaded with her to take a safe position at the main office in St. Louis. But no, she had braved the worst elements in society and put down roots in the rowdy city of Denver. Suddenly her determined crusade in life didn't matter one whit. She was about to be molested and murdered in some out-of-the-way shack five hundred miles from nowhere! Her father, in sheer desperation, would pay the ten-thousand-dollar ransom and still he would never see her again.

Curse it, why hadn't she listened to Kane? He'd urged her to pack up and leave town at least a dozen times. Now she'd been bound up and toted off, never to be seen or heard from again . . .

A choked sob exploded from Darcey's lips. She wasn't prone to tears and she had refused to allow herself to succumb to weak sentiment. But if ever there was a time to cry, now was that time. Despite her effort to gather her crumbling composure, a few scalding tears bled down her cheeks and a dispirited whimper echoed around her. Despair closed in like the darkness and Darcey found herself weeping like an abandoned child.

Kane steeled himself against the sound of Darcey's sobbing. The detective in him was committed to his assignment, distasteful though it had become. But the man in him balked at purposely tormenting this headstrong beauty. As much as he hated to admit it, and as obligated as he was to his cause of scaring her home where she belonged, it was pure and simple torment to know he was the one who had provoked her to tears. Darcey was being subjected to frustrating torture.

Oh, Patrick had implied that nothing short of a horrifying ordeal would make enough of an impression on Darcey to send her running. But Patrick wasn't the one who had to impose such torment on this spirited she-male. Kane knew she detested her own tears and her captivity. He was also aware that she would spit in his face when he finally worked up enough nerve to expose his true identity. Kane wasn't quite ready yet and he dreaded that moment. It would be a thousand times worse than when she had awakened from their night of passion to face her guilt and regret. All things considered, this emerald-eyed hellion would have every justifiable reason in the world to hate him with a vengeance.

Kane sagged in the saddle. In the past, he'd taken

several cases that had not appealed to him, but this one was positively the worst! He was forced to talk and behave exactly like the scoundrels he tracked. He wondered fleetingly if the criminal ever harbored feelings of regret. Only after he got caught, Kane reckoned. And in the case of Griz Vanhook, Kane doubted that murdering thief felt the slightest ounce of sympathy for all his victims.

Darcey didn't know how fortunate she was. She easily could have been carted off by Griz Vanhook himself. Kane had saved her from nine kinds of hell, but she would never know that. To her, Kane would always be a blackguard of the worst sort.

When this ordeal was over she would go back to her world and he'd go back to his. That was simply the way it had to be. And it was for the best, Kane convinced himself. If Darcey ever learned the truth about his mission she would still curse the ground he walked. What they'd shared during that night of reckless splendor was over as quickly as it had begun. Dwelling on it would be *his* torment.

It was midnight before Kane reached the obscure one-room shack that had been built into the looming precipices of the Rockies. There was a distinct chill in the air and a feeling of gloom in Kane's heart. He didn't like what he was doing, not one damned bit. And the next time he saw Patrick O'Roarke, he vowed to punch that pushy Irishman in the jaw for having such a stubborn daughter who demanded such drastic measures to reform her.

While Darcey hung there like a slug, Kane fished through Griz's saddlebag. As expected, Kane found an empty pouch that had been stamped with the O'Roarke Express emblem. When Kane dug a little deeper he came up with a handful of gold watches and rings that had once belonged to the unfortunate passengers of the O'Roarke stage line.

Darcey cursed fluently when she spied the familiar sack and stolen jewelry. It was just as she had suspected. Griz Vanhook and his ring of thieves had been terrorizing the stage. The only problem was that her captor had his grubby hands on the evidence and she was too far away from anywhere to point an accusing finger. She would probably take to her grave the knowledge of this secluded hideout and the identity of one of the gang's more ruthless members. She'd have delighted in telling the whole world that she'd discovered the outlaw gang which had hounded the stage. Unfortunately, she would never learn who the gentleman bandit was. It didn't appear likely she would live long enough to solve that frustrating riddle.

When Kane ambled over to cut the rope that secured Darcey to the saddle, she dropped headfirst and somersaulted over the loose rocks. A dull groan tripped from her lips when she was jerked up beside the brawny form and forced to jump toward the dilapidated shack like a grasshopper.

"At least untie my feet," Darcey demanded in frustration.

"No way, darlin'," Kane snorted in a tone that reflected not one ounce of sympathy. He had relied upon his acting ability a score of times in the past.

Treating this lovely but belligerent sprite so abominably tested his talents. "The only time you'll be able to spread yer feet is when ye're strapped to my bed."

The threat caused Darcey to become unhinged. She didn't care if this despicable varmint shot her in the back. She was making a run for her life! With a burst of energy, she wheeled about, using her bound hands as a club to knock her captor off balance and off guard. When her abductor instinctively staggered back from the unexpected blow, Darcey hopped toward a clump of underbrush beside the shack. She hadn't taken three jumps before her captor leaped on her like a pouncing panther. The cold ground flew up at her with incredible speed, and her breath was forced from her lungs in a grunt. She was left to mutter a string of curses into the grass and lie beneath the most disgusting snake ever to slither across the earth. Curse it, this renegade wouldn't even shoot her down when she practically sent him an engraved invitation!

"Get up," Kane growled in his most threatening tone. "You ain't ever gonna get away from me, witch, so don't waste yer energy and my time tryin'. I can think of better ways to expend yer strength."

"You won't enjoy it," Darcey spat venomously. "I swear you won't!"

"I'll enjoy it more than you will," Kane sneered. "And you can bet yer life on that, darlin'."

Clamping both arms around the squirming bundle of blind fury, Kane scooped Darcey off the ground and stalked purposefully toward the shack. With a swift kick, Kane sent the door flying open. It banged against the wall, sending a dribble of dirt onto Darcey's flushed cheeks. In two long effortless strides, Kane was beside the cot that was heaped with the quilts he had stashed there the previous day. Unceremoniously, he dropped Darcey onto the bed and listened to her growl and hiss like an angry cat. She hadn't even finished her last hiss before Kane grabbed her wrists and draped the rope over the rough-hewn bedpost, if one could call it that. The bed was so crude that only four poles, which had been lashed together with leather straps, supported the cot.

In the same inconsiderate manner, Kane clutched Darcey's feet and reached down to extract the long-bladed knife he kept in the scabbard on his belt. Darcey stared at the glittering blade and speculated on what he intended to do with it. Moonbeams spotlighted the cold steel blade as he swerved it threateningly toward her.

To her dismay or relief, he cut away one of the ropes so he could bind each leg to the posts at the foot of the bed. While Darcey lay strapped down like a victim of torture awaiting doom, Kane pivoted away.

"Damn that Patrick," Kane muttered to himself as he fumbled to light the lantern. "If he hadn't allowed his daughter to become such a termagant I wouldn't be doing this!"

Darcey peered at the wide expanse of her captor's back, straining in vain to decipher his muffled words. "If you were more of a man and less of an animal you wouldn't have to tie a woman down to have your way with her," Darcey taunted with incredible daring.

Kane lurched about, amazed at her challenge. It was becoming increasingly clear that this saucy little snip was inviting her own death. In fact, she seemed to prefer it to the thought of being taken by him. Well, she could antagonize him to her heart's content but it would do her no good whatsoever. She could lie there and fry in her own grease. Anticipating a merciless rape would be almost as bad as enduring it, Kane reckoned.

Honest to God, if this hellion knew the torment *he* was going through detesting his charade, she would have enjoyed a small amount of solace. Mistreating Darcey went against Kane's grain every step of the way. Forcing himself to be cruel was killing him, bit by agonizing bit. If ever there had been a woman he might have truly cared for, this auburn-haired elf came as close as any.

Day by day, Kane had begun to realize that it hadn't been a wounded heart that nagged at him when Melanie Brooks ran off with Jonathan Beezely. It was only his bruised pride that had been smarting. And when Kane finally ran headlong into the one woman he might have loved, if either of them would have given each other half a chance, he had tarnished golden opportunity. Darcey would hold a grudge, he'd bet his reputation on it. She would consign him to the farthest reaches of hell and never speak to him again.

Immersed in thought though Kane was, he came back to reality in one second flat. Darcey had opened her mouth to scream at the top of her lungs. The entire cabin shuddered at the high-pitched shriek that came dangerously close to shattering Kane's eardrums.

"Calm down, woman," Kane bellowed loudly.

"I won't . . . (wail) . . . shut up . . . (squawk) . . . ever . . . (shrill shriek, shrill shriek)!" Darcey sucked air and screamed blood murder all over again. "You'll have to . . . (eardrum-splitting yowl) . . . kill me first . . . (blare, howl)!"

"Oh no I won't, darlin'," Kane yelled over the banshee.

He knew what would shut her up. And now seemed the perfect moment for his unveiling. Kane clutched his hat and tossed it carelessly toward the crudely made table in the middle of the room. Swiftly, he tugged the black silk mask from his head.

For a half-second Kane swore Darcey would faint in surprise. Her elegant face turned white as milk and her jaws opened and closed like the damper on a chimney, but she emitted no sound whatsoever.

For that one brief second that froze time, Kane enjoyed his consolation. He had accomplished a most impressive feat that no other man had mastered. He had rendered this spitfire utterly speechless.

Chapter 11

Darcey gaped at Kane as if he'd sprouted devil's horns. Never in her worst nightmare had she expected to see his face behind that black mask! The shock of it all caused her overworked heart to slam against her ribs and stick there. Try though she might, she couldn't draw a breath without choking in pure rage. It was a full minute before her voice began to function properly. And when it did, only one croaked word burst from her lips.

"You!" Darcey glowered at the object of her scorn.

Kane struck a cocky pose and dropped into an exaggerated bow. "None other, darlin'," he drawled with infuriating nonchalance.

The color gushed back into her ashen cheeks. Darcey looked as if she might explode. And explode she did, just as Kane anticipated she would. Incoherent curses and hisses spewed from her curled lips. Her green eyes blazed like torches and her entire body strained against the confining ropes that held her to the bed. A lesser woman would have suffered heart seizure after expending so much futile energy to claw her way to freedom. But Darcey O'Roarke was made of sturdy stuff. She didn't burst a seam, but she *did* curse the air blue.

"Tsk, tsk," Kane chastised in sardonic amusement. "Ladies of high quality aren't supposed to use such foul language, especially in mixed company." Another grin crinkled his rugged features. "The Lord will get you for slandering His name."

"The Lord already did," Darcey muttered bitterly. "He let me get tangled up with you, didn't He?"

Like a duck repelling water, Kane shrugged off the insult and sauntered over to drop into a chair. Leisurely, he propped his booted feet on the edge of the table, linked his fingers behind his ruffled raven head, and studied her for a long moment. "It seems to me we both got exactly what we deserved. You're my hell on earth and I, it appears, am yours."

Darcey glared at the swarthy rake, begrudgingly marveling at his ability to change roles in life like a chameleon. He could portray a gambler, a gentleman, or a ruthless thief with amazing ease. And why shouldn't he be able to? Darcey thought bitterly. Kane Callahan was a deceiving rascal whose goal in life was to thoroughly fool and swindle as many people as possible.

"What do you want with me, you scoundrel?" Darcey spluttered in question.

"I thought we had already established that," Kane countered, settling into his role as the antagonist as best he could. After all, he didn't have any choices. He didn't have to *like* this distasteful assignment; he only had to do it. In this instance the unpleasant means justified the end. Darcey would have so many miserable memories of Denver that she'd never want to come back.

Darcey glowered murderously at the sinewy giant who sat sprawled on his wooden throne. She'd have given her eye teeth if she could have torn him limb from limb and fed his carcass to the wolves.

"I knew you were mixed up with Griz Vanhook all along," she seethed. "That's why you were the only one who dared to confront him. Then you put on that phony concern act of yours for my benefit. The whole lot of you staged every scene, didn't you?"

Darcey didn't wait for him to answer. She simply forged ahead, leaping from one incredible conclusion to another. "What a clever combination of personalities you are—the charismatic gambler, the deceitful Samaritan, and the odious outlaw."

She raked him with loathing disdain, wishing she could find one physical flaw to match his sneaky, dirty, rotten personality. Unfortunately, Kane had no noticeable physical flaws. And who knew that better than she, after he had used his masculine wiles to seduce her for his own lusty pleasures.

"You tried to get into my good graces and case the express office before you and Griz robbed it. Not that you cared if your cohort got shot down. That was all the better for you, wasn't it? Griz will take all the blame for the robberies against the express company while you drag me off to await a ransom. Not only did you spirit away with all the gold in the office, but you'll be

187

well paid for my return when my father learns of my kidnapping. I hate you! You disgust me!" she all but yelled at him.

There she went again, thought Kane. When this firebrand went on the rampage, she exhibited a most active imagination. She could really come up with some doozies when she got wound up!

In the first place, Kane had taken the gold and credit vouchers to ensure that they weren't stolen while the office was left unattended. It would have been a simple matter for someone who was down on his luck to pluck up a pouch of gold and stuff it in his pocket. And in the second place, Kane had brought Griz's horse and saddlebags along because they held important evidence that linked him to previous robberies.

Of course, Kane couldn't contest Darcey's weird theories and accomplish the task Patrick sent him to do. Darcey could believe what she wanted—the worst. She would have anyway. That was always her philosophy when it came to her dealings with men. It would take an act of God to change her opinions.

Heaving a tired sigh, Kane pulled off his boots and tossed them aside. It had been a long, trying night and he was exhausted—physically and emotionally.

"What are you doing?" Darcey hissed when he ambled toward the bed. "If you think to sleep here, think again! I loathe the thought of cuddling up with a snake."

"Loathe it all you want," Kane offered as he stretched out and draped one leg over Darcey's bound ankles to hold her in place. "But there is only one bed and we're sharing it, like it or not."

"I don't," she growled hatefully. "And I have had nothing to eat since noon. I expect—"

"I expect you'll be good and hungry by morning," Kane said with an unconcerned yawn.

"You plan to let me starve to death?"

She gaped at him in disbelief and then scolded herself for presuming this scalawag possessed one iota of compassion. He'd already proved he didn't have a sympathetic bone in his body. And all those softly uttered words he'd showered on her at the beginning of the week were nothing but poisonous lies. She was no more than a passing fancy, a temporary physical release for his male lust. She was his means to an end— a ransom that would enable him to live in the lap of luxury.

"Why should I feed you?" Kane questioned as he dangled his arm over her abdomen, infuriating her all the more with his reckless familiarity. "Your hatred for me should be nourishment enough to tide you over until dawn."

"I really do hate you," Darcey spumed. "I hope you are fully aware of that!"

"Oh, really, darlin'?" Kane expelled a mocking snort and tugged the quilt over them. "Who would have guessed? Certainly not I."

"I want you to know I'll shoot you down the first chance I get," she threatened.

"Thanks for the warning," Kane drawled drowsily. "Now clam up and go to sleep."

"I hardly see how that will be possible, considering I'm forced to lie with the likes of you. In fact, I don't imagine—"

Her voice drowned beneath the pillow Kane slammed over her face.

"My only fear is that you'll talk me to death trying to get in the last word," he smirked caustically.

Darcey said nothing more. She had enough trouble drawing in air with the down-filled pillow obstructing her breathing.

Despite the vow to stay awake by counting all the disgusting flaws in this hard-hearted scoundrel's personality, Darcey finally gave way to exhaustion. This was, without a doubt, the worst night of her life. It humiliated her beyond words that she had wasted one tittle of sentiment on this horrible, conniving rascal.

For the past few days she had battled her attraction for Kane, alphabetically listing all the reasons why she shouldn't permit him to burrow into her carefully guarded heart. And sure enough, all his whispered words had been tender lies which were voiced to soften her defenses and set her up for the kill. Kane Callahan was a silver-blue-eyed demon who had no conscience, no compassion, no noble sentiment. Why, if Kane hadn't already sold his wicked soul to the devil, it was only because he was holding out for the highest possible price!

Darcey sorely resented the fact that she had come to like Kane even a smidgen. But she would have died before she admitted it aloud. And a good thing it was that she hadn't in a weak moment. That would have been the ultimate humiliation. Then Kane truly would have had the last laugh on her!

Yet, somehow or another, Darcey would escape him. And this midnight-haired desperado would rue the day he met her. She would have the last word and the last laugh.

When Owen Graves reported for work the morning after Darcey's abduction, he was dismayed to find Lester Alridge at the helm. Owen had heard about the robbery attempt and Darcey's disappearance on his way to work. But the previous night he had been visiting his mistress on Ferry Street, which was located on the far side of town. His amorous rendezvous had prevented him from witnessing the celebration that hailed Lester as a hero.

To Owen's frustration, he was informed that Deputy Metcalf had appointed Lester manager until Patrick O'Roarke could be informed of the incident that resulted in his daughter's abduction. As for himself, Owen was glad that persnickety chit was out from underfoot. She was like a thorny rose that pricked a man's pride and tempted him beyond torment.

And to Owen's further exasperation, he found that Lester had gained an unexpected air of authority since he assumed the position of manager. Lester had stepped into Darcey's shoes and taken on that green-eyed terror's own image. Lester whizzed around the office with the same efficient stride, stacking every blessed object in alphabetical order. His stutter had disappeared and he now spoke with new confidence. Owen felt Darcey's irritating presence as if she had been there in body rather than spirit. Lester had become the epitome of organization and had begun bossing Owen about as if the demoted manager was no more than the company lackey.

"I don't have to take this from you, too," Owen grumbled as Lester thrust a stack of ledgers at him and gestured toward the back room.

"Oh yes you do," Lester contradicted in a no-nonsense tone that was startlingly reminiscent of Darcey's. "We have a service to perform for this community and we will carry on just as Miss O'Roarke would have done. She is counting on us . . . wherever she is."

"*If* she still *is,* "Owen amended with a snort before he stalked off with the ledgers.

"And we will have no more of that discouraging talk, either," Lester insisted as he adjusted his spectacles to glare at Owen's departing back. "File those books in alphabetical order, Owen. I want to be able to put my hands on them in a flash if I need them."

Owen rolled his eyes heavenward. He thought he'd seen the last of Darcey O'Roarke. But to his chagrin, she had somehow managed to mold Lester into a replica of her own efficient self. Lord, the express agency was plagued with another alphabetical monster!

While Owen organized the books, Lester manned the main counter and assisted the string of customers who filed in and out in a steady stream. A worried frown knitted Lester's face when he spied Pup Metcalf lumbering through the door.

"Did you see any sign of Miss O'Roarke?" Lester questioned apprehensively.

Pup gave his disheveled blond head a discouraged shake. "Nothing, not even a clue. God, I wish the sheriff was back on his feet. Maybe he would have handled the situation better than I did."

"I have notified Mr. O'Roarke," Lester informed the grim-faced deputy. "I'm afraid it will take a few days to get the message to him in St. Louis, but I'm sure he'll have every manhunter, bloodhound, and detective in the country on the trail."

Pup expelled a dispirited breath. "But that won't do Miss O'Roarke much good, now will it?" he replied before he spun himself around and trudged off.

Kane awoke to the sound of Darcey's grumbling stomach registering a complaint. When he pried open his eyes, she greeted him with a morning glare that was as hot as the hinges on hell's door.

Without uttering a word, Kane rolled out of bed and stuffed his feet in his boots. After working the kinks from his back, he built a fire in the hearth. Why he bothered, he didn't know, since Darcey started blowing enough hot air and flashed him enough blistering glares to keep the cabin toasty until midmorning.

"Not only am I starving half to death, but my appendages are numb . . . thanks to your heartless treatment," Darcey hissed in a bitter tone. "And besides that, I have been unable to tend to my needs. I don't expect much consideration from the likes of you, but I do demand the very minimum!"

Once the fire was crackling in the hearth, Kane strolled over to release the rope that was looped around the headpost of the bed. After he had untied Darcey's feet, he set her upright. Employing one of the ropes as a leash, he led Darcey outside and allowed her to wander behind the clump of bushes near the cabin. He knew full well she resented her captivity and lack of privacy, but he couldn't trust her. She would break into a run and attempt escape the first chance she got.

When Darcey emerged from the brush, she glared at Kane as if he were the most despicable creature ever to walk the face of the earth. Frustrated anger churned inside her. Never had she been treated so disrespectfully. She had felt betrayed once before when Michael used her as a stepping-stone to wealth. But the anguish she'd suffered was nothing compared to her dealings with this insufferable varmint!

"Even if I have to endure this captivity until my father gathers the money you demanded for my ransom, I will not tolerate living like a heathen," Darcey spewed. "I expect to bathe daily and to be fed nutritious meals and—"

Kane scooped her up so quickly that she was unable to finish raving at him. Before she realized his intent, Kane had sidestepped down the hill to toss her into the cold mountain stream that lay below the cabin.

That should cool off this fuming temper of hers, Kane decided with a wicked grin.

Darcey's shriek of disbelief echoed through the chasm when she landed slapbang in the stream. When Kane doused her with cold water, she swore instant icicles had formed on her flesh. In outrage, she floundered to her feet, cursing the soggy gown that weighed her down like an anchor, and the man who stood snickering in devilish glee.

From the creekbank, holding the rope that was

attached to her wrists, Kane dropped into an exaggerated bow. "Your bath, m'lady. Now, would you like to take your breakfast?" he asked in a mocking parody of politeness.

"What I would *like . . .*" Darcey fumed as she tramped from the creek, "is to see you shot, poisoned, stabbed, and hanged. But I doubt those are among my choices."

Difficult though it was, Kane didn't burst into a snicker. He swore he saw steam rising from the high collar of Darcey's dripping dress. He hadn't cooled her temper one tittle. If anything, he had made her madder than a wet hen.

Again Kane reminded himself that there were times when a man had to be cruel to be kind. He had to make her captivity a horrible nightmare, create agonizing memories of her trek through the mountains. Patrick wanted Kane to ensure that his rambunctious daughter never set foot in Colorado again. This rough treatment, Kane assured himself, would cure this hellion for life.

While Darcey spluttered hateful epithets to his name through her chattering teeth, Kane dragged her back to the cabin. Once inside, Kane yanked her to him to unfasten the stays of her saturated gown. With an indignant squawk, Darcey flung herself away, clutching the sagging gown to her breasts.

"I can do this myself, thank you very much," she hissed at him.

With a careless shrug, Kane plucked up a quilt and tossed it to her. "You can wear this until your gown dries out."

Darcey stared at the itchy blanket as if he were

offering her a live snake.

"It's this or nothing," Kane told her. An ornery grin dangled on the corner of his full lips. "I prefer to see you garbed in nothing at all, but—"

She snatched the quilt from his fingers and glared hot pokers at him. If looks could kill, Kane would have dropped dead at least twice.

Muttering under her breath, Darcey clamped the quilt in her teeth to protect herself from his leering gaze. She extended her hands for Kane to untie her wrists so she could worm from the gown. But she was extremely careful while wriggling from the dress into the quilt not to allow Kane an eye full of exposed flesh.

Kane, however, did glimpse an enticing view of cleavage, making him far more aware of this delectable beauty than he needed to be, considering the role he was forced to play. Trying to get a firm grip on himself, Kane tore his gaze away and glanced in the other direction. But it was difficult not to ogle this tempting minx.

After Kane secured the rope to the head of the bed, he built a makeshift rack in front of the hearth to dry her gown. While he prepared their breakfast, he could feel those blazing emerald eyes boring into him. Kane reminded himself that he couldn't become distracted by her sensual lure. Neither could he let up on Darcey for even a minute if he wanted to make a lasting impression on her.

Ah, how easy it would have been to apologize all over himself, to gather her close and offer compassion, which could easily transform into desire. But he couldn't, damn it. If he told her the whole truth, she would still despise him for deceiving her and she would curse her father for paying a professional detective to maneuver her into running home where Patrick thought she belonged.

"It is inconceivable to me how you can live with yourself, being the horrible man you are," Darcey said with scathing disdain. "You are cruel and cunning and despicable and—"

"Leave it to you to alphabetize my failing graces," Kane cut in. His voice reflected as little emotion as possible.

When their meal was sufficiently heated, Kane dipped up the broth that was flavored with chunks of dried beef. He purposely set the chunk of stale bread on the wrong side of the plate—completely out of order—knowing it would irritate Darcey. It did.

She stared at the rim of the tin plate from which greasy broth dripped into puddles on the table. Slabs of stringy beef floated like splinters of driftwood. "I said I desired a nutritious meal," she sniffed in complaint. "A coyote would turn up his nose at this inedible slop."

Kane folded himself onto the edge of the bed beside her and scooped up an appetizing spoonful of stew. "Open up. This isn't St. Louis, honey, and you don't have the choice of an extensive menu at the most elegant restaurant in town."

"I prefer . . ." Darcey strangled on her breath when Kane stuffed the spoon into her mouth. All that could be said for the distasteful breakfast that Kane force-fed her was that it warmed her frozen innards. Each time she opened her mouth trying to wedge in the last word,

197

Kane crammed food down her throat. When he decided she'd consumed enough of the "slop," he set her plate aside to eat his breakfast.

"I despise you, Kane Callahan," Darcey growled at him.

"I know," he replied between bites. "You've told me often enough."

When Kane had polished off his breakfast, he gestured toward the pitcher and basin on the end of the table. "I cooked. Now you can wash the dishes."

"Surely you jest!" Darcey scoffed. "I do not intend to become your servant."

Kane grabbed her by the shoulders and shoved her to her feet. In two strides he reached the table and dragged it toward her, since Darcey was already at the end of her rope—literally and figuratively.

"Wash 'em," he demanded tersely. "You were probably born with a silver spoon in your mouth, but if you want to eat with clean utensils next time, you'll have to sanitize them. And if you think I'm going to treat you like royalty just because your *daddy* owns the express company, you better think again."

Their eyes locked like doubled fists.

"I'll wash *my* spoon and plate and that is all," she gritted out between clenched teeth.

"And if you do, you won't eat again until your *daddy* comes to fetch you with a satchel of cash," Kane assured her in a harsh tone.

Darcey's temper, which had been sorely put upon already, burst loose. With a snarl she pressed her hands against the rock-hard wall of his chest and gave him a mighty shove. A surprised yelp erupted from Kane's lips when he slammed into the table. His boot hooked on the leg of a chair and he stumbled back into the improvised clothesline that held Darcey's gown. The rack plunged into the hearth with a crash and Darcey's clothes went up in smoke.

"You clumsy oaf! Now what am I supposed to wear?" Darcey wailed in exasperation.

Kane watched the gown smoldering on the log. It had nothing on Darcey. A wry grin bracketed his mouth. He knew Darcey was so frustrated that she was ready to spit tacks. Not that he blamed her and not that he could do much to console her. This was, to be sure, a hard lesson for this feisty female to learn. She was out of her element in the rugged mountains of Colorado. She belonged in Missouri, spinning in the social circles of the rich, employing her theories of efficient organization, taking her "nutritious" meals, and garbing herself in another fashionable gown when the one she wore suffered irreparable damage.

"Answer me," Darcey sputtered in outrage. "What am I supposed to wear? Surely you don't expect me to muck about in this quilt until my father comes to fetch me."

"Oh, I almost forgot," he fibbed. "I stopped by your hotel room to fetch a few of your things for the trip."

When Kane sauntered across the room to pull her nightgown from his saddlebag, Darcey exploded like a keg of blasting powder. "You loathsome swine! You planned this all, right from the very beginning." Another furious frown puckered her elegant features when he tossed the garment to her. "Surely you don't expect me to wear this frilly thing day and night!"

"Surely I do," he countered with an ornery smile.

Darcey resigned herself to the fact that Kane didn't intend to budge an inch. Every action was designed to humiliate and frustrate her. And damn if he wasn't exceptionally good at it!

"At least turn your back and allow me a meager amount of privacy," she insisted.

"Why should I?" he parried with an unsympathetic smirk. "It's not as if I haven't seen every gorgeous inch of you already, you know."

It was with extreme effort that Darcey held her tongue. She needed no reminder of their romantic escapade. In fact, even when she had been doing her damnedest to forget that careless night ever existed, it still tormented her thoughts.

"Haven't you mortified me enough?" Darcey choked out, on the verge of tears.

Kane relented. Seeing her standing there, clad in a quilt, her eyes misted with tears, left him wanting to hold her in the worst way. But he had pushed her far enough and she would probably come unhinged if he dared to circle her in his arms. But Kane had to admit that he found himself wishing she would accidentally drop the quilt and allow him a scant few seconds to gaze upon her beauty, just as he had that wondrous night.

Knowing Darcey was standing there wearing nothing but a blanket was damned hard on him. Kane had been giving her hell for her own good, but what he wanted was to transform her anger into fiery passion. Even after all they'd been through, and despite her well-earned hatred for him, he longed to recapture the magical moment that lingered in his mind. Beneath her shield of armor, Darcey was a warm, responsive woman. He yearned to drop this tormenting facade and lose himself in . . .

"Will you please turn your head and keep it turned!" Darcey railed in exasperation. "Haven't you tortured me enough for one morning?"

"All right, but be quick." Kane forced himself to stare at the wall instead of at the vision of absolute perfection.

In a flash, Darcey dropped the quilt, but she couldn't get her arms into the sleeves of the nightgown when her wrists were bound. Muttering sourly, Darcey clutched the gown around her bosom, leaving her chest and shoulders bare. Humiliated, she tapped Kane on the shoulder.

"I need your help," she begrudgingly admitted. "Untie me . . . please."

Kane pivoted, and his hungry eyes fell to the luscious swells that rose and fell beneath her flimsy gown. His gaze flooded over her alabaster skin, aching to touch what lay so temptingly before him. He took his own sweet time about loosening the rope from her wrists and Darcey turned all the colors of the rainbow while his masculine gaze devoured her to such a degree that she actually felt as if he *had* touched her.

Once she had wedged her arms into the garment, she realized this was her one and only chance to escape. Her arms were momentarily free, as were her legs. If she could find some way to incapacitate Kane she could dart toward the door and leap onto her horse before he caught up with her. This was a chance she had to take.

There might not be another.

Darcey moved like streak lightning. Her hand folded around the pitcher on the table and she slammed it against Kane's skull before he could react. When his knees folded beneath him, Darcey wheeled toward the door.

There was only one hitch in her plan. The blow to the head hadn't knocked Kane out. It only stunned him. Before she could veer around the table and whiz out the door, Kane clutched the hem of her gown. A tug of war began as Kane wilted to the floor.

Hissing and cursing, Darcey tried to yank the gown from his fist. But Kane was as determined to hold on to her as she was to take flight. Despite the throbbing pain in his skull, Kane clutched the fabric tightly while she dragged him halfway across the floor in her frantic attempt to escape. Once Kane's senses cleared, he reared back to jerk Darcey toward him. With a yelp, she tumbled off balance and fell—right smack dab on top of him.

Kane's arms and legs closed around her writhing body like a beaver trap. Darcey found herself squished against the hard wall of his chest. Her hips were meshed familiarly against the muscled columns of his thighs. This close contact reminded her of gentler moments they had shared. It triggered forbidden memories that had no right to bombard her at such a moment as this.

Although Darcey was valiantly trying to forget what they'd shared, Kane wasn't even trying at all. The feel of her delectable body molded suggestively to his was like dry kindling tossed on a smoldering fire. This wasn't the time and the hard floor wasn't the place, but burning desire demanded immediate satisfaction. Kane had held himself in check all through the night while he slept beside Darcey—wanting her, dozing, and then waking to want her all over again. Watching her disrobe twice was pure torment for him. And now that she had fallen into his arms, he couldn't let her go. He had denied himself as long as he could stand . . .

Chapter 12

"No!"

Panic chipped at Darcey's voice when she deciphered the spark of passion in Kane's silver-blue eyes. She knew he meant to kiss her and she refused to fall victim to the warm, tempting threat of his powerful body meshed to hers. She could feel his bold manhood against her thighs and she squirmed for release. But all that worming and squirming only made matters worse. Her betraying body began to respond and she cursed herself and Kane.

When his hands framed her face, tilting her lips to his kiss, Darcey died a dozen times. He courted her with unrivaled expertise, luring her deeper into his seductive spell. His sensual mouth was like liquid heat. His masculine body molded itself to hers, fanning flames of desire. She could feel her resistance melting beneath the fires that burned in the core of her being. She was starkly aware of the traitorous sensations that channeled through every muscle and nerve ending.

"No . . ." she rasped in protest when his mouth moved deliberately toward hers a second time.

Although her brain was shouting no, her betraying body answered yes the instant his lips whispered over hers in the slightest breath of a kiss. The feel of his gentle caresses coasting over her skin was her downfall. He knew where and how to touch to demolish the most determined woman's defenses. He wove a spell that thoroughly devastated and fervently aroused Darcey.

In that heart-stopping moment when their breath merged as one and his skillful hands flooded over her trembling flesh, Darcey knew she had lost the battle of mind over body. Kane was making her a slave to her own wanton needs. She could protest until she was blue in the face. She could curse him up one side and down the other, but it didn't change the way she felt—way down deep inside where it truly mattered—about this infuriating man.

Darcey decided right then and there that she was the worst judge of character this side of heaven. How could she respond so ardently to a man who had seduced her for his own lusty pleasure and abducted her for ransom? She meant nothing to Kane. She was only the place he went when he wanted to seek physical release. He had betrayed her time and time again . . .

And he had the most incredibly tender touch imaginable, a quiet voice whispered inside her. He could transform wrong into right. He could dissolve anger into passion with one soul-shattering kiss and bone-melting caress. He made her want what she knew she shouldn't want. He made her see things in him that weren't really there—things like concern and respect and mutual affection. He could make her feel wanted and so very special, as if she were the only woman in the world.

"Darcey . . ." Her name tumbled from his lips in a tormented moan. "I need you. Make this maddening ache go away. Feed this fire you ignite inside me."

They were only empty words, meant to shatter the last of her resistance. Darcey knew that as well as she knew her own name. But nothing could halt the fervent sensations that clamored through her quaking body when his caresses rediscovered each ultrasensitive point on her flesh and brought it to life.

A tiny whimper trickled from her lips when he moved her gown out of his way to greet every inch of her skin with titillating kisses and caresses. The warm draft of his breath fluttered over her throat, her shoulder, her collarbone. His tongue flicked at the taut peaks of her breasts. His questing hands migrated down her ribs to trace the indentation of her waist. Darcey felt herself melt into a puddle of bubbly desire. When he eased her down beside him to draw the gown completely away, Darcey felt the wave of warm caresses rolling over her like a tide flooding toward the seashore. Her traitorous body arched to meet his moist lips and exploring hands. She felt and heard his whispered words on her skin as he assured her of the pleasure she gave him, of the pleasure he yearned to return.

"I crave your touch," he murmured as he drew her hand beneath his shirt to make stimulating contact with his chest. "Love me, Darcey."

A hot sweet ache burned through her blood when he

took her hands on a sensual tour of his sinewy body. He guided her untutored fingertips over his flesh until she knew him far better than she knew herself. He taught her all the places he liked to be touched. He taught her how to arouse him, how to inflame his passions. Suddenly it seemed as if *she* were the one who had instigated their lovemaking, and Darcey found herself exploring his masculine body with a newfound sense of wonder.

Darcey marveled at the power she suddenly held over this muscular giant. Only now, only when she was in his arms, could she match this magnificent man. He had taught her the art of seduction, and seduce him she did, although that had not been her initial intention. Indeed, it had been anything but. Yet, when she touched him so familiarly, she wanted him to obsession.

Her hands swam over the hard planes and muscular contours of his body. She heard him groan in sweet torment and yet it wasn't enough to satisfy her. She wanted to taste him and touch him, to excite him until he was as vulnerable to her as she was to him.

When her hands investigated the rugged terrain of his flesh in languid strokes, Kane swore he would burn himself into a pile of frustrated ashes. He had practically begged for Darcey's touch. He had given her free license to caress him as intimately as he longed to caress her. But ah, at such cost to his composure! Each time her petal-soft lips drifted down his belly, Kane swore his thundering heart would leap clean out of his chest. Each time her hand trailed over his thighs, ardent need fed upon itself and multiplied by leaps and bounds. This tender torment would surely be the death of him. He'd never live long enough to appease the monstrous needs that raged out of control.

With each passing moment Darcey gained confidence in her ability to pleasure a man. In the past she'd been an expert in repelling advances and now she was inciting them! Her curious gaze swept down the full length of Kane's masculine body. He was like a sleek panther in repose—muscular, powerful, incredibly easy on the eye.

Darcey was amazed at her reckless abandon. Sweet mercy, it was as if she suddenly couldn't get enough of him! She thrilled to watching his muscles ripple beneath her inquisitive caresses, relished the feel of his lean, hair-roughened flesh beneath her prowling fingertips. Her hands refused to lie still for even a moment. They were restless in their eagerness to tantalize and explore. Darcey was confused by her own desire for a man she couldn't trust and was unable to resist. It frightened her to realize how vulnerable she was to this enigmatic man who could be infuriatingly cruel and yet remarkably tender.

Kane couldn't endure another moment of this maddening torment. Darcey had kissed and caressed him with magical inventiveness and he was bursting with the need to return the breathless pleasure she'd evoked from him. Passion such as this demanded to be prolonged and shared until it intensified and overwhelmed both of them.

During that moment, while Kane effortlessly pressed her down onto the discarded garments that formed their pallet, Darcey resented not being able to touch him. But in the next instant, when his skillful hands and warm lips feathered over her flesh, she couldn't voice a protest to save her soul.

Over and over again he kissed and caressed her, causing bullet-like sensations to rivet her. Darcey gasped in pleasure when profound need unfurled inside her. Like an ever-flowing river, his hands flooded over the roseate buds of her breasts and meandered down her body to the sensitive flesh of her thighs. And then, while his lithe body half covered hers, he bent his head to suckle at the taut peaks. Fire burned through every fiber of her being, and Darcey swore she'd never survive the divine torment. And when his moist kisses followed the evocative path of his hands, she forgot how to breathe and why she even needed to. It was as if her quaking body could survive on the exquisite pleasure he had aroused in her, as if she needed no more than his gentle touch and the soft whisper of his lips to exist.

And just when Darcey feared she would tumble over the edge into total abandon, his muscled body glided over hers. What Darcey had feared the instant she accidentally fell into his arms was now what she desired most. When his hips moved toward hers with intimate intentions, her body begged for his possession. She welcomed the ecstasy she knew awaited her when they were one beating, breathing essence, soaring past glittering stars to orbit around that wondrous dimension of time that defied description.

Suddenly they were clinging to each other in urgent desperation. The wild, gnawing needs that had sprung out of nowhere had consumed them. Their bodies moved in ageless rhythm, aching to appease the yearnings that burned like a thousand blazing suns.

Darcey met each hard, driving thrust, gloried in the sublime pleasure that enraptured the body, mind, and soul. She could feel her nails digging into Kane's taut back as the crescendo of passion built until it engulfed them.

And then it came, that mindless moment when every incredible sensation that had assaulted her converged like one sizzling ball of fire that blazed through the very core of her being. Darcey swore she had scattered in all directions at once when the tremendous force of passion hit her. Every ounce of energy she possessed drained from her pulsating body when Kane shuddered above her and clutched her to him as if the world had exploded. Darcey was positively certain it had. She was drifting somewhere in space, bedazzled by the quintessence of splendor, uncaring if she ever navigated her way back to reality.

Waves of contentment ribboned through her as she tumbled through the sensual darkness. And even in the aftermath of passion, Darcey couldn't draw a single breath without inhaling the man who cradled her so protectively in his arms. She couldn't have moved if she wanted to. Her brain and body refused to cooperate. She was so numb with the rapture of Kane's lovemaking that she wanted to linger forever in paradise.

Kane was suffering the same lethargy and lack of strength as Darcey. His mind was a blur and he felt sluggish. It amazed him that he had found himself amidst a battle one minute and in the heat of passion the next. He and Darcey, despite all their conflicts and differences, could ignite explosive sparks in each other. Never in his life had he experienced such devastation in a woman's arms. Darcey could demolish his self-control. He simply had no willpower when it came to this auburn-haired beauty. To see her was to want her in the worst possible way. To touch her was instant addiction. They had gone from fighting to loving in less than a minute and the rapid transition boggled the mind!

He knew they would be back to battling the second Darcey's senses cleared and guilt got the best of her. Kane dreaded that inevitable moment. How he longed to tell her the truth about himself, to make her understand that he wasn't the monster she believed him to be. But he knew that even the truth wouldn't be enough to dissolve the conflict between them. The solution to one problem would only create another. Darcey would resent him every bit as much as she did now, but for another set of reasons. Honest to God, there was no way out, Kane mused dispiritedly. He was damned if he told Darcey the truth and damned if he didn't. And, while he was at it, damn Patrick O'Roarke! He was the one who was going to come out of this whole distasteful affair looking like a saint while Kane emerged as the sinner.

When Darcey stirred beneath him, Kane dropped one last kiss to her heart-shaped lips. He knew for certain now that he had fallen in love with her. She cured the restlessness that plagued him all his life. She mattered in ways no other woman ever had. Even Melanie Brooks Beezely seemed a dim memory, a mere shadow in comparison to this flame-haired temptress who hated him as passionately as she had loved him.

"I love you, Darcey." Kane whispered without thinking.

There were some women who had waited all their lives to hear Kane Callahan murmur that confession. Unfortunately, Darcey O'Roarke was much too mistrusting of men to believe him for even a moment. To her, the words were a poisonous lie meant to manipulate her into dropping her resistance to his scheme to extract money from her wealthy father.

With an infuriated gasp, Darcey tried to bolt to her feet and make her escape. But she hadn't even levered onto one elbow before Kane flattened her against their makeshift pallet and shackled her wrists.

"Let me go!" Darcey screeched. "You wouldn't know love if it walked up and bit you! I don't want to hear any more of your lies!"

Kane cursed himself for allowing his innermost thoughts to escape. Darcey didn't want his love. He'd known she wouldn't believe the truth of his affection, considering the hell he'd put her through. She'd been a cynic before and she was even more skeptical of his intentions now. Damn, wouldn't you know that the one time in his life he admitted to being in love, his confession was not well received. Darcey was trying so hard to hate him that she refused to accept him. And as fiercely stubborn and determined as she was, there would come an ice age in hell long before she allowed herself to believe him.

"Fine," Kane growled into her flushed face. "So I don't love you. I wanted you because you were convenient. Any woman would have satisfied me, even a hellion like you . . ."

Kane, as quick as he was, wasn't fast enough to deflect the stinging slap that collided with his clenched jaw. Darcey had punched him a good one. Not that he didn't deserve it, but she made him every bit as frustrated as he made her! Hell, he'd only said what she been thinking. He'd *seen* her thinking it!

Muttering at the hopelessness of their situation, Kane reached over to pluck up Darcey's nightgown and thrust it at her. "Put this on. We still have a long ride ahead of us."

In angry jerks Darcey yanked her gown from his hand and glared flaming daggers at him. Kane couldn't have hurt her worse if he had slapped her as hard as she'd slapped him. His hateful words had confirmed her darkest suspicions and they cut through her like a rapier. But despite her valiant attempt to blink back the tears that clouded her eyes, they streamed over her cheeks.

Still keeping a firm hold on Darcey, Kane thrust his legs into his breeches and rolled to his feet. "I'm sorry," he muttered. "I didn't mean what I said. But damn it, sometimes you make me so mad I can't think straight!"

"Heaven forbid that I should boggle your criminal mind," Darcey said sarcastically. "At least you showed a smidgen of conscience. Until now I'd have sworn you didn't have one."

A reluctant smile pursed Kane's lips as he retrieved his shirt. He truly did admire Darcey's resilience. She could buckle to tears one minute and fling biting rejoinders the next. It was all part of her lure and the challenge of winning her affection. Taming a shrew like

Darcey O'Roarke would be a time-consuming task. She was bursting with spirit and, at the moment, bad temper.

Despite Darcey's mumbled protests, Kane bound her wrists and hobbled her to the bed while he gathered their gear and saddled the horses. It would take them more than a day to reach the cabin where he had left Noah and Giddeon to keep surveillance on the stage route. But Kane actually welcomed the company. He needed a distraction to help him forget the exasperation with this saucy nymph.

When Kane eased the door shut behind him, Darcey slumped defeatedly against the wall and cursed herself for surrendering to her foolish desire for Kane. He had seduced her into seducing him. That in itself was unforgivable. But then he'd had the unmitigated gall to profess his love. Curse it, how stupid did he think she was anyway? Well, she wasn't *that* stupid!

Darcey knew she was only the time he was killing. And she also imagined that a suave rake like Kane Callahan was in the habit of confessing love to every woman he bedded. He probably viewed his false admission as fair compensation for taking what he wanted from a female. Well, she didn't believe that softly uttered rubbish, not for one cussed minute!

Angrily, Darcey wiped away the infuriating tears that kept welling up in back of her eyes. She was so frustrated that she wanted to run home to her father, to accept all the compassion he could offer. Patrick had been right. She had bit off a damned sight more than she could chew when she rode off to Denver on her crusade. There was no telling what condition the express office was in these days. If Owen Graves was left in charge, business would suffer, just as it had before.

A heavy-hearted sigh escaped Darcey's lips as she stared at the door through which Kane had exited. Curse it, why did that man have to upset her so? Why was she so vulnerable to him? Hadn't she learned her lesson with Michael Dupris? Not well enough, Darcey decided. Kane was using her for his own selfish purposes and still she surrendered to him. How could he please her so thoroughly when she was in his arms and then incite her fury time and time again?

"Because you have rocks in your head," Darcey muttered aloud.

Her bitter thoughts evaporated when Kane swaggered back inside the cabin. Defiantly, Darcey refused to acknowledge his presence as he strode toward her.

After untying the rope that manacled her wrist to the bedpost, Kane set her on her feet. Still she refused to meet his gaze. Kane reached down to cup her chin and lifted her face to his.

"If you'll promise not to attempt escape, I won't tie you in the saddle," he bartered with her.

Darcey dodged his probing gaze. The way she had it figured, one lie deserved another. She could voice a pledge of submission without tormenting her conscience or feeling obliged to keep the vow. Kane had confessed to love her and she, in turn, would promise not to flee when she had the chance. Neither of them were bound to vows they really didn't expect each other to keep.

"Very well, I will behave myself," she announced.

Kane didn't believe her, of course. In fact, he didn't even know why he'd made the offer. And to ensure that she couldn't tear off through the mountains, he had taken the precaution of lowering the stirrups on Darcey's mount so that staying in the saddle would occupy all her energy. She would have to cling to the pommel of the saddle and clamp her legs to the horse's flanks to prevent toppling off as they picked their way across rugged terrain. With the stirrups out of reach, Darcey would have difficulty doing anything except maintaining her balance.

When Kane shepherded Darcey outside and attempted to assist her into the saddle she knocked his hand away with a hatchetlike blow of her bound wrists. "I can do this myself," she declared with her customary defiance.

But the task proved more difficult than she imagined. By the time she piled onto the horse, her hampering gown had ridden halfway up her thighs, exposing an indecent amount of bare leg. Kane had definitely noticed. He was grinning roguishly at her while he swung onto his own mount.

"Nice scenery," he chuckled, despite Darcey's reproachful glower. "I'm not going to begrudge this ride half as much as I first thought."

But Darcey begrudged it every step of the way. Kane spent as much time ogling her bare legs as he spent studying the perilous route over which they traveled. And to Darcey's outrage, she couldn't reach the stirrups to stand up and reach out to slap the leer off Kane's face. Clinging to her steed as it scrambled up steep slopes required tremendous effort. Darcey had to exert so much energy just to remain clamped to her animal that she couldn't slap Kane or race off in the opposite direction without the risk of catapulting off the saddle and over the jagged cliffs! Damn his ornery hide! He had misadjusted the length of her stirrups on purpose!

Chapter 13

After what seemed forever, they reached a rocky summit that overlooked the main stage route, which cut through the mountain valleys. The looming peaks towered over Darcey, encircling her like a war party of stony-faced giants. In the past, Darcey had been mesmerized by the sight of the craggy precipices, their granite shoulders cloaked with soft shades of pastels. But today the Rockies had a foreboding look about them. A parade of gloomy gray clouds marched across the heavens, swallowing the sun and plunging the world into shadows.

The dismal, overcast sky matched Darcey's mood. A distant rumble echoed around the stone walls of the mountains and Darcey glanced skyward. But the rumble wasn't caused by thunder, as she first thought. The clatter grew louder and expanded until it reverberated through the chasm. Darcey's sinking spirits soared with anticipation when she spied the stagecoach in the distance. If she could draw attention to herself, someone might notice her on the bluff and stop to lend assistance.

Darcey glanced discreetly at Kane and then stared speculatively at the road below. As the stage started up the steep incline which slowed the team of six horses to a walk, Darcey inhaled a deep breath, prepared to scream for all she was worth. To her dismay, the blast of a shotgun echoed through the chasm and the team of horses reared in fright. From her aerial vantage point she watched a lone highwayman emerge from the clump of brush to block the coach's path.

Suddenly Darcey forgot all about her own plight. The urge to prevent another robbery against O'Roarke Express became her primary objective. In a single bound she leaped off her horse and dashed to the edge of the precipice. With her hands still tied in front of her, she scooped up a rock and hurled it down at the bandit. The bouncing stone set off a trickle of pebbles and dirt which pelted the startled thief. Amid a barrage of gunfire between the guard and bandit, Darcey tried to supervise the battle, but she became so engrossed in shouting suggestions that she lost her footing and flapped her arms in attempt to regain her balance.

Frantically, Kane leaped from his horse to flatten Darcey to the ground before she teetered and tumbled off the edge. She hung there, half on, half off the perilous ridge, still spouting unheard instructions to the driver and guard. Despite her efforts, the highwayman dived for cover and appeared a few seconds later on a sure-footed mule that carried him away from danger.

"What in the name of heaven possessed you to take

such a risk?" Kane growled as he plucked Darcey up and deposited her, none too gently, in the saddle. "Honest to God, every time I think you've reached the pinnacle of idiocy you surpass yourself. You're crazy. There's no doubt about it! Are you trying to get yourself killed?"

"What do you care?" Darcey shot back. In frustration, she watched the key to her salvation rumble away at a fast clip. "If I get myself killed for any purpose, you'll probably still collect your blessed ransom. Who's to know the difference?"

"Forget about the damned money," Kane muttered as he glared into her enchanting but oh so belligerent face.

"If you feel that way, then let me go," she challenged him.

Kane threw up his hands in exasperation. He'd almost suffered heart seizure when Darcey had bounded off her steed with devil-may-care panache. He would have liked to track down that highwayman with his black silk mask, and black derby, and black linen duster, but he wasn't about to go thundering off, leaving Darcey to her own devices.

"You don't fool me for a second," Darcey fumed as she squirmed to cover herself as best she could in the saddle. "That scoundrel was a friend of yours, wasn't he? You couldn't care less if I got myself killed. You only wanted to prevent me from botching up the robbery attempt. You probably brought me this direction on purpose so you could ensure that your cohort met with success."

Kane rolled his eyes as he wheeled around to

continue on his way. This woman could link three unrelated events together and spin her sticky theories like a damned spider. And the terrifying thing about it was that she could make her hypothesis sound logical! Lord, she almost had him believing it himself.

"I suppose I'm going to have the displeasure of meeting that masked, mule-riding desperado later when the two of you rendezvous at your hideout," Darcey speculated as Kane blazed his way up another treacherous path.

"For your information, I don't have the foggiest notion who the Courtly Highwayman is. I wish I did," Kane grumbled.

"Naturally," Darcey smirked. "If you did, then you could dispose of him for trespassing on your territory. Competition among thieves must be bad for business."

"I wish you'd clam up. You're giving me a headache," Kane scowled.

"*You're* the headache," Darcey assured him spitefully. "You're the headache I've been having for almost two weeks."

"You weren't complaining about a headache a few hours ago," Kane shot back, knowing the remark would get her goat.

"I don't wish to discuss that," Darcey snapped.

"It seems to me that you like me more than you're willing to admit," Kane harassed her as his assessing gaze raked over the flimsy muslin gown that exposed far more than it concealed. "*You* seem to be the only one around here who doesn't know it."

"I do not!" she vehemently protested.

"I just said that," Kane teased unmercifully.

222

"That's not what I meant," she spluttered. "I meant that I know for a fact that I despise you with every beat of my heart."

"Really?" Kane broke into a mischievous grin. "Your kisses gave me a drastically different impression this morning."

"You are impossible!" Darcey wailed in frustration.

"And you should know all about impossible, being an expert on it yourself."

These days Darcey never seemed to be able to wedge in the last word. Kane drove her to the brink of fury and left her muttering inarticulate phrases. By the time she conjured up something suitably nasty to say, the moment had come and gone.

Silently brooding over his ridicule and her inability to return the insult, Darcey clung to the saddle. It was small consolation that she had mentally selected his most vulnerable spot and repeatedly stabbed him with an invisible knife. If Kane couldn't feel her daggerlike glares, then he was as insensitive as the boulders around which they rode.

Someday, somehow, she was going to repay this black-hearted scoundrel for all the frustration he'd heaped on her. If and when he let his guard down, she was going to blast him to smithereens with two loaded barrels!

The sound of booming thunder echoed through the clouds, demanding Darcey's attention. She glanced up at the mass of gray clouds that choked the Rockies and then she grinned spitefully. Better yet, she thought to herself, instead of blowing Kane to kingdom come, it would be more fitting if the Lord hurled down a lightning bolt to dispose of one of His more obvious sinners.

Darcey waited, hoping divine justice would be served. But the answer to her spiteful prayer must have been *no* because only a smattering of raindrops dribbled from the clouds.

At midday, Kane drew the procession to a halt and swung to the ground. Despite Darcey's protests, Kane plucked her off her horse and set her to her feet. When he handed her some pemmican and beef jerky to ward off the hunger pangs, she stared at the meager meal as if he'd offered her a three-day-old dead fish.

"Forgive me," Kane said in mock apology, then glanced at the food, "Knowing what a stickler you are for alphabetical order, you probably want to munch on the *j*erky before the *p*emmican." Quickly, he switched the order of their unappetizing meal.

"Must you poke fun at everything about me?" Darcey grumbled resentfully. And just to prove she could adapt, she chewed on the pemmican first. "There, you see? Pemmican before jerky."

"But never love before hate," Kane countered wryly.

"In your case, some things will never reverse their order," Darcey assured him. "You will always be my declared enemy."

Wasn't that the truth? Kane thought with a sigh. Resolved to the fact that he was in no position to change Darcey's stubborn mind, Kane swallowed down his meal. He was in the process of packing their supplies away when the skittering of rocks drew his attention. From between the craggy crevices that could hide man and beast, three wooly-faced scavengers emerged, clutching shotguns. Before Kane could retrieve his pistol, three rifles bore down on his chest.

"I wouldn't do that if I was you, mister," the first of the three Bishop brothers, Harley, advised. "Keep yer hand off that pistol. I don't claim to be no crackshot, but I kin hit what I aim at. If you don't cause us no trouble, me and my brothers will let you live." Harley's ravenous gaze swung to the shapely goddess in her revealing nightgown and he smiled like a starved shark. "All we want is yer whore. Me and my brothers ain't had a white wummun since we came trappin' for furs last winter."

Whore? Darcey glowered at the doughy-faced scoundrel who ogled her as if he were visualizing what she would look like in the altogether. Darcey had never been so insulted in all her life! She probably did resemble a soiled dove, since Kane had her traipsing around the Rockies in her nightgown, looking as if she were ready to appease a man's lust. And true, her hair lay around her shoulders in a mass of tangles, since she had no comb or brush to sweep the curly strands into a fashionable coiffure. But whore? *Kane's* whore? How dare these scalawags even think such things!

"I wouldn't touch the likes of you for all the gold in the Denver mint!" Darcey spewed.

Homer Bishop grinned, exposing the wide gap between his two front teeth. "I like my wimmun with lots of spunk." He visually devoured her, just as his older brother had done. "This piece of fluff is gonna be just what I need. I get a turn at her first, Harley."

225

"Oh no you don't, Homer," Henry Bishop piped up as he stared at Darcey with a bucktoothed leer. "*I* want her first."

When Henry peeled off his buckhide shirt and moved deliberately toward Darcey, she took off like a shot. Kane released the trailing end of the rope which was bound to her wrists. His keen gaze bounced back and forth between the three burly brothers and the fleeing hellion. The older men held Kane at gunpoint while their younger brother gave chase. When Darcey let out a yelp and wheeled to club Henry with her doubled fists, Homer and Harley became distracted and Kane kicked his steed, sending the startled animal plunging toward the mountain men. Kane was right behind the thundering horse, using it as his shield of defense. Before the Bishop brothers could gather their wits, Kane kicked the rifle from Homer's hand and buried his fist in Harley's stubbled jaw. Harley went down like a felled redwood tree, but Homer lunged for his rifle and rolled over in the grass to take quick aim. Another swift kick of Kane's boot sent the shotgun flipping end over end before it came to rest between two boulders.

With a furious growl, Homer launched himself at Kane to hammer his challenger with fists like hams. Emitting groans and grunts, Kane and Homer tumbled over the rocky terrain. Kane swore Homer's face was carved from wood; the powerful blows barely fazed him. When Kane rolled sideways to dodge an oncoming fist, he managed to grab his pistol. Flipping it in his hand, he employed the pearl handle of the Colt as a club to pound some manners into Homer. Still, it

226

took three hard whacks to the skull to put his lights out. With a heave-ho, Kane shoved the unconscious body off his lap and dashed to his horse to retrieve ropes. He bound the two unconscious men together and surged off in the direction Darcey and Henry had taken. The drizzling rain made the stone slabs slick as ice and Kane almost lost his footing twice while he made his mad dash to rescue Darcey. He had heard her terrified shriek a few moments earlier, but Kane had been too busy battling Homer to leap to her defense. Another cry for help, one with Kane's name attached to it, echoed through the canyon and put wings on Kane's feet. He leaped over boulders in his haste to locate Darcey.

A menacing snarl curled Kane's lips when he spied Henry sprawled atop Darcey. It sickened him to see the scoundrel clawing at her. Kane had made certain Darcey knew true lovemaking, but she was totally unprepared for animal lust and she was dangerously close to discovering the difference.

When he grabbed Henry, Kane thought he'd ripped the man's head off his shoulders. Blind fury had given Kane phenomenal strength. He lifted the surly brute as if he were as light as a feather and flung him away. Henry cartwheeled down the slope before he realized he was there. With a squawk and a groan, Henry slammed into an immovable boulder and slumped in a tangled heap. Kane was upon him, jerking him up by his greasy hair. He shook the miscreant until his teeth rattled and then reared back to deliver a blow that sent stars spinning around Henry's throbbing head.

After dropping Henry like a hot potato, Kane jerked

227

the last strand of rope from his pocket and tied the varmint in a knot. Hurriedly, he scaled the slick slope to make sure that Darcey had only suffered minimal discomfort after Henry's attempt to rape her. Kane had only set one foot on level ground when Darcey flew into his arms like a homing pigeon returning to roost. Kane hadn't expected to be the recipient of a fierce hug, but Darcey proceeded to squeeze the stuffing out of him.

"That horrible man tried to—" Darcey choked on the repulsive thought of what had almost happened. "He was going to—" Her voice broke completely and she burrowed into Kane's arms like a frightened mole.

"Sh . . . sh . . . it's all right now," Kane murmured as he cuddled her close and bent to replace the disgusting taste of her attacker's bruising assault with a gentle kiss.

When Darcey finally collected her wits and realized she had run to Kane for protection, she gasped in dismay. She had sworn to run *away* from this rake, never *to* him. She could have escaped him while he was preoccupied and he would have been left afoot. Curse it, even her instincts were conspiring against her!

"You men," Darcey muttered as she pushed away from the hard wall of his chest. "You're all alike. A woman is no more than an object of lust to the whole lot of you!"

Darcey had flung herself away so abruptly that Kane was left to flap his arms like a windmill to prevent plummeting backward down the cliff. While Darcey stomped back toward the horses, adjusting her gown into decency, Kane followed after her.

228

A wry smile twitched his lips as he appraised the graceful sway of her hips beneath the revealing gown. It seemed he was making some headway with Darcey, gradual though it was. In times of danger, Darcey found herself rushing to him for comfort and protection. She resented her spontaneous reaction, to be sure, but she had come into his arms nonetheless. On the outside, she despised what she thought he was. But on the inside, a small flame of affection flickered, and she couldn't smother it, as much as she would have liked to.

Sighing at the irony of the entire situation, Kane ambled over to collect the horses. Darcey stood aside, glaring at the two men who had yet to rouse from the blows Kane had delivered. Silently she studied Kane while he tugged both men's boots off and hurled them into the canyon below.

"Aren't you going to shoot them for what they tried to do?" she wanted to know.

Darcey didn't really expect him to blow the scoundrels away, she wasn't that bloodthirsty, only boiling mad. With a grin, Kane slid his Colt from his holster and handed it to her.

"They weren't trying to molest *me,*" he reminded her. "If you want to repay them, then *you* shoot them. I'll settle for letting them hobble over the rocks barefoot when they finally work the ropes loose . . ."

Kane's words died into silence when he realized what a careless blunder he'd made, all in jest. Like an imbecile, he'd offered Darcey a lethal weapon and now it was pointed directly at his chest. Suddenly the situation wasn't one damned bit amusing. If he

229

conducted all his assignments as carelessly as he had this one, he'd have been dead years ago! He knew better than to take this wildcat for granted, but he kept forgetting that her delicate beauty was only a distracting cover for the feisty witch who lurked beneath it.

"Take off your boots," she demanded abruptly.

Keeping a cautious eye on his Colt and the spiteful hellion who held it, Kane lifted his leg to tug at his left boot. But instead of dropping it on the ground, as Darcey expected him to do, he flung it at her. The Colt flipped over her bound wrists and misfired, echoing around the chasm like a cannon. Before she could recover, Kane snatched up his pistol and grabbed the trailing rope that was tied to her wrists.

"I should have shot you while I had the chance," she fumed.

Kane deposited her in the saddle and dallied the rope on the pommel. "Better luck next time, darlin'," he drawled, just to infuriate her. And sure as hell it did. She burst into another round of unintelligible hisses and he managed to get in the last word again, much to Darcey's outrage.

Leaving the Bishop brothers to manage as best they could, Kane pointed himself toward the mountain cabin where Noah and Giddeon waited. They had been cooped up in the middle of nowhere for more than two weeks. Kane couldn't help but wonder if the isolation had cured his overenthusiastic brother from wanting to be a detective. There would have been nothing for Noah to do but take his field glasses in hand and survey the area. Kane predicted Noah would be craving big-city life, convinced by now that staking out stage routes for possible holdups held no fascination whatsoever.

Kane only hoped Noah didn't react the same way the lusty mountain men did when he got a close look at Darcey. Kane inwardly groaned at the thought. Noah liked women. The prettier the better, and Darcey was as gorgeous as they came. Kane was going to have to remind him that Darcey was off limits. None of the men could treat Darcey all that well during her captivity. That would spoil everything. Noah would give them away in a minute if he started fawning all over her.

Maybe dragging Darcey to this obscure cabin wasn't such a good idea after all, Kane mused. He had enough difficulty handling this firebrand and he was supposed to be damned good at difficult people. Noah and Giddeon had virtually no experience in such situations . . .

"Why are you looking so glum?" Darcey questioned when she noticed the pensive expression that clouded Kane's rugged features. "After all, I'm the captive here, not you."

"I'm not so sure about that," Kane mumbled so quietly that Darcey couldn't decipher his remark.

No, Kane wasn't so sure about that at all. The more time he spent with this saucy elf the tighter the hold she had on his heart. He would eventually send Darcey back to her father, but Kane had the inescapable feeling that the delicious memories they'd made together were going to come back to haunt him.

Until this moment, Kane could say he'd never run across an assignment that got the best of him. A rueful smile quirked his lips as he maneuvered through the rocky ravine and pattering rain. He had finally met his match in Darcey O'Roarke. Patrick's words echoed in his mind and reverberated through Kane's heart.

"You haven't met my daughter yet," Patrick had declared with great conviction.

Kane had scoffed then but he wasn't scoffing now. He felt bruised. He was left wanting something he knew he could never have. This charade he was forced to play had spoiled any chance of finding happiness with Darcey. She planned on hating him until the day she died. And as determined as this spitfire was, she probably would!

Chapter 14

By late afternoon, the trickle of rain had become a steady downpour. Occasional flashes of lightning illuminated the sky like silvery spider webs. Although Kane had intended to forge ahead until nightfall, he was forced to locate some sort of shelter that would provide protection against inclement weather.

After tugging Darcey from the saddle, he secured her to the scrub brush that was located beside the mouth of the cave he had spotted. Without having to fear that Darcey would try to escape, Kane ducked into the cave to investigate. The last thing he wanted to do was hole up in a cavern which was already occupied by some creature that would resent the intrusion.

Kane had only wandered ten feet into the shadowed corridor of rock before he heard an echo that amplified movement somewhere in the inky darkness ahead of him. And, as if he hadn't already realized he'd stumbled into trouble, a low, threatening growl testified to that fact.

Reflexively, Kane took a cautious step of retreat and retrieved his Colt. He actually felt the deadly presence approach long before he spied the hoary form of the animal that emerged from the darkness to lumber toward him.

"How long do you plan to leave me standing out here in the rain?" Darcey glared into the shadowed confines of the cavern. "I'm already soaked to the bone and—"

Darcey's complaint transformed into a terrified shriek when Kane plunged out of the jaws of darkness with a grizzly bear hot on his heels. She had never seen such a look of desperation stamped on Kane's face.

Desperate, however, did not accurately describe Kane's state of mind. He had tethered Darcey so she couldn't escape, but now he wished she could. When he wrested the rope from the branches, one or the other of them would be left to contend with the enraged bear.

With eyes as wide as saucers, Darcey watched Kane dash from the cave to claw at the rope that held her fast. She never took her eyes off the deadly fangs of the grizzly plowing toward them in hasty pursuit.

"Hurry up!" Darcey wailed.

The mighty roar of the bear sounded like a death knell to Darcey. This was the end, she realized bleakly. She could see her life passing before her eyes as the snarling creature reared up on its hind legs, preparing to take a swat at the intruders with its sharp claws. Darcey swore the huge muscled monster stood eight feet tall if it stood an inch. It was the most terrifying creature she'd ever seen!

"Kane!" Darcey didn't know why that scoundrel's name burst from her lips, just as it had earlier in the day. Why should she bleat out *his* name with her last breath when she should have been praying for mercy?

Darcey had heard all the horrific stories about men being attacked by grizzlies. She shuddered, remembering how one man had practically been scalped when those daggerlike talons slashed across his head. Other unnerving tales spoke of humans being mauled beyond recognition, about arms and legs being instantaneously amputated as a result of ruthless attacks . . .

All thoughts froze in Darcey's mind when the growling monster took a vicious swipe at her. Darcey was too dazed and distressed to ascertain if she had been struck, but she found herself flat on the ground, staring up at Kane's bleak face. A split second later she realized Kane had freed the rope at the last possible moment and shoved her down, using his own body as a shield to protect her.

Kane twisted above her and his pistol barked just as the bear dropped onto all fours. The bullet drew blood, but not nearly enough to fell the enraged animal. It bounded toward them with a look in its beady black eyes that was as cold as a tombstone and fatal as the grave.

A shriek burst from Darcey's lips when she felt Kane roll away and jerk on her arm as if he meant to yank it clean out of its socket. The survival instinct was hard at work as they scrabbled up the rocky slope, heading for higher ground. Frantically, they clawed their way up the jagged, crumbling rock and then reached the place where every step became a death-defying leap. They were treading on unsure ground and the snarling beast seemed to have no intention whatsoever of aborting its pursuit. Each time she and Kane managed to put a safe distance between themselves and the bear, the ferocious beast gobbled up the space between them.

"Help me with this!" Kane ordered as he pulled Darcey behind the boulder that was perched on the cliff.

With her mouth set in a grim line, Darcey shoved at the huge mound of rock. Between them they mustered enough strength to cause the rock to budge a few inches. But it wasn't nearly enough to send the boulder tumbling down the path the grizzly was taking toward them.

"Again!" Kane demanded frantically.

In perfect precision, Kane and Darcey braced themselves against the perpendicular wall of the mountain and strained with every ounce of strength they possessed. To their relief—and just in the nick of time—the boulder teetered and rolled toward the approaching beast.

An echoing roar gushed from the bear's mouth as the boulder bounced down the side of the mountain. The falling rock, debris, and rolling bear startled the horses. Despite the fact that Kane had tethered the mounts to nearby trees, they bolted backward, fraying the rope to clatter across the rocky terrain in search of safety.

From the perch overlooking the narrow valley, Darcey assessed the situation. She knew for a fact that it took more than a bullet and a boulder to kill a bear the size of the one that had chased them. The grizzly dragged itself to its feet, shook itself off, and seemed to roar in outrage. When the beast bounded up the steep incline lickety-split, Darcey stared at Kane in horror and he stared back at her. Then they both stared at the bear.

"What now?" Darcey chirped on a strangled breath.

"What's left?" Kane muttered as he peered down at the bear that showed no signs of abandoning chase until it had ripped them to shreds.

"I don't know about you, but I think running is the only chance we have left," Darcey replied, her voice shattered with distress. "And I think . . ." She instinctively clutched at Kane's hand when the wooly creature reared up to intimidate them all over again. "I . . . think we both better start running *now!*"

Hand in hand, Kane and Darcey scuttled across the slippery rocks on a route that was perpendicular to the one the bear was taking. Darcey glanced over her shoulder at regular intervals to monitor the grizzly's progress. But nothing they did discouraged the creature. It seemed the animal was as intent on devouring them as its evening meal as they were to avoid becoming the honored guests for supper.

Darcey swore it was divine intervention that finally saved them. Just as the bear lunged onto the ledge to romp after them, the sky opened up. Sheets of driving rain pelted the mountains. The grizzly hadn't seemed to mind a shower but it didn't appear to be in the mood for a drenching. After casting the humans one last glance, the bear reversed direction and lumbered back to its dry cave.

In exhausted relief, Kane and Darcey slumped back against the slabbed wall of rock to watch the bear disappear into its den.

"Are you all right?" Kane panted.

"Aside from the fact that I scraped both knees and elbows, I was scared senseless, and my heart tried to beat me to death before the bear did, I'm in splendid shape," she wheezed.

"Good, because we have a long walk ahead of us," Kane said gloomily. "Our horses are scattered from here to only God knows where."

"And you wouldn't want to let all that gold in the saddlebags get away from you," she tacked on bitterly.

"At the moment, I'd give that damned gold away if my horse would waltz up here and pick me up," Kane grumbled before he sidestepped down the treacherous path.

Darcey glanced upward, only to have several huge raindrops slap her in the face. It seemed as if they were standing inside the gray cloud that enshrouded the jagged mountain peak. Lord, it exhausted her just to think of all that had gone wrong since she'd awakened this morning. First she had foolishly surrendered to Kane's masterful kisses . . .

After giving herself a mental slap for reflecting on that particular moment, Darcey pushed herself upright and inched down the cliff. She wasn't going to rehash her reckless tête-à-tête—or any other incident that had occurred during the course of this day.

"I suppose you're laying all the blame for this on me," Kane muttered as he glanced back to see Darcey trailing along behind him in her soggy nightgown that clung to her voluptuous figure.

"Well, I certainly wasn't the one who walked uninvited into a grizzly's den . . ." Darcey caught herself the instant before her foot slipped out from under her and she bounced down the mountain to wind up in a broken heap. "You really should stick to thievery. You're much better at it than warding off bear attacks."

Kane rolled his eyes and asked himself why he had broached the subject in the first place. He had practically invited her ridicule. But the truth was, he did feel responsible for nearly getting them mauled. And damn it, he was slightly out of his element himself. This was his first—and he hoped his last—confrontation with an eight-foot-tall monster that had fangs the likes he'd never seen and never wanted to see again!

By the time Kane and Darcey corraled their mounts, darkness had cloaked the mountains. The foggy mist that hovered in the air was thick enough to slice with a knife. Darcey was so tired she barely had the strength to place one foot in front of the other without falling flat on her face. When she finally reached her steed, she breathed a thankful sigh. With a groan, she piled onto the horse and slumped over its neck to hang there like wet laundry.

The faintest hint of a smile quirked Kane's lips as he watched Darcey sprawl on her horse. He had put her through more strenuous trials and tribulations than he'd originally intended when he abducted her from Denver. But Darcey had met each challenge with her customary determination. Most women wouldn't have had the courage or the stamina to endure what Darcey had suffered through during the short course of a day. But Darcey's fierce pride and undaunted spirit refused to allow her to buckle in the face of disaster. Weary though she was, she had defied catastrophe. Kane admired her fortitude. Darcey O'Roarke occasionally gave out, but she never gave up.

Lost in thought, Kane led the small procession through the V-shaped chasm until he spotted an overhanging ledge of rock that offered partial protection from the inclement weather. The location wasn't as suitable as the cave, but at least there were no bears, wolves, or mountain lions in sight. Kane did not, however, rule out the possibility that such creatures might wander by during the night. Kane hoped the rain would discourage nocturnal prowlers from venturing out, granting Darcey and him a few hours of peace.

Once Kane had dragged the saddlebags from their mounts, he unfolded the pallets and gestured for Darcey to sprawl upon them. Darcey gladly dropped to the ground without protest. She would have slept on a bed of rock and it wouldn't have mattered, exhausted as she was. The quilts felt heavenly, except for the soggy gown that clung to her skin, sending shivers down her spine.

Darcey didn't even put up a fuss when Kane peeled off his wet clothes in preparation for crawling inside his bedroll. When he shucked his garments, Darcey swore she'd have to stitch her eyelids down to prevent staring at him in appreciation. Kane was one hundred percent male, a magnificent work of art chiseled from rock-hard muscle. Darcey studied his shadowed profile, marveling at his powerful physique. She was entranced by the fascinating way his muscles flexed and rippled with each graceful movement . . .

MORE PASSION AND ADVENTURE AWAIT... YOUR TRIP TO A BIG ADVENTUROUS WORLD BEGINS WHEN YOU ACCEPT YOUR FIRST 4 NOVELS ABSOLUTELY *FREE* (AN $18.00 VALUE)

Accept your Free gift and start to experience more of the passion and adventure you like in a historical romance novel. Each Zebra novel is filled with proud men, spirited women and tempestuous love that you'll remember long after you turn the last page.

Zebra Historical Romances are the finest novels of their kind. They are written by authors who really know how to weave tales of romance and adventure in the historical settings you love. You'll feel like you've actually gone back in time with the thrilling stories that each Zebra novel offers.

GET YOUR FREE GIFT WITH THE START OF YOUR HOME SUBSCRIPTION

Our readers tell us that these books sell out very fast in book stores and often they miss the newest titles. So Zebra has made arrangements for you to receive the four newest novels published each month.

You'll be guaranteed that you'll never miss a title, and home delivery is so convenient. And to show you just how easy it is to get Zebra Historical Romances, we'll send you your first 4 books absolutely FREE! Our gift to you just for trying our home subscription service.

BIG SAVINGS AND FREE HOME DELIVERY

Each month, you'll receive the four newest titles as soon as they are published. You'll probably receive them even before the bookstores do. What's more, you may preview these exciting novels free for 10 days. If you like them as much as we think you will, just pay the low preferred subscriber's price of just $3.75 each. *You'll save $3.00 each month off the publisher's price.* AND, your savings are even greater because there are never any shipping, handling or other hidden charges—FREE Home Delivery. Of course you can return any shipment within 10 days for full credit, no questions asked. There is no minimum number of books you must buy.

"You're hurt!" Darcey suddenly realized when Kane half turned to expose the claw marks that left bloody gashes on his shoulder blade.

"It's just a scratch," he insisted as he folded himself into the warmth of his bedroll.

Darcey refused to let him shrug off his wound, knowing full well he had been clawed when he pushed her to the ground to protect her. "Turn over," she demanded. "I want to check your wound."

"It's nothing," Kane grumbled.

"Nothing, my eye!" Darcey sniffed as she ripped off a clean portion of the hem of her saturated gown. She pushed him to his belly and dabbed the fabric on the bloody wound. When Kane grimaced in pain she frowned in concern. "Did you bring any medical supplies with you for emergencies?"

Kane gestured toward the saddlebag behind her. Hastily, Darcey rummaged through the gear until she found the antiseptic and bandages she had purchased at the physician's office in Denver. When she dug a little deeper, she found the healing balm Kane had stashed in the bottom of the saddlebag.

Darcey suddenly forgot how tired she was. Her foremost concern was making certain that the deep gashes on Kane's shoulder didn't become infected. And why that concerned her, only God knew. She had spitefully wished for him to be lightning struck earlier in the day. Now she was helping this man she had vowed to hate forevermore.

While she carefully dabbed the salve on his shoulder, she contemplated this paradox of a man. Thief and extortioner though he appeared to be, Kane had placed her safety above his own when they had faced the growling monster of a bear. Darcey knew for a fact that Griz Vanhook would have left her staked to the bushes as a meal for the bear while he darted off to save his own selfish hide.

What it all boiled down to, Darcey decided, was that she was helplessly attracted to the tender, compassionate man who lurked beneath that tough, ornery surface.

A smile tugged at her lips as she bandaged Kane's wound. It seemed he knew her even better than she thought he did. He had declared that she expected the world and everyone in it to function according to her specifications. And perhaps she did, now that she thought about it. She wanted this raven-haired demon, who could make her come to life in his arms, to be the one man she could love and cherish until the end of time. But that was never going to happen . . .

"What are you thinking?" Kane questioned as he watched the multitude of indecipherable emotions sweep back and forth across her shadowed face.

Darcey sank back to survey Kane's rugged features in the scant light. Reflexively, she reached out to trace the smile lines that bracketed his sensual mouth. An odd combination of sentiment bombarded her. After all they had been through during the course of the day, Darcey wanted nothing more than to snuggle up in Kane's arms and forget everything that had any resemblance to reality. She didn't want to analyze or alphabetize. She justed wanted to be loved.

"I'm thinking that I'm tired of thinking," Darcey said in belated response.

Kane's hand glided up and down the soggy sleeve of her gown in a stroking caress. His gaze fastened on her emerald eyes that always burned with a fire that only hinted at her bottled vitality and spirit.

"Do you wish to sleep then?" he murmured, his voice husky with the side effects of having her so close and yet so tormentingly far away.

"Tired as I thought I was, I'm too unnerved to sleep," she admitted.

Kane held his breath, afraid to read too much into the twinkle that flickered in her eyes. "Then what do you want to do?" he questioned softly.

Darcey wasn't sure if it was the low, caressing whisper in his voice that caused her to sway toward him or if the forbidden yearnings of her own traitorous body compelled her toward him. But she inched closer and sighed when his arm stole around her waist to draw her down onto the thick carpet of hair that covered his broad chest.

Although she knew she was tripping along the borderline of dangerous territory once again, Darcey voiced no complaint when his warm lips feathered over hers in the gentlest whisper of a kiss. His mouth became hot and hard and faintly forceful as it moved deliberately deeper into hers. Darcey felt herself melting like a snowbank in spring sunshine. In a tenth of a second, her will to resist fled the ever-growing flame that flickered inside her.

Kane reached down to untie the rope that bound her wrists, offering her unlimited freedom. She easily could have dashed off into the darkness to escape him, but the sensual lure of this man had formed its own

243

invisible chain that held her captive. Darcey's need to escape was nowhere near as fierce as her need to be with Kane. Desire held her motionless.

God forgive her, but she did want to feel his arms encircling her. Her emotions were boiling after all they had endured together. Having come within a hairbreadth of death made every moment seem precious. Darcey yearned to forget all except the masterful magic of Kane's touch. She wanted to surrender to his overpowering spell. Darcey longed to feel his tender caresses massaging away the tension that had plagued her throughout the day. She yearned to overlook the obstacles that loomed between them, to pretend there was more between them than this explosive attraction. And yet pride refused to let her buckle without putting up token resistance.

Kane could sense the wavering indecision in Darcey's kiss. He knew she was battling her own desires and her fierce sense of pride. Kane swore he would burn alive if Darcey pulled away from him and retreated inside her shell. He wanted to hold her and forget how close they had both come to an early grave a few hours earlier.

The moment the growling grizzly had reared up, Kane had suffered all the torments of the damned. He had been frantically trying to free the rope that tied Darcey down. It had scared the hell out of him to think what would have happened if he hadn't loosed the knotted rope when he did. In those tense seconds when he envisioned Darcey being permanently scarred or killed by the bear, he had very nearly suffered heart seizure. Now he longed to hold her in his arms and create a sweet dream to replace that horrifying nightmare. He wanted to love her the way she deserved to be loved—thoroughly and completely.

That tantalizing thought burned through his mind as he eased the damp gown away to warm every inch of her chilled flesh with hot, greedy kisses. His hand roamed everywhere at once—massaging, soothing, arousing her. Kane couldn't seem to get close enough to her to satisfy himself. Touching her so intimately instilled monstrous needs in him that left him burning. He was oblivious to the pain on his shoulder and it didn't inconvenience him in the least when he shifted sideways to bring Darcey's body down beside his. As if she were a delicious treat that he'd been denied for weeks on end, he savored the feel of her satiny skin, her utterly feminine scent.

All Darcey's reserve fled when Kane showered her body with bone-melting caresses and heart-stopping kisses. Profound need shook the very roots of her soul. Hundreds of pulsating tremors wracked her body. It was if she was suddenly living only for his touch, as if she could survive on it alone. She yearned to return each caress for caress, each kiss for steamy kiss. She felt the need to share the rapture that unfurled inside her and sizzled along every nerve ending. Her pride bowed down to instincts that were as ancient as time itself. Darcey wanted to be loved and protected, even if Kane could only offer one splendorous moment. In this space of time when the world faded into oblivion, there was no past or future, only the glorious present and the one man who could make her want him in the wildest ways.

In shameless abandon, Darcey succumbed to the

cravings that gnawed at her. She gave his hands free license to her body and surrendered to the desire to reacquaint herself with every steel-honed inch of his muscled flesh. She longed to taste him, to breathe him, to absorb his strength. It no longer mattered who or what he was to the rest of the world. To her, he was the one man who could push her past the point of no return and make her ever so glad she was there.

Darcey wanted him desperately, though she couldn't bring herself to voice that confession. It was enough that her kisses and caresses communicated her desire to be a part of him. Despite her better judgment, Darcey was unable to resist the temptation of this enigmatic man. He was the hopeless battle she constantly waged and never won. He always seemed to know what she needed better than she knew herself. He was sensitive to her moods and aware of the yearnings that hounded her from the instant they touched.

That was the last sane thought to spear through the foggy haze that clouded Darcey's mind. The feel of Kane's exploring hands migrating across the ultrasensitive points of her flesh banished all except the wondrous sensations that splintered through her body. She could feel herself arching upward to meet each titillating kiss and caress while her hands struck out on their own journey of discovery.

Darcey gasped in pleasure when his moist lips whispered over the dusky peaks of her breasts. Her heart stopped beating when his roaming hands glided over her abdomen to sensitize the silky flesh of her thighs. Another coil of fire burned in the core of her being when his fingertips delved and aroused her beyond bearing. Spasms of ecstasy riveted her and she cried out to him to appease the ache he had instilled in her.

"Do you want me, sweet witch?" Kane questioned, his voice rattling with unfulfilled passion.

"Yes," Darcey moaned.

"Then say the words," he murmured against her trembling lips. "I need to know you want me as much as I want you."

A whimper trickled from her throat when his intimate fondling evoked another wave of uncontrollable shudders.

"Say it," Kane commanded. "I need to hear the words from your lips."

Kane didn't know why he felt the urge to draw a confession from her, but it mattered a great deal to him. Perhaps he could never earn her love and devotion, but for now, for this one splendorous moment, he had to know that he was what she wanted to make her feel whole and alive. Although they couldn't enjoy forever together, he intended to create a living memory that would tide him over in the long, empty years to come.

Darcey's tangled lashes fluttered up to study the shadowed giant who hovered above her. Even in the darkness she could see those glittering silver-blue eyes boring down on her, making demands she was helpless to refuse. "I . . . I want you . . ." she admitted brokenly. "No one but you . . ." Her hands lifted to frame his rugged face, drawing his lips to hers. "No one but you . . . Kane."

When his mouth slanted over hers to steal the last

ounce of breath from her, his body settled upon exactly hers. His hands drifted over her hips, pulling them into intimate contact with his while he whispered promises of the delicious pleasures to come.

Darcey welcomed him without the slightest hesitation. Only when she became a part of his boundless energy did she feel complete. Only when he was the pulsating flame within her did she know the meaning of contentment. Only when they were one living, breathing essence, wafting their way across the boundless horizon, did she comprehend the meaning of eternity. When Kane held her tightly in his sinewy arms, she felt wildly free of all of life's limitations. She could see forever in his eyes.

One indescribable sensation after another swamped and buffeted her as Kane's body drove into hers, seeking ultimate depths of intimacy. An urgency that was far too intense to be measured bombarded her. Darcey clung to him. Her senses reeled and her pounding heart beat in frantic rhythm with his as they set sail on a wondrous journey through a universe of ineffable sensations.

Darcey marveled at the pleasure that engulfed her. The wild union of hearts, bodies, and souls defied description. Each time she surrendered to Kane, it always seemed like the very first time, only better. The sensations felt so new, so exciting. Even the tantalizing memories of their lovemaking was never as sweet and fulfilling as it was each time they lost themselves in each other's arms.

A cry of pleasure burst from Darcey's lips when the fiery sensations recoiled upon her all at once. She clung to Kane as if she never meant to let him go. It was impossible to measure time while she was soaring through this dark, sensual dimension, but she felt somewhere beyond the moon and stars, drifting in a world that only existed when she was in Kane's arms.

Shock waves rippled through her body and she felt herself floating through space. In the aftermath of passion, Darcey tried to draw a steadying breath, but she was paralyzed by sublime fulfillment.

With a heavy sigh, Kane nuzzled against the swanlike column of Darcey's throat and waited for the numbing pleasure to subside. He would have braved the attack of an entire den of bears if he could be assured he would wind up in Darcey's arms, reveling in glorious splendor. This night was worth every challenge he had confronted, each sacrifice he had to make.

Yet, as wondrous as their night together had been, Kane wasn't foolish enough to believe Darcey wouldn't withdraw into her shell come sunrise. But for now, she seemed content. Kane yearned to brand his memory on her mind, to make her confront the realization that they *did* share something rare, despite what she believed about him.

When Darcey cuddled up beside him like a purring kitten, Kane smiled to himself. This stubborn beauty wouldn't admit it, never in a million years, but she had come to rely and depend on him for comfort, companionship, and protection, as well as for passion. The fragile bond between them had strengthened, hour by hour. They had come to each other's defense a dozen times the past two weeks. Guarding each other had become a natural, instinctive reaction. Darcey had come to count on him, and he on her. They had become like two pieces of a puzzle that fit together. But Darcey, independent and stubborn as she was, would deny the truth because of her damnable pride.

More than anything, Kane had wanted to hear her admit that she had begun to love him just a little. He had coaxed her into confessing she wanted him. Yet that wasn't enough to satisfy him. He wanted her total love, the kind that defied all boundaries.

When Darcey drifted off to sleep, Kane reached over to retrieve the rope to handcuff her wrist to his. Although she had refused to flee when he had given her the chance, he didn't trust her not to slip away if she awakened during the night. He knew it would infuriate her to find herself chained to him, that she would think the worst of him for doing it. But he couldn't risk having her sneak away from him, not in this unfamiliar neck of the woods. There were too many dangers lurking in the mountains. Kane preferred to face her outrage rather than endure the agony of losing her forever. He was dismally aware that, very soon, she would be whisked from his life. But he couldn't bear the thought of living in a world without Darcey in it . . . somewhere . . .

Unnerved by that depressing thought, Kane cuddled her body protectively against his. He was going to relish every moment of their night together because he was never sure if there would be another night of splendor with this feisty elf.

Kane wondered if Darcey really knew what she wanted or felt. He'd forced her to endure so much that he had thoroughly confused her. And once her alphabetical sense of order was all askew, she seemed in a state of chaos.

And the saddest part of all was that, considering what he had led Darcey to believe about him, Kane couldn't honestly blame her for refusing his affection and for mistrusting him. Thanks to Patrick O'Roarke, Kane found himself and Darcey in the most impossible situation imaginable. Now, the truth would drive as many wedges between them as the lie.

Chapter 15

Just as Kane predicted, Darcey erupted in irritated hisses when she awakened to find herself bound to him. She cursed herself and him. It infuriated her that she had disregarded the opportunity to flee the previous night, just to lie in his arms. But he hadn't trusted her to remain with him until dawn. When the lovemaking was over, it was business as usual for Kane Callahan. And to add insult to injury, Kane rummaged through his saddlebags to retrieve one of the two calico dresses he hadn't bothered to tell Darcey that he had purchased for her to wear during the last leg of their journey.

Seething, Darcey glared at the garment and the man who extended it to her. "There were more decent clothes for me than my nightgown and you purposely made me clomp through these mountains in it!" she spat disdainfully. "That was unforgivable!"

Kane ignored her scathing remark and fuming glare and draped the dress over her arm. "I doubt this gown is the same high quality you're accustomed to wearing.

But as you said, it's far more practical than your nightgown. Considering the effect you had on those mountain men yesterday, I decided to garb you in something more concealing. I would hate to have to shoot my own friends for trying to take advantage of you."

"Your friends?" Darcey stared dubiously at him. "I wasn't aware you had any."

A faint smile quirked Kane's lips. After Darcey's nerve-shattering experience with the Bishop brothers, she probably expected his so-called "friends" to be cut from the same scrap of wood. All the better that she disliked Noah and Giddeon, sight unseen. Kane made a mental note to brief his companions to ensure that they played convincing roles in this distasteful charade.

"Last night meant nothing to you, did it?" Darcey blurted out, and then cursed herself for blundering onto the subject that hounded her.

Kane peered down into her elegant face and clamped an iron grip on his emotions. "Should it have?" he questioned her question. "Did it mean something special to you?" Despite his attempt to hold himself in check, his hand lifted to limn the exquisite lines of her face. "Could it be that, beneath all your contempt, you might have actually fallen in love with me and you would like to see the affection returned?"

Stubborn pride came to her rescue in the nick of time. "And you mock *me* for leaping to ludicrous conclusions!" Darcey sniffed caustically. "That is the most preposterous theory I ever heard!"

"Then I suppose you gave yourself to me, hoping I'd be so enthralled by passion that I would forget to tie you up, which would give you the opportunity to escape." Kane returned her looks glare for glare. "Has desperation finally taken you to the point that you actually consented to a night in my arms in hopes of eluding me when I let my guard down?"

The thought soured his mood. He wanted Darcey on *his* terms, but he knew he'd never get his way.

"That is exactly what I was thinking when I allowed you to seduce me," Darcey replied to save face. She'd cut out her tongue before she admitted that she had been a captive of her own foolish desires. "But I was too exhausted to remain awake until you fell asleep. And I cannot tell you how much I regret my weariness . . . and everything else."

"That's just what I thought," Kane scowled. "Now get dressed. We have places to go."

"The only place I wish *you* were going was to hell," she snapped in a spiteful tone.

"Where do you think I've been for the past few days?" Kane muttered. "And it might not have been so bad, except for the company I've been keeping."

"My sentiments exactly," Darcey flung nastily before she yanked the green calico gown over her nightgown.

After Darcey had dressed in the more appropriate apparel, Kane deposited her in the saddle. Curbing his irritation and formulating his thoughts, he led Darcey through the winding chasms. It was a good while later before he spotted the thin curl of smoke drifting above the cabin that was nestled in a clump of pines.

Kane had the unshakable feeling that Giddeon and Noah were going to have difficulty treating Darcey with less courtesy and respect than she demanded. It had taken Kane several days to adjust to the role himself. Kane was tormented by this charade and the emotional turmoil it provoked. Kane flung his brooding companion a brief glance. He was letting her get under his skin and he had years of experience to his credit. Noah and Giddeon didn't. Damn, how he wished they had!

Noah paced aimlessly around the main room of the cabin while Giddeon prepared their afternoon meal. "How much longer do you suppose we'll have to stay cooped up here?" Noah grumbled.

Giddeon stirred the slumgullion and shrugged.

"I've spent two weeks monitoring the stage coach when it passes and I haven't seen even one robbery attempt," Noah muttered disappointedly. "I don't see how this is supposed to prepare me to become a skilled detective."

A sly smile pursed Giddeon's lips as he watched Noah walk off his frustrations the same way Kane did. It was a Callahan trait, Giddeon decided. Daniel Callahan had passed that characteristic of pacing on to his sons.

"It seems to me that this detective business isn't as glamorous and exciting as you had imagined," Giddeon pointed out. "All we ever heard was the glowing praise that was heaped on Kane. I'm sure your brother has spent days staking out routes in his attempt to apprehend criminals. He just never bothered to divulge the boring details to us. In fact, I don't recall Kane ever boasting about any of his cases. He simply applies himself quietly and efficiently."

"Well, I thought there would be more to investigation than this," Noah groused. "Boring isn't the word to describe this humdrum life!"

The nicker of the horses caused Noah to freeze in midstep. He lurched toward the window in anxious anticipation to pull back the curtain. "Well, it's about time Kane showed up."

Even Giddeon was grateful for the break in monotony. To while away the hours, Giddeon had tried his hand at trapping wild game. He'd nearly cut off his fingers before he figured out how to use those confounded traps. Finally, he'd gotten the hang of it and had even skinned his game to add some variety to their bland diet.

Having the dynamic Kane Callahan back would be a welcome change. Enjoyable company though young Noah was, he wasn't quite as entertaining as his older brother. Anxious to greet his employer, Giddeon set the spoon aside and scurried across the room. Both men tried to dart out the door at the same moment. They stuck there shoulder to shoulder when they spied the auburn-haired beauty who was bound with rope.

"What the hell does Kane think he's doing?" Noah croaked at Giddeon. His astounded gaze was glued to the knotted rope that held Darcey captive.

Giddeon couldn't shrug the way he usually did when he was miffed by a question. His shoulders were wedged against the doorjamb and Noah. "Darned if I know."

Kane almost burst out laughing at the two men who

were lodged in the doorway like frozen statues. They were both gaping at Darcey as if it was the first time they'd seen a female. No doubt they were shocked to find Darcey to be a raving beauty after Kane had made so many derogatory remarks about Witch O'Roarke before he'd actually met her . . . And if the bug-eyed expressions that were plastered on Noah and Giddeon's faces weren't enough, they looked terrible. Neither man had been within ten feet of a razor since Kane had stashed them in this obscure cabin for safekeeping. He had purchased buckskin clothes and jackets for them to wear so they would fit in with the mountains.

Although they looked the part of ragtag mountaineers, it would take a stern lecture to ensure that these two city dwellers portrayed the thieves Darcey assumed them to be. Thank the Lord Darcey already thought the worst about Kane's "gang." It would never do for her to know Noah and Giddeon were both tender-hearted softies when it came to women.

Before Giddeon or Noah could utter a blundering remark, Kane yanked on the rope that was tied to Darcey's wrists. "I kidnapped O'Roarke's daughter for ransom," he announced.

Kane planted himself solidly between Darcey and his "gang" so she couldn't see the shock on Giddeon and Noah's faces. Kane shot his brother a silencing glare when he opened his mouth to speak.

"Take Darcey inside and tie her to the bedpost, Noah. Then I want to talk to both of you . . . outside."

Stunned to the bone though he was, Noah followed his older brother's orders. While Noah was inside, practicing his knot-tying, Giddeon closed the door and peered incredulously at Kane.

"What in heaven's name is going on?" Giddeon asked.

"Some assignments demand drastic measures," Kane assured him. "Darcey is everything Patrick said she was—stubborn, independent, and defiant. She's almost gotten herself killed four times trying to protect that cussed express company. Physically removing her from harm's way was my last resort."

"But, sir, she's an heiress," Giddeon bleated, aghast.

"And if you don't drop that formality of address, Darcey will become suspicious," Kane said brusquely. "Don't call me sir again!"

At the moment there were several names Giddeon would have liked to call Kane. He was outraged by what his employer was suggesting. "How could you tie that young lady up and drag her around like a dog?" Giddeon shook his shaggy head in dismay. "I was right. It *is* high time you gave up the business you're in. I know you've always claimed that a detective has to think like the miscreants and scoundrels he tracks down, but my Lord! I didn't realize you also had to *behave* like them."

Kane latched onto the outraged servant and shepherded him out of earshot. "Damn it, Giddeon, keep your voice down. I know exactly what I'm doing. If there had been any other choice I would have utilized it. Believe me, there wasn't. I tried everything else first. And if you are foolish enough to take that little hellcat for granted while she's underfoot, we will all be in serious trouble." Kane gestured for Noah to join them. While Kane unsaddled the horses, he offered a brief account of the events that had forced him to take Darcey captive and swipe the gold and credit vouchers from the express office. And while the men gasped and groaned, Kane described the incidents with Griz Vanhook that testified to Darcey's daring.

"And so," Kane concluded, "I had no choice but to let Darcey think I was part of Vanhook's outlaw gang and that I abducted her for ransom." His silver-blue eyes narrowed solemnly on one goggle-eyed man and then the other. "Sometimes in investigative assignments, you are both going to have to pretend to be someone you're not. This sojourn in the mountains has to be made very nearly intolerable for Darcey. If not, she'll trot right back to Denver to resume her crusade."

"You want us to treat that lovely vision like a hostage?" Noah squeaked in astonishment. "I can think of several things I'd like to do to her, but behaving abominably isn't even on the list. I don't think I can do it. I've been trained to treat a lady like a lady!"

"So have I." Giddeon added his two cents' worth.

Kane flashed both men the glare that had stopped several criminals dead in their tracks. "I'm not asking you, I'm *telling* you how you are to behave around Darcey," he growled menacingly. "I spotted the gentleman bandit who has been plaguing the stage yesterday morning. Now I intend to track that varmint down while the two of you ride herd over Darcey. If I return to the cabin to find you waiting on her, the both of you are going to have hell to pay. Now, do you . . . understand . . . me?"

Noah and Giddeon winced when Kane's threatening

voice rolled over them like thunder. Rarely had he jumped down either of their throats, but he was doing it now. Reluctantly, they nodded in compliance.

When Kane wheeled around and stalked off, Noah stared uneasily at Giddeon. "Are you going to do what he is demanding?" he questioned quietly.

Giddeon sighed in defeat. "To tell the truth, I'm afraid *not* to. Kane assured me that he knows what he's doing. He is, after all, the expert in such matters."

"All I know is, the idea of treating that pretty lady without respect goes against my grain," Noah grumbled.

"Better that it goes against your grain than against your own brother," Giddeon replied grimly. "I for one don't think it wise to cross him."

Resolved to his distasteful duty, Giddeon marched back to the cabin to put the finishing touches on their meal. Perhaps he was to offer the poor woman meager portions of food and treat her as if she counted for nothing, but he didn't have to serve burned biscuits. And they would be charred if he didn't quicken his step!

Noah proceeded at a slower pace, growing more disenchanted with the detective life with each passing second. Where was all the glamour? Thus far, Noah had seen none of it. Nor had he experienced even a minimal degree of success in tracking the lone bandit. Kane had accidentally happened on to the thief en route while Noah had spent days searching for him. And now, to top off a perfectly dull fortnight in a remote region of the Rockies that left him one hundred miles from nowhere, he was ordered to behave like a bandit. He was supposed to antagonize that poor little bluestocking Kane had abducted in a moment of madness? This was insane!

Grumbling at the whole distasteful affair, Noah stamped back into the cabin and plunked down at the table, just as he had been ordered to do. It was difficult not to toss Darcey, whom Kane had chained to her chair, a sympathetic glance. But Noah managed to stare only at his empty tin plate and await his meal.

While Giddeon clanked the pots and pans on the stove, Darcey assessed the boyish face of the man who appeared to be only one or two years her senior. It had taken only a moment to deduce that Noah was Kane's younger brother. They bore a striking family resemblance, even though a mustache and bristly beard hugged Noah's jaws and surrounded his lips. Both Kane and Noah had a crop of raven-black hair that rippled with natural waves. Noah's eyes were a darker shade of blue than his older brother's and he bore no evidence of the rugged lines of experience on Kane's tanned face. As far as Darcey could tell, the younger Callahan was in training for his life of crime. Clearly, his older brother's influence had caused him to veer from the straight and narrow path. In ten years Noah would be every bit as formidable as his brother, Darcey predicted. What a shame that would be.

Although Darcey didn't think Noah was as cold or calloused as Kane yet, she cautiously reminded herself that behind many a boyish face lurked the soul of a killer. She'd seen enough wanted posters around Denver to know that. She would be naive if she didn't consider Noah as a threat.

Casting the thought aside, Darcey focused her

attention on the thin, brown-haired man who dipped slumgullion into a bowl and then pried open a can of fruit. Giddeon didn't appear all that much of a threat, either, she mused. In fact, his manner resembled a gentleman's, or at the very least a gentleman's servant. How Giddeon had gotten mixed up with the Callahan brothers Darcey would probably never know. From the look of things, Giddeon was more of a cook and housekeeper for these thieves rather than a bloodthirsty killer. She supposed desperation led some men into associating with criminals. Giddeon truly must have been desperate to team up with a scoundrel like Kane Callahan, handsome though he was. And oh how she wished he wasn't! Then maybe she would stop making such a fool of herself where he was concerned.

When Giddeon set the food on the table, Kane picked up the huge bowl of slumgullion. Since Darcey had only one free hand with which to eat, Kane slopped a meager portion onto Darcey's plate.

In mounting irritation, Darcey watched Kane dribble food all over her plate, leaving globs of meat and potatoes teetering on the edge. Then, just to annoy her further, knowing how particular she was about her meal, he dropped a perfectly good biscuit in the middle of the stew so that it would become spongy with juice.

Glaring mutinously, Darcey rescued the fluffy biscuit before it was ruined. "Must you purposely irritate me?" she muttered at the grinning rake. "Tolerating you and your disgusting friends is bad enough. But you don't have to spoil the only pleasure to be had during my stint in hell."

"If I had my—" Noah piped up and then groaned

when Kane kicked him in the shins under the table.

"I'm only trying to ensure that your time with me is the most memorable you've ever had," Kane taunted her before casting his brother a discreet glare.

"You needn't fret on that count," Darcey hurled at him, along with a poisonous glower. "I'll never forget how much I despise you."

From there, the meal progressed in stilted silence, broken only by the clatter of silverware against tin plates. When Darcey polished off her meal, she requested another helping. Kane flatly refused. Annoyed beyond words, Darcey was forced to watch the three men devour their meal while she sat there, still hungry.

Darcey was beginning to understand why Kane had convinced Giddeon to join his gang. Kane might have engaged in a life of crime, but he definitely had a taste for fine cuisine. Giddeon provided a much-wanted service for this midnight-haired rapscallion. Giddeon could cook as well as the chef her father had hired to prepare meals at their St. Louis estate. What a shame that Giddeon was wasting his talents and loyalty on two thieves in this remote region of the Rockies!

"Darcey can do the dishes," Kane volunteered for her when Giddeon began gathering up the bowls and plates.

"And then I should like a bath," she added, tilting her chin to that determined angle Kane had come to recognize.

"I'll fetch—" Noah tried to offer, but Kane kicked his shins again.

"Darcey can wait until evening for her bath," Kane

insisted. "You and I are going to take a look around the area to make sure I wasn't followed."

His gaze swung to Giddeon, who was staring at the plates he had clasped in his hands. "You fetch a hammer and nails to board up the window to Darcey's room. I don't want her to use it as an escape route while we're gone."

Bleakly, Giddeon obeyed. He was appalled by the way Kane was treating this saucy sprite. Tying her to chairs? Shackling her to the stove so she couldn't escape while she was supposed to be washing dishes? This was outrageous!

It was a good thing Patrick O'Roarke wasn't here to see the way his daughter was being abused. Surely Patrick would have protested this inhumane treatment. Giddeon wanted to and he wasn't even the poor girl's father! But of one thing Giddeon was certain. Darcey would walk away from her captivity hating Kane with a passion. Giddeon supposed that was the whole point of this distasteful ordeal. If he was Darcey he would have been more than eager to dash back to St. Louis for protection and compassion.

When they were alone, Kane secured Darcey to the cast-iron stove and pulled the dish pan within easy reach. After dumping the dishes in the water he pivoted toward the door.

"You really don't have a conscience, do you?" Darcey hissed at his departing back. "You've dragged Noah and Giddeon into your loathsome criminal activities. Neither of them seem the type. But your influence will ruin them for life."

"They're here because they want to be," Kane

265

assured her. "Just wash your dishes in alphabetical order and leave me to scout the area. If you badger me or cause Giddeon trouble while I'm gone, you won't get your bath when I come back."

Darcey clamped her mouth shut and wheeled toward the dishes. She couldn't wait to sink into a warm bath and cleanse away the lingering fragrance of the man who constantly deceived her and hounded her every minute of the day.

A frustrated sigh escaped Darcey's lips as she scrubbed the polish off the bowl. Cursing her fate, she snatched up the skillet and attacked it with a vengeance. She would show that ornery scoundrel! She would wash these damned dishes helter-skelter instead of in alphabetical order. And if she didn't detest the idea of eating off dirty dishes, she would have left the scum on each and every one of them!

Darcey plucked up the baking pan and plunged it into the water, but not before she swiped the last biscuit Kane had neglected to remove from it. Spitefully, she popped the biscuit in her mouth and chewed vigorously on it. No doubt, leaving her the extra scraps of food was an oversight on Kane's part. He wanted to starve her half to death as part of his torture.

The truth was Kane had purposely left the last biscuit within her reach. He would never have offered it to her at the table, but he did allow her to think she had gotten away with something. He couldn't permit her to know how sympathetic he and his companions really were. She had to think she was being mistreated, even if she couldn't have been in better hands.

Darcey silently seethed at the way Kane had

tormented and ridiculed her. How she hated herself for being the least bit attracted to him. The conflict that warred inside her was taking its toll on her composure. Darcey cringed at the thought of how she had responded to that blackguard the previous night. And to further humiliate herself, she had run straight into his arms after her terrifying ordeal with one of the Bishop brothers.

It was glaringly apparent that this entire ordeal had caused her brain to malfunction. She had contradicted herself all over the place and turned into a full-fledged hypocrite. There was no reason why she should care in the least for a man who treated her with mocking disrespect. But damn it, every time she stared into those hypnotic silver-blue eyes, her resistance crumbled. Each time he touched her, she wilted beneath temptation.

Darcey bit back the frustrated tears when Giddeon tied her to the bedpost and locked the door behind him. Willfully, she tried to get herself in hand. She was every kind of fool for caring about Kane when he clearly viewed her as nothing but his convenient harlot. Kane had bedeviled her with his charm.

Well, there would be no more touching and kissing, she vowed fiercely. She would never let that rapscallion come near her again without putting up one helluva fight. She was much too vulnerable to him and simply couldn't trust herself with him anymore. Kane was her declared enemy, and if she knew what was good for her, she would never allow herself to forget that ever again. She was going to survive this ordeal and then have him hunted down like the lowdown, good-for-nothing varmint he was. He could mildew in jail for all she cared. He could be placed in front of a firing squad and blown to smithereens and she would applaud!

On that spiteful thought Darcey plopped back on the bed and glared at the cobwebs on the ceiling. This journey across the rugged terrain of the mountains and her captivity in this cabin was nothing short of hell. And Kane Callahan was the resident demon who was tormenting her to no end!

Chapter 16

While Noah and Giddeon scuttled back and forth, heating and carrying water into Darcey's room for her evening bath, Kane sat on the edge of the bed sketching a map of the area he and his brother had surveyed that afternoon. Noah dared not glance in Darcey's direction for fear Kane would jerk him aside and chew him up one side and down the other for flinging sympathetic stares at their captive. But despite Noah's attempt to appear unmoved by Darcey's plight, Kane was vividly aware that his brother and Giddeon were severely frustrated. He was asking them to do things that were in contrast to their sense of integrity, but they both had to learn to handle the duplicity, Kane reminded himself bleakly. Both men were blithely ignorant of what went on behind the scenes of detective investigation and clandestine assignments. Sometimes a man had to pretend to be what he wasn't. He had to lie and to deceive . . .

"The three of you can leave now," Darcey announced,

jostling Kane from his deliberations. "The tub is full and I'm anxious to enjoy a warm bath."

Although Noah and Giddeon instantly took their leave, Kane refused to budge from his spot. "I'm not going anywhere," he told her point-blank. "I'm here to make sure you don't try anything. After you admitted what you planned to do last night while I slept, I don't trust you."

Darcey glared holes in his tan chambray shirt and cursed herself for making that spiteful comment just to salvage her pride. Sure as hell, it had come back to haunt her. "I have no intention of disrobing until you are gone and it's safe," she declared firmly.

Kane folded his arms over his broad chest and grinned rakishly. "Are you suggesting I'm dangerous, little minx?"

Extremely dangerous, she silently corrected, but she wasn't about to give him the satisfaction of hearing her admit it aloud. Why, if the truth be known, when he flashed her one of those disarming smiles that accentuated every rugged feature on his face, it was impossible to not be affected by it. But a thief was still a thief, Darcey reminded herself. Even if Kane Callahan had the phenomenal ability to make her forget who he was when he swept her up in the tide of passion, he was still a scoundrel.

Defiant to the bitter end, Darcey lifted her skirts and plopped into the bath, fully dressed. This wasn't exactly how she envisioned her long-awaited bath, but she would *not,* under any circumstances, doff her clothes in front of Kane ever again!

A burst of laughter exploded from Kane's lips while

270

he watched Darcey snatch up the soap and scrub her gown and herself. It was better this way, Kane decided. Staring overly long at this delectable beauty always caused his blood to ignite. And seeing her in the altogether was damned hard on his male anatomy, but having Giddeon and Noah underfoot prevented Kane from fulfilling his desires, so there was no sense tempting himself if he didn't have to.

"You realize, of course, that if you bed down in your wet nightgown, which is under your dress, you will catch your death of cold," Kane pointed out. "Now you'll have to sleep in the buff."

"If dying ensures that I will be away from you forevermore, death does have its advantages," Darcey flung at him as she scrubbed her face until it shone like a polished apple.

"You're making this worse than it has to be," Kane said with a ridiculing smirk.

"Nothing could make this situation worse than it is," she countered in a bitter tone.

"No?" One thick black brow elevated in contradiction.

"No," Darcey confirmed with perfect assurance.

Kane snatched up the bucket of water beside the tub and dumped it on Darcey. A mischievous grin curved his mouth upward while she sputtered and clawed at the wet mass of auburn hair that clung to her face. Still hissing like an incensed cat, Darcey bounded to her feet to repay the ornery rake for dousing her with cold water.

With her hands cupped, she flung her bath water at him. Kane retaliated by dipping up another bucket to

271

splash on her. Halfway through their childish water fight Darcey realized she was giggling and actually enjoying their playful battle. Then another thought hit her like a falling boulder and she very nearly stumbled in her tub. Her gaze flew to Kane, who was grinning back at her. When their eyes locked and she saw those silver-blue pools sparkling with amusement, Darcey's heart sank to the bottom of the tub in which she was standing.

What she had feared was happening had truly happened! God have mercy on her wretched soul! Despite Kane's contemptible flaws of character, there was something about him that lured her against her will. She had fought these traitorous feelings tooth and nail, but it had done her not one whit of good. At first, to soothe her nagging conscience, she had declared her ill-founded feelings for this man to be nothing but newly awakened female curiosity and mere physical attraction. But she was ashamed to admit that there was far more to it than that. She had actually fallen . . .

Darcey gulped audibly and her eyes rounded like dinner plates. Bewildered, she peered up into Kane's craggy, bronzed features. She had actually fallen . . . in love with this undeserving rascal!

A muddled frown furrowed Kane's brow when Darcey collapsed on the edge of the tub and gaped at him. "Darcey? Are you all right?" he questioned.

He clutched her hand and drew her onto her wobbly legs. When her knees threatened to buckle beneath her and her face turned white as the snow that capped the looming mountains, Kane scowled at himself. He and his ornery pranks! It wasn't enough that he had dumped her in the cold mountain stream and had forced her to muck about in that flimsy gown for his own devilish purpose of admiring her appetizing figure and forced her to ride through driving rain. Now he had dumped cold water on her. She had probably caught the grippe. Damn it, hadn't he pushed her far enough in the past few days?

When Kane clamped a steadying arm around her, Darcey jerked away. She shot out of his arms, but he lunged to capture her all over again.

"Don't touch me," she croaked.

Kane flagrantly ignored her demand and swept her up in his arms and carried her across the room. "We've got to get you out of these wet clothes and into bed," he insisted before he set her to her feet.

"Just leave me alone!" Darcey all but screamed at him.

Her protest had no effect whatsoever. Kane made quick work of removing the calico dress and the nightgown beneath it. And that was when he realized he'd made matters worse for himself. Suddenly he was devouring this luscious beauty as if she were a feast he longed to consume. His hungry gaze pored over her curvaceous body, aching to touch her, to re-create those precious moments of splendor.

"Are you cold?" he murmured as he stared down into her emerald eyes.

Darcey wasn't cold. She was afraid he was going to take her in his arms and she would melt all over him. It was moments such as these, when Kane displayed gentleness and concern, that had made her love him all the more. Deep down inside, beneath that thieving

273

mind and ornery temperament, there was a man who had been able to do what no other man had done since Michael Dupris broke her heart. Kane had made her love him.

When Kane Callahan was in one of his gentler moods he was positively devastating. Perhaps it was a flaw in her character to think she could transform this outlaw into a respectable gentleman. Whatever external influences had caused Kane to turn to a life of crime had molded him into a paradox of a man. Darcey was drawn to him, but she was afraid she was only seeing things in him that she wanted to see. Until now, she refused to admit just how much she cared for him. Yet, it frightened her to know she loved a man who was all wrong for her . . .

"Darcey, for God's sake, what's the matter with you?" Kane demanded when she continued to stare at him in a daze.

Kane could see a flicker of fear in those glistening pools. Fear? Kane did a double take. Why should Darcey be afraid of him now? He had done everything under the sun to her and she had defied him every step of the way. But damned if she didn't look frightened now. Of what, Kane couldn't begin to imagine.

A protective instinct bubbled up from inside him just as naturally as blood flowed through his veins. This charade was playing havoc with his emotions. He had pretended not to care, but whatever had upset her was really upsetting *him*. He wanted to hold her close until whatever frightened her had subsided.

"Darcey . . . ?" His voice was low. Gently he framed her face in his hands and lifted her face to his. "Tell me what's wrong."

Kane hadn't meant to take her lips beneath his or draw her quaking body against his muscular frame until she told him what was bothering her. But holding her close had become as natural as the batting of an eyelash. One would have thought that it had been weeks since he had felt the imprint of her supple body on his. A shudder of need wracked his very soul as his lips rolled over hers, savoring the honeyed taste of her. Instinctively, he pulled her quivering body against his hard contours and felt her melt against him. Kane didn't stop to analyze why this feisty hellion had surrendered without a fight. She had never come into his arms without some degree of resistance. But there was no reluctance in her kiss or the tantalizing way she wound her arms around his neck and pushed up on tiptoe to greet his lips.

A tiny moan rattled in Darcey's throat when she felt herself teetering on the edge of abandon. Loving this silver-blue-eyed devil was her curse in life. But she could no more stop the fervent sensations that channeled through her when he caressed her than she could halt a rockslide. When Kane made wild, sweet love to her the walls of her defenses came tumbling down. He had taught her expertly where these sensations led, made her long for all he had to give. He never seemed to demand more than she wanted to offer him and yet she always wound up yielding to him completely. Kane had an uncanny knack of making her feel as if her will was his, whether it started out that way or not . . . which it hadn't.

"You're the most beautiful creature I've ever seen,"

Kane rasped as his hands and lips migrated over her trembling flesh, caressing her as he'd longed to do since the instant he'd gotten her alone. "You take my breath away . . ."

That was when Darcey folded at the knees and admitted defeat. She not only heard his whispered words but she felt them vibrating across the throbbing peaks of her breasts. His masterful touch warmed her from inside out. She was suddenly at a loss for words. Her voice refused to function during Kane's sensual assault on her body and her senses. She couldn't draw a breath without inhaling his alluring male scent. She couldn't reach out without touching the hard length of him. And even when she closed her eyes he was there, hypnotizing her with softly uttered incantations of magic.

For one brief moment Darcey thought she had mustered enough will to resist. But the instant came and went when Kane drew her onto the bed. Her lashes swept up to watch him shuck the damp clothes that clung to his physique as if they had been painted there. Darcey marveled at each rippling muscle, at his flat belly and the long hard columns of his legs. Darcey couldn't have glanced away from the awe-inspiring picture he presented, even if her life depended on it. This man matched the rugged mountains. He could be ominous and imposing and yet his very presence demanded admiration and respect.

Without a hint of reserve, Darcey reached out to touch the rock-hard wall of his chest, to coast her fingertips over the dark thatch of hair that covered the lean muscles of his belly. When Kane stretched out beside her to return her adoring touch caress for caress, Darcey couldn't think of one sensible reason why she should battle the burning needs that uncoiled inside her. She and Kane could have been the world's worst enemies and yet they were as close as two people could get.

Darcey wanted him beyond bearing. It was as simple and, ironically, as complicated as that. When the armor of her anger and stubborn pride fell away, Kane's lovemaking overshadowed reality.

"I want you." The quiet confession tripped from her lips before she could think to bite it back.

Her words inflamed Kane's passions. There was a world of difference between wanting and loving. Kane knew that. But having this defiant hellion admit she needed him, even for the moment, was a monumental milestone in their stormy relationship. Her words resounded in his mind as he kissed her with growing impatience.

His hands moved restlessly over her flesh, eager to rediscover every delicious inch of her, as if he could have forgotten how it felt to caress perfection! She was like a fire in his blood. These rapture-filled moments pursued and captured time. And yet, when the lovemaking was over, he was left wanting more. Thoughts of her tormented his days and haunted his nights. Knowing that one day she would walk away from him was pure and simple hell. And knowing that, Kane clung to every wondrous sensation, savored each intimate caress.

When Darcey set her hands upon him to return the tantalizing pleasure, Kane swore he had gold dust in his lungs. Breathing was next to impossible. His senses were saturated with the scent, feel, and taste of her. Undulations of hungry desire rippled through him. His body craved her gentle touch, her intoxicating kisses and arousing caresses.

A groan of unholy torment rumbled in his chest when Darcey's hands and lips scaled down his belly to limn the ultrasensitive flesh of his thigh. She drove him over the edge into oblivion and left him clinging to one thin thread. She invented imaginative ways to seduce him, using her body in one long erotic caress. The sheer impact of her flesh moving provocatively over his left him begging her to stop tormenting him so, and at the same time praying she wouldn't quit what she was doing.

Darcey was completely overwhelmed by the power she seemed to hold over this magnificent man. He had become her willing captive, an obedient slave who bowed to the passions that burst between them. She was the victor in this tender conquest, the one in absolute control. She could make him move upon command, leave him trembling with the want of her.

Darcey knew she could never earn his love, since he wasn't the kind of man who understood total, heartfelt affection, but she longed to leave her imprint on his body and burn her memory on his mind for all eternity. His torment would come in seeing her face each time he took another woman in his arms.

Given the time, Darcey might have gotten around to convincing herself that she was seducing Kane for mere spite, but when he pushed her to the mattress to shower her with kisses and caresses she knew spite had nothing to do with her desire to touch and be touched so intimately. She wanted and needed to share this delicious moment. Loving him had become pleasure in itself.

Kane battled for composure over his raging passion. He ached to satisfy the gigantic needs Darcey had instilled in him. Yet, the need to arouse her to the very limits of her sanity compelled him to prolong that moment of final possession. He wanted to tease her into mindless abandon, to leave her begging for him to come to her. And tease her he did. His hands and lips were everywhere at once, teaching her things he had never revealed to her about the mystical world of desire. He wanted to tantalize and torment her with his *c*aresses and *k*isses . . .

Sweet mercy, now she had *him* doing it, Kane thought as he smiled against the peak of her breasts. Darcey even had him thinking in alphabetical order. Well, it was time *she* learned, from A to Z, all the wondrous sensations passion could offer. And Kane was more than eager to teach her all he had learned about love—the selfless giving, the breathless sharing, the sublime magic . . .

A gasp of surprise trickled from Darcey's lips when Kane employed the most intimate techniques imaginable to arouse her to the limits of sanity. Spasms of unappeased desire riveted her body and left her quaking in explosive response. He had taken her from one dizzying plateau to another, leaving her aching with the want of him. And yet he refused to satisfy the monstrous needs that rocked her very soul.

Urgently, Darcey reached out to guide him to her,

anxious to end the divine torment of having him so close and yet so intolerably far away. Shamelessly, she arched toward him, wanting him with every fiber of her being. And when he came to her, the world split asunder . . .

And so did their rickety bed!

A low growl burst from Kane's lips when the mattress and broken slats plummeted to the floor with a resounding crash. He decided, there and then, that this crudely constructed stick of furniture had been built for nothing more strenuous than sleeping.

His tormented gaze darted to the door, wondering what Noah and Giddeon would make of the racket that shattered the silence. At the moment, Kane was too engulfed in passion to care what anyone thought, as long as they didn't come stampeding inside the room. If either of them did, Kane would cheerfully kill them.

A bubble of laughter erupted from Darcey's lips as she stared up into Kane's face. Her eyes danced with amusement when Kane glanced at her and then stared expectantly at the door.

"They probably think you're tormenting me to death," she tittered before moving provocatively beneath him.

"Is that what you think I'm doing to you?" Kane queried as his male body eagerly responded to the feel of her silky flesh stirring under his.

Her hand glided over the hard tendons of his neck, drawing his tanned face back to hers. "What else would you call it?" she murmured against his sensual lips. "You're denying me what I want most . . ."

What Kane wasn't calling it was *quits,* just because

the bed folded up beneath him and his companions were waiting outside, wondering what the devil was going on. Nothing mattered in all the world except taking this witch-angel to paradise with him. When Darcey was ardent and responsive in his arms, the rest of the universe was lost in oblivion. Kane wanted her so badly that the real torment would have come if he denied himself the ecstasy he knew awaited him.

The playful smile vanished from Darcey's lips when passion clouded her thoughts like an incoming fog. Her body moved instinctively toward his, flowing in the rhythmic cadence of lovemaking. She hadn't meant to cry out in the splendor of it all, but she possessed not one smidgen of control when passion burst between them like a keg of blasting powder, sending her thoughts scattering in all directions at once.

Spasms of ineffable splendor ribboned through her, and she clutched Kane to her and held on to him for all she was worth. The world shattered like exploding meteors, and sensation after indescribable sensation riveted her. Darcey was left suspended in a universe that could be seen, felt, and heard. She was bombarded by one wild shudder after another. It was an eternity before she could breathe normally, and forever before she could navigate her way back across the star-studded expanse of infinity.

Noah fidgeted in his chair and stared apprehensively at the closed door. He had heard the splashes, yelps, muffled voice, and Kane's rumbling growls. Then the crash of furniture had Noah squirming like a restless tiger. "What the devil do you think he's doing to her?" he questioned Giddeon.

Giddeon shrugged and stared grimly at the door. His imagination was running wild. "I don't think either of us want to know what Kane has resorted to in his effort to terrorize that poor woman," he grumbled in reply.

"He's probably torturing her and enjoying every minute of it," Noah speculated. "That's what this mischievous game of his is all about, isn't it? He's scaring the living daylights out of her, just for the spite of it."

"Surely he wouldn't actually hurt her," Giddeon said hopefully. "Maybe he just wants her to think he might if she doesn't toe the line. She is rather feisty, after all."

"And gorgeous," Noah tacked on. "It is beyond me how any man could be cruel to that spirited beauty. I don't care how stubborn and determined he says she is. Kane doesn't have to scare her to the extreme." He bolted to his feet. "I'm going in there and give Kane a piece of my mind. This whole affair is ridic-ulous . . ."

Giddeon grabbed Noah and stuffed him back in his chair so quickly that it ripped the last word off his lips. "You heard what your brother said about interfering. This is *his* assignment. We are just the props."

"Well, if he leaves one mark on Darcey he's going to answer to me," Noah fumed. "I'll not be a party to torturing women. I don't care what Kane says! And I'm not going into this branch of detective work, either. I don't have the stomach for it."

"If we ever get back to Independence, I may never set foot out of there again," Giddeon vowed as he stared resentfully at the closed door. "I don't want to know what that brother of yours does while on assignment, either. It's already giving me nightmares."

When the racket stopped, Noah slouched back in his chair to breathe a sigh of relief. "God, I'm glad that's over. Knowing what a maniac Kane has turned out to be, he'll probably expect us to molest Darcey while he's off tracking that highwayman. And I won't do it, I tell you!"

"Neither will I," Giddeon said with firm conviction. "We'll just tell him we tortured her, and what he won't know won't hurt him."

When the door whined open and Kane emerged, both men sat like statues, glaring at him. Composing himself, Kane strode across the room toward the front door.

"Now what are you going to do, big brother, stalk off to fetch the thumbscrews? I hear they are quite painful."

Kane stifled his wry smile before he pivoted to face Giddeon and Noah's condescending glowers. "She is still in one piece, if that's what you're worried about." Another grin struggled to curve the corner of his mouth upward. Kane bit it back and glared at his companions. "If either of you go in that room, you'll regret it, I promise you. Leave her alone. She doesn't need your sympathy and you'd best not give her any. Do I make myself clear?"

"Like hell she doesn't need sympathy!" Noah spouted. "Honestly, Kane, I don't even know you these days. You've turned into a monster."

"You'll find out just how much of one I am if you go rushing in there," he scowled in ominous threat. Then his arm shot toward the door that led into the other bedroom. "Now get to bed, both of you. I have tasks to tend outside. When I get back, you'd damned well better be tucked beneath your quilts."

Reluctantly, Noah and Giddeon skulked to their room, but not without casting a sympathetic glance at Darcey's door and a disdainful glare at Kane.

Wheeling about, Kane continued on his way. A frustrated sigh gushed from his lips the moment he slammed the front door behind him. He was between a rock and one helluva hard spot. If he told Noah and Giddeon what had really happened, they would be even more outraged than they already were. They simply didn't understand what was going on between him and Darcey. Hell, Kane didn't understand it too well himself! Darcey's eager responses baffled him, but when she was in one of her tender moods he wasn't going to interrogate her about it. That would only infuriate her. No, it was better just to accept the pleasure she'd offered without trying to analyze her reasons. She probably didn't even know why herself.

Absently, Kane paced to and fro—away from the scrutinizing gazes of Noah and Giddeon. He couldn't let the men know this situation was getting to him, too. With a long-suffering sigh, Kane paused and knelt to pluck up a clump of wildflowers that glowed in the moonlight. Lord, there was so little he could offer that feisty beauty. Flowers seemed a meager gift to convey his feelings.

What Kane wanted, more than anything, was to win Darcey's heart. He didn't want this love to be the temporary kind Melanie Brooks had offered. Hers was

284

a fairweather love. She had been far more intrigued by Kane's material wealth than the man himself. Kane wanted Darcey to love him, in spite of everything. That was asking a lot, but he had to know he really mattered to her, way down deep inside where it really counted. He had an inkling that Darcey had finally come to realize there *was* magic between them, despite all else. And if he could nurture that tiny bud, she might find it in her heart to forgive him one day.

"Of course she will, Callahan," Kane scoffed at himself. He was living on false hope if he allowed himself to believe that hogwash. But no matter what, Kane vowed to ride off the following morning, leaving their wondrous lovemaking fresh on Darcey's mind. They didn't have forever, but they had the rest of the night and Kane intended to make the most of it, even if that would never be enough to satisfy him in the years to come.

That disturbing thought caused Kane to quicken his step. If he left that sassy hellion alone for too long she'd start thinking, and he didn't want her to think, only to *feel* the magic they created when they were in each other's arms. And if this night was all the time Kane had left to assure her that there was more to him than the bandit she saw him as, then he intended for this to be a night neither of them would ever forget!

Chapter 17

Darcey stirred beneath the cozy quilts and sighed contentedly. Although Kane had eased off their broken bed to confront Noah and Giddeon, he had left Darcey with a gentle kiss and a quiet promise of pleasures to come. The long, grueling days and the sweet sensations of passion had worked on Darcey like a sedative. She had drifted off to sleep, only to be awakened by the faint creak of the bedroom door.

The spell had yet to be shattered. As crisscrossed shadows and moonbeams sprayed through the barred window, Darcey watched Kane shed his clothes. The mere sight of him unfolded invisible tentacles that wrapped around her heart. An adoring smile pursed her lips when he revealed every hair-roughened inch of his muscular body to her appreciative gaze. Tomorrow she would return to her senses and scold herself for her vulnerability and desire for this man. Tomorrow, thought Darcey with a sigh of longing, but not tonight.

Oh, to be sure, she would regret loving him, but she

would cope with her noble conscience later. Just for tonight she would let herself imagine what her life would be like if Kane gave up his evil ways and truly fell in love with her . . .

Darcey blinked when Kane extended the bouquet of wildflowers to her and eased down beside her. The thoughtful gesture tugged at her heartstrings. She accepted the gift with a quiet murmur of appreciation and a tender kiss.

"I wish I had more to offer," Kane whispered as he snuggled against her shapely contours. "But no gift can match your beauty." Slowly he peeled away the quilt, allowing the spotlight of moonbeams to glow on her flawless skin. "I love looking at you. I could spend the whole night marveling at the absolute perfection of you."

"And what is it that you expect in return for all this flattery?" Darcey teased with a smile that melted him.

Lord, when she blessed him with that elfin grin, he swore he'd died and gone straight to heaven. "All I want in return is *you*," he rasped. "Even if only for this one night . . . Make this moment last forever."

Darcey responded instinctively to his husky request. She gave herself up—body, mind, and soul—to the love she felt for him. And each time she roused from her dreams, inviting lips were there to greet her. And, over and over again, Kane sent her sailing on a sea of ecstasy.

It was with great reluctance that Kane unfolded himself from the collapsed bed at the crack of dawn.

But he forced himself to roll to his feet and gather his strewn clothes. In the first place, he didn't want to explain to Noah and Giddeon why he was walking out of Darcey's room when he had intended to bed down on the small cot in the main chamber of the cabin. And in the second place, he had a wily thief to catch.

A melancholy smile pursed Kane's lips as he peered down at the angelic face, so soft in repose. Sunlight flickered through the barred window, to glitter in the glorious mass of auburn hair that cascaded over the pillow like a waterfall of molten lava. Longingly, Kane's gaze swept over Darcey's satiny arms, which protruded from the edge of the quilt. Her hand rested on the pillow where he'd slept, as if she were reaching out to touch him as wondrously as she had the previous night, as if she were waiting to rekindle the fires of desire that had consumed them.

Kane clamped an iron grip on his willpower and stabbed his legs into his breeches. Lord, leaving Darcey was worse than tearing off an arm! But he had made a commitment to Patrick and he had to leave her where she slept. He regretted that he wouldn't be there when she roused. Kane had the inescapable feeling, things wouldn't be the same when he returned. Darcey would gird herself up in her protective armor just the way she always did, convincing herself that what they shared was only a passing fancy.

Muttering, Kane eased the door shut and tiptoed across the room to ruffle the quilts on the cot, making it look as though he'd slept there. Blast it, he wished he knew exactly how Darcey felt about him. He knew he had made her want him. But being stubborn to the core, Darcey balked at admitting her feelings ran deeper than physical satisfaction. He had thought perhaps she might have fallen a little bit in love with him.

"Wishful thinking on your part, Callahan," Kane chastised himself, then, with swift efficiency, he tossed the blanket over his steed and dropped the saddle in place. "She's never going to let herself love you. Why should she? She thinks you're a criminal, for crying out loud! You're expecting a helluva lot from her. How many heiresses do you know who have fallen head over heels for supposed outlaws?" Kane asked himself.

The horse nickered, stamped his foot, and Kane chuckled at his own soliloquy. "You could have jumped into the conversation any time, nag, instead of letting me do all the talking."

The instant Kane swung into the saddle, he tucked his troubled thoughts in the corner of his heart. If he didn't concentrate on the business at hand, he might be wandering around these mountains for weeks on end. Heaving a frustrated sigh, Kane glanced back at the cabin, visualizing the beauty inside it. God, how he wished things would be the same when he got back. But they wouldn't be, he told himself realistically. Darcey would fortify her defenses and he would have to woo her all over again. Only once had she come willingly into his arms. Kane dared not expect her to do it twice. He knew he was going to lose her because of the circumstances of his assignment. He might as well prepare himself for the day when Darcey walked out of his life.

On that bleak note Kane trotted his mount through

the meandering valleys in search of the gentleman bandit who stalked the mountain passes and stage route. He hoped like hell that it wouldn't take long to track the thief because his heart just wasn't in a long, exhausting search when that auburn-haired angel weighed so heavily on his mind.

A contented sigh tripped from Darcey's lips as she roused from sleep. Instinctively, her hand glided down the hard, muscular . . .

Darcey came awake with a start when her hand landed on the empty space that had once held Kane. When she glanced around the room to find him gone, a wave of disappointment swept over her. She supposed she should have appreciated his consideration. No doubt, he had tiptoed back to his cot so his cohorts wouldn't know he had spent the night with her.

Her pensive gaze swung to the coiled rope that lay on the nightstand. She wondered if Kane had intended to tie her up again but had just neglected to do so. Before she had time to contemplate the thought, a knock sounded on her door. Hurriedly, Darcey scrambled into the gown that was still a mite damp after the previous night's escapade. When she had dressed, she scuttled toward the door.

To her chagrin, it was Noah who greeted her rather than Kane. Anxiously, Darcey peered around Noah's shoulders, only to see Giddeon huddled over the stove. Kane was nowhere in sight.

"You'll be glad to know the tyrant is gone," Noah informed her. "He's—" He caught himself before he divulged information that was not meant for Darcey's ears. "He's scouting the area."

A dubious frown knitted Darcey's brow. So Kane was up to his old tricks again, was he? Curse the man. He made love to her as if there were no tomorrow and then he tramped off to plot another robbery against her father's express company. He had no scruples whatsoever!

Noah cleared his throat and shifted awkwardly from one foot to the other. His gaze darted to the nightstand where the discarded rope lay and then fell to the collapsed bed. "If you promise not to try to escape, Giddeon and I won't stake you down. You can have the run of your room."

Darcey was relieved to learn Noah wasn't as hard-hearted as his brother. The younger man clearly possessed a smidgen of compassion for her plight.

"I'll bring your breakfast to you as soon as Giddeon has prepared it. And I won't cut your rations in half the way Kane did, either," he assured her emphatically.

While Noah was making his generous offers, Darcey's mind was humming with possible solutions. If she could get these men to let their guard down, she could escape while Kane wasn't underfoot. First she needed to scout the area around the cabin to determine whether the horses had been tethered or if they had been staked to graze. And later, when Noah and Giddeon least expected it, she would make her flight to freedom.

With that practical plan in mind, Darcey glanced humbly down at the scuffed toes of her shoes and wrung her hands in front of her. "I have to see to my needs, Noah. If you accompany me outside without putting that humiliating leash on me, I promise not to attempt escape."

Darcey was pouring on the coy charm like she'd seen some of her flirtatious schoolmates do when they were trying to bedazzle a man. Darcey had always scorned such pretentiousness. But now it suited her purpose extremely well.

Lord, she had become just like Kane Callahan! she realized. She was behaving just as deviously as he had.

Noah nodded agreeably and followed Darcey out the door. All the while they were outside, she was surveying the area, plotting every minute detail of her escape. She calculated the distance from the door to the grazing horses. None of them had been saddled. That would present a problem. Darcey would be forced to ride bareback when she made her getaway. And when she did, she would have to scatter the other horses so her captors would be forced to chase down their mounts before pursuing her. That would buy her precious time and allow her a head start.

Darcey ambled back into the cabin with Noah one step behind her. She was escorted back to her room and left alone for several minutes. When Noah reappeared with her breakfast plate heaping with food, Darcey had the feeling there was something he wanted to say. He glanced at the broken bed. His mind, no doubt, was reeling with speculation, and Darcey tensed, wondering what assessments Noah was making. A hot blush worked its way up from the base of her throat into her cheeks and she turned away from his curious gaze before embarrassment betrayed her.

"That scoundrel!" Noah exploded. "He roughed you around last night, didn't he? Did he leave bruises on you while he was tearing this place upside down so you would have to sleep on the floor?"

Darcey breathed a sigh of relief when Noah leaped to his erroneous conclusion about why the bed had collapsed.

Suddenly Noah was pacing the floor, just as his older brother was in the habit of doing. A muffled growl gushed from his lips as he stamped hither and yon. "I don't know what's gotten into Kane." He paused, jerked up his head, and frowned. "Well, damn, maybe I do know why he's treating you so abominably."

Noah lurched around and paced some more before halting to peer at the elegant beauty in calico. Even the dowdy gown couldn't detract from her alluring assets. This curvaceous female always looked gorgeous. And blast it, she had the right to know why Kane had become such a spiteful devil of late, Noah decided. It might not ease Darcey's miserable situation when Kane returned, but at least she would understand what made him tick.

"I think Kane is using you as his scapegoat," Noah blurted out. "It's nothing personal, you understand, but—"

"His scapegoat?" Darcey stared inquisitively at Noah.

He nodded affirmatively. "Kane was engaged to a very tempting little blonde by the name of Melanie Brooks. While Kane was lollygagging all over creation, as he has a habit of doing to cure his restlessness,

294

Melanie found herself a rich businessman and eloped without notifying Kane."

Darcey felt as if Noah had punched her in the midsection with a doubled fist. Knowing what she knew about Kane, she formed a distorted view of the incident. Apparently, Kane had been off doing what he did best—gambling and thieving. His paramour had worked her wiles on some wealthy dandy and then she'd flitted off with him.

"Giddeon and I figure Kane is still bitter about the whole affair. That's why he's taking his frustration for Melanie out on you. He's being cruel to you, but it's really *her* that he wants to hurt," Noah speculated, making matters even worse than he could possibly imagine.

Inwardly groaning at her foolishness, Darcey stared unseeingly at the rough-hewn wall. So she had been right all along. She didn't mean anything to Kane, not in the ways that really mattered. He had whispered his love for her again the previous night and, imbecile that she was, Darcey had allowed herself to believe he had begun to develop an attachment to her. But he had obviously envisioned himself in Melanie's arms and his hushed words were meant for her, not Darcey. Kane had never said those words to her in the light of day. He spoke them only during the heat of passion while another woman was on his mind, not in his arms. He must really have cared deeply for Melanie what's-her-name. She had hurt him and he was using Darcey as a substitute for the woman he really wanted. It was Melanie's face he saw in the moonlight! Damn him!

Damn her for loving a hopeless cause!

Noah expelled a heavy sigh and ambled toward the door. "I cannot change things, you understand. Kane is in command and I'm obliged to do what he tells me. But I just wanted you to know he hasn't always been like this. Melanie Brooks Beezely just soured him on women and unfortunately you are the one who is paying for it. I'm truly sorry."

When Noah closed the door, Darcey cursed the air blue. Now she was even more determined than ever to escape! She never wanted to see that midnight-haired devil again. She couldn't retest her vulnerability until she had time to get herself in hand and put this bittersweet romance in proper perspective. And by damned, she didn't love Kane Callahan; she hated him!

Giddeon stared at the closed door to Darcey's room and then sighed heavily. "I'm never going off on one of Kane's deplorable adventures again," he vowed sourly. "I'll quit my position first."

"And I'll disown him," Noah chimed in. He peered sympathetically toward the door which held Giddeon's undivided attention. "You should have seen what Kane did to Darcey's bed. He tore it to pieces and left them in a pile on the floor for her to sleep there."

A frown plowed Giddeon's brow. He reflected on the commotion he'd heard coming from the room the previous night and a wave of disgust buffeted him. Good God, surely Kane hadn't . . . He wouldn't have . . . would he?

Giddeon scowled at the offensive thought. There was

more than one way to break a bed, even if Noah had yet to puzzle out the other possibility. That rascal! Giddeon silently fumed. Kane *had* become a monster. He had taken this assignment a mite too seriously. If Kane had lowered himself to molesting the innocents of this world . . .

"Giddeon? You don't look well," Noah said when he observed the servant's face had turned pea green. "Didn't your breakfast agree with you?"

It was the repulsive thoughts Giddeon was thinking that settled on his stomach like an indigestible meal. What he had deduced about Kane had sickened him. "I think I'll get a breath of fresh air," Giddeon mumbled as he got up from the chair.

Once outside, Giddeon lowered himself to swearing colorful curses. Confound that Kane! He'd really gone too far this time. Noah hadn't figured out what really happened the previous night, but Giddeon had the uneasy feeling he knew exactly what had transpired. Damn that man! He had been raised better than that. And Kane would answer for his transgressions, Giddeon would see to that!

After gathering his composure, Giddeon stamped back inside to discreetly check the cot on which Kane had supposedly slept. Under the pretense of straightening the sheets and quilts that Kane had purposely ruffled, Giddeon shrewdly appraised the cot. He was positively certain the bed hadn't been slept in. He'd made enough beds in his time to know when one had been used and when it hadn't. This one had been made to *look* as if it had been occupied, but it had been anything but!

Still fuming, Giddeon made a mental note to confront Kane the instant he returned. Forcing himself on Miss O'Roarke was not part of the assignment. Kane had been sent here to protect the young lady, not soil her upstanding reputation. And by God, Kane would answer for this, whether he wanted to or not!

By midafternoon, Darcey had formulated her scheme and plotted each step of her escape in an efficient, organized manner, right down to the letter. Employing her sweetest smile, she eased open the door to find Giddeon and Noah peering questioningly at her.

"I wonder if I might have a bath," she requested hopefully. Her gaze dropped to the planked floor. "Kane refused to leave the room last night so I had no opportunity to bathe. And there seems very little else to do here. It is bad enough that I've been confined to my quarters until I don't know when . . ."

Her voice trailed off before she went into a speech designed to milk sympathy. Darcey doubted she was very convincing since she had never relied on such tactics to get her way before. But to her surprise the technique worked.

When both men bounded to their feet to comply with her request, their chairs scraped across the floor. While Giddeon stoked the fire in the stove and retrieved several pots to boil water, Noah scampered outside to fetch the buckets. In less than fifteen minutes, warm water was being carted into the tub. Both men were so eager to please her that they forgot she was supposed to be kept under constant surveillance during Kane's absence.

When Darcey volunteered to pour more water into the pot on the stove, Giddeon nodded agreeably without suspecting her true motive. While both men were in her bedroom, testing the water temperature, Darcey sprang into action. Like a shot, she dashed out the front door. Retrieving the rope from her pocket, she hooked the looped end of braid over the door latch and then secured the other end to the supporting post of the cabin, barring the exit. As she raced toward the horses she heard surprised yelps erupting inside the shack. The frantic men wrestled with the door, quickly abandoned their attempt, and then set about to pry open a window. But by that time, Darcey was sitting astride one steed and had scattered the other horses in all directions.

It was her intention to wind her way down the steep slopes until she reached the stage route. Then she would follow the path back to Denver. As she maneuvered between the boulders she could hear Giddeon and Noah calling out to her, warning her to return for her own safety. But Darcey wasn't about to reverse direction. She wasn't going to be around when Kane came back, not for all the gold in Pike's Peak! She was going to the express office and put it under solid management. Then she was hightailing it back to St. Louis to place herself as far away from Kane Callahan as she could get!

With that determined thought buzzing in her mind, Darcey dismounted to lead her horse over the treacherous trail that zigzagged down the mountain.

When she reached the winding road, she bounded onto his back once again and thundered off, holding on for dear life. She had never claimed to be a skilled equestrian and it showed. Without the pommel of a saddle upon which to anchor herself, Darcey was forced to hug the horse and flatten her body against his. And with any luck at all, the afternoon stage would roll by and she could hitch a ride, O'Roarke Express-style. Since she was the one who set the schedules, she knew the coach would be along within the next two hours.

By nightfall, she would be bedded down in one of the stage stations and by the following day she would return to Denver. Her first order of business would be to direct a posse to Kane's hideout. And wouldn't he be surprised when he returned from his latest robbery to find Deputy Metcalf waiting to greet him. Justice at last, Darcey thought spitefully. Scapegoat indeed! She would never be any man's scapegoat, or his object of pleasure ever again as long as she lived. She was going to fall out of love with that thieving rakehell. From this day forward he would mean nothing to her, nothing whatsoever. He was a closed chapter in her past, a painful reminder of how deceitful and treacherous men could be.

This time, she was really swearing off men for good!

A gloomy stare glazed Giddeon's eyes as he grasped the lead rope to the horse he had been chasing on foot. Gasping for breath, he glanced northward to see that Noah had finally tracked down his runaway horse. Grumbling over the fact that he had committed the

300

unpardonable sin of taking Darcey for granted after Kane had cautioned him not to, Giddeon trudged toward Noah.

Giddeon was outraged with Kane. But at the moment, he was none too happy with Darcey, either. She could get herself lost, or wounded or killed in these perilous mountains. That woman was definitely long on determination and short on sense. How the devil did she think she could survive out here alone?

"Kane will kill us, sure as hell," Noah predicted as he paced toward Giddeon. "Damn it, I had planned to be sympathetic toward Darcey, but I didn't expect her to take advantage of us!"

Giddeon stared off at some distant point and sighed audibly. "It seems Kane knew the lady better than we thought. We gave her an inch and she repaid us by taking the full mile."

"Well, there is only one thing to do," Noah announced with a decisive nod. "We'll have to chase her down and hope we can tow her back here before Kane returns to bite off our heads for being incompetent." He swung onto his horse and muttered under his breath for several frustrating moments. "I wish I'd waited until another assignment came along before I begged Kane to teach me this business."

"I wish you had, too," Giddeon grumbled bitterly. "But this ordeal has taught me one thing. I'm not cut out for this kind of life. I do much better in a predictable environment. I only hope I live long enough to return to civilization where I belong."

"I wouldn't count on it," Noah said grimly. "If we don't apprehend Darcey, and quickly, Kane will bury us up here in this pile of rocks!"

Grappling with that depressing thought, Noah and Giddeon trotted along the cliff, trying to locate the path Darcey had taken. They had to overtake that daredevil before she managed to kill herself and leave them to face Kane's wrath.

Chapter 18

Kane had searched the stage route for hours on end, trying to outguess his quarry. Knowing the lone bandit's robbery attempt had been thwarted the previous day, he wondered if the thief would do the exact opposite of what one might expect. Instead of lying low for a few days and thanking his lucky stars he'd escaped, the thief might strike somewere in the same vicinity on a stage that had yet to be informed of the previous holdup attempt.

After surveying the rough terrain, Kane found three steep inclines which would slow the team of horses to a walk when pulling a heavy load. All three sites would make perfect locations for holdups because of the clump of bushes on either side of the path. One location in particular seemed most advantageous. From the ridge above, a bandit could monitor the stagecoach's approach for almost a mile. In the other two areas, huge chunks of protruding rock and scraggly trees blocked the view of the road below. If Kane was going to rob a stage, this was the site he would have selected.

Lying in wait, Kane had munched on the beef jerky he'd brought along for his meal. And sure enough, late in the afternoon, he heard the clomp of a mule. From his concealed position in a canopy of aspens and cedars, Kane watched the man in black pause atop the lookout point and check his timepiece.

Kane couldn't get a positive identification of the man in the long black linen duster. His hat was pulled low on his forehead and a mask covered his face. It was also difficult to get a good description of his size and stature because the full length coat concealed his form. But Kane was certain this was the same man who had attempted to halt the stage a day earlier . . .

Something unexpected happened while Kane was lost in thought. The thief shrank away from the precipice and ducked into the underbrush. The pounding of hooves echoed along the steep grade of the road and Kane was quick to realize that a single rider was beating a hasty path toward Denver. Cautiously, he pulled his feet under him to survey the road.

"Damnation," he hissed furiously. "How in the hell? Darcey?" His voice evaporated into sour expletives. He might have known Noah and Giddeon couldn't keep close tabs on that hellion without resorting to nailing her feet to the floor. This was the very last time he ever brought those two incompetent dolts along with him. They would have been more assistance to him if they had stayed home. They both had turned out to be more trouble than they were worth.

Muttering sourly, Kane sank down to hastily review

his choices. With Darcey on the loose, he didn't have time to wait around to catch the thief in the act, not without letting that terror in green calico escape him. If she returned to Denver, the deputy would guard her like a dragon and Darcey would inform the whole damned town that Kane was a member of Griz Vanhook's brigands. That would never do!

Kane had allowed this lone bandit to escape earlier because Darcey was riding with him. But Kane refused to waste precious time tracking this scoundrel again.

Still scowling at Darcey's appearance, Kane weaved around the bolders until he spied the bandit scrunched down in the scrub brush. With the silence of a stalking jungle cat, Kane pounced. He made a spectacular leap through the air, knocking the bandit off balance. The highwayman never knew what hit him until two hundred fifteen pounds of solid muscle flew down at him. Although the thief was squashed flat, his will to survive gave him additional strength. In wild desperation, the bandit scrabbled with his hands and feet to crawl away from his assailant. The instant he shook himself loose, he dashed toward his waiting mule. The highwayman had just stuffed one foot in the stirrup and was in the process of swinging into the saddle when Kane clamped one hand on the nape of the black linen duster. With his free hand, Kane clutched his Colt by the barrel, using it to whallop the bandit over the head.

Kane cursed fluently when his unconscious victim toppled backward from his mule. Before Kane could remove himself, the bandit collapsed on top of him, knocking him off balance. They both wound up on the ground—Kane on the bottom with dead weight sprawled atop him. Muttering at the inconvenient delay, Kane heaved the bandit away and bolted to his feet.

Quick as a wink, Kane lashed the man's wrists behind him and dragged his victim's limp body over to the nearest tree. When Kane rolled the highwayman over and removed the mask, a muddled frown puckered his brow. The face looked vaguely familiar, but he couldn't place it. He couldn't recall meeting this man during his stay in Denver, but yet there was something . . .

Kane shook off his puzzled thoughts and jogged toward his horse. He didn't have time to figure out who the bandit was. If he didn't chase Darcey down she would be halfway to Denver before he caught up with her. And if the stage whizzed by on time and she piled into it, he'd have to hold up the damned coach to retrieve her.

Honest to God, that woman was worth her weight in trouble. She would have his name blabbed from one end of the stage line to the other before he could shut her up. Then what would he do? Take the whole stage company and all its passengers hostage? And what the hell good would that do?

Cursing fifty words a minute, Kane put his mount through tedious obstacle maneuvers to cut Darcey off at the pass. He had to find some way to get ahead of her, to chop the distance between them in half. She was on open road and he was picking his way through a maze of boulders and trees.

Frantically, Kane glanced around, searching for a hasty solution. He had been up and down this rugged terrain several times the past few hours. Somewhere there had to be a site that he could use to his advantage. And if he hadn't used his lariat to stake his robbery suspect to the tree, he would have considered lassoing that auburn-haired witch and anchoring *her* to the nearest boulder!

He had to think of something and he'd better think fast. The coach was approaching from the northwest. Just his luck that it was right on time. Curse it, the only luck he seemed to have lately was the luck he made on his own. Fate certainly seemed to be plotting against him!

Unaware that potential danger lurked on the ridge above her, Darcey raced along the weaving path, awaiting the coach. She was positively certain her fingers would remain forever frozen in a clenched position. She was clinging to the horse's mane for dear life and her body was clamped on the galloping steed in a vise grip.

Just as she swerved around a sharp bend in the road, a shower of dirt and rocks pelted her. The dancing stones startled the horse, already apprehensive about the rider who kept sliding from one side to the other in an effort to maintain her position. When an oversize boulder bounced off the stone wall of the mountain and landed with a thud five feet in front of him, the chestnut gelding reared in fright and spun around to lunge off in the direction he'd come.

The instant the horse braced on its hind legs and reared to spin about in midair, Darcey was yanked loose. The horse's whirling momentum sent her flying sideways, jerking her fingers from the mane. Darcey hit the ground with a bone-jarring groan. Her clenched fists held several strands of horse hair, but her mount raced off in a cloud of dust.

Intense pain throbbed in her hip as she clutched at her hampering skirts and wobbled onto her knees. Darcey hadn't even maneuvered her feet beneath her before another avalanche of debris rolled over her. Blinded by dirt, Darcey groped to steady herself against the craggy face of the mountain. But instead of bracing on solid rock, her hand collided with the hard wall of a man's chest. Gasping in surprise, Darcey stumbled back and wiped her eyes in an attempt to clear her vision.

"Goin' somewhere, darlin'?" Kane drawled in mock amusement.

"Damn, you're everywhere!" Darcey hissed before wheeling around to make a mad dash in every direction at once.

She hadn't taken two steps before Kane snaked out a hand to shackle her wrists. With a back-wrenching jolt he snatched her under his arm and strode toward the protective rim of boulders that formed a ridge ten feet above the road.

The jingle of harnesses and the clatter of hooves heralded the approach of the afternoon stage, which Darcey had hoped to catch. Before she could send up a shout of alarm, Kane shoved her behind an oversize boulder and squished her flat. Darcey couldn't have screamed if she'd wanted to. Kane had successfully managed to force every ounce of air from her lungs when he plunked down on top of her. When Darcey opened her mouth, only a weak chirp erupted.

Darcey sucked in a scant breath and tried again. This time Kane pushed her face down until she swore her nose had become an indentation rather than a protrusion on her face. Outraged fury pulsated through her veins. She bucked and writhed, but still she couldn't unseat the brawny giant who straddled her hips and kept her plastered to the ground.

Frustrated to no end, Darcey listened to the coach rumble on its way, leaving her alone with the last man she ever wanted to see. Confound it, what did it take to shake this scoundrel off her trail? He seemed to show up at the most unexpected moments. Kane would have made a sensational lawman, Darcey decided. He had a natural instinct that enabled him to be in the right place at the right time. If she hadn't known better, she would have sworn Kane had read her mind and knew just where she'd be when he went looking for her.

When the coast was clear, Kane jerked Darcey up by the sleeve of her gown and dragged her along with his swift impatient strides. "Come on, there's someone I want you to meet," he growled unpleasantly.

Darcey was baffled by his remark, to say the least. She had expected him to curse her for escaping, but he dispensed with the lecture and herded her up the slope where his steed waited.

The horse didn't seem all that thrilled to see Kane again, either, and with good reason. Kane had taken his mount through rigorous paces in his desperate effort to reach the peak before Darcey veered around the bend. The winded gelding had barely recovered his breath in the high altitudes before Kane showed up to pile extra baggage on his back.

"Hold still, damn it," Kane snapped when Darcey wormed and squirmed in front of him in the saddle. "My horse is having enough trouble maneuvering around these rocks with the additional weight without you throwing him off balance."

"Fine," Darcey muttered resentfully. "Give what little consideration you possess to your blessed horse. Don't worry one tittle about me. I just had ten years scared off my life when I thought I was about to be buried under a rockslide. But before that could happen I was catapulted into the middle of the road."

"I'm sorry about that," Kane apologized.

"Aren't you just!" Darcey sputtered. "If you think my father is going to pay his full price for bruised and broken merchandise, you'd better think again. And I've had just about enough of your rough treatment. You nearly got me killed!"

"I said I was sorry," Kane grumbled, trying to clamp down on his temper and failing miserably.

"Sorry doesn't raise the dead!" Darcey yelled at him.

"For God's sake, you're still alive, aren't you?" Kane growled irritably.

"No thanks to you," she spat at him.

The militant tilt of her chin and the hostility in her voice provoked Kane's muddled frown. He knew Darcey was in a snit because he'd recaptured her. But there was something about the venomous glares she flung over her shoulder at him that suggested more than her customary burst of temper. Kane knew

Darcey was regretting their night of passion. Indeed, he had already anticipated her defensive reaction, but he hadn't expected to be the recipient of glares that were hot enough to melt the mountains.

"What's really bothering you?" he wanted to know that very second.

"What's bothering me?" Darcey parroted furiously.

"That was the question," Kane growled back at her. "Now answer it!"

"I hate you. That's what's the matter," she exploded.

"Give me some new information," Kane scoffed. "When didn't you hate me?"

Last night I didn't hate him at all. I loved him, Darcey thought with a sharp pang of remorse. Last night she had realized she had fallen in love with him and he had bruised her heart blue and black. His scapegoat, was she? His object of lust? He was the cruelest, most insensitive snake ever to slither across this earth!

"Who is this mysterious person you want me to meet?" Darcey demanded, quickly changing the subject.

"I was hoping you could tell me," Kane mumbled.

"I have a thing or three I'd like to tell you," Darcey spewed insultingly. "You are the most horrible man I've ever met, for one. And secondly, I do not appreciate being—"

Kane cut her off with a harsh growl. "It's bad enough that you always try to have the last word, but must you be so long-winded about it?"

Darcey puffed up with indignation. "I hardly ever

get the last word with you and you know it."

"Oh, no? You're trying to get it now, aren't you?" he smirked.

"It seems hollow solace, in light of everything you've put me through," she spouted self-righteously.

"Fine, have the last word if that's what it takes to make you happy," Kane conceded in a sarcastic tone.

"Thank you."

Small gratification indeed, thought she. A lot of good having the last word would do her broken heart. It didn't heal the wounds of knowing she counted for nothing with Kane. But she would take a dagger through the chest before she let this blackguard know she'd fallen in love with him, despite all the torment he'd forced her to endure. And why she cared for him, only God knew. Darcey certainly couldn't figure it out!

Darcey sniffed caustically when she spied the bandit who lay facedown, his arms staked to the base of a tree. "It seems there is no code of ethics among thieves," she declared as Kane hoisted her out of the saddle. "What happened? Did this highwayman cut into your profit so severely that you decided to put him out of commission?"

There were times, like now, that Kane would have liked to strangle this sassy spitfire. He had done the O'Roarke Express Company—and her—a favor, but as cynical as Darcey was, she refused to realize it.

"Unless I miss my guess, and I doubt that I have," he said with a sigh, "this is the Courtly Highwayman, gentleman bandit who has been robbing stages and

312

leaving his thank-you notes to infuriate you."

Darcey shoved her bitter thoughts aside and stared down at the unidentified stranger. When Kane ambled over to push the man to his back, Darcey gasped in disbelief.

"Mr. Alridge! What in heaven's name are you doing here?" she croaked.

"Alridge?" Kane's bewildered gaze bounced from Darcey to the scowling thief. Suddenly, he realized why this bandit seemed familiar. "Is this Lester Alridge's older brother?" he questioned, astounded.

"None other," Darcey confirmed.

In swift strides, Kane approached the mule Peter Alridge had been riding. After a thorough search of the saddlebags, Kane located a discarded pouch and a note written with the flourished strokes of a pen.

"Let me see that," Darcey insisted as she snatched the message away to read its contents. Sure enough, it was the same elegant handwriting and taunting reminder she received each time the bandit held up a stage and left his ridiculing note behind.

Darcey peered down at their captive. "Is your brother in this with you, Peter?" she wanted to know.

Peter Alridge glanced the other way and clamped his mouth shut like a crocodile.

"Well, answer me!" Darcey demanded as she planted herself firmly between Peter and the distant point at which he was staring. "Is Lester informing you of stage schedules and revisions or isn't he?"

"I wish to consult my lawyer," Peter replied.

"You *are* a lawyer. Or at least that is what you have pretended to be," Darcey snapped at him. "I hope you have something to say in your own defense or I'll—"

"He's a lawyer?" Kane croaked. His gaze drifted over the bandit's scarecrowlike frame, wondering why Peter had taken to robbing the express company where Lester worked. The family ties between them didn't bode well for Lester.

"The shingle that hangs outside his clapboard office says Peter is a lawyer, but he hasn't been doing much business," Darcey reported. "And it's little wonder that he hasn't been. How can he uphold the law while he's out here breaking it?"

"I have nothing to say," Peter declared in a belligerent tone.

Like a pouncing lion, Kane jerked Peter to his feet and shook him until his teeth very nearly fell out. Still Peter was as tightlipped as a clam. With a menacing growl, Kane slammed the smaller man against the tree bark, causing him to groan in agony.

Still, nothing but moans and muffled curses tumbled from Peter's lips.

Kane then resorted to his more persuasive tactics of investigation. He didn't want to have to become so forceful, with Darcey as witness. But since she thought so little of him anyway, Kane doubted his drastic methods of eliciting information would shock her. She thought he was a no-account outlaw already.

The blow Kane delivered to Peter's soft underbelly worked effectively. Peter howled in pain and blurted out his confession.

"Robbing stages was my idea," he squeaked on what was left of the breath Kane hadn't succeeded in hammering out of him. "I received information from

314

Lester each time you changed the schedules."

Darcey slumped in disappointment. She had hoped Lester was free from any wrongdoing. He was such a meek, mild little man who had seemed to accommodate and cooperate since she took control of the agency. But, from the sound of things, Lester was as guilty as his brother. No doubt he was also the one who was embezzling money from the accounts. No wonder Darcey couldn't get the books to balance!

The clatter of hooves dragged Darcey from her reverie. She wheeled around to see Noah and Giddeon galloping toward them. The glare Kane flung at the approaching men testified to the full extent of his irritation with them. Aware of his distraction, Darcey took her cue and dashed toward Kane's horse. This was her last chance to make her escape and she was taking it!

Like a bat out of hell, Darcey bounded onto the gelding and dug her heels into its flanks. Before Kane could stop her, she raced along the slope and on to freedom. Kane had two choices. He could straddle Peter's mule to give chase or he could wait until his brother and their servant reached him so he could confiscate one of their horses. Desperation and impatience prompted Kane's split-second decision.

Kane leaped onto the mule in a single bound, reining the reluctant creature in the direction Darcey had taken. But the mule was no match for the sturdy steed Kane had purchased in Denver. Neither did the mule possess a pleasant disposition, living up to every expectation of his breed. Contrariness was an inborn trait, Kane concluded halfway across the valley that led down to open road. The mule's one speed was a bone-jolting trot. Kane swore furiously when, after yelling and kicking the ornery creature to switch speeds, the animal refused to stir another step. By that time Kane was good and mad. Darcey had reached the road and sailed off like a flying carpet.

With another flurry of ear-scorching curses, Kane swung to the ground, stuck his face in the mule's, and chewed the stubborn animal up one side and down the other. It did no good whatsoever.

While Kane was getting nowhere with the mule, Noah and Giddeon trotted down the slope with the captured bandit in tow. Neither Noah nor Giddeon was anticipating Kane's reception. He was already giving the mule hell; they shuddered to speculate on what Kane was going to say to them. And sure enough, it was every bit as bad as they expected.

"This is all your fault," Kane exploded. "I asked one simple request of the two of you and you couldn't even manage that! Now Darcey is on her way back to Denver to tell the whole damned town who—"

Kane clamped his mouth shut so quickly that he very nearly bit off his tongue. In his fit of temper, he had almost divulged information the gentleman bandit didn't need to hear.

"Gimme your horse, Noah," Kane demanded impatiently.

Noah couldn't swing from the saddle quickly enough to satisfy his frustrated brother. Kane reached up and jerked Noah off his perch and left him stumbling to regain his balance.

"The two of you bring our captive along. I'll meet

you on the west side of town. And don't either of you bungling morons come sashaying into town until I come to get you!" Kane ordered before he wheeled the horse around to race off in the direction Darcey had taken.

With a muted growl, Kane thundered through the valley and charged down the road. He wasn't sure what in the hell he was going to do if Darcey reached town before he could overtake her. Although he had telegraphed Patrick O'Roarke before the kidnapping to save time, Kane didn't expect his client to arrive for another few days. Damn, Darcey would whiz into Denver like a cyclone and spoil everything. Hell, she'd have every able-bodied man in town rounded up to form a posse before he got hold of her. Kane would find himself lynched before Patrick arrived to explain the situation. And Patrick would be in one helluva spot himself. Patrick would have to expose his part in this unfortunate escapade and Darcey would never forgive her father. At the moment, Kane didn't want to be either of them—Patrick or himself. That auburn-haired terror would hold this incident over both their heads for the rest of their natural lives!

Chapter 19

For once, good fortune seemed to be riding on Darcey's side. She managed to stay a few steps ahead of her pursuer without being recaptured. Knowing Kane was following in her shadow, Darcey rode all through the night in her eagerness to reach Denver.

It was her intention to confront Lester Alridge with what she had learned. She didn't want to believe Lester had undermined the workings of the agency by conspiring with his worthless brother to steal gold shipments. But under duress, Peter had blurted out the incriminating confession.

Darcey's second dilemma was nearer and more painful to the heart—Kane Callahan. His name whispered through her mind. A complex image formed, frustrating her. She loved him; she hated him. She didn't understand him! He had tormented her out of pure orneriness and then he made love to her as if she meant all the world to him. He had stolen the pouches of gold and held her for ransom. Then he had captured the other bandit who preyed on the stage. Why had he done that? *To appease my curiosity and stifle his own competition,* she reckoned. But only the Lord knew what had really been on Kane Callahan's mind. Darcey certainly didn't!

If she had a grain of sense she would spare Kane not the slightest consideration. Yet, her heart warred with her sense of integrity. That infuriating man constantly put her in a mental wrestling match, pitting sentiment against sensibility. Kane deserved to be behind bars or swinging from the Cherry Creek bridge where known criminals were hanged in front of lynch mobs. And yet Darcey couldn't quite bring herself to condemn that midnight-haired devil to his well-deserved fate.

Curse it, she should have been totally objective where Kane was concerned. His skillful seduction was clearly a ploy to gain her loyalty. He wanted her to fall in love with him. In the event that he got caught for robbery and kidnapping he could rely on her affection to save his neck. Well, she would testify against him in the people's court, which convened when solid cases against offenders could be presented . . . Or at least she *should* testify. It was definitely against the law to have Kane Callahan running around loose. He was a menace to women in general and to the O'Roarke Express Company in particular!

Darcey sighed and peered into the distance to see the buildings of Denver silhouetted against the morning sunlight. Just what *was* she going to say when Pup Metcalf asked her for a description of the man who had abducted her? Why was her decision so tormentingly difficult? She knew exactly what she should say and do, so why was she battling this frustrating tug of war of emotions?

Because you love that scoundrel, you ninny! Darcey cursed herself for carrying a torch for a man who had plied her with empty confessions of love and used her as a scapegoat to compensate for his own painful wounds of the heart. Melanie Brooks, wherever she was, deserved a medal for breaking Kane's heart. At least one female on the planet had been able to accomplish that remarkable feat. Darcey's only consolation was that Kane didn't know she felt betrayed and broken-hearted. It was meager consolation, to be sure, but it was all Darcey had.

Flinging her glum thoughts aside, Darcey circled around Denver to make her discreet entry into the express office. She wanted to confront Lester before the entire town knew she had returned.

Darcey knew she was procrastinating. She was unsure about what to tell Pup Metcalf. But sooner or later she would have to decide what was to be done about Kane. Damn the man for forcing her to choose between her ill-founded affection for him and her sense of honor.

"Miss O'Roarke! You're back. Thank God you're all right!" Lester choked out when he saw the disheveled beauty breeze through the back door of the agency.

Darcey stopped short when her assessing gaze circled the office to find it just as she had left it—clean, organized, and running like a well-oiled machine. She blinked, surprised to see the meek, mild-mannered man who had an aversion to dealing with customers. Lester seemed to possess a newfound confidence. Was this the same self-conscious little man who had conspired with his brother to commit robbery against the stage company?

Before Darcey could answer that puzzling question to her satisfaction, the swarm of customers closed in around her to fire a barrage of questions about her captivity. Darcey fielded their questions, assuring them that she was in splendid condition, considering her exhausting ordeal. She thanked them kindly for their concern and offered very little in the way of specific details.

Her attention focused on Lester, who was stacking the ledgers in alphabetical order and placing equipment back in its proper place . . . just as she would have done! Curse it, how was she to condemn the very man who had stepped in to fill her shoes during her absence? And where the devil was Owen Graves? Probably in the back room, doing what he did best—little of nothing.

The commotion in the outer office drew the attention of the two men who were closeted in one of the back rooms. Darcey glanced over her shoulder to see Owen Graves swaggering down the hall. The look on his face suggested disappointment rather than relief to see she had returned unharmed. No doubt, Owen had been enjoying the fact that Darcey hadn't been looking over his shoulder, trying to train him to become an efficient manager.

When the man behind Owen stepped around the corner, Darcey gasped in disbelief. Patrick O'Roarke seemed to be as shocked to see her as she was to see him. Instinctively Darcey ran into her father's outstretched arms to give him an affectionate squeeze, which he zealously returned.

"What are you doing here?" Father and daughter questioned in unison.

"I thought you had been kidnapped!" Patrick gasped.

"I was, but I escaped," Darcey informed him and then frowned bemusedly. "How did you get here so quickly?"

Patrick's mind raced in an attempt to supply a believable answer. He had known from the very beginning that his master detective would have to resort to kidnapping in order to rout Darcey from Denver. He had given Kane a week to realize he had no other alternative. Then Patrick began his trek westward from St. Louis.

"I was on my way through Kansas to visit you when a letter passed through the Leavenworth office with my name on it," Patrick answered, pleased with himself for conjuring up the explanation.

Darcey watched her father shift nervously beneath her scrutinizing stare. "Leavenworth is several hundred miles away," she pointed out.

"We own the stage company, for heaven's sake," Patrick snorted. "I pulled all the right strings to get myself a private coach and fresh teams at every relay station."

Patrick breathed a discreet sigh of relief when Darcey finally nodded acceptance of his explanation. But damn it, now that Darcey was back, having escaped Kane . . . And how had she managed that? Wasn't there one man on the planet who could control this feisty daughter of his? Patrick was beginning to doubt it.

While Patrick speculated on how Darcey had fled her captor, she pivoted to stare solemnly at Lester Alridge. "Lester, I would like a few words with you. Owen can tend to the customers while we have a private chat."

After casting Darcey an annoyed glance, Owen manned the counter. He detested being told what to do, especially by a woman—by this woman in particular. When Lester had rattled off a few instructions to Owen, his pride took another beating—right in front of the owner of the express agency. Swearing under his breath, Owen assumed his task. For a man who had once been the manager of the office, he suddenly found himself at the bottom of the totem pole, a position that put another dent in his pride.

Darcey paced down the hall in measured strides. After seating herself beside her father, she gestured for Lester to plant himself in the vacant chair. Inhaling a deep breath, Darcey formulated her thoughts.

"I'm grateful to you for keeping the agency running smoothly in my absence," she began.

"Thank you," Lester murmured modestly. "I did what I thought you would have wanted me to do."

"We seem to have a hero in our midst," Patrick inserted. He flashed Lester a pleased smile before glancing at Darcey. "According to reports, Lester saved you from the first wave of disaster and saved our company and the town from its worst menace. Lester has made quite a name for himself in Denver."

And that made it all the more difficult for Darcey to

say what she had to say. "While I was in the mountains, I happened on to the bandit who has been preying on our stage."

Lester slouched in his chair, looking in every direction except at Darcey.

"You captured him?" Patrick was incredulous. "How ever did you manage that?"

"I'll explain later," Darcey replied, waving the question away to cut to the heart of the matter. "The problem is that the gentleman bandit, who always seemed to know I had jostled the schedules to throw him off track, is Lester's older brother."

The news hit Patrick like a sledgehammer. Wide green eyes—ones that were the same vivid shade as his daughter's—drilled into the man, who sank a little deeper in his chair. "What?"

Lester sighed miserably and stared at his lap. "I'm ashamed to admit that it's true. When Peter first began quizzing me about my duties at the office and our schedule, I thought he was only showing an interest in my work." He raked his bony hand through his hair and let it droop loosely back to his lap. "It didn't dawn on me until Darcey arrived to juggle schedules that Peter was using me to gain vital information about gold shipments."

"Why didn't you come forward and tell me of your suspicions?" Darcey questioned point-blank.

Slowly, Lester elevated his dismal gaze to meet Darcey's inquisitive eyes. "Because, despite everything else, Peter is my brother. I have always tried to repay him as best I could, since he took care of me when we were orphaned at a tender age. But Peter always seemed to hold a grudge against the world and expected something for nothing."

Lester expelled a deflated sigh. "My brother is a con artist. He has roamed from town to town, pretending to be someone he's not, hanging a shingle outside his office. He has claimed to do one sort of skilled work or another. Once the townfolk figured out he was a charlatan looking for quick money, they ran him out of town. He's sold land which doesn't even exist to gullible speculators. He's passed himself off as a barber, a dentist, and once even a doctor until he was asked to perform surgery that he knew nothing about. At least his conscience bade him to hotfoot it out of town before he killed somebody with his deceptive charade."

"You must have known Peter was up to something when he arrived in Denver, claiming to be a lawyer," Darcey declared, fighting back the sympathy she was beginning to feel for Lester.

Lester nodded bleakly. "I knew Peter was up to no good. I just didn't realize what it was until it was too late. The saddest part of all is that Peter could have been anything he aspired to be. He was a bright, imaginative child who always made sure we got by when times were hard. But he never had the patience to follow through to certify himself for anything. I'm deeply sorry I didn't turn him in," he finished regretfully.

Dragging his feet beneath him, Lester stood up. "I'm awfully glad you have returned unscathed, Miss O'Roarke. I will hand myself over to Deputy Metcalf. I have been saving every spare penny of my salary, hoping to repay the company for Peter's thieving. It's all here in the office. I just haven't been able to figure out a way to enter it into the books without drawing your suspicion."

"Sit down, Lester," Patrick boomed in the gruff voice he employed when he wanted control of the conversation. It always worked well on everyone except Darcey, who was immune to it.

Meekly, Lester plunked down in his chair.

"There is another matter I need to discuss with you, Lester," Darcey insisted before her father leaped into the discussion. "According to my calculations, no money has been added to the accounts, only *embezzled* from them."

"Embezzled?" Lester croaked.

"Embezzled?" Patrick howled in repetition. "Good Lord, this agency is in worse shape than I thought!"

"You think I have been swindling the company out of funds while my brother . . . ?" Lester looked hurt and disappointed. "I assure you, Miss O'Roarke, I would not . . . have not!"

"Then who the devil has?" Patrick mused, then clamped his mouth shut when he heard the clatter of footsteps down the hall.

All three occupants of the room bounded to their feet to ascertain who had been eavesdropping. Darcey darted out the door to see Owen Graves skidding around the corner to zoom out the back exit as if pursued by demons. She should have known that weasel was responsible for swindling the funds. Owen also suffered from the disease of wanting something for nothing. Peter should have been Owen's brother. They were a matched pair!

"Stop that man!" Darcey yelped as she surged through the office. But the customers had come and gone and so had Owen.

By the time Darcey whizzed into the alley to glance in every direction at once, she could see hide nor hair of that swindling dandy. Obviously Owen had tiptoed back to the office to eavesdrop on the conversation. Having realized he'd been found out, he made his escape before Darcey had him bound over for trial.

"I'll have an all-points bulletin sent out to every relay station and agency on the route," Patrick vowed. "I sat there for an hour and listened to that blowhard boast about how he gave *you* a few tips on managing the agency, how he had trained Lester to assume the tasks he had allowed *you* to undertake while you were here. That deceitful scamp! He's nothing but an arrogant windbag!"

"Amen to that," Darcey sniffed disgustedly. "Why you put that cocky oaf in charge in the first place was a wonder to me."

"He talks a good story," Patrick grumbled in defense. "Obviously he boasts much better than he works."

When Darcey tried to bound off, Patrick grabbed her by the arm and towed her back inside. "I'll hire a detective to hunt Owen Graves down. I happen to know one of the best in the country. And you, young lady, have endured one ordeal already." How Darcey had eluded Kane was a question that was tormenting Patrick, but he was in no position to ask his daughter about Kane without exposing his part in the scheme.

328

And if she ever found out the truth, she would never let him live it down!

"We have to make a decision about Lester," Patrick insisted as he closed the office door for a private conference.

Lester hung his head in a posture of defeat and abject regret. "I expect no consideration, Mr. O'Roarke. I should have come forward to declare my suspicions about Peter. I am prepared to give myself up and pay my penance."

Darcey stared at the frail man who stood with head downcast and an expression of sincere apology stamped on his face. She, of all people, knew the difficulty Patrick faced when confronted with the frustrating decision about whether to follow sentiment or a sense of integrity. Darcey had wrestled with the same dilemma in terms of divulging Kane's name as her abductor. How could she condemn Lester when she still had found no solution to her difficult situation?

After her tormenting ordeal, Darcey had acquired a generous fund of sympathetic sentiment. She now found herself compassionate toward those who experienced similar soul-wrenching decisions. She simply couldn't condemn Lester because she knew exactly how he felt. Peter was all the family Lester had in the world and he couldn't forsake his brother despite his criminal offenses.

"I can't fire him," Darcey said finally. "You'll have to do it, if you want it done, Papa. But it seems to me that Lester has redeemed himself to the company during my absence. He could have allowed the agency to fall into ruin. Instead, he assumed command. My conscience will not allow me to press charges against Lester for what Peter did. Considering the perplexing circumstances, I'm not sure I would have handled the situation any differently."

Patrick exhaled a long sigh. "You realize, of course, Lester, that I will have to press charges against your brother. I also expect you to help me recover the lost money if at all possible."

Lester nodded somberly. "I understand, sir. And I'm sure most of the money Peter stole is hidden somewhere nearby. He's obviously been too busy planning his robberies and covering his tracks to spend his loot. Only last week he mentioned plans of moving to California at the end of the month, just to see what the state had to offer. The truth is, I was relieved to hear he was considering leaving. But the fact remains that I was guilty of withholding information from you. I expect to receive my just punishment for that."

"You would have me lock up the hero of the city?" Patrick snorted. "Can you imagine what that would do to my business? Why, the townspeople would refuse to set foot in this office. That would never do!"

The faintest hint of a smile found its way to Lester's turned-down mouth. "I'm no hero, you know. That night, when I confronted Griz Vanhook, I was sure I was staring certain death in the face. But I couldn't back away without trying to save Miss O'Roarke."

"Then it's settled," Darcey interjected. "Lester is still in charge of the agency and this whole dreadful affair is behind us. Your brother will be bound over to the law officials in Missouri to save you the embarrassment in Denver."

"Just where the devil is Peter now?" Patrick inquired with a muddled frown.

Darcey glanced the other way, wondering how she was going to explain that Kane had taken Peter captive. Curse it, she felt as handcuffed as Lester did!

Darcey brushed her wild mane of auburn hair away from her face and glanced pleadingly at her father. "Let's fret over Peter later. I've had a most exhausting night, with no sleep. I would like to lie down."

Leaving Lester in command of the office, Patrick ushered Darcey down the street to her hotel. They had just veered around the corner onto Cherry Street when Deputy Metcalf, having heard the news of Darcey's return, came upon the scene.

"Miss O'Roarke, thank the Lord!" Pup breathed delightedly. "I've searched high and low for you the past few days, but I couldn't find your trail. What happened? Who kidnapped you?"

Darcey had been dreading that question. Now that it had been posed, she still couldn't bring herself to respond honestly to it. Blast it, what a foolish sentimentalist she had turned out to be.

"My daughter has been through hell the past few days," Patrick insisted as he pushed past the well-meaning deputy. "She needs to rest and recuperate. I suggest we wait until later before we interrogate her about her ordeal."

"But—" That was all Pup was allowed to say before Patrick whisked Darcey away.

A bemused frown knitted Darcey's brow. She glanced curiously at her father as he marched her down the boardwalk, zigzagging around passersby. Knowing

331

what a penchant Patrick had for seeing to all business matters quickly and efficiently, it surprised her that he had shrugged the deputy off.

Although Patrick seemed concerned about her, he wasn't as vindictive as she thought he'd be about hunting down her abductor. And now that she thought about it, wasn't it an odd coincidence that the ransom note found its way into Patrick's hands en route? True, Patrick always possessed the luck of the Irish, but Darcey had the feeling that something was amiss. She had expected Patrick to say "I told you so" after she had deputized herself to solve the problems in the Denver office and wound up kidnapped. He hadn't wanted her to come and yet he'd bypassed the chance to scold her. She knew her father better than anyone alive. He wasn't reacting as she had predicted.

"Now you just rest and I'll take care of everything," Patrick declared with a wave of his hands that seemed to magically resolve all problems. He steered Darcey into her room and enveloped her in his arms. "I'm thankful you returned safe and sound. And once I have interviewed several people to determine who is most capable of filling Owen's position and hire a replacement, we're going back to St. Louis. I have a company meeting next week and our investors will be relieved to hear you have put this floundering office back on its feet."

After planting a kiss on Darcey's smudged cheek, Patrick breezed toward the door. "I'll have the clerk send up water for your bath. Tonight we'll have a quiet dinner in your room and forget this unfortunate incident happened."

When the door clinked shut behind Patrick, Darcey stared at her father's lingering image. No siree, Patrick O'Roarke was *not* behaving the way she anticipated. In fact, he seemed in an all-fired rush to deposit her in her room and be on his way.

Mulling over Patrick's peculiar behavior, Darcey plunked down on the edge of her bed to await her bath. She had intended to curl up on her feather mattress and sleep the rest of the day away. But considering her father's early arrival and his mysterious handling of the situation, Darcey wondered if perhaps she should keep an eye on *him*. If their situation had been reversed, Darcey would have put every citizen in town on a horse and sent them bundling off to track down her father's abductor. Patrick hadn't even demanded a description of the man or allowed the deputy to get one, either. Darcey's well-developed intuition shouted that the theory sounded not at all like normal procedure for Patrick.

Chapter 20

Kane was so exasperated and apprehensive about what he would encounter when he reached Denver that he squirmed in the saddle. It was dusk by the time he arrived at the outskirts of town. He expected to confront at least three search parties of mounted men whose pistols were loaded with bullets that had his name on them. But to his surprise and relief, he had passed almost no one on the road. If there was a warrant out for his arrest, the posses must have gotten their directions mixed up. Kane couldn't imagine how that could have happened with Darcey—the epitome of efficient organization—in command.

Steering clear of the main thoroughfares, Kane took the long way to the express office. Knowing Darcey O'Roarke, Kane expected her to be conducting her search from the office. Kane didn't have the foggiest idea what in the hell he was going to do when he located Darcey. But he couldn't prepare himself for whatever trouble awaited him until he discovered what she had done.

For all Kane knew, he could walk right smack dab into a trap. That was probably what he was doing, come to think of it. That firebrand was trying to second-guess him. Well, *he* was legendary in his ability to second-guess his quarry's second guesses. And he had taught himself to rely on instinct. As clever as that green-eyed elf was, *she* had nothing on *him!*

Kane felt a smidgen better after giving himself that silent encouragement. Expecting the unexpected, Kane dismounted and weaved through the alley to tiptoe toward the back door of the express agency. When he inched beneath the window where a single lantern flickered, he stopped dead in his tracks. Lo and behold, there sat Patrick O'Roarke. His bushy red head was bent over a mound of papers. Irritably, Patrick drummed his fingers on the desk and grumbled to himself.

Quietly, Kane stepped back to peer in the other window that opened into the main office. Assured that Patrick was alone, Kane ambled back to tap on the windowpane.

Patrick jerked upright and very nearly launched himself out of his chair. When it reared back, Patrick thrust his stout body forward to brace himself against the desk. "Good Lord, man, you scared twenty years off my life," he muttered when he recognized the shadowed face in the window.

Gesturing toward the back door, Patrick bolted from his chair to stalk down the hall. By the time he felt his way along the dark corridor, Kane was there to greet him.

"Where the devil have you been and what the blazes

is going on? I thought I left the most capable detective in the country in charge of my daughter."

"That green-eyed horror you call your daughter escaped me," Kane grumbled sourly.

"Obviously," Patrick snorted.

"She is the most contrary creature I've ever run across," Kane muttered. "I tried friendly persuasion and gentlemanly charm. When those didn't work, I resorted to scare tactics and force to remove her from town. And when I finally had her where I wanted her—away from trouble—she escaped me. When I wanted her to leave, she stayed. When I wanted her to stay, she left!"

"And she came bursting in here all by herself this morning," Patrick reported. "And just where the devil were *you?*"

"What the hell are *you* doing here already?" Kane questioned the question. "I just sent you that note four days ago."

"I saw no sense of waiting," Patrick replied. "I knew you would have to rely on scare tactics to drag Darcey out of town. But now that she has escaped you, we've got a tangled mess on our hands. If she divulges your name to that dimwitted deputy, I don't know what we're going to do!"

"You mean she hasn't told him yet?" Kane questioned in disbelief.

"I didn't let her," Patrick clarified. "I told the deputy that Darcey needed to rest first and answer questions later. But I can't put him off indefinitely. And if you think I'm going to pay you the full ten thousand dollars I offered when I hired you to investigate the robberies

337

and scare Darcey out of town, then you'll be sorely disappointed. I don't—"

"You! My own father! How could you . . . ?"

The voice that hissed out of the deepening shadows caused Patrick and Kane to stiffen in gloomy recognition. The tension in the air was as thick as mud and the alley suddenly became as silent as the grave.

Kane wasn't the only one who had used the alley to sneak into the express office. Darcey had been keeping surveillance on her father for almost two hours. She didn't know what she expected to learn, but it certainly wasn't this!

Dressed fit to kill, Darcey stamped into the shaft of light that splintered through the window. The elegant blue silk gown displayed her beauty, but the expression that puckered her bewitching features did her no justice whatsoever. It testified to the full extent of her fury.

"My own father conspired against me?" She shot Patrick a glower that branded him a traitor. "My own flesh and blood? Your only living heir? You hired this . . ." She pointed an accusing finger at Kane and cursed him but good. "You hired Kane Callahan . . ." The bell of recognition clamored through her head, and Darcey muttered under her breath. Now she remembered where she had heard that name before, or to be more accurate, had *seen* that name on the ledgers for services rendered. "He's the man you hired four years ago to track down the desperadoes who were harassing the stage company in California! And now you sicced him on me!" Darcey all but spat at her father.

Her breasts heaved with every indignant breath. Icy

338

disdain glazed her eyes as she glared first at one guilty man and then the other. "You tried to scare me out of Denver for the sum of ten thousand dollars?" Her voice quivered with outrage. "Of all the deceitful, devious, underhanded schemes! And you . . ."

Darcey stalked toward Kane, seeing him in an entirely different light, knowing he had gotten the last laugh and the last word . . . Or at least he had until now. But Darcey intended to blast him to kingdom come for tricking her!

"You let me think you were a gambler and a thief, which you still are in my opinion," she raged. "You dragged me out of town. You flung me over the back of a horse and let me think I would be mauled, killed, and tossed over a ledge to break in a hundred different pieces! And then you—"

An explosive curse burst from Darcey's lips. She honestly didn't know which was worse—thinking Kane was a criminal or knowing he had purposely deceived her. But when she considered all the turmoil she'd been through, then and now, it made her so aggravated she wanted to throw things—starting with Kane and ending with her own father!

Giving way to the infuriated impulse, Darcey snatched up the empty crates and hurled them at Kane and her father. To her dismay they both artfully dodged the oncoming missiles.

"And I've got news for you, Papa," Darcey fumed. "This wily detective of yours pranced off with the gold Griz Vanhook tried to steal from the agency. He's even more devious than you are because he double-crossed you!"

Patrick gaped incredulously and Kane scowled sourly.

"I didn't steal the gold," Kane defended when Patrick glared at him. "I took it for safekeeping. I couldn't very well leave all that money and those credit vouchers lying around while the office was unattended, now could I? Giddeon has the gold with him and Noah is keeping an eye on Peter Alridge. They are awaiting my orders about what to do with the loot and the captured thief."

Darcey felt as if the world had been pulled out from under her. She had never been so mortified in all her life. She had been played for an absolute fool so many times the past two weeks that it made her sick to think about it! All of Kane's threats and scare tactics had been a ploy to send her running home to her father—the very man who had paid Kane—*paid* him, mind you!—to rout her from Denver! They both deserved to be shot and hanged a couple of times for good measure.

"Now, Darcey, before you completely lose your temper . . ." Patrick began, and then ducked when another crate sailed through the air.

"It's too late," she hissed contemptuously. "I lost the last of my temper when I overheard the two of you talking. And I don't care if I never see either of you again! What a rotten trick to pull on a person!"

In a flurry of muttered oaths and fuming glares, Darcey lurched around and stamped down the alley. Her own father! She couldn't believe he'd do such a thing. And Kane, that scoundrel! He should have told her the truth in the beginning. But he was committed to his assignment and he didn't really care what she thought or how she felt. And *she,* ignoramus that she was, had hesitated in naming him as her abductor! She should have shouted accusations to high heaven.

Well, I certainly know what to do now, Darcey told herself as she stormed toward the hotel. She was leaving Denver for good. And when she returned to St. Louis she was going to pack her belongings and find a place of her own. She wasn't living under the same roof as her father. And she was never going to speak to Kane Callahan again as long as she lived. He had used her to appease his lusts, to satisfying his personal vendetta against Melanie What's-her-name. He had tormented her for the very last time, damn him.

"Now look what you've done," Patrick glared at Kane as if the entire situation was his fault.

"What *I've* done?" Kane blustered. "This was your idea, not mine. I wasn't the one who came to you with this proposal." In a flash, Kane was pacing back and forth in the alley with his hands clasped behind him, muttering an oath with every step he took.

"Why I came to you for assistance I'll never know." Patrick flung Kane a furious glare when the frustrated detective wheeled around to pace in the opposite direction. "It was Lester who put an end to that Griz Vanhook character. And if the truth be known, Darcey probably apprehended Lester's brother on her way back to town. I don't know what you did to earn a cent of your fee!"

Kane spun around to answer Patrick—glower for glower. "Lester didn't shoot Griz," he rapped out in staccato. "I did."

When Kane took the wind out of Patrick's sails, he blinked bewilderedly. *"You* shot Griz Vanhook?" he said.

"I was on my way to kidnap Darcey, out of sheer desperation," Kane explained as he went back to his pacing. "That's when Griz showed up. He had attempted to rob the stage the previous day and met with difficulty, so he came to the express office to steal the loot. Lester blundered in and I was afraid he was going to accidentally shoot Darcey while he was trying to save her from Griz."

"Well, why didn't you say so?" Patrick muttered.

"I was hardly in any position to discredit Lester, now was I?" Kane parried sardonically. "I had to get that spitfire out of town, and quickly! She had almost gotten herself killed several times already. I tried to warn her, beg her, reason with her. Nothing worked. And even when I abducted her and put the fear of God in her, she still defied me."

Kane paced some more. "Then I made the mistake of leaving Darcey in the care of Noah and Giddeon. Those tender-hearted morons let her outfox them. I had just tracked Peter Alridge down when, lo and behold, there came Darcey thundering down the road, hightailing it to Denver. Hell, I had to stake Peter to a tree and race after her. And when Noah and Giddeon showed up, Darcey flew off again. I had no idea what kind of reception awaited me in town. I could have been the honored guest at my lynching, for all I knew."

Kane wheeled around. His chest swelled like an inflated bagpipe with every agitated breath he took.

"And I don't want your damned money, either. I didn't need the *a*ssignment, the *c*ash, or an ounce of *p*raise."

God, just listen to me, thought Kane. *I can't even talk these days without alphabetizing the words!*

"Well, you won't hear me begging you to take another assignment after you bungled things with my daughter," Patrick spumed. "As far as I'm concerned, Lester saved the day and you botched it up. I'm keeping him on as manager and you can haul Peter back to Missouri to stand trial. I don't want that bandit to blemish his brother's reputation in Denver."

"I'm relieved to hear you won't be coming to me to solve your problems again," Kane scowled. "I've had my fill of O'Roarkes!"

"You needn't worry on that count. We've had our fill of you, too!" Patrick hurled nastily. "As far as I'm concerned, you've been overrated as a detective. I'll hire someone else to hunt Owen Graves down. He's the one who was embezzling money from the agency, not that you were smart enough to figure that out. Darcey did. And now Owen has dashed off into parts unknown. But you couldn't catch him. Hell, you couldn't track a hippopotamus through the mud!"

"And you won't win any awards for the world's best father, either," Kane smirked sarcastically. "What kind of man would even suggest having his daughter kidnapped, for crying out loud! If Darcey is cold to you, know that you deserve it. And if you had showed a little sense before you started running off at the mouth about our dealings, she wouldn't have overheard us!"

"Get out of my office, Callahan," Patrick shouted, green eyes blazing like a forest fire.

343

"I'm not in it," Kane smirked sarcastically. "The alley isn't your personal property."

"Then I'll buy it and have you thrown in jail for trespassing."

"Honest to God, Patrick, your daughter is your spitting image. You both have to have the last word, don't you? It must be an inbred O'Roarke trait. One, I might add, that I have come to detest!"

"Get out of my sight before I officially lose my temper!" Patrick boomed.

"I'm gone!" Kane blared.

"Good!" Patrick bellowed before he entered the office and slammed the door with such ferocity that the stone-and-timber structure shuddered and groaned.

"I'm not going to cry," Darcey vowed as she flounced on her bed and pummeled the pillow with her fists. "I'm not wasting one iota of emotion of either of those despicable men!"

A green-eyed horror? Is that what Kane thought of her? He must! He'd said those very words to her father! And he had also declared that his friendly persuasion and seductive charm had only been his attempt to get what he wanted. He cared nothing for her. She was the biggest fool ever to walk the earth!

When her eyes misted over, Darcey blinked determinedly. She was not going to reduce herself to tears. It was a sign of weakness and she detested weepy displays . . .

Was that a whimper she heard bubbling from her throat? Her ears must have deceived her. She was *not*

344

going to cry!

A muffled sniffle broke the silence, followed by a huge sobbing gulp. And before Darcey could clamp a firm grip on her crumbling composure, a shuddering sob wracked her body and she cried her eyes out. Her emotions were in such a state of turmoil that she wanted to scream at the top of her lungs. She was never going to allow Kane Callahan to come near her again. He was out of her life forever and she was eternally glad of it . . .

No, you aren't, the pesky voice deep down inside her scoffed in contradiction.

"Oh yes I am!" Darcey blubbered to the darkness at large.

Then what are you bawling about? came the infuriating voice.

Darcey hated having this conversation with herself. Her bruised pride smarted; her heart wrenched in her chest, and her spirits scraped rock bottom. She desperately needed to sort her sensible thoughts from her emotions, to spread them all out and analyze them one by one. But curse it, thought and emotion kept leaping up at her in tangles, frustrating her to no end.

Inhaling a determined breath, Darcey started by focusing on the source of her exasperation—Kane Callahan. He was a shrewd, cunning detective who could change roles at the drop of a hat. He could pretend to be anyone he wanted to be—a gambler, a gunslinger, a renegade, a charismatic lover. Every action of his, every word, was a ploy to manipulate and maneuver her. She had only been part of the game he had been playing. He had conspired with her father, and that was unforgivable. Both of them had decided that, since she was a woman, she was incapable of taking care of herself.

With a soul-wracking sob, Darcey mopped the tears from her eyes. Men were so cock sure of their superiority. Kane's sense of protectiveness was to be scorned, not praised. If Patrick hadn't interfered, Darcey wouldn't have fallen in love with that deceptive detective.

No wonder Kane could portray so many conflicting roles and keep her thoroughly confused! No wonder Darcey hadn't been able to figure him out. She well remembered, after making the connection, that her father had sung Kane Callahan's praises before the war. Kane had lived up to his legendary reputation when he defied Griz Vanhook on the streets and tracked Peter Alridge down. He had quietly and efficiently applied himself to his assignment. He had done what he had been paid to do . . . Of course, stealing Darcey's heart wasn't supposed to have been part of the assignment . . .

"Get out of my mind, you horrible man," Darcey muttered at the taunting image that floated above her.

No doubt Kane was gloating all over himself for making her look the fool and using her trampled heart as his doormat. He had accomplished his mission. Now Darcey couldn't wait to leave Denver and the bittersweet memories that haunted her. Even this room held forbidden images of the night Kane had introduced her to the splendors of passion. She could still hear his voice whispering in her mind. And now that he'd had the last laugh, Darcey was humiliated beyond words. She thought she had learned her lesson when she'd fled Philadelphia and Michael Dupris. But no, she had buckled beneath Kane's magnetic charm and he'd shattered her heart.

Inhaling a shuddering breath, Darcey struggled for hard-won composure. She wasn't waiting for tomorrow's stage to make her departure. She was hotfooting it out of town tonight! She was not about to leave herself open to a chance meeting with Kane ever again, not on the streets, not in the office . . . nowhere!

On that determined thought, Darcey bounded off the bed and crammed her belongings into her satchels. She intended to catch the train in Cheyenne, Wyoming. Let Patrick take the stage if he wished, but she was using another mode of transportation. And by damned, when she returned to St. Louis, she was going to interview for a job with the railroad, just to spite her father. Patrick had scorned the rails, but locomotives were making their mark on this widespread nation. Darcey had encouraged him to invest in the railroads, but he had stubbornly balked at the suggestion. In the next few years, Darcey predicted the railroads would span from coast to coast and the stage company would become obsolete. And then where would Patrick O'Roarke be? He would be out of business and without his daughter, that's where!

Feeling angry and spiteful, Darcey whipped open the door to make her exit. But to her disgust, the last man she ever wanted to see blocked the doorway as effectively as a boulder. Damn the man. He truly was everywhere! Darcey couldn't even turn around without bumping into this infuriating rascal!

Chapter 21

"Get out my way," Darcey demanded as she attempted to elbow her way past the human blockade.

Kane refused to budge an inch. "You're not going anywhere until we talk this out," he growled into her belligerent face.

"I'm through talking to you," she muttered contemptuously.

"Good, then you can stand here and listen."

"Not interested," Darcey smarted off, tilting a rebellious chin.

Kane pushed his way forward and slammed the door behind him. Darcey refused to be closeted in the same room with this man who had already run her emotions through a meat grinder. With a curse and a hiss she flung herself at him, pelting his chest with her doubled fists. Before she could expend all her frustration, the source of it grabbed her by the arms and jerked her against him, causing her head to snap backward with a painful jolt.

"You're not leaving here hating me," Kane assured her sharply. "You can think what you want about my assignment, but you aren't about to traipse off without knowing how I feel."

"I couldn't care less how you feel," Darcey spewed, on the verge of more tears. "You disgust me! Your feelings are of no concern to me, just as mine are of no concern to you! The sight of you nauseates me!"

"Does it?" Kane scoffed, battling for control of his temper after Darcey had completely lost hers. "That's not what you said the first time we made love, right here in this room."

Darcey's face flamed with fury. In a burst of temper she tried to hurl herself away from him, but Kane only clamped a tighter grip on her. "Let me go!" she railed. "I never want—"

His lips came down hard on hers, smothering her protest. Kane hadn't meant to resort to kissing her into silence, but damn it, she wouldn't clam up long enough to allow him to wedge in more than a few words.

Darcey told herself she wasn't giving in to his demanding kisses. She refused to let her frigid defenses thaw. She wanted to feel nothing for him, But the harder she fought to escape his arms, the closer Kane pressed her to him.

Kane hadn't meant to hurt her, only to hold her to him until she calmed down. But Darcey was like a wild creature who was terrified of captivity. She struck out with her feet to kick him in the shins and grind her heels into the toes of his boots. Kane was holding his own until Darcey bit a chunk out of his hand. Reflexively, he shrank back, and Darcey darted across the room. After locating the farthest corner, she planted herself in it and glared poison arrows at him. Every time she came within ten feet of the man, her body forgot it had a brain attached to it. She wasn't going to take that risk again!

"I can't bear to have you touch me," she spat at him. "Now get out. All you will ever get from me is my contempt."

Kane exhaled a deep sigh. "I want to start all over again with you." His voice was much calmer now, his expression sincere. "Let's forget the past, shall we?"

"It's already forgotten," Darcey snapped with finality. "And so are you."

"Am I?" One dark brow elevated to a challenging angle. "Then come here and prove to me that you don't remember the way we make sparks fly each time we kiss, each time I touch you and you touch me . . ."

It was at that moment that Darcey cursed her inability to retreat from a challenge. Kane had dared her to kiss him and walk away without feeling anything whatsoever. Well, she possessed more willpower than he did! She would pretend she was kissing a stone statue and then she would laugh in his face and walk away without looking back.

"You want proof, do you?" she smirked as she squared her shoulders and marched deliberately toward him.

"I most certainly do," Kane guaranteed. "And I don't expect one of those brotherly pecks on the cheek, either."

Darcey gnashed her teeth, marshaled her defenses, and switched her tactics in midstream. It seemed she was going to have to call upon her theatrical ability. She would deliver a sizzling kiss that knocked him to his knees. When this lusty rake dripped into a puddle of unappeased desire, then she would laugh in his face and sashay out the door.

Determined to outfox Kane with her clever strategy, Darcey glided her hands over the massive wall of his chest. Her fingertips trailed over his shoulder to toy with the thick, wavy hair that lay at the nape of his neck. She was going to make his heart pound like hailstones, beating him to death. She was going to burn this rogue into a pile of frustrated ashes, just see if she didn't!

In a provocative manner, Darcey molded her feminine curves into his masculine contours. Using her body in a seductive, suggestive caress, she moved against him. She would whet his appetite and then leave him on the brink of starvation. She would tease and torment him until she raised his temperature several degrees and then leave him to fry alive. She, the picture of self-control, would bid him good-bye and good riddance. She would sail off without being the least bit affected by their parting embrace.

Darcey had it all planned. There was just one small hitch. Her betraying body forgot that it was merely playing a spiteful role to avenge her bruised pride and broken heart. When Kane's hands splayed over her hips, pulling her intimately against his bold manhood, Darcey's heart hammered. When she tried to draw a steadying breath, she inhaled the masculine scent that was so much a part of him, one that had somehow become a part of her.

It was nothing but physical attraction, Darcey assured herself sensibly. It was a natural reaction to this wildly sensual man. Any woman would have had difficulty resisting his lure. But it didn't mean a thing. Her mind was still in control of her wayward body. Her determination was still stronger than wanton desire.

Famous last words . . .

The instant their eyes locked and their lips met, Darcey knew she was in serious trouble. Their embrace did phenomenal things to her equilibrium, and she involuntarily swayed toward him. Her traitorous body wasn't paying the slightest attention to the messages sent out by her brain. Warning signals flashed in her mind. Her nerves shattered and her composure threatened to crack wide open. Those old familiar feelings pulsated through her veins with fierce intensity. Suddenly she was trembling from the uncontrollable onslaught of forbidden desire. Darcey had wanted to feel nothing for Kane after the heartache and humiliation he'd put her through. But deep down inside, beneath the injured pride and stubborn defiance, the flame of love still burned brightly.

The instant Darcey had moved seductively against

him, Kane realized her intention. Oh, she was a clever little witch, that was for sure. She was seeking her own kind of vengeance against his deceit. But two could play her cunning game, Kane reminded himself. Time would tell which one of them would walk away the least affected by their embrace. He would make her face the truth of her own feelings and she would be unable to deny the existence of the bond that linked them together.

Like a bee courting nectar, Kane brushed his parted lips over hers. He felt her tremble in his arms, and he took advantage of her momentary weakness. His mouth slanted over hers savoring her kiss, taking only what she offered, making no overpowering demands. His hands drifted up her hips to scale her ribs and linger just beneath the luscious curve of her breasts. Slowly and deliberately, he traced his fingers over the taut peaks that lay beneath the blue silk bodice. But Kane made no move to delve his fingertips beneath the fabric. He merely sensitized her without actually making direct contact with her satiny flesh.

Darcey suddenly found herself wondering who was tormenting whom. She had launched this amorous assault to teach him a lesson, but she was the one who had been assaulted with nerve-tingling sensations and compelling needs. She had been trapped in the devastating aura of masculinity that surrounded him. Waves of heightened awareness crested in her blood. She couldn't concentrate on her purpose when her body practically called out to him to continue his tantalizing caresses.

Courageous to the bitter end, Darcey tunneled her hands beneath his chambray shirt to make arousing contact with his hair-roughened flesh. She was determined to match every sensuous tactic, to best him at his own seductive game. He had taught her how to excite and arouse him. She knew all the places he liked to be touched. She knew how to kiss him until savage passion fogged his senses and he lost control.

Employing the devastating techniques he had used on her and utilizing her own inventiveness, she conjured up new ways to torment him with desire. She spun silken webs of pleasure over his flesh and drew lazy circles around his male nipples with her fingertips. With a seductive purr, she leaned close to place whispering kisses on his bronzed skin. Her hands glided over his ribs and traced the band of his breeches. When she heard Kane's sharp intake of breath she knew she had managed to counter his provocative ploy with feminine effectiveness.

Kane groaned in torment when lips as moist as morning dew lit on his skin and then fluttered over his chest like velvety butterfly wings. He hadn't realized what a skillful temptress Darcey had become until he challenged her to a duel with seduction as its deadly weapon.

"So you want to play rough, do you?" Kane growled when Darcey smiled in smug satisfaction.

"The rougher the better," she parried confidently. "I enjoy living dangerously, don't you, Mister Detective?"

When Darcey's adventurous hands dipped beneath the band of his breeches, Kane swore there wasn't enough air on the planet, much less in this room, to fill his lungs. His pulse leapfrogged through his bloodstream and his heart slammed against his ribs, but he did muster enough control to return the titillating assault, touch for erotic touch.

He bent to spread a row of hot kisses along the scooped neck of her gown. He was thankful Darcey hadn't donned one of those high-collared garments she usually wore. His hands were too shaky to fight their way through all those pesky little buttons to reveal the tempting flesh beneath it. This particular gown worked to *his* advantage, not hers.

With a gentle tug of her sleeve, Kane exposed the sheer chemise. His index finger curled over the edge of the fabric to glide between the valley of her breasts. He teased her with his light touch, left her wondering what other sweet tortures he had in mind for her.

A smile of male arrogance quirked his lips when he felt Darcey respond to the scintillating threat of his caress. His lips dipped to the dusky peaks while his hands cupped and kneaded the soft mounds. His tongue flicked and his mouth suckled, drawing helpless responses from her lips. His hips moved intimately against hers, making subtle promises of the pleasures he could offer. He resented the hindering garments that separated them when desire pulsed through his loins. His caresses became more demanding. His ravishing kisses stole her breath away and refused to give it back until she surrendered in his arms.

Suddenly, neither Darcey nor Kane could remember this was purely a battle of wills. What had begun as a daring challenge had transformed into wild, intense longing. Impatience overwhelmed both of them. They couldn't seem to remove each other's clothes quickly enough to satisfy themselves. Their caresses spoke of hungry needs that had lain dormant far too long. Their kisses demanded all the other had to give. And give they did—instinctively, spontaneously.

Darcey couldn't even remember how and when they had come to be on her bed. But they were there, lying naked in each other's arms, kissing and caressing as if it had been months instead of days since they had lost themselves to this wondrous brand of passion.

The challenge had gotten out of hand somewhere along the way, Darcey realized. Desire had sneaked up to engulf her, and her body throbbed with remembered passion. She was in the throes of such wild needs that no thought could penetrate the dense fog that enshrouded her. She had become a creature of impulsive desire, surviving only on Kane's masterful kisses and practiced caresses. Her body glowed with the warmth of his intimate touch. It was as if she knew this would be the last night she spent in his arms, as if each moment was as priceless as precious jewels.

Devastating sensations bombarded her as Kane worked his magic, creating a spell that no amount of willpower could counteract. The needs he instilled in her yearned to be shared until they heightened and expanded to consume both of them.

Darcey caressed every muscular inch of his body; she committed the feel of his masculine contours and muscled planes to memory. She absorbed his awesome strength and reveled in every white-hot sensation that echoed from her body to his and back again. She returned each fervent kiss and arched upward to meet his restless hands. She matched his fiery passion and returned it until breathless urgency throbbed through the very core of her being and vibrated back to his.

When his sleek, powerful body glided over hers, Darcey glanced up to see the intense hunger that blazed in his silver-blue eyes. She had unleashed his savage desire and, in turn, he had ignited hers. The swift, impatient descent of his lips caught her breathless gasp as the warm, demanding threat of his body enveloped hers. His tongue darted into her mouth, imitating the intimacy that was to come. When Kane guided her thighs apart with his knees and lifted her to him, Darcey welcomed his possession, craved the seductive fire that she knew would soon inflame every part of her.

It was a wild, breathless coming together. Darcey answered each hard, driving thrust and dug her nails into his back, mindless of the mending wound. But Kane didn't even grimace when she clung to the tender flesh on his shoulder blade. He was oblivious to all except the hypnotic cadence of her silken body moving in perfect rhythm with his.

As he drove into her, lost to the savage urgency of unrivaled passion, one maddening sensation after another gripped him. And suddenly, every splendorous feeling recoiled upon him like an avalanche of living fire. Ineffable pleasure consumed him as his shuddering body surged toward hers. His pounding heart throbbed as pulsating ecstasy streamed through his body. When torrents of rapture drenched him, Kane feared he would squeeze the life out of Darcey. He clung fiercely to her, riding out the tidal wave that crested upon him and sent him plummeting into a sea of unparalleled passion.

When the sensual curtain of darkness that covered Darcey's eyes finally lifted, she choked on a humiliated sob. She had accomplished nothing when she accepted Kane's cunning challenge. This was yet another of his shrewd ploys to get her into bed to appease his voracious appetite. Fool that she was, she thought she could defeat him at his own game. But she lacked his experience. He would always be a master and she the novice.

Darcey had intended to deliver a parting kiss that would bring this awesome giant to his knees, not land them both in bed! Damn it, did she have not one ounce of pride left? Kane could take her in his arms and pretend she was any other woman—Melanie, in particular. Darcey was no more to him than she had ever been—a challenge, a conquest, a substitute for the woman he really wanted.

"You got what you wanted, now let me up," Darcey hissed in mortification. When Kane refused to roll away, Darcey tweaked the hair on his chest and reached up to yank on his ruffled raven hair.

"Darcey, damn it . . ." Kane growled when she tried to pull his hair out by the roots.

The instant he moved away, Darcey bolted off the

bed and jerked up her discarded clothes. And all the while, her mind was racing in an attempt to salvage what was left of her bruised pride. Her heart, she would leave behind, but by damn, she was taking her last smidgen of pride with her when she went! She would turn this humiliating incident around and play it to *her* advantage.

"There, you see, even I can pretend to be someone I'm not," she flung at him, wanting to hurt him the same way she was hurting. "I can even pretend to feel something I don't. I just proved to myself that I can feign love, just for the satisfaction of a few moments of passion. You have taught me well, Kane. Now I have become as uncaring and feeling as you."

Her spiteful words stung like a scorpion. Kane gnashed his teeth until he very nearly ground them smooth. "Is that what you think this was? A test?"

He had just come close to strangling her. Damn her, she was trying to spoil something that was rare and unique. But, of course, she hadn't lived long enough to know that passion never got better than this.

"That's all it was. A test," she confirmed as she rammed her arms through the sleeves of her gown and yanked the garment into decency. "Did you actually think that after all the hell you've put me through that I would forgive you and let you make a fool of me again? Did you think you could love away my anger?"

She didn't wait for him to respond; she rushed on, her voice growing wilder by the second. "Well, it didn't happen. It seems to me that if a man can seduce a woman for the mere pleasure of it and waltz away

360

unaffected, then so can a woman. There will be other men in my bed, Kane Callahan. You can bet your ten-thousand dollar-fee on that!"

That was a boldfaced lie, of course. Darcey couldn't bear the thought of another man touching her as intimately as Kane had. She would always be making love to this rascal, even when he wasn't the one in her aching arms.

"Now wait just a damned minute, woman," Kane growled as he came up off the bed, stark-bone naked. "I was the one who taught you all you know about passion. You belong to me and—"

"Belong?" Darcey pounced on his poor choice of wording with both feet. "Do you see your initials engraved on my skin like a tattoo? Hell would sooner be frozen in a polar ice cap before I gave my heart to a sneaky, deceitful varmint like you! Why, for ten thousand dollars, I could even pretend to love Pup Metcalf. At least he would be more honest and considerate than you!"

"Pup isn't man enough to satisfy you, and you know it," Kane muttered when the jealous green monster took a bite out of him.

"Then maybe I'll find someone who is," she hurled at him. "There has to be one deserving man on this continent."

This was not the way Kane had envisioned his encounter with Darcey, not at all! He had intended to apologize for his role in this charade, to declare his feelings for her, to assure her that when he was making wild, sweet love to her, it was no act. She had never been the time he was killing. But reasoning with her was impossible. She dragged him into one argument after another before he even realized he was there!

"I have one thing to say, and by damned you're going to listen!" Kane snapped brusquely.

When he reached out to clutch her arm and pull her close enough to thrust his face into hers to ensure that she listened, Darcey leaped backward. Swiftly, she scooped up his strewn garments and her satchels. Like a mountain goat, Darcey bounded toward the door, leaving Kane two alternatives: He could pursue her without a stitch of clothes or he could remain where he was.

"Damn you, woman, come here!" Kane blared at her departing back.

Darcey didn't break stride. She simply tossed Kane's garments on the floor and stamped on them as she stalked off. She only hoped Kane felt half as frustrated and humiliated as she did. Childish vindictiveness had put hateful words on her tongue.

She was St. Louis-bound. And never ever again would she fall prey to disarming smiles and persuasive kisses. She had been taught by the master that love was only an illusion, a self-maiming emotion whose aftereffects offered far more pain than the temporary pleasure derived from it.

With a muffled sob, Darcey whizzed toward the livery stable to fetch a mount. She didn't want to think or feel anything. She just wanted to ride against the wind, letting the breeze dry the tears that clouded her eyes. It was over, Darcey told herself firmly. She was going to get on with the rest of her life and profit from the heart-breaking mistakes she had made in Denver. Kane Callahan was a page from her past—and an unpleasant page at that!

When Kane darted out to the hall to retrieve his clothes he visibly distressed the poor unfortunate old woman who had poked her head around her hotel door to determine what had caused the commotion. Kane rather thought it sounded like the woman had fainted after she jerked back and slammed her head against the edge of her door. But Kane didn't stick around to administer first aid or apologize. He decided the matron had seen enough of him already.

By the time he located Noah and Giddeon, who waited on the edge of town, he was in the worst of all possible moods. He'd had his heart trampled. He'd exposed himself to a woman who was old enough to be his grandmother, and Patrick O'Roarke thought he was the most incompetent detective on the planet. Although Noah and Giddeon lambasted him with questions about his sour disposition, Kane refused to answer. He merely grabbed the reins to Peter Alridge's mule and pointed himself east toward the nearest stage station.

Two miles later, Noah demanded answers. "Confound it, Kane. We want to know what happened in Denver!"

"Nothing happened," Kane bit off testily. "The case has been solved. Peter is being transported back to

Missouri to stand trial for robbery and that is that."

"And what about Darcey?" Giddeon wanted to know. "Did she arrive without mishap?"

"The incorrigible Miss O'Roarke is still incorrigible," Kane muttered resentfully. "Now kindly clamp down on your tongue and grant me peace. Our prisoner is not privileged to hear any details."

Noah eased his steed up beside Kane and leaned over to relay confidential information. "Peter tried to bribe us into letting him go if he divulged where he stashed the money."

Kane reined his mount to a halt and cursed under his breath. He had been in such a stew after his encounter with Patrick and the frustrating confrontation with Darcey that he'd forgotten about the stolen loot.

"I deceived Peter into thinking we would release him," Noah said proudly. "He told me that he'd hidden the money in the file cabinet in his law office. There, you see, I do have the right qualities to become a detective. I can be as devious and sneaky as you are."

Darcey had made a similar comment the previous hour and Kane was in no mood to hear his own brother repeat it. "I prefer to consider myself clever and cunning," Kane qualified.

Without preamble, Kane handed Peter over to Noah and reversed direction.

"Now where are you going?" Giddeon questioned.

"To Denver to consult with Patrick," Kane explained.

"What's he doing there already?" Giddeon queried.

"Fouling things up," Kane scowled before he thundered off into the darkness.

The instant Kane arrived in Denver he made a beeline for the law office to recover the stolen loot. That done, he deposited the money in Patrick's lap and abruptly informed him that his feisty daughter was on her way back to St. Louis. The news did nothing for Patrick's irascible temperament. He called Kane a few more names for being unable to prevent his daughter from stamping off. Their conversation was as unpleasant as the first one and they parted on the worst of terms . . . again.

Once Kane had tied up all loose ends, he aimed his steed in the direction Noah and Giddeon had taken. But even the darkness couldn't conceal the haunting image that floated above him. He could hear Darcey's voice in the wind, see the lively twinkle in her eyes when he glanced up at the glittering stars, feel her tormenting presence.

"I'm going to miss you more than you will let yourself believe, sweet witch," he said to the vision of bedazzling beauty that hovered beside him.

Even now, Kane could see Darcey leaping over every obstacle he'd placed in her path during her captivity. He had given her hell for her own good and she had given as good as she got. Her indestructible spirit always saw her through every crisis. She possessed remarkable resilience, courage, beauty, and she had ridden away . . .

Kane couldn't quite bring himself to face the reality that Darcey had walked out of his life.

"It isn't over yet," Kane vowed as he urged his horse into a trot. "Not by a long shot! I have something to say to you, woman, and by damned, you'll hear me out, even if I have to tie you to a chair and *make* you listen!"

It wasn't in Kane's nature to admit defeat, not in his challenging profession. He had never called it quits until he had tracked down fugitives of justice. And he wasn't calling it quits with Darcey, either! She hadn't seen the last of him. Just wait! She hadn't seen anything yet! She wasn't having the last word, by God, *he* was! He was going to hound her every step until she realized she loved him as much as he loved her. And she did, Kane convinced himself. She had to! No woman could pretend to respond so ardently unless she cared for him—especially a woman like Darcey, who had no experience in deception. All that malarky she'd fed him before she stomped off was her way of defending that infuriating pride of hers.

Hate him, did she? Well, maybe she did hate him for deceiving her, but there was far more between them than passion for passion's sake. Kane was prepared to bet his fortune and his reputation on it. He had given his soul to her. They were a matched pair, and if Darcey couldn't see that, then it was only her monumental stubbornness that prevented her from recognizing the truth.

A sly smile hovered on Kane's lips as he galloped toward the stage station to meet Giddeon and Noah. He wasn't giving up on Darcey O'Roarke and he wasn't going to let her give up on him, either. Kane vowed to plow through every obstacle Darcey hurled in his path. He had fallen in love for the first time in his life and he liked what he was feeling. He enjoyed being protective and possessive of that high-spirited woman, faults and all. He adored her. He had finally found the part of himself that had eluded him all his life. Darcey was his missing link with happiness. Even if she was on her way to Missouri, burning bridges behind her, he was going to make her realize what she was throwing away.

Chapter 22

Independence, Missouri
1866

Kane tossed his file for Peter Alridge's court case on his desk and plunked down in his chair. After Kane's testimony, Peter had been sentenced to spend the next five years in the penitentiary. Patrick O'Roarke had been in court for the trial, but Kane had made it a point to avoid him. Since Patrick had declared that he didn't want any association with Kane, he had made no attempt to smooth things over with the fiery Irishman. But there would come a time when he and Patrick would meet again, face-to-face, for Kane had every intention of following Darcey to St. Louis and declaring his feelings for her, whether she wanted to hear them or not.

The past month had been hell for Kane. Darcey had hounded his every step and clouded every conversation. Her memory seemed to stretch in every direction

Kane glanced. Her name had attached itself to every thought. He hadn't even made it through Peter's trial without thinking about her at least two dozen times. In fact . . .

"I thought perhaps you could use a brandy just about now," Giddeon predicted as he strode into the study with silver tray in hand.

Kane experienced an odd feeling of déjà vu. More than two months earlier he had been haunted by a woman's memory, and Giddeon had sailed into the same room with much-needed brandy to numb Kane's frustration. But brandy couldn't cure what ailed Kane, and it didn't soothe the painful symptoms all that much, either. But what the hell, Kane thought. If he drank until he couldn't think or feel, he would enjoy temporary relief from the woman who was tormenting him.

The glass clinked on the desk in front of Kane. In his customary formal fashion, Giddeon drew himself up and stared down at Kane. "Now that the trial is over, would you like for me to see to your packing?"

"Just where is it you think I'm going?" Kane inquired before downing his brandy in one swallow.

Giddeon promptly refilled the glass and poured one for himself. "Why, to St. Louis, of course. You have obligations there, in case you have forgotten."

Kane's dark brows jackknifed when Giddeon glared accusingly at him. Since he returned from Denver, Kane had been keeping his own counsel. Not once had he mentioned his plans of following Darcey.

"Please get to the point you seem intent on making," Kane demanded impatiently.

"My point, sir," Giddeon began with a condescending stare, "is that you and Miss O'Roarke..." His voice trailed off as he leaned forward to brace his hands on the front of the desk. "Although you made great efforts to conceal your less than gentlemanly dealings with the aforementioned young lady, I happen to know what transpired between you. And might I also add that I find your behavior distasteful."

Kane squirmed uncomfortably in his chair and glanced at his father's portrait on the wall to avoid Giddeon's pointed glare.

"We both know you employed far more than scare tactics on that young lady," Giddeon told him plainspokenly. "And if you intend to ignore your responsibilities where she is concerned, then you will leave me no choice but to go to Patrick and inform him. And it will not take me long to find him. He is, at this very moment, standing in the vestibule, awaiting an audience with you."

"He is?" Kane croaked, and bolted to his feet.

"He is," Giddeon confirmed. "Now will you tell him or shall I?"

Kane's silver-blue eyes were fixed on the closed door behind which Patrick stood. "I'll handle this," he said, distracted.

Giddeon expelled a sarcastic snort. "That is the same thing you said when you dragged Miss O'Roarke to our headquarters in the mountains, as I recall. And we both know that turned out disastrously. For a man who is famous for solving everybody else's problems, you certainly have an astounding habit of royally botching up your own personal affairs. It seems to me—"

Kane stalked up to loom over his outspoken servant. "It seems to me that you should mind your own business and let me deal with mine."

"If you could do so effectively, I wouldn't have to poke my nose in your affairs," Giddeon said audaciously. "Had I known you were in the habit of gallivanting all over creation, deflowering young maids under the pretense of solving cases, I would have—"

"Enough!" Kane's voice was like a judge pounding his gavel.

"My sentiments exactly," Giddeon shot back in a caustic tone. "You have soiled Miss O'Roarke's reputation and you should marry her."

Kane didn't bother informing Giddeon that he had already proposed to that firebrand once and she had turned him down flat. Giddeon, who already thought the worst, probably wouldn't believe Kane anyway. It was for certain that Kane had offended Giddeon's sense of propriety and he wasn't going to be satisfied until a marriage to Darcey had been arranged. The fact was, Kane was willing and eager. But Darcey wasn't. She despised him and she'd had a full month to nurture her hatred for him.

"Why don't you summon Patrick," Kane suggested. "I'm sure he's growing impatient and annoyed with the delay."

"And I'm positively certain he would be furious to learn that the man he sent to *protect* his precious daughter was the very one who—"

"I said that was enough," Kane growled menacingly. "You have a choice, Giddeon. I can forcefully remove

372

you from this room or you can leave of your own free will."

Giddeon chose the latter option. Since he had said his piece, he drew himself up and took himself off before Kane lost his temper and tossed him out by the seat of his breeches.

Within a matter of seconds, Patrick breezed into the study and stopped in the middle of the room to stand as erect as a marble statue. "I came to thank you for seeing justice served and for returning my money."

"You're welcome," Kane acknowledged in the same clipped tone.

The breath Patrick had been holding came out in a rush. "I also have another assignment I wish you to take on my behalf."

Kane blinked in astonishment. "If memory serves, you vowed never to speak to me, much less deal with me ever again."

"I've changed my mind," Patrick muttered. "It's my daughter again, as well as that pesky Owen Graves who has eluded the incompetent moron I sent to hunt him down."

"What about Darcey?" Kane wanted to know that very instant.

Patrick grumbled under his breath and plopped into the nearest chair. "By the time I reorganized the Denver office, hired more help, and returned to St. Louis, Darcey had moved out. She refused to see me, even when I called on her at the cottage she rented on the west side of town. And to annoy me to death, she applied for and acquired a job with an up-and-coming railroad company owned by a young upstart by the name of Edward Talbert." He inhaled a quick breath, raked his blunt fingers through his crop of bushy red hair and plunged on. "She is doing this to retaliate for my deceiving her. She knows I'm leery of railway companies and their shrewd dealings for government contracts. Neither do I condone tactics of passing information to land speculators who buy up right-of-ways from unsuspecting citizens whose property lies along the tracks. I want you to check into Talbert's firm to ensure that it is legitimate. I don't want Darcey mixed up with a bunch of crooks. And I also want Owen Graves apprehended and convicted, just as Peter Alridge was."

"It will be difficult for me to be in two places at once," Kane reminded the exasperated Irishman.

"Then send Noah to track down Owen Graves," Patrick suggested. "I want you in St. Louis. Name your price."

Kane crossed his arms over his broad chest and stared at Patrick for a long, pensive moment. "Any price, Patrick?"

"Didn't I just give you free license to set your own fee?" Patrick snorted as he bounded to his feet. "I want to be back in my daughter's good graces. But if I can't have that, then, at least, I want to make certain she isn't involved with a railroad company that is cheating landowners out of fair prices for the property which lies beside those confounded steel rails! Now, are you going to take this assignment or aren't you?" he yelled into Kane's amused face.

374

Kane was positively certain that Darcey had inherited her volatile temper from her father. He wondered how Patrick would react when he heard the price Kane demanded for his services. After all, they were barely on speaking terms after their encounter in Denver.

"I'll investigate Talbert's company," Kane agreed. "If, in return, you will give me permission to marry your daughter."

Patrick's knees buckled and he sat down before he fell down. He stared bug-eyed at the ruggedly handsome detective. "Marry her? Good God, she detests you as much as she does me. If I inform her that I have contracted her into marriage with you, we'll both be cutting our throats again! I refuse to—"

Kane flung up his hand to forestall Patrick. "I did not mean to imply that you would force her against her will, only that you give your blessing if she consents to my proposal," he clarified.

Patrick's wide green eyes rounded in disbelief. "Your fee is my blessing? That's all?" After a moment, his gaze narrowed suspiciously. "Is this your way of getting your revenge after our falling out in Denver? For if it is—"

"This is my way of getting what I want," Kane told him point-blank. "And what I want is your daughter."

Patrick didn't know what to make of Kane's unexpected demand. "And what in hades are you going to do with her if you get her?"

"Love her the way she deserves to be loved . . . if she'll let me," Kane answered honestly.

375

Patrick's face dropped. "You're in love with my daughter?" he croaked. "You know how she feels about you and you are still willing to approach her? I shudder to think what she'll throw at you this time!"

Kane knew perfectly well that Darcey detested being deceived. But that changed nothing. He'd been miserable this past month without her, and he had no intention of being miserable for the rest of his life, not if he could help it.

"I know exactly what I want, Patrick, difficult though it will probably be to obtain. Now, do I have your permission to marry her or don't I?"

The Irishman's pensive gaze flooded over Kane's muscular physique. Despite the circumstances that had put them at odds, Patrick still had a great deal of respect for Kane. Otherwise, he wouldn't have come crawling back, requesting Kane's assistance. And for certain, it would take a man such as this to handle Darcey. She had more spunk than a woman naturally ought to possess.

Patrick finally nodded his consent. "Very well then, you have my blessing. But if you tell my daughter I agreed to this, prior to your engagement, I will vehemently deny having had this conversation. She is irritated enough with me as it is. I will not have her thinking I conspired to plan her future!"

"What conversation?" Kane questioned with feigned innocence.

A wry smile pursed Patrick's lips as he levered his stout body out of the chair to clasp Kane's hand. "Good luck with all your endeavors. I will be waiting in St. Louis for a report at your earliest convenience."

"And I will inform Noah that you have hired him to track down Owen Graves. The two of you can bicker over his fee after he takes Graves into custody."

Patrick voiced his agreement before he sailed out the door.

Kane had just poured himself another brandy when Giddeon emerged from the shadowed foyer. Kane jerked his head up to see the servant regarding him with an amused smile.

"What do you find so funny?" Kane demanded before chugging his drink.

"You, sir," Giddeon replied. "All this time you let me think you were a heartless womanizer who had—"

"I know what you thought." Kane cut Giddeon off in midsentence.

"Well, I must say I could not have arranged a more perfect match," he announced with absolute conviction.

Kane glared at the servant, who had obviously eavesdropped on the private conversation. "Giddeon, you missed your calling. You can spy with the best of them."

An embarrassed blush stained the servant's features. "It appears your and Noah's talents have rubbed off on me."

"And speaking of Noah, where the devil is he?"

Giddeon's shoulders lifted in a noncommittal shrug.

Kane sighed audibly. "I'll find that brother of mine and inform him of his assignment while you pack our

377

belongings. I intend to be on the next train to St. Louis."

"Our belongings, sir?" Giddeon questioned in surprise.

"I'm bringing you along for moral support. I'll need it if I propose to Darcey. I'm sure she will prove to be a most reluctant bride."

"But a most worthy one," Giddeon added with an approving smile. "A much better one than flighty Melanie Brooks, if you ask me."

Kane blinked. "I thought you liked Melanie."

"What I *liked,*" Giddeon corrected, "was the possibility of seeing you settle down at long last. Had I been doing the picking, Melanie would not have been on my list."

"I don't know how she got on mine, either," Kane admitted with a snort. "I must have been going through an indiscriminate phase of my life. I knew there must have been a logical reason why I never could bring myself to set an official wedding date."

"Thank God for that," Giddeon breathed in relief. "And I want you to know that I highly approve of Miss O'Roarke. In this instance, I think both the lady and marriage will agree with you."

"With me, perhaps," Kane qualified. "But not with her."

A sly smile twitched Giddeon's lips. "Knowing how persistent you can be during your most difficult assignments, I'm sure you will find a way to convince the young lady that she belongs with you."

"I wish I shared your confidence, Giddeon," he

replied with less enthusiasm than his servant had exhibited.

"I shall speak to her on your behalf, sir," Giddeon volunteered.

"Lord, no!" Kane howled. "If you hound her with your lecture on honorable obligation and propriety, she will flatly refuse, just to be contrary. That woman is stubborn to the core, in case you hadn't noticed."

"Very well, then, I will leave you to your dilemma while I pack," Giddeon obliged.

When Giddeon took his leave, Kane paced back and forth. Damn, just what was he going to say to convince Darcey that he was sincere? How did a man go about courting a woman who had her heart set on hating him?

Pausing to gulp a drink of brandy, Kane wrestled with that unsettling question. Darcey wouldn't be the least bit receptive to his attention, that was for sure. But damn it all, if she'd stop being so stubborn for five minutes, she might realize that they needed each other for all the right reasons.

Kane heaved a worried sigh and resumed his pacing. Never had he undertaken a task where he was so uncertain of its outcome. Even now, after a month, he could still visualize that furious expression on her face when she learned he and Patrick had tricked her. She had glared at him as if he had betrayed her, deceived her, disappointed her. And the worst part of all was that he *had* betrayed the small amount of trust she had finally put in him. But it had been for her own good, although in her estimation, that counted for nothing. She refused to trust what she couldn't understand. All

379

she knew was what she felt. And what she felt, Kane was sorry to say, was anger, regret, and resentment.

Yes, indeed, convincing Darcey that he honestly cared for her and that he had no ulterior motives would be the most taxing assignment he'd ever undertaken. If he were a betting man, which he often had been during numerous investigations, he wouldn't have wagered a plug nickel on his success. Darcey had been very nearly impossible when he dealt with her in Denver. And, thanks to him and Patrick, she was even more of a cynic than she had been then.

Chapter 23

A look of utter boredom etched Darcey's elegant features. She had spent the past ten minutes enclosed in a carriage with Edward Talbert. He had been rattling nonstop since he rapped on her cottage door to accompany her to the grand ball he was hosting at his mansion. It amazed Darcey that Edward had managed to begin every sentence with *I*. The man was incredibly proud of himself, though Darcey couldn't fathom why. When she compared Edward to Ka—

Darcey trampled on the betraying thought before it took root. Although she had vowed never to waste another emotion on that raven-haired rascal, Kane Callahan had taken up permanent residence in her mind. She had spent almost six weeks trying not to think about him, but his memory kept popping up at the most unexpected moments to torment her. Darcey

381

had hoped that forgetting her bittersweet love affair in Colorado would be easier than this. But that certainly hadn't been the case.

Oh, she had delivered herself all the consoling platitudes and alphabetically listed all the reasons why she was glad Kane was out of her life. Then she had set about to keep herself so busy that she met herself coming and going. The problem was that Kane's blessed memory had been coming and going with her, following like an ever-constant shadow.

"I managed to convince a very influential entrepreneur to invest in our railroad company yesterday," Edward announced with colossal pride. "I assured him that trains are the coming thing and nothing can hold them back. I predict we will be able to reach Denver in at least three years and soon after I will be able to connect the east line with the west."

Darcey inwardly grimaced at the reference to Denver, but she managed to force a smile. "I'm sure you'll reach your goal, Edward," she replied absently.

Although Darcey knew she had been offered her new position in Edward's company because of her looks rather than her efficiency, she had quickly accepted the new job. There had been a time not so long ago when she would have been insulted, just as she had been when Owen Graves tried to patronize her because she was a woman. But those things which had once been so important to her—things like making a place for herself in this man's world—just didn't seem to matter anymore.

"I invited many of our investors to the party tonight," Edward was saying when Darcey finally got around to listening. "I want you to charm them all, Darcey. I want them to be impressed by our lovely new addition to the company."

Darcey gnashed her teeth. So Edward expected her to flirt with his investors, did he? And why shouldn't she? She, after all, had gotten very good at that sort of thing, at Edward's insistence. He made the same aggravating request before they arrived at every business meeting and social function they attended together. And why had she obliged him? Darcey wasn't quite certain. Maybe it was to reassure herself that she could attract men if she wanted to. Maybe it was like salve to soothe her wounded heart. Of course, all this flirtation meant nothing. It was simply a childish game she played to counteract the devastating effect Kane had had on her. She hadn't been able to make him love her. Lord, she hadn't even tried; she had been too busy being defensive and fighting her vulnerability to him. And the worst part of all was that now *she* was reacting just as Kane had done to compensate for the heartache Melanie What's-her-name had caused him.

Honest to God, she didn't even know herself at all these days . . . And just listen to her! She had even resorted to using Kane's favorite expression! Damn . . .

"I don't expect you to spend all your time with me, love," Edward murmured as he leaned over to drop a kiss to Darcey's petal-soft lips. "I think we both need to socialize for business reasons. I hope that later . . . when the party's over . . ." He blessed her with his most charming smile. "I have heard through the grapevine that we have become the talk of St. Louis, since we have been keeping constant company. I think we should be doing some of the things the gossips speculate we're doing."

Darcey caught herself the split-second before the angry retort which stampeded to the tip of her tongue leaped off. If Edward Talbert thought this relationship of theirs was going to progress into an intimate phase, he would be sorely disappointed. After all, she had only taken this position and tolerated his arrogance to teach her father a lesson about meddling in her life.

"Ah, I believe we're here," Edward declared as the coach rolled to a halt in front of his magnificent three-story mansion. "I want you to put on that bewitching smile of yours, sweeting, and make my investors glad they are part of my company."

With graceful ease, Darcey pulled the flowing gold satin skirts around her and stepped from the coach. Her gaze swept across the immaculate grounds that were illuminated by lanterns that spotlighted the rows of elegant phaetons which lined the circular driveway. It seemed that everyone who was anyone in St. Louis was in attendance, awaiting the return of their host.

Darcey braced herself for a long evening of idle conversation and sugar-coated smiles. Although she had attended several of these grand parties on Edward's arm since her return from Colorado, she always felt alone in the crowds. Curse it, sometimes she even felt as if she were the only living soul on the planet. And when she crawled into bed each night, the emptiness very nearly suffocated her. She only seemed to be going through the mechanical paces of living. There were no challenges, no one with whom to match wits, no one who touched her emotionally. She was living in a vacuum and the restlessness that seized her never seemed to go away.

"I want you to be sure to give Jonathan Beezely plenty of attention," Edward coached her. "I know he has recently wed, but he still has an eye for beauty and has scads of money. I've been trying to persuade him to invest more heavily in our western expansion. I think he will be more generous if you make it worth his while."

Darcey pasted on her most bedazzling smile and swept into the crowded vestibule. Once or twice, she chided herself for playing this charade for Edward. But, she reminded herself determinedly, this was all part of a necessary distraction designed to rout every last thought of Kane Callahan from her mind. And once she had succeeded, she would tell Edward Talbert what he could do with this job and the intimacy he expected to be having with her in the near future.

A frown knitted Darcey's brow when her thoughts circled back to Edward's last remark. Beezely . . . Where had she heard that name before? It rang a distant bell. Ah well, Darcey mused as she extended her hand to greet one of the guests. She would probably recall the name soon enough since Edward planned to thrust her at Jonathan Beezely for his own selfish intentions.

Projecting an air of enthusiasm she didn't really feel,

Darcey made all the proper rounds of how-do-you-do's. When Edward guided her into the overflowing ballroom, he singled out the investors he expected her to charm for business reasons. After fifteen minutes of leaving Darcey to mingle with one stuffed shirt and then another, Edward returned to her side to propel her through the congested crowd.

"I finally located our newest investor," Edward told her. "I want you to keep company with him and make him feel welcome." He gestured across the room to the dashing raven-haired man who was decked out in the fancy trappings of a gentleman.

Darcey's legs very nearly folded up at the knees when her startled gaze locked with a sparkling pair of silver-blue eyes. Her chest caved in when her heart began hammering furiously against her ribs. It was at that precise moment that Darcey realized just how deep the taproot of Kane's memory ran.

Willfully, she dragged her gaze away to note there wasn't a woman in the room who wasn't admiring St. Louis's tall, dark, and handsome newcomer. Curse it, what was Kane doing here, all dressed up like this? No man deserved to look so damned attractive, especially this one!

"Darcey, I want you to meet Kane Callahan. Although his family made their fortune in riverboats, this shrewd businessman has fully realized that rails are the mode of the future." Edward smiled down at his stunned escort. "Kane, this is Darcey O'Roarke."

Striking a sophisticated pose, Kane drew Darcey's clammy hand into his and brushed his lips over her wrist. It was the slightest breath of a touch, but he could feel her instantaneous reaction. Good, he thought in relief. The spark was still there. Now all he had to do was convince this stubborn sprite that the spark could ignite love's raging flame. All he needed was a little cooperation on her part.

"The pleasure is all mine, my dear," Kane drawled in a low, caressing tone. "I've only seen such rare beauty once before in my life."

"Oh?" Edward chuckled in amusement. "And where, I wonder, could there be another woman to match our lovely Darcey?"

Our Darcey? Kane gnashed his teeth. She was *his,* not *ours.* Edward Talbert was loose with his possessive pronouns, at least Kane hoped so. The thought of Darcey encircled in another man's arms stabbed him like a cactus needle.

"During my travels in Colorado, I met a most remarkable young woman," Kane explained, never taking his eyes off Darcey's flushed face for even a moment. "But even her exquisite beauty is a dim memory in comparison to such divine elegance."

If Darcey could have gotten away with it without causing embarrassment to herself, she would have wheeled around and plunged through the crowd to race out the front door. The last man she expected to see kept turning up to stir up old memories faster than a witch could boil her magic brew. The instant he touched her and stared down at her with that roguish grin, Darcey felt as if she'd been run over by a locomotive. A rush of forbidden memories rumbled through her and a riptide of emotion tormented her to no end.

"Well, I'll leave the two of you to become better acquainted," Edward commented before spinning on his heel. "But don't try to steal my lady away from me, Callahan. And you will also have to answer to the other investors if you deprive them of Darcey's entertaining company."

When Edward ambled over to converse with his other associates, Darcey got herself in hand and glared at the midnight-haired rogue who had put her emotions in a tailspin and her heart on a drumroll in one second flat.

Kane smiled to himself. He hadn't forgotten the way she tilted her chin when she was put out with him, the way her eyes sparkled like emerald fire when she was angry. Darcey was defiance personified, ever ready to fend off the world and everyone in it.

"What are you doing here?" Darcey hissed, half under her breath. "I swear you have played so many contrasting roles that I wonder if *you* even know who you really are." She raked him up and down with consternation. "A former riverboat tycoon turned to railroads expansion? My Lord, don't tell me I have the misfortune of getting caught in the middle of another of your clandestine investigations?"

"Yes and no," Kane replied with a smile.

"I love your definite answers," Darcey grumbled in a resentful tone.

Like a connoisseur of fine art scrutinizing a masterpiece, his probing gaze swept over her. "And I love the way you look tonight," Kane complimented unexpectedly. "This gown displays all your tantalizing assets to their best advantage."

It really griped him that she had worn such a seductive gown for Edward Talbert's benefit, especially when she had fastened herself into such modest apparel in Kane's presence. And he told her as much.

"This creation is far more alluring than those high-collared garments you bundled yourself into in Denver," he said, "But no one knows better than I that your beauty is—"

"Stop it," Darcey muttered. "I asked you a question. Don't think I'm so dim-witted that I can be distracted by your flattery and your insinuations."

Sure enough, Darcey wasn't cooperating one tittle. Kane hadn't expected her to, but it would have made his courtship a damned sight easier if she'd meet him halfway.

When Kane didn't immediately respond, Darcey glared at him. "What is it you want?"

"I wanted to tell you I love you. I did in Colorado and I still do now." Kane told her simply and directly. "I want you with me always."

Darcey blinked like an owl adjusting to bright sunlight. There had been a time when she swore she would believe those softly uttered confessions if he offered them to her when he wasn't overcome by passion. Now he had said the words flat out and she still couldn't bring herself to believe him, not after what Noah had told her about Melanie Something-or-other. That was also a good while before she discovered Kane and Patrick had conspired to forcefully remove her from Denver. Everything had changed since those nights they had spent in the mountains.

"You still won't let yourself believe me, will you? Or is it that you are just so incredibly stubborn that you don't *want* to believe me?" His hand curled beneath her chin, forcing her to meet his unwavering gaze. "I love you, Darcey."

Darcey retreated a safe distance away and inhaled a steadying breath. It rattled her that this man could only touch her lightly and she could melt like hot glue. "I believed you were a wastrel, a gambler and a thief and—"

"Gambler, thief, and wastrel," Kane corrected her with a teasing grin. "It seems your sense of alphabetical order is askew."

"Whatever." She waved him off in her eagerness to make her point. "You turned out to be none of those things. I cannot believe what I see because you are only an illusion. And I cannot believe what I hear because you have plied me with so many lies that I couldn't recognize the truth if it walked up, sat down, and squashed me flat!"

"Then believe what you feel," Kane challenged as he moved toward her.

The endless rabble of guests faded into oblivion. To Darcey, the room suddenly seemed no larger than the space this handsome giant occupied.

"Believe what I feel when I take you in my arms," Kane whispered. "Let the memories come to life."

Darcey swallowed hard when Kane's arm stole

around her to pull her quivering body against his rock-hard contours. In fluid rhythm with the music that reverberated around the room, Kane made intimate movements that suggested far more erotic activities than were usually found on the dance floor. Darcey's pulse leaped and the imprint of his powerful body molded to hers burned like fire.

"Stop it," she demanded, her voice wobbly.

"Stop what?" Kane quested as his lips sought out that ultrasensitive point just beneath her ear. "Stop dancing? Stop loving you? I can do one, but not the other. I want you in my arms. I want to touch you, to kiss you, to make wild, sweet love to you the way we did when we were . . ."

With a strangled gasp, Darcey pushed away as far as his encircling arms would allow. "My father put you up to this, didn't he?" Darcey accused, her voice two octaves higher than normal.

He was getting to her; he could sense it. Kane beamed in satisfaction. He could feel her trembling in his arms and it wasn't from fury. Her body remembered the sweet magic, even if her intractable mind refused to let her buckle to his seductive assault.

"Papa paid you to hound and torment me so I would finally give up and go home where he thinks I belong, didn't he?" Darcey quizzed him. "Well, I'm not giving up my cottage and my life here to go home and twiddle my thumbs. And I suppose Papa is also paying you to investigate Edward's railroad company, too. He detests the threat and competition of the rails. He'd like nothing better than to find corruption in the ranks and send every railroad company plunging into bankruptcy."

Darcey was gathering momentum. As usual, her active imagination was off and running. But she was partially right about his reasons for being here. Kane had spent the past two weeks snooping around, posing questions about Edward Talbert.

"Your father misses you," Kane did admit without completely giving himself away.

"I knew it," Darcey muttered resentfully. "He *is* up to no good and so are you!"

"Patrick and I both have your best interest at heart," Kane assured her as he spun her around the dance floor.

"My best interest? My eye!" Darcey spewed, wishing she could be anywhere except in this man's powerful arms. He stirred up too many forbidden memories. His touch reminded her of more intimate moments she had tried so hard to forget. But one casual caress from him and he resurrected those titillating sensations that Darcey wanted dead and buried.

"Patrick loves you as much as I do," Kane murmured against her cheek.

"You're repeating yourself," Darcey admonished. "I didn't believe you then and I'd be an even bigger fool to believe you now. And since I refused to cooperate with you or Papa, I suppose I can expect to be dragged off to some secluded spot to be terrorized all over again."

Kane had cautioned himself against losing his temper. He knew he had his work cut out for him with this skeptical sprite, but all his well-meaning sermons to himself on the necessity of patience and understanding flew out the window when Darcey flung accusations at him and glared at him as if he were a snake that had slithered out from under a rock.

"Damn it, woman, I came here on my best behavior, but you are as immovable as a stone wall. What does it take to get through that slab of rock you call a brain?" he muttered acrimoniously.

"What does it take to get it through that chunk of wood you call a skull that I'm immune to your tactics of deceptive persuasion?" Darcey countered. "I know perfectly well that I mean nothing to you, so don't try to charm me into doing your bidding. Noah told me all about your broken engagement to Melanie What's-her-name. Your own brother told me that you were only using me to compensate for your own rejection. You were tormenting me, just to hurt me the way you were hurting."

There, it was out in the open. Let him talk himself out of this one. Darcey dared him to try!

Kane looked as if he'd bitten into something sour. Damn it to hell! Noah had the biggest mouth this side of the Continental Divide. Kane couldn't wait to stuff his fist into his little brother's face a couple of times. So that was what had turned Darcey completely against him. No wonder she refused to accept his love. Noah had botched up royally, curse his well-meaning hide!

Satisfied that she'd gotten the last word, Darcey lurched around to find a safe corner to stand in. But the woman who was regally poised behind her, staring through her as she wasn't even there, blocked Darcey's exit.

"Kane . . . what are you doing in St. Louis?"

Kane cursed his damnable luck. Of all the people in all the world, why did Melanie have to waltz up during his verbal battle with Darcey?

Darcey's curious gaze bounced back and forth between the willowy blonde in burgundy and the fashionably dressed rake whose bronzed face had bleached flour-white.

When Kane made no attempt at introductions, Melanie glanced briefly at Darcey before fixing her gaze on Kane. Melanie had been groomed in all the social graces. Even though she was shocked to find her ex-fiancé at the party, she was still aware of her social obligations.

"We have yet to be introduced," Melanie said with a cordial smile. "I am Melanie Beezely."

Darcey assessed the voluptuous beauty and realized whom she was addressing. She could also understand why Kane and every other man would be attracted to this seductive blonde. Sensuality oozed from her pores and her curvaceous assets very nearly poured from the skintight gown that dipped dangerously low on her bosom. Melanie had regal poise, dazzling good looks, an arresting figure and the expensive garments which accentuated what Mother Nature had generously bestowed on her. Expensive jewels were draped all over her—glittering rings, sparkling diamond bracelets and a stunning necklace.

The provocative blonde also possessed a flirtatious

394

smile that had undoubtedly caught many a man's eye, Kane's included. It looked as though Melanie had practiced seduction to perfection. Even if Darcey tried to emulate this sophisticated beauty, she doubted she could match her in any arena. Obviously Melanie had made it her life's profession to tantalize men with her beauty and tempt them with her feminine charms.

"I'm Darcey O'Roarke," she murmured unenthusiastically.

"Ah, yes, Edward has been singing your praises for weeks now," Melanie reported before tossing another provocative smile in Kane's direction. Her pale-blue eyes momentarily shifted back to Darcey. "Edward seems quite taken with you."

Mustering a faint smile, Darcey excused herself and edged past the stunning beauty. No wonder Kane was still carrying a torch for her. Melanie was everything a man could ever want—lovely, and willing, if the glances she flung at Kane were any indication. And unless Darcey missed her guess, which she seriously doubted she had, the new Mrs. Beezely wasn't opposed to reckless affairs any more than her husband reportedly was.

And within the next few minutes, Jonathan Beezely confirmed Darcey's suspicions. After Edward introduced them, Darcey found herself the recipient of several leering smiles that visually undressed her. Although Darcey tried to impart information about the western expansion, Jonathan was far more interested in flinging suggestive innuendos that had nothing to do with locomotives and steel rails. And why he was plying her with so much attention when he had a wife like Melanie was beyond Darcey. Marriage, it appeared, hadn't slowed either of the Beezelys. They seemed to delight in other conquests.

Darcey found herself bombarded by incredible feelings of inadequacy when she glanced over to see Melanie melting in Kane's arms on the dance floor. If she wasn't sure there were still sparks flying between Kane and Melanie before, she was now. Darcey could never compete with her. Darcey's father had taught her to succeed and to excel, to live up to her full intellectual potential. But when it came to luring a man, Darcey felt . . .

A miserable sigh tripped from her lips. Darcey was so frustrated and confused that she didn't know how she felt or what she wanted. Not that it mattered now. Kane was holding the woman he really wanted. He had only pursued Darcey as a substitute for the woman he really needed. Darcey had never been anything but a convenience for Kane. And he probably had known Melanie would be among Edward's guests, too. That was another reason he had arrived upon the scene—rekindle old flames.

The sooner she accepted the fact that she was only torturing herself by harboring this illogical affection for Kane, the happier she'd be. If she had a lick of sense she would pack up and go home to her father. Then Patrick would be satisfied and there would be no further reason for Kane to remain in St. Louis, except to pursue the love of his life and lure her away from her new husband.

And by damned, she *was* going to go home. There was no sense being unnecessarily stubborn. She missed her father, and this estrangement between them felt unnatural. They had both suffered long enough. It was time she forgave Patrick. Maybe Kane was right. Even though Patrick had tried to frighten her home from Denver, his heart was in the right place; he had just gone about getting her home in the wrong fashion. It was time she squelched her pride and returned home where she belonged. She could still keep her position in the Talbert Railroad Company. Her father wouldn't like it, but Darcey needed the distraction to help her forget the man who had turned her wrong side out and bruised her heart as if it were his punching bag.

Chapter 24

"I've missed you, Kane," Melanie whispered as she sidled a little closer than respectability allowed. While Kane waltzed her around the ballroom at her request, Melanie gazed up into his expressionless face. "It was you I always wanted. You know that, don't you?"

"Was it?" Kane questioned, his tone conveying none of the emotions that coursed through him.

If nothing else, this unwanted encounter had assured Kane that his liaison with Melanie had only been a passing fancy, his half-hearted attempt to settle down. He had always wondered why he felt the need to procrastinate about tying the matrimonial knot. To be sure, Melanie knew all the sensual, provocative ways to make a man glad he was a man. And true, she could be amusing company when she wasn't fretting over her climb up the social ladder. But as desirable as Melanie was, she lacked Darcey's spunk, magnificent spirit, and keen intellect.

Until this moment, Kane hadn't realized just how

deeply he was involved with Darcey. He didn't just crave that delicious body of hers. He loved her to distraction and he actually *liked* her. Why, he even found himself organizing his life in alphabetical order nowadays! It seemed the most sensible thing to do. And any woman who wasn't Darcey seemed dull in comparison.

"Oh, Kane, you needn't pretend I didn't hurt you," Melanie cooed, flashing him a disarming smile. "I behaved abominably and I know it. I was put out with you because you wouldn't set the marriage date. And like a fool, I looked elsewhere for someone to replace you."

"You seem to have done well for yourself," Kane replied before glancing in Darcey's direction.

It annoyed him to see Darcey in Jonathan Beezely's arms. That rake had attached himself to her like a limpet to a rock. It seemed to Kane that the four of them needed to exchange partners. Everybody was in the wrong set of arms. At least he knew who *he* wanted to hold. Melanie felt all wrong. Luckily, he'd realized that before it was too late.

"Perhaps I've done well for myself in outward appearance," Melanie conceded, pressing closer. "But Jonathan is not you, Kane." Her pale-blue eyes lifted to his. "I want what we once had."

Invitation was written all over her face. Kane would have had to be blind not to read the blatant offer. But he knew exactly what he wanted and it wasn't Melanie Brooks Beezely.

An annoyed frown creased Melanie's brow. Kane's lack of interest incensed her. She had noticed where his attention had strayed for the umpteenth time during their conversation and she set about to correct any misconceptions Kane had.

"You are wasting your time if you've decided to make me jealous by courting Darcey O'Roarke," Melanie sniffed. "Edward has set his cap for her. In fact, from what I've heard, they are already as close as two people can get. Although Darcey's praises have been sung at the company because of her remarkable head for business, we all know why Edward hired her . . ."

Kane silently cursed at the news. If Darcey had turned to another man for consolation he'd skin her alive. She had betrayed him. Her beauty had been meant for his eyes only. He had taught her all she knew about passion and now she had employed the tactics *he* had taught her on that prancing dandy! The bitter taste of jealousy almost gagged him.

Damn it, he and Darcey had been through hell together. And they had also seen glimpses of paradise in each other's arms. How dare she give herself to that cocky rake! Kane hadn't even wanted to touch another woman after Darcey walked out of his life. If that didn't signify his devotion to her, he didn't know what did!

"Melanie, let's get one thing straight right here and now," Kane muttered. "I have no desire to become one of your many conquests. You made your bed when you flitted off to St. Louis. And now that you've made your bed, you can sleep in it with your husband who, from the look of things, is as intrigued with Miss O'Roarke as you claim Edward to be."

Melanie gasped indignantly at his comments and her face turned purple. "Well, I never!"

Kane regained his self-control and smiled with sardonic amusement. "Oh yes you have. A number of times. And not just with me. If you ask me, you and Jonathan deserve each other."

Kane swaggered toward the terrace door and evaporated into the shadows. Melanie silently fumed as she glared at the auburn-haired beauty who had captured Jonathan's undivided attention. She knew perfectly well that her husband indulged himself in the arms of others, and so had she. She would lure Kane Callahan back, just to prove the power she held over him.

Reject her, would he? Well, she would see how firm-willed he was! She would ruin his fascination with Miss O'Roarke just to spite him! He deserved to be taught a lesson!

Darcey mentally prepared herself for the moment when Edward escorted her to the door of her cottage. He had made his intentions known earlier. After her unnerving confrontation with Kane, Darcey fully intended to let Edward kiss away all thoughts of that dark-haired devil.

When Edward bent to press a kiss to her waiting lips, Darcey found herself making comparisons. It only took a moment to realize the difference in Edward's embrace. Darcey was sad that this very eligible railroad magnate couldn't compete with Kane Callahan in any arena. There were kisses and then there were Kane's explosive brand of kisses. She knew there and then that Edward could never take Kane's place in her heart, even if that silver-blue-eyed man was ornery and deceptive and constantly toying with her emotions.

"I want you," Edward whispered as he clutched her supple body to his. "You know I do—"

Darcey pressed her palms to his chest to hold him at bay. "Edward, I'm not in the habit of—"

"I know," Edward murmured. "But I will teach you how to—"

"You didn't let me finish," Darcey insisted before dodging the oncoming kiss. "I don't think—"

Edward refused to be put off. His mouth came down on hers with demanding possessiveness.

When he finally let her come up for air, Darcey glared at him. "Enough! I have something to say and I expect you to listen!"

"Confound it, woman, how long do you intend to make me wait? What is it you want? A marriage proposal? It's yours," Edward graciously offered.

Darcey gnashed her teeth and cast diplomacy to the wind. "What I *don't* want is to be squished in a bear hug. And believe you me, I know how bears hug! And what I *do* want is to retire to my bed! It has been a long evening."

"I want you to retire to bed, too . . . with me," Edward rasped before attempting to steal another kiss.

Darcey had to resort to giving Edward a swift kick in the shins to free herself from his possessive grasp. But that only frustrated him more than he already was.

"Don't forget that I gave you the position in my company," Edward growled into her glare. "I can fire you as quickly as I hired you."

Darcey puffed up with so much indignation that her breasts very nearly burst from the daring décolleté of her gown. "Are you suggesting that if I don't let you have your way, I will lose my position?"

"You said it. I didn't." Edward scowled. "Surely you're not naive enough to think I hired you and have been courting you just because of your brilliant mind! I am, above all else, a man and you arouse me."

"Good night, Edward. I think perhaps you should get yourself under control before our next conversation," Darcey advised. "And if maintaining my position in your company depends on my acquiescing to your lust, I don't want the job."

"Darcey, wait a minute . . ." Edward slumped in a posture of dejection when the door slammed shut in his face. Hurriedly, he rapped on the door, but he was met only with a furious "Go away!" And so he did. It seemed the sensible thing to do, considering he had bungled his amorous assault and put that elusive beauty on immediate defense.

"My, you certainly handled that nicely," Kane snickered as he disengaged himself from the inky shadows of the hall and swaggered forward.

Darcey jumped as if she'd been stung when the teasing voice rolled toward her. "Honest to God, what does it take to get rid of you? How did you get in here?" she demanded, glaring daggers at the shadowed figure that was propped negligently against the staircase.

"I'm a detective, remember?" he mocked dryly.

"Sneaking around is one of the things I do best."

It had come as a great relief when Kane overheard the conversation that had taken place on Darcey's stoop. Edward's remarks had dissolved Kane's worst fears. Darcey had not turned to another man to punish him for what she considered betrayal. Melanie had lied to him for her own selfish purposes.

When Kane sauntered toward her, Darcey shot into the parlor to light the lantern. She wasn't afraid of the dark, only the temptation which darkness presented when she found herself alone with Kane. As the light filled the immaculate parlor, Darcey placed herself behind the sofa for protection and tilted a determined chin. She was not giving in to her wanton desires for this man. He had come here to play his mischievous games again and she would not tolerate them.

"Your mission has been accomplished," she informed him tartly. "I have thought it over and you can tell Papa I have decided to come home. You needn't try to persuade me with all your seductive tactics. I'll go home the first chance I get and you can trot off to assume your next assignment, Mister Detective. You win. I admit defeat."

A curious frown knitted Kane's brow as he ambled across the room, watching Darcey retreat, step for step. "Why? Because you think your father can protect you from your overzealous suitor's advances?"

"No," Darcey protested. "I can take care of myself . . ."

A dull thud resounded around the room when Darcey backed herself into the farthest corner. But it offered no protection. Kane approached like an infantry, leaving nowhere else to retreat.

Darcey threw up a hand in a deterring gesture before he pulled her into his arms and she buckled to her vulnerability. "I have had my fill of amorous advances for one night . . . if that's what you're planning. I already told you that you have accomplished your purpose here. I'm sure Papa will pay you handsomely for your assignment." Darcey showed him the door, as if he didn't know where it was. "Good night and goodbye, Kane. I'm sure Melanie is expecting you. I'm also sure the two of you will have a very enjoyable evening making up for lost time."

Kane braced his arms on either side of her, refuting any attempt of her escape. Damn it all, Kane hadn't expected her to give in the moment he approached her. But the least she could have done was cut him a little slack here. But no, it was going to be a battle to the end.

"*A,* I didn't take a penny of your father's money after our fiasco in Denver," he told her point-blank.

"You didn't?" Darcey gaped at him. Valiantly, she fought the devastating effect his sheer physical presence was having on her. But if he didn't move away from her and quickly, she feared she'd melt on the spot.

"No, I did not," he confirmed. "I don't need the money. I never did. My father *did* own a fleet of riverboats that navigated up and down the Missouri. I happen to be stinking rich, if it matters. I just never quite fit into the life of the independently wealthy. *B,* I invested in Edward Talbert's railroad company because it seems to be solid and above board. Patrick and I both wanted to be absolutely certain of that before we sank our money into it."

406

"You did?" Darcey squeaked in disbelief.

"We did," Kane affirmed. "And *C,* I demanded no monetary compensation for investigating Talbert's company. He may be a mite overeager in his romantic pursuits, but he seems to be an honest businessman whose noble standards match your father's."

Darcey struggled to draw a breath that wasn't thick with the musky scent of this seductive rogue who eclipsed the lanternlight and left her quaking in his looming shadow. "That is all very interesting. And unless there is a *D,* I would like to retire to bed. I have considerable packing to do tomorrow. And let us not forget dear Melanie who seemed all too eager to see you again."

"Will *you* forget about Melanie," Kane scowled. *"I* forgot all about her a long time ago."

"Not according to Noah," Darcey parried, her chin tilting to that characteristically rebellious angle.

"Just because my little brother was named after a biblical figure does not mean his word is gospel," Kane muttered. "Noah can barely manage his own life and I certainly wouldn't turn him loose with mine. He has only just succeeded in tracking Owen Graves down, and it certainly took him long enough, I might add. Noah has a lot to learn about investigation and about poking his nose in places it doesn't belong—my personal affairs for one."

"Why are you telling me all this?" Darcey quizzed him, shifting nervously beneath his probing gaze. "All I really want is for you to leave so I can go to bed. All you have succeeded in doing is giving me a hellish headache."

"I'm telling you this because there is no Melanie," Kane murmured as his head dipped deliberately toward hers.

"No? She certainly looked real enough to me," Darcey smirked as she artfully eluded his kiss. "It also seemed to me she had *invitation* stamped all over her."

"Would I be here now if I wanted Melanie?" Kane questioned reasonably.

"Only if she couldn't detach herself from her husband, which she probably couldn't until late at night since they arrived *at* and departed *from* the party together. But I'm sure she'll find a way to sneak off. And if she can't, there is always tomorrow," she insisted, spinning another sticky theory like a spider. "I suppose I'm the time you're killing until Melanie can rendezvous with you in some quaint little out-of-the-way tavern."

Kane hadn't meant to burst out in incredulous laughter but he couldn't contain himself. Darcey's imagination was an absolute marvel. She could concoct some of the most farfetched conjectures he'd ever heard and make them sound so logical it was absolutely amazing. He combed his fingers through the lustrous auburn strands. "I find your wild deductions highly amusing."

Darcey slapped his hand away as if it were a pesky mosquito. "I want you to leave. *Now . . .*"

"I want you to love me forever," Kane countered as he glided his arms around the tiny indentation of her waist and bent her into the hard-muscled planes of his body.

"Of all the things you want from any woman, love isn't

even on the list!" Darcey growled, trying in vain to escape him. It was a waste of time and energy. Kane had meshed her betraying body into his, and her traitorous flesh responded instinctively.

"I love you, damn it," Kane growled in vexation. "What the hell do I have to do to convince you?"

"Try strapping anchors to your ankles and leaping into the river," she suggested, fighting like the devil for control of the fiery sensations that swamped her. "That ought to do it."

Kane finally admitted defeat. He knew how infuriatingly stubborn Darcey could be once she had made up her mind. He would wind up forcing himself on her as Edward had tried to do. That would only provoke her defensive instincts. As much as he hated the thought of walking away when he wanted her so badly that he ached all over, he had damned few choices available. She had to come to him willingly. Only then could he make headway.

"Have it your way, minx. You usually do," Kane grumbled as he stepped away from her. "But I intend to have the last word, at least." His silver-blue eyes pinned Darcey to the wall, the one to which she was clinging for support. "Melanie did offer me an invitation. It seems the bonds of matrimony are very flexible in her and Jonathan's case. But the minute I saw her tonight, I asked myself what I had ever seen in her besides a pretty face."

"A comely figure, regal poise, a taste for the fine things in life," Darcey couldn't help to add. Her tone was bitter in spite of her attempt to disguise it.

"That, too," Kane confessed honestly. "But I didn't

love her. In fact, I didn't even know what love was until you came along. And what my well-meaning little brother thought was a bad case of vindictiveness directed toward you was my inability to cope with my own frustrations where you were concerned."

Kane raked his fingers through his raven hair and sighed. And then suddenly, he was pacing all over the place. "You thought *I* put *you* through hell, but you didn't know the half of it, Darcey. I was committed to a role I detested, trying to frighten you back to your father for your own good. I had to let you think the worst about me. That was killing me bit by excruciating bit. And I couldn't let Giddeon and Noah pamper you during your captivity, either. They thought I was being unnecessarily cruel and you thought I was the worst form of life on the planet. I had to live with your scorn when all I really wanted was your love and respect."

He spun around to glare at her, a victim of his own exasperation. "How would you feel if you fell in love with someone who had been forced to think the worst about you? Don't you understand the torment I endured? I couldn't confess the truth without betraying the confidence of my client—your own father. And what Patrick didn't want to happen *did* happen. You turned against him when you accidentally overheard our private conversation. Not only had I lost you because you considered me a deceitful bastard, but you begrudged a father's heartfelt concern for your safety."

Kane brandished his finger in her face. "You, little imp, were too damned daring and independent for your own good. You forced Patrick to come to me for assistance. And I was committed to my assignment, which included protecting you from the rough elements of Denver society. The only crime I ever committed was loving you. And believe me, I've paid dearly for it. Now, no matter what I say, you refuse to believe the truth. I'm beginning to realize love isn't everything it is cracked up to be. My own father warned me of that when my mother traipsed off with another man, leaving him to raise two young sons on the river. We learned things we didn't need to know at a tender age. Wandering from one place to another like the restless river became a way of life for me. And then, when I finally made a stab at settling down instead of roaming all over creation like a nomad, Melanie—social butterfly that she is—found Jonathan Beezely who could afford to keep her in the manner to which she had grown accustomed."

Kane didn't know why he was rattling on. He doubted it was doing him one whit of good. Darcey just stood there, watching him circumnavigate the room, staring at him as if . . . he didn't know what!

"And then along came a green-eyed imp who was so incredibly stubborn that she refused to listen to reason. She defied every plea to leave Denver for her own protection. I got myself beaten to a pulp trying to protect her. And all I have received for my bruises and efforts on her behalf is her hatred, her mistrust, and her scorn. And if that's all there is to loving a woman to utter distraction, then maybe I should ride the rails back to Independence and become a hermit. Honest to God, I'm not sure women are worth all the trouble a man has to tolerate!"

For the first time ever, Darcey began to understand what Kane had been through. His mother's abandonment had left hidden scars. Melanie's betrayal had reinforced his belief that women were too selfish and temperamental to be deserving of a man's love. And her own bitter liaison with Michael Dupris had made her so wary of men that she defied the one man who had taught her the true meaning of love. She had come to care for Kane, even when she believed the worst about him. And she had unintentionally dealt him more misery in her effort to protect her own bleeding heart. They had gotten off on the wrong foot and it had been downhill from there. But through it all, she had loved him and nothing had been the same since she rode out of his life. There were no challenges, no one with whom to share the smallest of victories. She was a shell of a woman who could find no purpose to make her happy.

Kane heaved a frustrated sigh, wishing Darcey would say something . . . anything! But the woman who usually had a counter for every remark just stood there gaping up at him with those dazzling emerald eyes that cut all the way to the heart.

"I'll drop by in the morning to tell Patrick you'll be coming home. That should delight him," he mumbled as he strode toward the door. "It seems you despise me a helluva lot more than I let myself believe. I cared enough about you to keep trying to win your love and respect, but it appears you want nothing I have to give you."

He paused beside the door and glanced back at the lovely vision who stood there like a statue. "I'm walking out of your life for good, Darcey. Obviously that's what you want. I've certainly been told enough times to leave you alone." The door slammed shut on the last word.

Alone . . . The haunting sound echoed through the foyer and died into deafening silence.

Darcey inhaled a shallow breath and struggled to swallow. She hadn't been the least bit prepared for the confessions Kane had offered her. And like a senseless ninny, she had stood there, peering at him as if he were a creature from another planet. But she couldn't let Kane walk out of her life, thinking she didn't love him! She had sworn never to pledge her love after Michael had trifled with her. Now it was difficult to express her feelings. She had bottled them up inside her for too long, especially after guarding her heart so closely these past three months. But the words of love were there, waiting for just the right moment to tumble from her lips. And if she didn't stop Kane he would be gone for good.

That panicky thought put Darcey to flight. By the time she raced across the parlor to open the door, Kane had whizzed off in his carriage. Muttering at the inconvenience of having to chase him down on foot, Darcey zoomed down the street. When she spied a horse tethered in front of one of the local taverns, she swung into the saddle to follow after the speeding coach.

Wasn't this a switch? thought Darcey in wry amusement. She had spent most of her time running away from that handsome rake. And now she was thundering after him, afraid she was going to lose him forever.

And she very well might if he didn't slow that blessed carriage down! She didn't have the foggiest idea where Kane was staying, and if she lost track of him, it could be hours before she traced him to his sleeping quarters.

When Kane's rumbling carriage screeched to a halt outside of St. Louis's most elegant hotel, Darcey breathed a sigh of relief. Now she knew where he was, even if it took her a few extra moments to locate his room.

Frantically, Darcey rehearsed what she intended to say to Kane. She wanted to explain why she had been so mistrusting of his intentions and to divulge her heart-breaking relationship with Michael. She had been too humiliated to speak of it, but now Kane needed to know what influences had made her so cynical of all men.

Reining the steed to a halt, Darcey bounded from the saddle and scurried up the steps to the lobby. Without ado, she marched toward the clerk's desk to ask directions to Kane's room. Clutching her hampering skirts, she scaled the steps two at a time.

This was the moment of reckoning, she told herself shakily. She had allowed herself to believe that Kane truly cared for her. Now she had to assure him that he was what she needed to make her life complete. And he better have been telling her the truth this time or she would feel like a fool all over again. Darcey winced at the frustrating thought of laying her heart on the line and having it squashed flat a second time.

Feeling as depressed as one man could get, Kane

fumbled his way across his dark room, stumbling against the furniture as he went. Finally he managed to locate the lantern and tinderbox. In a few moments, the flickering flame engulfed the shadows.

Shock registered on Kane's face when he glanced down at his bed to see the uninvited guest who had snuggled beneath the quilts.

"Melanie . . ." Kane croaked.

"Kane . . ." An inviting smile played on her lips as her bare arms lifted to him in seductive invitation.

Without warning, the door creaked open and an unannounced visitor barged into the room. Kane glanced up and scowled when he realized how damaging these circumstances would look to a woman who possessed an incredibly active imagination. Darcey's timing was terrible and Kane wished the floor would open so he could drop out of sight. The thought of explaining himself out of this incriminating situation made him cringe in gloomy apprehension.

The sight of Melanie sprawled in Kane's bed as if she belonged there struck Darcey like a physical blow. She glared at Melanie, who glared right back at her. With a silent curse, Darcey focused her absolute attention on Kane, who grimaced as if he'd been stabbed.

In that crucial moment, Kane pondered and discarded a dozen possible explanations, none of which seemed worth the waste of breath.

"Well, damn," he finally said, expelling the breath he had been holding until he very nearly choked on it. It was all over but the shouting. There was no doubt about it, Kane thought deflatedly. This time he had lost Darcey for good.

Chapter 25

The look that was frozen on Darcey's face when she glanced in Kane's direction a second time was one he swore would haunt him through all eternity. The very fact that this nymph had followed him back to his hotel indicated that she had begun to believe in him, to trust him enough to try to make a new beginning. But the anger and hurt in her eyes was like a dagger in Kane's heart. He knew what she was thinking and it killed him to watch her think it.

Smug satisfaction pursed Melanie's lips when she observed the wounded expression on Darcey's face. No doubt, this chit had fallen beneath Kane's charms and had come to offer herself to him. But she wasn't going to get him. Few men could match Kane Callahan's prowess and Melanie fully intended to be the one who spent a portion of this night in his arms.

Melanie had plotted her departure from her home the moment after Kane walked out of the party. Once Jonathan had dozed off, Melanie had sneaked away.

And it hadn't taken her long to locate Kane . . .

With time to spare, she had tiptoed up to Kane's room and climbed into his bed to await his return. She hadn't expected extra company, but things had worked out superbly. Melanie could make sure this auburn-haired chit steered clear of Kane in the future, leaving him in Melanie's capable hands.

Humiliated to the bone, Darcey wheeled toward the door. Curse Kane Callahan to the far reaches of hell! Like an idiotic fool, she had believed he had come to love her and she had chased him down to bare her heart to him. Instead, she caught him in his own lie, just as she had caught Michael with his paramour. Kane had only come to torment her before dashing back to Melanie's arms. Damn him.

Before Darcey could sail out the door, Kane thrust out an arm to snare her. His hand clamped around her elbow, towing her back inside the room.

"I didn't know Melanie was going to be here when I returned," Kane growled down into Darcey's blanched face.

"Didn't you?" she countered with loathing.

"Tell her, Melanie," Kane demanded without taking his eyes off Darcey. He was operating under the theory that if he looked away, even for a second, she would disintegrate into a puff of smoke.

Melanie clutched the sheet over her ample bosom and sighed theatrically. "Oh for heaven's sake, sweetheart. I don't see why I should have to lie for you," she declared with a pretty pout. "Darcey may as well know how it is between us, how it will always be."

Kane had never wanted to strike a woman as much

as he wanted to clobber Melanie at this crucial moment. She was purposely trying to destroy Darcey's trust in him to protect her own vanity and feminine pride. Well, Kane wouldn't have it!

"She's lying," he muttered.

"There seems to be a lot of that going around," Darcey hissed. The glare she flung at Kane pinpointed him as the biggest liar of all.

Kane was on the verge of pulling out his hair, strand by strand. "Damn it, woman, I love you, and I don't care who knows it. And that includes Melanie, who can't find what she wants in her marriage bed—or any other bed for that matter."

That blunt declaration brought Melanie upright with an indignant yelp. Now, more than ever, she was determined to spoil Kane's feeling for Darcey. "Don't be swayed by him," Melanie jeered bitterly. "For a year, I waited for him to return from wherever he kept going to do only the Lord knew what! He's as restless as a tumbleweed and he will only break your heart. If you have a grain of sense you will leave while you still can!"

Darcey wavered in indecision. Melanie was warning her that Kane would never settle down with one woman. But the compelling glow in those silver-blue eyes bade her to stay.

"Get dressed, Melanie," Kane ordered brusquely. "What we had was over long ago. Go back to your husband. I don't want you here."

Furious, and humiliated beyond words, Melanie wrapped the sheet around herself and stamped behind the dressing screen. In a matter of minutes, she had stuffed herself in her clothes and was on her way out the door.

"You are a fool if you stay, Darcey O'Roarke," Melanie assured her, holding her head as high as possible, considering the mortifying circumstances. "If you are expecting more than a night of reckless pleasure, you won't find it here, not with *him*. He couldn't settle down, even if you planted him and watered him twice a week. And if you do stay, you can expect to pay for your foolishness. I shall see to it that word spreads like wildfire, and then you can contend with the gossip and Edward's scorn. In fact, I wouldn't be surprised if this lusty tête-à-tête doesn't cost you your position with the railroad."

After delivering her threat, Melanie exited with more speed than dignity.

Darcey glanced toward the now-vacant bed and then back at the man who hadn't moved a muscle in five minutes. The fact that he had sent Melanie on her way with words that would refuse to allow her colossal pride to bring her back stirred Darcey's emotions, which had undergone such incredible turmoil that evening.

"People can change," Kane murmured as he loosed his tight grasp on Darcey's arms. "I couldn't change for Melanie because she wasn't woman enough to hold me. Unlike you, she is shallow and social-minded. But for you . . ." He sighed as his hand lifted to reverently limn the elegant features. "You started an eternal fire in me that refuses to burn itself out."

Kane was pressing her, forcing her to make her decision, despite the unfortunate incident with Melanie. But damn it, the frustration of not knowing if she would admit there was something special between them was driving him crazy.

His index finger traced her velvet-soft lips, aching to take them under his. "Make up your mind what you want—to stay or to go. I told you how I feel about you. Now what are *you* going to do about it?"

Darcey peered up into his ruggedly handsome face and made her decision. It was Kane's open, honest need to be accepted and to be believed that tugged so fiercely on her heartstrings. He found himself in a very incriminating situation and she could sense his frustration. The single most important sensation that vibrated from him to her was that what *she* thought mattered to him.

It was time to put her humiliating romance with Michael out of her mind and make a new beginning with the one man who had proved he would be there for her, through thick and thin.

"Well?" Kane demanded, at the end of his patience.

"I'm going to do what I should have done a long time ago," Darcey announced with great conviction.

"That's what I was afraid you were going to say," Kane grumbled defeatedly.

Unfortunately, he'd read her all wrong. Kane was sure she was going to call it quits forevermore. He flipped back the hem of his black velvet jacket and retrieved the pistol.

"Here." He slammed the Colt into her hand. "Why don't you just put me out of my misery. Then we'll both be satisfied."

"Thank you, I'd like that very much," Darcey said politely as she trained the pistol on his broad chest.

"Now kindly take off your clothes, Mister Detective. All of them . . ."

Kane promptly swallowed his tongue and stared goggle-eyed at her.

Darcey gestured the barrel of the pistol toward his jacket. *"Now* will be soon enough," she prompted with a devilish smile.

When Kane flagrantly ignored her order, Darcey jabbed him a good one with the pistol. "I know how to use this thing, don't think I don't. Now do as you're told."

"I suppose you're going to claim self-defense when the constable shows up to investigate my murder," Kane concluded bitterly. "Since I'll be undressed, you can claim I tried to molest you. And knowing your wild imagination, I'm sure you can dream up a believable tale to justify your drastic actions."

Darcey clamped hold of the nape of his jacket and jerked it off his shoulders. Carelessly, she tossed the garment aside, and Kane thought how that gesture of dropping his jacket in a wrinkled heap was highly irregular behavior for a woman who was such a stickler for order.

"Now the shirt," Darcey demanded in a no-nonsense tone.

"I swear you would go to the most remarkable extremes to make your point," Kane muttered grouchily. He was sure Darcey intended to put him through the same frustrating torture that he'd used when he had kidnapped her. She was repaying him for all the torment she had endured at his hands.

"Now the breeches and shoes," she ordered impatiently.

"I don't want to upset your alphabetical order, but it is ten times easier to remove the shoes first," Kane said flippantly.

After Kane had shucked every article of clothing and wore nothing but an annoyed frown, Darcey indicated the bed. "Lie down."

"No, I prefer to die standing up, if you don't mind."

"I do mind, quite a bit actually," she countered. "And to add just the right touch, I'll fetch the ropes." Darcey backed toward the drapes. Still holding Kane at gunpoint, she jerked on the tasseled cord and then flung the improvised rope to him. "Tie yourself to the bedposts. You're familiar with the procedure, I believe. After all, I learned the tactic from you."

"Darcey, I think this has gone far enough . . ."

"Do it!" she all but shouted at him.

He did it. Kane knew better than to argue with a loaded gun, especially when it was in the hands of a hot-tempered female like Darcey O'Roarke.

While he lay there with his arms looped to the bedpost, playing out the role he had originally designed for her in the remote cabin in the mountains, Darcey set the pistol aside. A bemused frown plowed Kane's brow when she proceeded to doff her elegant gold gown in the most seductive manner imaginable. Kane groaned in torment as the golden light flowed over every inch of satiny flesh she exposed to his hungry gaze.

So this was to be his final torture before she blew him

to kingdom come! Kane would have preferred to take a single bullet through the heart. But no, Darcey wanted him to suffer all the torments of the damned before she was through with him. And sure enough, only hell multiplied by three could compare to this! Watching her peel off every last garment was killing him. Knowing he would be forbidden to touch her before she launched him into eternity sent his spirits plunging to rock bottom.

"And now, Mister Master Detective," Darcey purred as she eased down to glide her hand over the carpet of hair that covered his chest and belly. "Clever as you are, let's see if you can figure out why I held you at gunpoint and tied you in bed."

Her moist lips flicked at his male nipples and then whispered across the wide expanse of his chest. Kane moaned in frustrated desire, one he was positively certain he would never be able to appease. He was destined to die wanting what he could never have.

Her hands wandered to and fro, employing all the divine tortures he'd taught her. The sensations she evoked crippled his mind and body. And if that wasn't enough to drive a sane man mad she assaulted him with kisses that boiled his brain and his body. She blazed paths of fiery kisses over his flesh and over and over again, she stroked and teased him until his need for her surpassed all rational bounds.

Darcey felt deliciously wicked as she coaxed him to moan in unholy torment. For once she had Kane exactly where she wanted him and she was rediscovering every muscled inch of his magnificent body without the distraction of his masterful caresses. Since he was bound to the bed, he couldn't encircle her in his arms, even if he had wanted to.

"Say the words again," Darcey commanded as her lips skimmed across the muscles of his belly.

"No," Kane chirped. "I refuse to die with a profession of love on my lips. I've said it too damned many times already, for all the good it did me."

"Then I'll say it." Darcey propped up on her elbow to peer down into his tormented face. "I love you, Kane Callahan. I did then and I still do now. Even if Melanie and an endless rabble of women try to take you away from me, it doesn't change the way I feel about you. Nothing has yet and nothing ever will."

Her hand coasted over his hips to swirl over the lean columns of his thighs. Kane flinched at her intimate touch and then strangled on his breath.

"It's true, you know," she assured him as she lifted her hand to trace the sensual curve of his lips. "I've spent six weeks trying to forget you, but nothing worked. And Edward Talbert is hardly a satisfactory substitute. I couldn't bear the thought of his touch when all I wanted was you."

Kane stared up into those emerald eyes to see love glittering down on him. It was the same expression he had noted that night in the cabin when Darcey had stopped splashing water on him and stood there, staring up at him with a look he hadn't been able to decipher. But it had been love all along. She really did love him! He knew it now, just as surely as he knew his own name.

"Let me loose, Darcey," he rasped, his voice barely above a whisper.

She gave her head a negative shake, sending the thick auburn curls cascading over his laboring chest. "I'm never going to let you loose again," she informed him with a saucy smile. "Now, do I have to have my way with you in order to drag that confession from your lips or will you offer it freely?"

Kane returned her mischievous grin. "Have your way with me," he invited with a seductive growl.

"I was hoping you'd say that."

Darcey took up where she left off a moment earlier. Lord, the things she did to him! And the things he ached to do to her in return! But he was tied to the bedpost and no matter which way he wormed and squirmed he couldn't wriggle loose.

This was the end, he thought to himself. He had already caught fire and now he was going to burn alive. Darcey's bold caresses glided over his body, worshipping him, arousing him beyond bearing. Her hands enfolded him and her lips followed, and then, when her curvaceous body moved upon his in the most erotic caress imaginable, there didn't seem to be enough air in the room to sustain him. God! He couldn't endure much more of this!

"Darcey . . . please . . ." Kane gasped.

Her soft laughter and alluring scent fogged his senses. "Please what, my handsome rogue?" she whispered against his parted lips.

"Untie me," Kane demanded in a hoarse voice.

"Why?" she teased unmercifully.

Her hands still wandered at will, memorizing every inch of his muscled flesh, setting off a chain reaction of sensations that demolished every smidgen of his self-control.

"Because you showed me your love. Now I want to show you mine."

He groaned again when her hands set out on another journey of discovery, leaving him to sizzle and burn.

"But I'm not finished with you yet," she replied.

She proceeded to lure him far past the point of no return. Her butterfly kisses fluttered over his flesh until he moaned aloud and strained against the confining cords that held him down. Again and again she dragged him to the edge of mindless abandon and then drew him back, leaving him to groan in torment.

"Come here, damn you," Kane growled in ragged breaths.

And she did come to him then. Her body settled intimately upon his, ending the torment of having her so close and yet so frustratingly far away. When she set the cadence of lovemaking with a hypnotic rhythm that was as ancient as time itself, Kane trembled helplessly. His masculine body moved of its own accord, arching toward her in urgent desperation, living and dying in that one fantastic moment that captured time. He was the possession of this wild-hearted, highly imaginative witch who sent him skyrocketing through time and space. Ineffable sensations pelted him like rapid-fire bullets, penetrating flesh, bone, and soul. Sublime rapture riveted his body when Darcey clutched him to her and shuddered at the same breathless instant that he found sweet release from the boiling pleasure that churned inside him.

A contented sigh escaped Darcey's lips as she nuzzled against Kane's neck. She hadn't believed it possible to become so aroused, but exploring Kane's muscular body and making him groan with unappeased desire evoked erotic sensations which demanded their own fulfillment. Watching him want her with every fiber of his being was a memory that would sustain her during those long lonely days while he was roaming around the country, doing one of the many things he did so well. She hoped the memory of their night together would bring him back to her.

The need to feel his arms around her overwhelmed her in that sentimental moment. Darcey reached up to untangle the knotted cord and sighed appreciatively when Kane wrapped her in his possessive embrace and cradled her against his broad chest.

"Would you mind telling me what that was all about?" he murmured against her forehead.

Darcey cuddled a little closer and then leaned her head back to peer up at him with an elfin smile. "Even though I'm not the only woman you've ever—"

Kane pressed a light kiss to her dewy lips. "I don't ever remember being with anyone but you," he whispered softly.

"Well, at least this was the first time any female tied you down and—"

"Drove me crazy?" Kane chortled huskily. "Mmm . . . you most certainly did that and much more, little witch. But it wasn't necessary to make such a point. Every moment I've spent with you since the day I met you has burned every other memory from my mind. There are some things a man can never forget. The sweetest memories I've ever known begin and end with you."

"Do they truly?" Darcey folded her arms over his chest. She propped up her chin on her hands and peered into those mystical pools of silver-blue. "And what if Melanie comes stealing back to your room?"

"Then I'll tell her to take another hike," Kane said with absolute assurance. "All I need is you."

"And what if some pretty female catches your eye while you are gadding about from one side of the continent to the other pretending to be someone you aren't in your effort to catch someone who is?" Darcey quizzed him.

Kane cocked a dark brow. "Who said I was going to go mucking about and leave you to the Edward Talberts and Jonathan Beezelys of the world?"

Darcey blinked, bemused. "Well, aren't you?"

"No, I *aren't,*" Kane chortled as he tilted her pert chin to his kiss. "My investigative days are over. You said you loved me and I'm holding you to it. You're not getting rid of me that easily and you're not working for Edward anymore, either. He has designs on you and I won't have him coveting what belongs to me."

Darcey's mind whirled, trying to absorb what he was telling her. Kane planned to quit his job because of her? And she was going to quit hers? That was preposterous.

"But what are we going to do with all the spare time we have on our hands?" she questioned.

A roguish grin pursed his lips and his hands began to roam over her supple curves. "What spare time? You won't have any . . ." His raven head inched steadily toward hers. His smile held the sensual promise of the pleasure he longed to offer her. "And now, my wild sweet love, it's time I taught you a few more things you didn't know about passion embroidered with love."

Darcey deftly eluded his kiss. "I don't want what any other woman has ever had from you," she demanded of him.

Kane halted. His brows knitted together in a speculative frown. Was she truly jealous that he hadn't been a stranger to women's arms before she came into his life? It flattered him to know she cared so much to be possessive, that she resented the other females in the past.

Reverently, he framed her face in his hands. He leaned close to feather his lips over her petal-soft mouth. The tenderness in his kiss paralyzed her brain. Entranced, Darcey watched his sensual lips whisper over hers. He nipped gently at the corner of her mouth before his tongue slowly tasted the inner core of her lips. Darcey felt her bones melt like wax on a burning candle.

Kane eased away to gaze into those lively green pools and he smiled adoringly at her. "Darcey, there are some things a man cannot change, no matter how much he'd like to. One of them is his past and those who were a part of it. Before you came along to give my life a new purpose, I was haunted by restless need. Another thing I can't change is the hell I put you through in Denver. It went against the grain and I regretted my assignment the moment I felt myself falling in love with you. When I asked you to marry me the first time we made love, I had never been more serious in all my life. I would have packed up and walked away with you and returned later to fulfill my obligation to Patrick. But you, little nymph, have a certain tendency toward stubbornness, no matter what the circumstances. Yet, I knew from the very beginning that what we had was special and worth keeping."

"Stubbornness *is* one of my worst faults, I'll admit." Darcey sighed, touched by his quiet confession. Her eyes lanced off his, floundering to formulate an explanation that would help him understand why she had been so cynical and mistrusting. This seemed to be the time for baring the soul.

"I was afraid to believe you were serious about marriage. You see, I thought I was in love once before I met you. I was young and foolish and unaware of the heartless motives of a suave but greedy adventurer. He proposed, of course, and pledged his undying love to me. And when I went to his cottage to give myself . . ."

When her voice trailed off, Kane realized his speculations had been correct after all. There had been someone who had betrayed her. He winced at the very thought of Darcey giving herself to another man. He suddenly realized that he was as resentful of every man who had courted her as she was of his previous liaisons.

"Another woman was in his bed," Darcey finished in a demoralized voice. "Later I learned the truth about his courtship with me. Michael and his paramour supported themselves by borrowing money for his 'investments' from his would-be brides while his courtesan used the same seductive methods on the men she lured."

Darcey gnashed her teeth, remembering how gullible and foolish she had been. "The reason I was so determined to take an active part in my father's business was to reimburse the money I had loaned to Michael from my trust fund. I was too embarrassed to tell my father what had happened. I suppose I was trying to prove that I could be more than a man's meal ticket and to replenish the money I had lost."

"Michael who?" Kane wanted to know that very second.

"It doesn't matter now," Darcey assured him. "I only wanted you to be aware of why I was so cautious and defensive, so mistrusting of the gambler and adventurer you seemed to be."

"Michael who?" Kane persisted.

"Michael Dupris, if you must know," Darcey grumbled.

A deep skirl of laughter rumbled in Kane's chest as he levered up on an elbow. "Michael Dupris from Philadelphia?"

Darcey frowned dubiously. "You know him?"

"Uh, yes. I do . . ."

Now it was Kane who refused to meet her penetrating gaze. He wasn't sure he wanted to divulge the details of that particular undercover assignment for the government. Darcey would be perturbed all over again if she knew he had used Michael's harlot to glean information and to prove the accusations brought against Angela and Michael Dupris.

"It seems your friend Michael turned to other avenues to make money during the war. He and his lady friend were selling information about the Union forces and planned offenses to the Confederates. In fact, he is now serving a sentence in the Pennsylvania penetentiary. And he and his accomplice will be there for a good long while."

Darcey was ever so thankful Michael had gotten what he deserved after all the naive heiresses he had swindled. The man had no scruples whatsoever if he had turned traitor to support his lavish lifestyle.

"Darcey?" Kane's quiet voice jostled her from her musings.

"Yes?" Her eyes lifted to peer intently into his.

"I love you. I want to spend the rest of my life with you. I asked you once to marry me and you turned me down. I'm asking you again. Not because you're an heiress. And not because our lovemaking is magic . . . because it most certainly is . . ." he added in a rustling whisper. "But because I look at you and I see a new world waiting to open its doors to me."

Darcey felt every last barrier of resistance evaporate when he leaned over to breathe new life into her with his adoring kiss. All the unpleasant memories of her past seemed so insignificant in comparison to the wondrous memories that awaited her in Kane's arms. She'd never felt so loved, so cherished, so needed.

As her lips parted in invitation, her arms twined around his neck, offering all the love she had to give. It was his for the taking. Suddenly it didn't matter so much that there had been other women in his past, as long as he was hers forevermore.

"I love you," she whispered with all her heart.

"Does that mean yes?" Kane queried huskily.

"Yes," she assured him.

He wrapped her tightly in his arms. The fierce emotions that gushed through him made him wonder if he would squeeze the stuffing out of her before he regained control of himself.

Darcey graced him with a provocative smile. "Now, about that magic you mentioned earlier . . ."

A low rumble of amusement filled the narrow space between them. "You mean that O'Roarke and Callahan style of magic?"

"Callahan and O'Roarke," she automatically corrected when he got his alphabet out of order.

"Ah, yes," he tittered as his caresses flowed over her satiny flesh, leaving fires burning in their wake. "Ours is love from *A* to *Z*, omitting nothing in between."

Darcey realized how very thorough Kane Callahan could be. After all, he was a master investigator. And investigate every possible avenue of sublime passion he did! He pursued every pulsating sensation he aroused in her to its very source. He sensitized every fiber of her being until her nerves screamed for release. He tantalized her by whispering his intentions against her quivering flesh and then he left her to burn like a thousand blazing suns.

Her body arched instinctively toward his as his masterful caresses traveled along her rib cage to draw lazy circles around the roseate peaks of her breasts. His greedy lips suckled at the tender buds until an array of shocking sensations blossomed inside her. Darcey trembled in breathless anticipation as his kisses and caresses drifted lower, seeking each ultrasensitive point and bringing it to life. Indescribable pleasure throbbed through her nerves and muscles. Shamelessly, she begged him to appease the wild cravings he had instilled in her.

"Not yet, sweet nymph," Kane murmured as his lips moved seductively over her and his fingertips delved and teased until Darcey gasped with the maddening want of him. "I'm just halfway through the alphabet. Wait until you see what *Q* stands for."

"Quit?" Darcey breathed hopefully. If he didn't *quit* torturing her like this she wouldn't survive to see *Z!*

"No, it stands for *quiet,*" he said with a provocative chuckle. "And that's what I want you to be. You're distracting me."

And *R,* Darcey decided was *really* going to drive her mad. He had coaxed her into rapturous submission and she had reached the point that it no longer mattered how much more delicious torment he put her through. The riveting sensations that buffeted her left her gasping for breath. Her body was no more than a shell that housed this wild, pulsating need to be one with him, to be heart to heart and soul to soul.

"Kane," Darcey moaned in sweet agony. "Why are you torturing me when I want you so desperately?"

"Y?" he growled playfully. *"Y,* because I'm madly in love with you."

Darcey would have giggled at his foolishness if she hadn't been so engulfed with a need that refused to be ignored. And when he finally came to her, his muscular body taking absolute possession, Darcey felt the splendorous flame burning inside her. She met each hard driving thrust with fervent urgency. Pulsating tremors rippled through her like breakers on the sea—rolling, cresting, engulfing, and rising to consume again. She clung to him as the world spun out of control. She could taste him, feel his body molded intimately to hers, inhale the masculine fragrance that was so much a part of him, a vital part of her . . .

And then it came, that wild burgeoning sensation that filled her to overflowing. With a muffled cry of ecstasy, Darcey clutched him to her and trembled with spasms of rapture. She was suspended in motionless flight, marveling at the dark, sensual dimensions of passion that knew no end when she was in Kane's magical arms.

"And that, alphabetically speaking . . ." Kane breathed a good while later. "Is all the ways I love you." His lips slanted over hers, sealing his heartfelt confession with a worshipping kiss.

Darcey grinned up into his face, her eyes flickering with animated sparkles of love. "And *Z*, it seems, stands for no *zest* left."

Kane stared down into that bewitching smile that radiated from her exquisite face and felt the fires blaze anew. This night was a time for secret confessions, for compensating for all those lonely nights he'd spent wanting her and wondering if he would ever again experience the splendor he had discovered in her arms. When he detected that glimmer of love in her emerald eyes, he felt his body rouse by leaps and bounds. Wanting this auburn-haired sprite had become as natural and instinctive as breathing. Loving her and knowing she loved him, too, seemed the very essence of his being.

Darcey felt the flame of passion sizzle through her again when Kane moved suggestively toward her. Another playful smile tugged at her lips, realizing that, for them, the end only signified a wondrous new beginning. And when Kane plied her with practiced caresses and steamy kisses, the world faded into oblivion. Darcey gave herself up body and soul to the pleasure he aroused in her and she returned it wholeheartedly.

It was a joyous coming together, a rapturous moment in time that left the world dangling in space. Flesh became flesh. One heart beat only for the other in perfect harmony. This love that had been put through every test, had withstood the winds of trouble and misunderstanding. It had burst forth into full blossom . . .

But the trouble was, there were still those who wished to spoil what was so glorious and so long in coming. If Kane had been blessed with the gift of foresight he might not have slept quite so peacefully that night.

Chapter 26

Kane awoke to the feel of the morning sun beaming through the window. A contented smile played on his lips. His thick lashes fluttered up to peer at the curvaceous beauty who slept peacefully beside him. Silently, Kane reflected on the past few months that had turned his life around.

There had been a time not so long ago when the challenge of tracking down the country's most wanted criminals had lured him away from the serene life that could have been his for the taking. But he had discovered more adventure in his pursuit of this high-spirited sprite than he ever believed possible. Honest to God, he seemed to have no other goal in life but keeping this cherished love he had worked so hard to win. After years of restless roving he had found his heart mate . . .

When Darcey stirred beside him, Kane bent to press an adoring kiss to her lips. It amazed him that he had found such peace with himself when he had uttered his confession to Darcey and she had returned it. Lord, he was filled with such affection for this lovely elf that he was afraid he would burst like a balloon! And when Darcey graced him with that dazzling smile of hers, Kane swore the sun was burning twice as bright.

"My, you seem to be in good humor this morning," Darcey observed as she looped her arms over Kane's shoulders and glided her leg intimately between his.

Kane's body automatically reacted to the feel of her silky curves blending into his masculine contours. And when Darcey's gentle caresses began to drift hither and yon, Kane had to force himself to shackle her hands.

"Good mood though I'm in, and a much better mood I would be in if we could spend the whole day doing what we did last night, we can't. Now is not the time," Kane insisted before dropping a kiss to her lips.

Darcey pouted playfully before she wormed her hands free to investigate the corded muscles of his thighs.

"Quit that," Kane ordered with a tormented groan. "It's impossible for me to think straight when you tempt me with that delectable body of yours. I'm trying to be sensible."

"I liked you better when you weren't," she murmured provocatively.

"Your father is expecting me. Noah managed to track down Owen Graves. His telegram stated he would be arriving with his fugitive this morning. And it seems to me that we should announce our marriage before your friend Melanie wags her poisonous tongue

440

all over town about who was seen in whose room last night."

The last remark put a halt to Darcey's amorous assault in a hurry. "*My* friend Melanie?" she scoffed, giving her auburn curls an indignant toss. "Let's not forget who arrived here to find *whom* in *whose* bed!"

A rakish grin quirked his lips as he tugged away the sheet to leer at the lovely angel who had taken him to heaven. "And let's not forget *who* wound up with *whom* while you know *who* stalked away with her nose out of joint. Now get dressed, minx."

Darcey expelled a reluctant sigh, but she did as she was told. Later she would compensate for being forced to forego her impulsive desire to have her way with this handsome rogue. In all her born days, she had never felt so free to express her affection. It was all so new, so intriguing, this love of theirs.

"Are you angry?" Kane queried as he watched Darcey hastily scoop up her discarded garments and dress herself in them.

"Positively livid," Darcey declared, sticking her tongue out at him in playful vindication. "Don't think I won't hold a grudge against you for refusing me this morning. You could very well find yourself staked out in bed, never to rise again."

Two dark brows jackknifed and he grinned in rakish anticipation. "I'll hold you to that threat."

Darcey betrayed herself by returning his mischievous grin. When their eyes locked, desire flashed between them like lightning.

"I'll get the marriage license this afternoon," Kane

promised in a throaty growl.

"I'll fetch plenty of rope," she countered with a suggestive glance that melted Kane's knees.

It was with impatient intent that Kane rammed his legs into his breeches and jammed his arms into his shirt. He had the feeling he was going to be in an all-fired rush the whole day, anticipating their night together. Damn, if not for the loose ends he had to wrap up, he would have dragged Darcey to the justice of the peace to speak the vows right there and then. It seemed one thing or another had gotten in the way of what he wanted since Darcey had sailed into his life like a misdirected hurricane. But after tonight, she was going to be his forevermore. And the next time Darcey awoke with loving on her mind, he wasn't going to resist her. He had spent more than a month yearning for her to come willingly to him. And the one time she instigated their lovemaking he was obliged to get up and leave. Blast it!

Patrick sighed in relief when Darcey appeared at the door of the parlor, laden down with her belongings. Behind her, clutching several more of Darcey's satchels, stood Kane Callahan, looking tremendously relaxed—and Patrick had a sneaking suspicion why Kane looked the way he did. Although Patrick was annoyed with his speculation, he surged out of his chair to wrap Darcey and her satchels in a welcome-home hug that very nearly squeezed her in two.

"Lord, I'm glad you're back," Patrick murmured affectionately before he pressed a kiss to her forehead. "I hope this means you've forgiven me for . . . Well, you know . . ."

Darcey couldn't reply. Her father had squished her nose and mouth so tightly against his shoulder and hugged her so hard that there was barely enough air in her lungs to breathe. Speaking was impossible.

"She's back, but she isn't staying," Kane informed Patrick, since Darcey was unable to speak for herself. "Your daughter has agreed to marry me before the day is out."

"Not staying?" Patrick hooted. "But she just got here! We have barely spent a full day together in the last five months. And I have every intention of organizing a huge wedding, complete with every appropriate manner of all paraphernalia. I intend to give my only daughter away in the proper fashion."

"I think a quiet wedding would be best," Kane advised, his gaze dropping to Darcey's enchanting face. "I have waited long enough already."

Unless I miss my guess, you haven't waited at all, you scoundrel, Patrick silently fumed. "No." He emphasized his rejection of Kane's request with an adamant shake of his bushy red head.

"Patrick . . ." Kane shot his father-in-law-to-be a challenging glance.

The firm rap at the door brought quick death to the argument in progress. Scowling, Patrick stamped through the vestibule to whip open the door. Owen Graves stood on the stoop, bookended by the beaming

Noah Callahan and the solemn-faced Giddeon Fox. His hands were manacled in front of him and his glare testified to his disgust in being apprehended.

"I thought you might want to interrogate Owen about the missing funds he embezzled in Denver," Noah announced before herding his captive inside the house.

A proud smile spread across Noah's lips when he saw his brother propped leisurely against the doorjamb. "I followed your instructions to the letter," he declared, quite pleased with himself. "Owen had taken a new job at a railroad depot in Omaha, Nebraska. He didn't put up much of a fight." Noah looked disappointed. "It was a simple matter to haul him back by train."

Kane grinned at his younger brother. Noah seemed so delighted with his success that he was bursting with newfound confidence. "You've done well for yourself, little brother," he complimented.

Noah lapped up the flattery like a thirsty puppy. "Thank you, big brother. I had a most accomplished instructor to teach me the tricks of the trade—"

Noah committed a critical mistake by focusing more attention on his brother than his desperate captive. In the batting of an eyelash, Owen launched himself across the room and pounced on Darcey. Before she realized what he was about, Owen had looped his shackled hands around her throat and slammed her body to his like a protective shield.

Kane reacted instinctively, but he was unable to intercept Owen before he clutched Darcey in a threatening position that put her at risk. While Kane

444

stood there growling at himself for not paying closer attention, the other three men gaped at Owen in disbelief.

"You neglected the most important rule of all, Noah," Kane muttered, still glaring at the man who had taken Darcey hostage. "Never, *ever,* take a captive for granted."

"Hand Darcey the key to these cuffs," Owen demanded impatiently.

Noah tilted a defiant chin and glowered resentfully at the man who had made him look the fool in front of his brother.

"*Now,* damn it," Owen snarled. "I'll break her neck, so help me I will!" To emphasize the threat, he jerked his hands backward, causing the metal cuffs to bite into Darcey's throat.

When Darcey choked on her breath and clutched at the shackles which dug into her windpipe, Kane cursed fluently. "Give him the key," he barked.

"But—" Noah tried to object.

"Do it!" Kane roared.

Noah obeyed. In a matter of seconds, Darcey had unlocked the cuffs and Owen clamped her tightly in his arms.

Raw fury boiled inside Kane's taut body. With mounting concern he watched Owen drag Darcey toward the door. He could see the wild desperation in Owen's eyes. Owen had been captured once and and he had no intention of being apprehended again, no matter who he had to hurt to escape. Kane had detected that look too many times on a fugitive's face not to take

Owen seriously.

"I want all the money you have in this house," Owen demanded as he backed against the wall for protection. "And a pistol," he added in afterthought. "I want a pistol, too."

"Give him your Colt, Noah," Kane demanded. He wasn't about to give up his, should he have the opportunity to use it.

"But—"

"Give it to me!" Owen shouted as he clamped his fingers around Darcey's neck to convince the men that he meant business.

With great reluctance, Noah stepped forward to extend the weapon to Owen. But his pride rebelled against being outfoxed by this thieving dandy. With a lurch, Noah tried to jerk Owen off balance and save the day. All he got, instead, was an instant headache. Owen took control of the Colt in time to part Noah's hair and leave him with a knot on his head. Noah folded at the knees and dropped into an untidy heap at Darcey's feet.

Attempting to take advantage of Owen's distraction, Darcey gouged him in the belly with her elbow and attempted to fling herself from his restraining arms. But all she received for her courageous efforts was the jab of the Colt in her ribs.

"Damn it, Darcey, don't fight him," Kane snapped, frustrated to no end. He cursed himself soundly for being more preoccupied by Patrick's resistance to a hasty marriage than the seemingly subdued captive. That distraction could very well cost Darcey her life.

"Get the money," Owen demanded with a snarl.

"Not until you tell me what you're planning to do with my daughter," Patrick snarled back at him.

"That depends on a number of things," Owen countered. "If she doesn't battle me every step of the way and you don't come charging out the door hot on my heels, I might release her."

Kane cautiously stepped forward. "Take me instead of her," he requested. His gaze locked with Owen's desperate stare. "I'll ensure that you get out of town scot-free."

"No," Owen snorted. "Women are easier to handle than—"

The comment ignited Darcey's temper in one second flat. She lifted her foot to strike Owen in the shin. That was also a mistake, she realized a half second too late. The pistol clanked against her skull and she wilted over Owen's arm, unwillingly surrendering to the swirling darkness that quickly engulfed her.

Kane felt as if he had taken the mind-boggling blow himself. Owen had become more desperate and violent with each passing minute. Now two of his victims were unconscious, and each time Owen lashed out to protect himself, it became infinitely easier for him to inflict bodily harm on those who stood in his way.

"Lay the cash on the sofa," Owen ordered as he propped Darcey's limp weight over his left arm and held the pistol to her head.

Cursing the air blue, Patrick emptied his pockets and laid their contents on the couch. In single file, each man grimly followed the procedure.

"Now drag Noah into that closet." Owen gestured

his ruffled blond head toward the small niche in the far corner of the room. "The rest of you join him there."

Growling under his breath, Kane reached down to grab Noah by the ankles and pulled him across the carpet. When they were all wedged into the tiny cubicle like sardines, Owen released his grasp on Darcey long enough to bound across the room to lock his captives in the closet. After scooping up the cash from the sofa, Owen fastened Darcey into the shackles and hoisted her over his shoulder like a feed sack.

He was out the door in a single bound, staring in every direction at once. When he spied Kane's carriage, he aimed himself toward it, lickety-split. Sparing a brief glance over his shoulder to make sure he wasn't being followed, Owen dumped Darcey on the buggy floor, braced his feet on her back, and popped the reins over the steed. The carriage lurched off and rumbled down the street, narrowly missing the pedestrians who had the misfortune of standing directly in its path.

"Noah . . . Noah . . . ?"

Noah blinked and stared up into the fuzzy darkness. He saw only a distant beam of light which seeped under the crack of the door. Noah couldn't imagine where else he could have been at the moment.

"Noah?" The booming voice crackled through his pounding brain again.

"Is that you, Lord?" Noah mumbled groggily.

Kane rolled his eyes and grumbled under his breath. "No, it's me—Kane. You have to stand up. If you don't

448

I'll have to trample all over you to break down this blessed door!"

Noah wobbled onto his knees, but bodies seemed to be everywhere. He could feel them, but he couldn't see them. "Where are we?"

Kane hooked his elbows under Noah's arms and hoisted him to his feet, and none too gently, either. "Hold him up, Giddeon," he commanded as he stuffed his brother into the corner.

Giddeon braced himself against the stunned man and scrunched down to give Kane space.

"Will you move over, Patrick," Kane snapped impatiently as he tried to wedge himself past the stout man who was blocking his path.

"Move to where?" Patrick scowled. "There are four bodies crammed in this closet!"

With a growl and a curse, Kane slammed back into Patrick and then launched himself toward the door. The door groaned and creaked, but it didn't give way. Kane retreated to try again. The third time, wood splintered and the door sagged beneath sheer masculine strength and determined will. Like a shot, Kane blazed across the room and darted out the front door. With the rescue brigade one step behind him, Kane vaulted onto the nearest horse and thundered off in search of his stolen buggy.

Frustrated anger spurred him. He kept seeing flashbacks of the wild desperation in Owen's eyes. The man had panicked and his instinct to survive was hard at work. Owen had been pushed to a point that he didn't care what he had to do to escape a jail sentence.

449

The fact that Owen had taken the best part of Kane's world as hostage was killing him, bit by agonizing bit. If that scoundrel harmed even one hair on Darcey's auburn head . . .

Kane exploded in a venomous growl and shook off the dreadful visions. Damnation, he had to get himself in hand. He couldn't go charging after Owen without a sensible plan of action. Owen would be prepared to sacrifice Darcey's life to save his own.

Forcing himself to keep a cool head rather than allow his emotions and imagination to run rampant, Kane skidded his steed to a halt and wheeled around. The rest of the rescue party swerved to miss the obstacle that blocked their path. And Noah, who wasn't performing at full capacity just quite yet, was catapulted off his mount and landed with a thud in the street.

With swift ease, Kane leaned down to clutch his brother by the jacket and jerk him to his feet. "The three of you follow the carriage," Kane ordered hurriedly. "I'll circle through the alley to see if I can cut Owen off before he reaches the edge of town."

While the cavalcade clattered down the street, Kane veered into the alley, dodging the maze of clutter that blocked his path. Wild-eyed, the steed sidestepped around the obstacle course, straining to race at its swiftest speed when its rider demanded it. Kane prayed nonstop, hoping he had accurately guessed the direction Owen had taken—toward the sparsely settled area to the north rather than toward the wharf that banked the Mississippi River. If he were Owen Graves,

450

he wouldn't head toward a cluster of humanity. He would race along the river where he could dive into the thickets at the first sign of trouble.

And if by chance Darcey awoke and began screaming her head off, it wouldn't draw the kind of attention Owen didn't want. No, Kane predicted, the scoundrel was headed for the country road and the cover of dense underbrush and thick foliage to the north. He had tracked enough fugitives in his time to second-guess his quarry. He just hoped like hell this wasn't the one time he turned out to be wrong!

Chapter 27

The feel of her chin bouncing on the wooden floorboard brought Darcey back to harsh reality. A pained groan tumbled from her lips. Her head was throbbing in tormenting rhythm with the rumbling carriage that raced over washboarded roads. The bite of metal nipped at her wrists and the heels of Owen's boots smashed into her spine, keeping her pinned facedown.

Darcey blinked once, and then twice. Frantically, she struggled to orient herself and formulate an escape attempt. The metal cuffs that manacled her wrists would become her improvised weapon. Ponderously, Darcey peered down at the handcuffs. The way she had it figured, one blow to the head deserved another. If she could worm free quickly enough to whack Owen and stun him, she could make her daring leap to freedom.

The instant her senses and her vision cleared, Darcey sprang into action. To Darcey's good fortune, Owen was busily concentrating on steering the carriage down the rough path and darting expectant glances over his shoulder. When Darcey jerked her legs beneath her and pounced like a cougar, Owen didn't have enough time to deflect the oncoming blow caused by the metal shackles. The second blow sent Owen's senses reeling. Wildly, he shoved Darcey away before she could inflict more pain on him.

A shriek of horror burst from Darcey's lips when Owen knocked her sideways. As the carriage careened around the bend in the road that overlooked the river, Darcey toppled from her precarious perch. The bare rock cliff was strewn with pebbles that made it impossible for her to maintain her balance. Although Darcey tried to land on her feet and lurch backward to prevent pitching off the jagged bluff, the loose rock and her forward momentum sent her skidding.

A stab of terror shot through every nerve and muscle in Darcey's body as she fell through the expanse of nothingness and splashed into the swift-flowing channel. Icy dread numbed her throat and she struggled to expel a scream for assistance, but before she could gasp for much-needed air, a wall of water toppled over her, swallowing her alive . . .

Kane gouged his laboring mount the instant he spotted the cloud of dust on the road ahead of him. He had burst into several obscene oaths when he reached the outskirts of town long after Owen had sailed past. It was a wonder to Kane that Owen hadn't run down one-fourth of the population of St. Louis in his desperate effort to escape!

Kane bounded down the road, unaware that Darcey had been launched into the river during her attempt to elude Owen. While Darcey was being swept downstream, battling for breath, Kane was galloping off in the wrong direction, pursuing the coach.

A quick glance over his shoulder assured him that the threesome wasn't far behind. Since Kane had been unable to cut Owen off before he reached the edge of town, he had no other alternative but to run the man down . . .

Kane instinctively ducked away when a bullet whined in the distance. As much as Kane would have liked to return the gunfire, he didn't dare for fear of hitting Darcey, who, unbeknownst to him, was in far more danger of drowning than being plugged by a stray bullet!

Slowly but surely, Kane's steed gobbled up the distance between him and wobbling carriage. Kane practically dared Owen to take his best shot as he swerved from side to side, forcing the fugitive to waste his ammunition. When, in total exasperation, Owen flung the empty pistol at him, Kane launched his fierce attack.

Wild-eyed, Owen stared at the formidable form of the man who charged at him with a vengeance. His frantic gaze darted toward the thicket of underbrush that skirted the right side of the road. Before Kane could leap off his steed and into the carriage, Owen dived for cover. The carriage teetered precariously and the runaway horse bolted sideways in fright.

In stark horror, Kane watched the buggy flip onto its side when one of the front wheels bounced off the cliff that overlooked the river. The steed floundered to maintain his balance as the toppling carriage tugged against him. In sickening dread, Kane saw the upended carriage scrape across the perilous ledge, knowing for certain that Darcey was pinned beneath it. With his heart hammering, Kane bounded from his mount and braced himself against the buggy before it dropped off the cliff.

After what seemed forever, Giddeon, Noah, and Patrick arrived upon the scene to lend assistance. With strains and groans, the men shoved the carriage upright . . .

No Darcey? Kane blinked in disbelief. Where the hell was she? His worried gaze dropped to the river searching for some sign that she had been flung over the edge.

Nothing . . . Darcey was nowhere to be found.

"Noah, you and Giddeon go hunt Owen down," Kane growled. "He's no longer armed, but for God's sake, don't take him for granted again!"

Having roared the order, Kane charged toward his horse and bolted into the saddle. Kane found himself conjuring up the most horrible nightmares imaginable while he retraced his tracks along the river, searching for Darcey's mangled body in the brush.

She must have tried to leap to freedom the minute she regained consciousness, Kane speculated. He was sure Owen hadn't shot her dead in desperation. Kane would have heard the discharging pistol. He knew Owen had emptied every chamber of the Colt in an effort to discourage Kane. He had counted six shots. And damn it, he had to remember to tell Noah never to

456

load all six chambers in a pistol again. That was foolish. The nitwit could blast off his toes while he was trying to retrieve his pistol from his holster in a rush. If he accidentally pulled the trigger, Noah could get himself hurt . . .

Kane shoved the thought aside and stared down at the rolling river . . . Was Darcey . . . ?

A wordless scowl gushed from his lips. He wasn't going to flounder in pessimistic thought. Honest to God, he'd been around that feisty she-male so long that her overactive imagination had rubbed off on him. He was not going to leap to wild conclusions until he knew for certain what had become of her!

"H . . . E . . . L . . . P!!"

A waterlogged cry erupted from somewhere beneath Kane.

Jerking his mount to a halt, Kane bounded to the ground. In reckless haste, he scuttled down the vine-tangled slope, searching for the source of the sound. He wound up falling flat on his face twice.

"Somebody . . . H . . . E . . . L . . . P!!" Darcey croaked.

To Kane's terrified amazement, he found Darcey snagged by her handcuffs on the sawyer of tree limbs and debris that clogged the river. Every other second, a wave of water crested over her like frothy brine. She barely had time to gasp for breath before she was doused again.

Kane glanced frantically around him. What he needed was a canoe, but there wasn't one within five miles. Scowling in frustration, Kane slopped through the mud in search of driftwood which could serve as his rescue raft. The current was too swift for him to swim through. And he wasn't sure he could navigate toward Darcey by raft, either, now that he thought about it. Blast it, he would have even settled for a long rope and an anchor to steady himself.

"Curse it!" Darcey screeched when she spied Kane darting up and down the river. A wall of water rolled over her and she strained to lift her face from the muddy depths. "Do something!"

"I'm doing the best I can!" Kane bellowed, as if the perilous situation in which she found herself was all her fault. And it probably was, he thought furiously. If Darcey wasn't such a daredevil she would have been pinned under the upended coach, her body broken in a zillion pieces . . . "Lord, what am I thinking?" Kane muttered crossly.

"Kane!" Darcey's voice rattled with sheer desperation. The force of the water had sapped her strength. It was all she could do to lift her head and inhale an occasional breath.

Scolding himself for being so rattled in the face of disaster, Kane tugged on the driftwood and dragged it upstream. If he was going to reach Darcey he would have to be far enough upriver to employ the current to his advantage. With a prayer on his lips, he shoved the soggy tree limb into the river and paddled for all he was worth to prevent his improvised raft from heading downriver rather than into midstream.

Intent on his progress, Kane flapped his arms like oars and battled the current. His breath came out in a long sigh of relief when the driftwood lodged against the sawyer. Scrambling atop the half-floating tree trunk and tangled debris, Kane stretched out to untangle Darcey's wrist from the limbs. Finally, he dragged her atop the sawyer and whacked her between the shoulder blades to ensure that she was still breathing.

With a sputter and a cough, Darcey sucked in air and wheezed to catch her breath. "It's about time you showed up," she chirped. "I nearly drowned."

"Of all the times I've saved you from certain catastrophe, I would think, just once, you could thank me instead of criticizing me," he grumbled resentfully.

"Thank you," she gasped.

"You're welcome. Now, how in the hell did you get here in the first place?" he demanded. "By all rights you should be dead."

"Is that what you would have preferred?" she questioned as she dragged herself into a sitting position on the bobbing sawyer.

"Hell no!" Kane exploded. "I love you, woman. I'm just wondering if I can keep you alive long enough to marry you! The way our luck has been running and the way your father is dragging his feet, demanding a wedding with all the traditional trimmings, we'll never be married!"

Once danger had passed and Darcey had regained her composure, she looped her handcuffs over Kane's neck and blessed him with a kiss that was hot enough to turn the river into a cloud of steam. "You truly are something, Kane Callahan," she murmured admiringly. "Did I ever tell you that?"

All the frustration that had nagged at him since

Owen took Darcey hostage drained out of Kane. When she pressed temptingly against him, all thought and previous torment fled. He could feel her supple curves through their soggy garments, feel the heat of pleasure engulf him. He had found little satisfaction in hearing his praises sung when he accomplished his dangerous missions for the government or private enterprises. But receiving a genuine compliment from a woman who was as difficult to please as Darcey O'Roarke touched him to the bone.

"Well, now what do we do, Master Detective?" Darcey questioned as she stared thoughtfully at the distant shore.

"We paddle," Kane informed her with a decisive nod.

"In these handcuffs?" she sniffed.

"You take the right side of the driftwood and I'll take the left." Kane drew her to her feet and carefully inched across the sawyer, which dipped and swayed with the current.

Kane sprawled atop the driftwood and motioned for Darcey to cushion herself on his hips—her head positioned on his derriere, her body cradled between his legs. A muffled giggle tripped from her lips when she realized how ridiculous they would look to passersby.

"What's so damned funny?" Kane questioned as he pushed away from the sawyer.

"I was just admiring my pillow," Darcey snickered before paddling against the current. "This gives an entirely new meaning to cuddling cheek to cheek."

Kane glanced over his shoulder at the grinning imp

on top of him. "You are outrageous," he chastised her.

She flashed him a sultry smile. "And you have a nice—"

"Darcey, for God's sake!" Kane croaked, amazed at the uninhibited sprite who had emerged from her shell to voice the most outrageously ribald remarks. "What has gotten into you?"

"Paddle, Kane," she insisted, managing a straight face. "You're steering us sideways."

Kane did as he was told, but he couldn't smother the amused grin that quivered on his lips. He was seeing a new facet of Darcey's complex personality. And if the truth be known, he delighted in her playfulness. It made his heart soar to know he was the one who had lured this bewitching butterfly from her restrictive cocoon.

"Good Lord!" Patrick hooted when he peered over the bluff to see his daughter sprawled half on, half off Kane's backside, paddling—handcuffed—across the river.

Leaving Noah in charge of the recaptured fugitive, Giddeon swung from the saddle to scurry down the steep slope. Hurriedly, he located a long sturdy branch that would serve as a pole to anchor Kane when he drifted past.

Arching backward, Kane clasped the branch and clamped his legs around the driftwood while Giddeon pulled him ashore. Before he could gain his feet, Giddeon had plucked Darcey up and set her on solid ground. A condescending frown knitted Giddeon's brow as he scrutinized the soggy sprite who always seemed to embroil herself in more than her fair share of trouble.

"Young lady, if I may be so bold to say so, both you and Kane should strive for a more sedate way of life. I never saw two people cutting their time short with such dangerous escapades!"

A mischievous smile pursed Darcey's lips as she peered up into Giddeon's concerned face. "Are you the same man who took pity on me when I was being held hostage in the mountains?" she mocked dryly.

Giddeon's mouth opened and closed like the damper on a chimney. Finally, he regained control of his voice. "That was before I discovered what a spirited young woman you are," he defended before glancing quickly at Kane. "I was warned ahead of time about you, but I was skeptical of what I'd heard. It seems Kane was right about you after all."

"Does this mean you don't approve of our marriage?" Darcey questioned him outright.

"Approve?" Giddeon erupted in an explosive chuckle and beamed like a lantern on a long wick. "Indeed yes, I approve! Most heartily, in fact. If you ask me, Kane should have married you before he—" A pained grunt gushed from his lips when Kane gouged him in the midsection in silent reprisal.

"I think it's time we ventured back to town, don't you, Giddeon? I, for one, would like to get out of these wet clothes," Kane insisted, hastily changing the subject before his servant's runaway tongue got them both in trouble.

Darcey's puzzled gaze bounced back and forth

between the suddenly tight-lipped Giddeon Fox and Kane. "What was he going to say that you didn't want me to hear?" Darcey questioned as Kane shepherded her up the slope.

"Nothing important, I'm sure," Kane said with a dismissive shrug.

He wasn't about to embarrass Darcey by allowing her to know that Giddeon was aware of what had transpired between them in the mountain cabin. Giddeon was as good as gold, but sometimes he didn't think before he spoke his mind.

"Sorry, sir," Giddeon murmured in quiet apology after they scaled the bluff. "I forgot myself for a moment."

Once atop the cliff, Patrick stared down at his bedraggled daughter and then focused his stern attention on the man beside her. "Taking all things into consideration, I have decided an immediate wedding is for the best."

An amused grin quirked Kane's lips as he regarded the bushy-haired Irishman who sat rigidly in the saddle. "What made you reverse your decision, if you don't mind my asking?"

Patrick squirmed uneasily on his perch and peered solemnly at his daughter. "I think she needs round-the-clock protection to keep her out of trouble," he admitted frankly.

"Papa!" Darcey gasped in indignation.

"Well, it's the truth," Patrick declared with absolute conviction. "You have always had more spirit than can be contained within the acceptable confines of womanhood. And I can think of no other man better qualified to handle you. The sooner you and Kane are wed the better off we'll all be."

"Amen to that!" Giddeon chimed in.

"Well, thank all of you very much for your vote of confidence," Darcey said huffily.

Her gaze swung to the man who had been led along behind Noah's mount with his hands bound with rope. Her indignation momentarily forgotten, Darcey marched over to retrieve the key from Owen's jacket and quickly freed her hands. Then, with malice and forethought, she cocked her arm, doubled her fist, and clobbered him a good one.

"That's for very nearly getting me killed, you patronizing womanizer!" she fumed. "I've been wanting to do that since the day I walked into the Denver office to endure your repulsive flirtations and your snide insults. I hope you mildew in jail!"

When she lurched around, Noah, Kane, Giddeon, and Patrick were grinning in amusement. "He had it coming," she defended self-righteously. "And woman or no, I was determined to see that he got it."

"I would have been happy to take care of the matter for you," Kane teased the sassy spitfire.

"There was no need," Darcey insisted. "I can take care of—"

"Yourself" all four men finished for her in unison.

A becoming blush stained Darcey's cheeks. Her emerald gaze swung back to Kane. "Are you certain you want to marry me? Even my own father is glaringly aware of all my faults. Perhaps I do possess a mite more spirit than necessary. And I suppose I am a tad too independent for my own good. And, as you are so fond of reminding me, I do have this peculiar penchant for putting my life in alphabetical order and—"

Kane reached out to press his index finger to her lips, shushing her. His eyes twinkled as he stared at the corkscrew ringlets of auburn hair that framed her animated features. "I want you just the way you are," he assured her before he bent to whisper a kiss across her forehead.

A pleased smile blossomed on Darcey's face. "And I will try to control myself in the future," she promised faithfully.

Kane broke into a roguish grin. He leaned close to convey a confidential comment that was meant for her ears only. "I'd really rather you wouldn't. I love it when you're completely out of control."

Darcey blushed profusely and stepped away. "Now about this wedding of ours—"

"I'll see to all the arrangements myself," Patrick volunteered. "By the time Noah returns from incarcerating Owen and you and Kane have a chance to make yourselves presentable, we'll have the ceremony."

"And none too soon, if you ask me," Giddeon mumbled, only to have Kane jab him in the ribs again. "Sorry, sir."

"Kane," he corrected his servant for the umpteenth time. "I hate being called sir. And do try to keep your thoughts to yourself. I'd prefer Darcey didn't overhear them."

"Yes, si—Kane," Giddeon replied, drawing himself up to stand at attention.

With their prisoner in tow, the cavalcade trotted

back to St. Louis. Kane curled his arms possessively around the soggy bundle of femininity who sat in front of him on the saddle. A peculiar feeling overcame Kane. Impulsively, he hugged Darcey close. Every time he thought about how close he had come to losing her, he was overwhelmed by so much sentimental emotion that he very nearly drowned in it.

During those terrifying minutes while he searched for Darcey, fearing the worst and praying for the best, he'd asked himself how he could survive without her. The answer was so painfully clear that he'd shuddered in bleak resignation. He hadn't even wanted to speculate about how he would live without her. She was a part of him that time and distance could never erase. She owned his very soul. Without her he would have been half a man, a man without purpose.

"Kane? Are you all right?" Darcey questioned when he suddenly tried to squeeze every bit of water out of her saturated clothes while she was in them.

"I am now," Kane admitted with a relieved sigh. "I just realized that it scared the living daylights out of me when I thought I'd lost you. I never want to go through that again. Maybe Giddeon is right. Maybe we'd both be better off if we confined ourselves to a peaceful existence and avoided life-threatening situations."

Darcey smiled to herself. Perhaps Kane was overcome by sentimentality at the moment, but she seriously doubted that he or she could thrive without challenges and excitement. It simply wasn't the nature of either of them. In fact, she predicted that within a few months the need for adventure would seize them both. Oh, Kane had vowed to merely oversee his investments and lounge in the lap of luxury. And he'd probably try, thought Darcey. But he wouldn't have to for her benefit because she wasn't going to watch the world pass her by without being involved in it.

An impish grin surfaced on her lips as she peered into the distance. Private investigation had always sounded very intriguing to her. She had done a bit of it herself while trying to search out the embezzler in Denver. In fact, she might be rather good at detective work if she had just the right instructor to train her.

Chapter 28

Darcey thumbed through the stack of letters, absently arranging the names on the return addresses in alphabetical order. Since her hasty marriage in St. Louis four months earlier, she and Kane had invented hundreds of ways to amuse themselves at his palatial home in Independence. There had been afternoons at the horse races, evenings at the theater, and short jaunts up the Missouri by steamboat. They had been entertained by several troupes of traveling singers, dancers, and actors and they had attended all the posh parties in town. In fact, there was very little of the "good life" they hadn't enjoyed together. They had crammed as many activities as possible into their days and filled their nights with enough passion to melt the moon and leave it dripping on the night sky.

It wasn't that Darcey found fault with even one facet of her life as Kane Callahan's wife. Kane was the ideal husband and lover. He was devoted, warm, attentive and . . .

A curious frown knitted Darcey's brow when she glanced down at the official-looking letter in her hand. Her gaze flicked toward the door to ensure that no one was around to catch her tampering with Kane's mail. Casting glances at the door at irregular intervals, Darcey plucked off the seal and unfolded the letter. The note was from a congressman in Washington who requested that Kane investigate the rumors of corruption in a railroad company headquartered in Chicago, one from which the congressman had been offered a bribe the previous week.

Darcey contemplated the letter for the next few minutes. Drumming her fingers on the desk, she let her imagination run rampant, conjuring up ingenious ways to infiltrate the company and examine their ledgers in hopes of learning who was reponsible for the unscrupulous dispersal of funds. After her dealings in Denver and her experience with Talbert's Railway Company in St. Louis, she had developed an eye for detecting foul play and a nose for sniffing out trouble . . .

"What are you doing in here, madam?"

Kane's rich baritone voice echoed through the paneled office, causing Darcey to bolt straight up in her chair. A muffled curse tumbled from her lips. Kane had always had the silent tread of a cat. He could sneak up on her before she realized he was there. Another of the talents that made him such a skillful detective, Darcey reminded herself.

"I'm not doing anything in particular," she replied with an innocent smile.

His dark brows narrowed over scrutinizing silver-blue eyes. Darcey suddenly looked so angelic that Kane expected her to sprout wings and a halo any second now. That made him higly suspicious. Staring at his wife, Kane ambled across the room to snatch up the letter she had crumpled into her clenched fist.

"No," he said firmly, having read the contents of the note from Congressman Pedigrew. "Giddeon will be sending off a letter to Pedigrew, as well as my other would-be clients, informing them that my brother is available for assignment. I have retired from the detective business. You know perfectly well that Noah has become quite capable of replacing me."

Darcey eased back in her chair to regard her handsome husband with an assessing stare. "Are you going to stand there and tell me you don't miss the active life you had before we married?"

She dared him to deny it. In fact, she had noticed that the same restlessness that hounded her had also begun to hound him, even when he made a conscious effort to disguise his emotions. But Darcey had come to know Kane well. And a time or two she had caught him pacing when he didn't realize she was around to observe him. He always paced when he was frustrated or restless . . .

Kane tramped back and forth across the carpet in swift, precise strides. He was as happy and content as one man could possibly be, that was for sure. But yes, he *was* having slight difficulty adjusting to the life of the idle rich. And yet, the thought of accepting an assignment that would take him away from his saucy, green-eyed wife for several weeks cut him to the quick. This new brand of restlessness that tormented him wasn't the same kind that had bothered him before. But honest to God, how many Shakespearean plays and musical performances could a man attend before he was bored to tears?

"Well? Are you going to admit you are restless or shall I do it for you?" Darcey prompted with a wry smile. She could see the turmoil of emotions working on her husband as he paced the study like a caged tiger.

"All right, yes," Kane finally acknowledged, but with extreme reluctance. He screeched to a halt and wheeled to face Darcey's smug smile. "I suppose I do thrive on challenges, but I have no intention of leaving you alone."

One delicately arched brow elevated. "Who said you had to?"

"Oh, no," Kane muttered, flinging up his hands to forestall the thought that was buzzing through her head. He knew what she was thinking. He could see that sparkle of anticipated adventure in her emerald eyes. "I've watched you flirt with disaster and court catastrophe one too many times the past few months. And if you think for one minute that I would involve you in this or any other assignment you, my dear wife, have rocks in your head!"

With graceful ease, Darcey rose from her chair and sashayed over to loop her arms around Kane's neck. "I'm not suggesting we team up to track down the James Gang that has been plundering Missouri, Arkansas, and Indian Territory," she assured him before pressing full length against him. Her lips hovered invitingly beneath his, tempting him to the

472

extreme. "But we could pose as husband and wife and I could—"

"We *are* husband and wife," Kane corrected.

He was feeling the instantaneous effects of her seductive assault and battling to keep his wits about him. Lord, when Darcey was this close to him he never had been able to think rationally. Marriage hadn't helped all that much, either. He was still vulnerable to this gorgeous nymph and he was positively certain he always would be. Some things, it seemed, were not subject to change. His explosive response to her was one of them.

"Or I could infiltrate the company as an employee to study the ledgers," Darcey went on to say as she limned the rugged lines of his face. "And you could do the same thing you did when you investigated Talbert's company. If I could get my hands on the books to examine the expenditures I could—"

"No," Kane said firmly.

"I can be very efficient and thorough when I set my mind to it," Darcey whispered as her roving hands tunneled inside his shirt to make titillating contact with his flesh.

"No," Kane said again in a half-strangled voice and then groaned when the stimulating warmth of her practiced caresses melted his bones and his resistance.

"You are being unnecessarily stubborn," Darcey murmured as she peeled away the shirt to press moist lips to his chest. "And you know we both live for thrills. That's why we make such a perfect match . . ."

Her hands and lips whispered across his sensitive

skin, setting fires that had never burned themselves out and gave no indication that they ever would! Kane expelled a breath. He knew he was losing this argument, as well as his self-control. When Darcey worked her potent magic on him he had never been able to deny her anything . . .

The whine of the front door caused Kane to flinch involuntarily. He glanced over his shoulder to see that Giddeon had returned from the railroad depot with Noah, who had just completed his latest assignment in Louisiana.

Noah's discerning gaze flickered over his brother's gaping shirt. He darted a quick glance at the desk where the letter lay open. Then he surveyed the very determined expression on his sister-in-law's enchanting features. Noah grinned wryly. Unless he missed his guess, Darcey was using her potent powers of persuasion to bring Kane out of retirement. And from all indications, Darcey's tactics were working superbly.

"We . . . were . . . um . . . discussing the possibility of teaming up to take a case in Chicago," Kane chirped, his voice nowhere near as steady as he hoped.

Giddeon rolled his eyes and groaned in dismay. He knew it would come to this eventually. Four months was a long time to confine two such rambunctious individuals to a normal, sedate way of life.

"Close the door on your way out, Giddeon," Kane requested. "I think it best if Darcey and I continue this conversation in private."

Before Giddeon could do Kane's bidding, Noah zipped across the room to scoop up the stack of mail that Darcey had alphabetized. Flinging his older

474

brother a wry smile, Noah swaggered back to the door. "From the look of things, you two won't be reading these letters any time soon. I'll look them over while you're ... er ... deeply involved in ... um ... discussion—or whatever it is the two of you plan on doing in private."

"As good a detective as you've become, little brother, I do wish you would figure out a way to make yourself invisible ... and take Giddeon with you," Kane muttered into Noah's ornery smile.

Giddeon cast husband and wife a disapproving glance before he eased the door shut behind him. An exasperated sigh gushed from his lips. "I knew this was going to happen sooner or later. Darcey is so much like Kane that it's downright scary! And in the years to come there will probably be pint-sized private investigators running around all over this place. I only hope that couch in the study is sturdier than that cot in the mountains on which those two—" Giddeon clamped his mouth shut like a drawer and cursed his wagging tongue.

An amused chuckle burst from Noah's lips as he studied the grumbling servant. "You needn't worry that you have divulged any confidential secrets, my friend," he consoled Giddeon. "It took me a while to figure out what was going on that night. But now that I've come of age, I'm beginning to understand my brother better than I used to. Before, I only idolized him without really knowing him." His gaze darted back to the closed door of the office. "And as for that delightfully vivacious wife of his ..."

Noah sighed audibly. "They'll make a sensational

team of detectives, with her distracting beauty and keen wit and Kane's remarkable ability of spotting trouble before it begins and resolving it quickly and efficiently. Why, before you know it, the Callahan Detective Agency will be passed down through several generations." His blue eyes twinkled as he ambled up the steps beside Giddeon. "Take heart, Giddeon. There will come a time when Kane and Darcey will have to stay home to raise the flock of infants they're bound to have, what with all the 'private discussions' they keep having."

Giddeon broke into a smile. "You do have a point. And knowing how Kane felt about your father hauling the two of you up- and downriver during your early years, he'll make certain his children have a stable home. I'll bet my salary on that!"

Noah grinned broadly. "I'll bet your salary on that, too, Giddeon. Kane won't allow his children to grow up the way we did. Of course, these future children of theirs won't see much of their parents, since Kane and Darcey can't seem to keep their hands off each other for more than a few hours at a time." He expelled a wistful sigh. "I wish I could find . . ."

Giddeon comfortingly patted Noah on the shoulder. "Someday you will," he said with perfect assurance. "And when you do, you'll understand your big brother even better than you do now. Love gives a man a wider perspective of life."

Noah frowned bemusedly. "When did you become such an authority on love?"

A secretive smile pursed Giddeon's lips. "Watching your brother hover around his bride has given me a few ideas of my own. For almost two years I've had my eye on the housemaid who works down the street for the Dunbars. I think it's high time the two of us got better acquainted. It looks as if I'm going to have more free time on my hands with the three of you out cracking one case after another."

"A wise decision," Noah snickered as his gaze strayed back down the steps to contemplate the muffled noises that wafted their way out of the office. "I don't think we should bother waiting lunch for my brother. With his past history, I doubt we'll see much of him until late afternoon."

Noah, of course, was right. Lunch was the farthest thing from Kane's mind.

Kane peered down at the beguiling face and kiss-swollen lips that hovered a hairbreadth away from his. He'd known the instant Darcey set her hands upon him that he was going to buckle under and agree to her request to assist him in the assignment in Chicago. She could be a very persuasive woman when she wanted to be.

Oh, to be sure, Kane would keep a watchful eye on his feisty wife during every investigation they accepted in the future. He would allow her to participate to a certain degree in every adventure that took them hither and yon. But there would be no excessively dangerous missions that could put her life in jeopardy. He, like she, had experienced that yearning for new challenges and excitement. They both had begun to miss the opportunity to match wits with those who defied the

477

laws. But Kane intended to use extreme caution because what he needed most in his life was this delightful angel in his arms. He would always be there to guide and instruct her. And she, in turn, would be his beacon in the darkness.

"I just want you to promise me one thing," Kane demanded, his voice still thick with the aftereffects of passion. "While we are on assignment, I want you to proceed cautiously at all times. I'll have none of those daredevil tactics that leave you tripping on the borderline of disaster. Do you understand me, wife?"

Darcey combed her fingers through Kane's thick raven hair and guided his sensual lips to hers for a sizzling kiss. "I'll be on my best behavior," she vowed.

"And you had best not use these same mind-boggling methods of persuasion on any suspicious parties in hopes of dragging out useful information, either," Kane warned. "In short, I'll not have you taking 'undercover' detective work literally."

Soft, tantalizing laughter filled the small gap between them. "Do you honestly believe I would settle for less when I've had the very best 'undercover' agent in this business?" she asked as her hands set out on another adventure of discovery. "I wouldn't think of using the same tactics on any other man and *you'd* best not use them on other women." Darcey eyed him suspiciously. "You've probably utilized such strategy yourself in the past; otherwise, you wouldn't have brought it up."

"Let's just forget I said anything," Kane whispered before he settled down to the arousing business of making love to his wife all over again.

Eagerly, Darcey pressed even closer to the warm, hard length of his masculine body. Kane kissed and caressed her, fueling that eternal flame into a raging blaze. And she fanned the billowing fire, returning each intimate kiss and caress.

A soft moan gurgled in Kane's throat when Darcey invented imaginative ways to reassure him that she needed and wanted no other man to pleasure and love her until the end of eternity. This one beautiful woman who shared his thirst for adventure had made his life complete.

"Oh, Darcey . . ." Kane groaned as he clutched her fiercely to him, overcome by waves of emotion. "I love you so much it frightens me to think how I would ever survive without you . . ."

"Then come here, my love," she urged with a provocative smile and a seductive caress. "I'll love all your fears away . . ."

"You've done it again," Kane pointed out as his sinewy body settled intimately over hers.

"Done what?"

"Wedged in the last word," Kane replied in a tone that was too full of hungry passion to sound the least bit condemning. "You do it every blessed time."

Darcey moved suggestively beneath him, inflaming him with monstrous needs that demanded fulfillment. "I thought you once told me that the Q in lovemaking stood for *quiet,*"she whispered in reminder. "And what does it really matter if I do have the last word, as long as the last word is love. And I do love you, more than you'll ever know."

A smile traced his lips as he drew her possessively

against him and felt that wild, sweet magic channel through every fiber of his being. Words failed Kane when he lost himself to the splendor of loving and being loved so totally. It was for this high-spirited female that Kane had searched all his life. And quite honestly, Kane didn't care if Darcey did have the last word. He had won her love. That was all that really mattered to him anyway. All else was a dim shadow in comparison to this moonlight enchantress who put stars in his eyes and fulfilled his every dream.